After Paris

—

Renny deGroot

Also by Renny deGroot

Family Business

ISBN-10: 1532823932
ISBN-13: 9781532823930

Toadhollow Publishing
88 Elder Avenue
Toronto, Ontario
M8W 1S4

Contact Renny at
http://www.rennydegroot.com

Dedication

To the memory of my grandparents: Mary
Thomson-Meijer and Max Meijer, who met and
served together in Paris during WW1

And

To the memory of Mary Arsenault of Antigonish, N.S.,
who could turn any hardship into a great story; some
of which have found their way to these pages.

"Each mortal thing does one thing and the same:
Deals out that being indoors each one dwells,
Selves—goes itself; *myself* it speaks and spells,
Crying *What I do is me; for that I came.*"
Gerard Manley Hopkins

Neuilly-sur-Seine, Paris

I

Spring 1916 – Arrival in Paris

Liesbeth paused to savour the heady fragrance of the mild Parisian afternoon, a welcome contrast to the smell of winter-weary travellers of the Amsterdam train station where she had shivered with a fleeting sense that she was making a terrible mistake. She could have turned back then, but instead she had gripped the medical bag, and pulled herself up into the crowded train, turning her back as her sister Alida gave one last hug to each of their grim-faced parents before joining her.

Liesbeth's mind raced with fragmented thoughts of the past five days. Her stomach was settled now, but her heart still pounded with the same excitement as when she'd boarded the train with four other nurses, including her sister, and one doctor. The dirt, sweat and general griminess of the long, exhausting journey by train and by ship through Folkestone and Dieppe clung to her now, making her itch. But all that melted away as she comprehended that finally, she was here in Paris. The March sun was warm and the breeze carried the scent of budding flowers to Liesbeth as she stood beside her sister on the wide gravel boulevard, gazing at the hospital. Its beauty was deceptive, hiding, like a sepulchre, the horrors that she knew would be within.

Liesbeth blinked, taking in the grandeur of the building shining whitely in the sun. Le Pré Catelan in the Bois de Boulogne, now transformed into a hospital for the duration of the war, still retained the splendour that had made it a famous restaurant. A man on the third floor looked down at them, seeming to study the new arrivals. He appeared small, framed in the tall window. Liesbeth looked away, unsettled.

"It's beautiful, isn't it?" Alida opened her arms to gesture at the magnificent rounded pavillion.

Liesbeth nodded. "Did you see that man?" She tilted back her head to look up at the third floor window again.

Alida shook her head. "I didn't see anyone. Come, we're going in." Alida's voice quavered and she crowded forward to stay with the group. She glanced back over her shoulder at her sister.

Liesbeth smiled at Alida, stood for another second, then followed the others a few steps behind. She caught up as they gathered in the foyer in front of the matron, a thin woman dressed all in crisp white with a high, stiff collar. A younger nurse, holding a clipboard, stood by Matron's side. Matron waited to speak as a tired-looking man wearing what was once a white coat but now stained with rusty brown and red, separated the new doctor from the group and led him away.

"Welcome. I'm Matron Hoff and this is Sister MacIsaac. I'm going to have Sister show you where you are staying and give you half an hour to get settled. Then we will meet back here for a short tour and orders." Matron turned away, then back again. "You're lucky. It's a little bit quiet at the moment so you'll have time to catch your breath, but it won't last." She nodded and hurried off.

Sister MacIsaac was a short, round-faced girl in her early twenties. Strawberry-blonde curls framed her face, held in place by the draping white cap. Liesbeth nudged her way through the group and walked beside the sister as the other girls followed, heels echoing on the marble floors.

"Have you been here long?" Liesbeth shortened her stride to match Sister MacIsaac's as they made their way down one corridor, then turned right into another.

"Since November, so four months now."

"Where are you from? You're not Dutch, yet you speak it perfectly."

"I'm Canadian. My mother is from Amsterdam originally and my father is Canadian. Since we have so many French neighbours, I can speak that quite well also. That's the language you'll find most people speak here."

Sister MacIsaac stopped and looked at the clipboard. "Sisters Piek, and deKort, you're in here." She swung open a door, pointed inside, then moved to the next room. "Sisters Zwart, Zwart again." She glanced up at Liesbeth and Alida "Sisters?" Without waiting for Liesbeth's nod, she looked back at her clipboard. "And Sisters Hoorn and Van Egmond, you're in here."

Liesbeth stepped into the room as Sister MacIsaac called out to all the girls. "I'll see you back in the front lobby in twenty minutes."

Alida, Trudy Hoorn, and Martina Van Egmond crowded in after Liesbeth and stood, looking around the room.

"Well, I'll take this bed." Liesbeth set her bag down on one of the beds closest to the door, leaving the window beds free.

There was a narrow wooden wardrobe to one side of the bed that she opened to reveal a shelf and a bar with four empty wooden hangers. Inside the door was a small mirror, and Liesbeth made a face when she saw what a mess she was. She had to stoop to get a good look at herself because, at five feet and ten inches, she was taller than most women. Her chestnut hair was parted in the middle and pulled back into a bun at the nape of her neck. She usually wore two carefully curled loops at the sides in an effort to hide her large ears, but now the curls were gone and only long wispy strands framed her face. She peered at herself through her small, round glasses and attempted to pin back the wisps. Frowning wrinkled her forehead and chin, giving her a severe appearance. She sighed and turned away from the mirror.

On the other side of the bed was a short wooden locker that also had a shelf. This doubled as a bedside table and had a hasp on it with a lock and key dangling.

Her sister was unpacking her few items into her own wardrobe. Alida had the same straight nose and dark hair parted in the middle, but her hair was thicker and still looked tidy. Where Liesbeth's eyes were pale blue and round behind her glasses, Alida had their father's wider dark blue eyes with perfect vision and a pretty oval face. Alida always looked ready to smile.

Alida glanced up. "Are you unpacked already?"

"No, but it will only take a moment."

True to her word, Liesbeth unpacked her things, wasting no movements to hang, fold, and place spare clothing and toiletries. She placed her writing case into the locker along with her purse, locked it, and slipped the key into her deep pocket.

Liesbeth walked over to the window and admired the beautiful grounds before pulling out her watch from her waistband. "Twenty minutes, ladies. Shall we go down?"

———

Sister MacIsaac was waiting for them, folder in hand. The other girls were already there as Liesbeth and her roommates hurried down the narrow, winding steps to the left of the main entrance.

Sister MacIsaac began. "I'll take you on a tour now to show you the different wards, operating rooms, administration area, kitchen, and storage. You'll need to learn your way around quickly because there is no time to lose when you're working."

One girl's stomach growled and a few sniggers erupted. "The patients are served lunch at ten forty-five after which the staff take it in turns to eat." MacIsaac smiled at the guilty-looking girl.

Sister MacIsaac led them first into a long room lined with beds along both walls, plus another row down the middle. The three rows of utilitarian beds, some with elaborate frames for supporting arms or legs, contrasted with the ornate chandeliers, elaborately sculpted friezes, and the marble tile on the floors and walls. The tall windows let in sunshine, made even brighter by reflecting off the mirrored panels along parts of the wall. A massive sculpture of three women reaching for the ceiling frowned down on the beds below, while larger-than-life cherubs balanced an antique plate in a window alcove at the far end of the salon.

Liesbeth blinked in the bright light, then focused on the patients. Men dressed in everything from pajamas to full uniforms lay, sat, or stood throughout the room. Some balanced on crutches as they looked up at the new group of girls crowding in the doorway.

"This is where the men who are going through therapy and rehabilitation are. These are the men in the best condition." MacIsaac's voice held a note of caution.

After forty-five minutes of dizzying explanations and touring the three-storey building and the smaller outbuilding, lovingly called the 'cowshed', which contained more storage and additional staff quarters, it was time to get to work. Liesbeth was assigned to the first ward they had seen, while Alida was momentarily put to work handing out the soup for lunch. Alida was very new while Liesbeth had already been nursing for a year in Amsterdam.

MacIsaac made a circular motion with her hand before leaving Liesbeth to her work. "The director of the hospital, Mr. Bierens deHaan, does rounds every afternoon, accompanied by Matron and the assistant director, Mr. Bos. Just go about your business, but be ready to answer any questions they might have."

Liesbeth nodded. "Very good, Sister"

Liesbeth took the small cart loaded with supplies and set to work. She had plenty of experience changing dressings from her work at the Red Cross Hospital in the Hague, and knew how to manage it

without too much added pain for the patient. She had only completed the dressing changes for a few when lunch arrived. She
stopped and sat with the armless man whose dressings she had just
replaced. She helped spoon soup into his mouth.

The young man nodded his thanks. "Not much use to myself with
no arms."

"You'll be good as new once you get the hooks." The man in
the next bed waved his arm with a spoon clasped between the split
metal hooks.

"Maybe." The patient opened his mouth for another spoonful.

Liesbeth smiled. "What's your name?"

"Bany, Jean-Michel, from the 97th Infantry Regiment." He ate
another two spoonfuls, then turned his head away. "That's enough,
thank you." He lay back and closed his eyes.

Liesbeth coaxed the patient to eat some more when Sister
MacIsaac came by. "May I have a word please, Sister Zwart?"

They stepped away from the bed. MacIsaac leaned in to whisper.
"You've spent enough time on him now. Move on. You can't get
caught up with one patient when the whole ward is ahead of you,
waiting for your help." She patted Liesbeth on the arm before moving away.

Liesbeth nodded and took the half-finished bowl of food back to
the cart.

She was halfway through the ward, focused on peeling the
dressing off an amputated leg when she realized there were people
standing behind her, watching her. She threw a quick glance over
her shoulder and took a sharp breath, startled to meet the dark
eyes of the man she had seen standing in the window. He, along
with another man and Matron Hoff stepped closer to see better.
Liesbeth felt herself flush. *Don't be a ninny. Just think about your
work.* Liesbeth was always confident when it came to her work.

Matron Hoff nodded at her. "This is one of our new nurses, Sister
Zwart." She introduced Liesbeth to the two men, but didn't intro-
duce them in return. "Carry on, Sister." They moved down the row of

patients, stopping once in a while to look at a chart or have a word with the man in the bed.

Liesbeth took a second to watch their progress, wondering about the man from the window. *Is he the director or the assistant director or someone else altogether?* He was, in fact, tall. His jacket hung on him as though he had lost weight. From her first glance, she had seen that he wore square, wire-rimmed glasses which magnified his dark blue eyes. He moved with an easy grace, sometimes stepping ahead of the other man, sometimes falling back to have a further word with someone. *He seems kind.*

Liesbeth's patient groaned and she gave him her full attention, finishing the painful task as quickly as she could. When she next looked up, the trio was leaving the ward.

The day was busy, despite Matron's comment that the hospital was enjoying a quiet period. She saw Alida at supper but they did not have a chance to really talk until they returned to their room in the evening.

"Seven o'clock. My back is killing me." Alida stretched before sitting down on the edge of her bed. The four roommates had become good friends on their five-day journey together from Amsterdam and were already relaxed in each other's company.

"Will it be this late every evening, do you think?" Trudy Hoorn was the same age as Alida, twenty, and came from a wealthy Amsterdam family.

"I suspect we've been let off early today." Liesbeth was tired herself but under no illusions.

Martina Van Egmond stretched out on her bed and groaned. "I don't think I've recovered from the travelling yet. I could have gone straight to bed this morning already if I'd been allowed." Martina, at nineteen, was the youngest in the room, while Liesbeth, at twenty-two, was the oldest.

Liesbeth walked over to look out the window as the evening sun filtered through the trees, then turned to her sister. "I know you're tired, but what about a little walk to get some fresh air before bed?"

"Mmmm. Can I manage it? Yes, I can." Alida pushed herself back up to her feet and looked at the other two. "Come on you two, come and get some air with us."

After a chorus of groans, they also got back to their feet and followed behind Liesbeth and Alida.

Outside, Alida linked arms with Liesbeth. "This was a good idea. It's so beautiful here. Look at how tall the trees are." Alida walked along with her head tilted back to watch the breeze swinging the tops of the trees with their green fuzz of new buds.

Trudy smiled at Alida. "I guess you have no trees in Zandvoort? It's all sand dunes and sea, I suppose?"

"That's not quite true. We have a lovely forest area to go for picnics by bicycle in Kennermerland, don't we, Lies?" Alida's voice was sharp in defense of her home village.

"We do, but it's true that there's nothing like this." Liesbeth was quiet in contrast with her sister's outburst.

"It reminds me of Vondelpark at home in Amsterdam." Trudy sighed.

Martina nodded. "Or the trees along the canal by the Herengracht."

"Except we don't see many people like this." Martina nodded toward two patients, almost hidden by the trees. One was in a wheelchair with the other pushing the chair with his one arm.

The girls walked on, each lost in her own thoughts as they made a circuit around the hospital, skirting the rose garden and bringing them back across the gravel driveway to the building. The walk had done them good but they were all ready for an early night.

II

Summer 1916 – New Relationships

Liesbeth took a deep breath of clean evening air. "I can't believe we've been here for four weeks already." She and Alida were out for a walk again. The evenings were growing longer every day, and now at eight-thirty it was still light enough for a few moments outside.

"My hands believe it." Alida held up her red, chafed hands. "I dream about boiling, boiling, and boiling."

Liesbeth laughed. "I'm sure it's not fun doing all that sterilizing, but it really is important work."

Alida sighed. "Yes, I know."

"Anyway, I heard that you'll be moved on to the ward in a couple of days. There are a couple of new porters and they are taking over some of the sterilizing work."

"I'll believe it when I see it."

They strolled arm-in-arm along a well-tended pathway through the deep woods of the Bois de Boulogne. The leaves were fully out now and fluttered in the evening breeze. It was quiet, the sounds of the ambulances coming and going muffled. They stopped to listen to the tick-tick-tick of a woodpecker.

Liesbeth pointed. "Look up there in that tree. You can hardly see it because it's all black, but look at the red cap it has. How wonderful."

Alida leaned in close to her sister and they both stood, staring up at the bird as it hammered away.

"Quite something, isn't it?"

Both girls yelped and turned at the deep voice behind them.

Alida placed her hand on her pounding heart. "My God."

Liesbeth blinked. "We didn't hear you coming."

Liesbeth knew Assistant Director Bos by sight now. The man she had first seen standing in the window of his office on her first day was familiar to her, but she had never spoken directly to him. He wore a peaked cap and brown serge uniform with red crosses on the lapels. His tan-coloured shirt was tidy, but the matching tie was loose.

"I'm so sorry. You were both so intent. I didn't want to scare the bird away by making too much noise. There. I *have* scared him away now."

They all looked up to watch the large bird fly off into the depth of the woods.

The man nodded. "A black woodpecker. I've noticed a few in these woods. I've seen you"—he looked at Liesbeth—"a few times. You work primarily in the rehabilitation ward, don't you?"

"Yes. I'm Sister Zwart. Liesbeth." She touched Alida's arm. "This is my sister, Alida Zwart."

He leaned forward to shake hands, first Liesbeth's, then Alida's. "A pleasure to meet you both, Sister Zwart and Sister Zwart. I'm Max Bos."

Liesbeth nodded. "Assistant Director Bos,"

"Yes, but not here in the quiet of the evening forest. I'd like to forget that person for just a little while." He smiled and took his hat off to run his hand through his hair. "I find that nothing is quite as refreshing as a short walk through the woods. It gives me renewed energy. Don't you find it so?"

"Yes." Liesbeth couldn't think of anything to add. She glanced at her sister, who smiled.

"Oh yes. We often walk here, don't we, Lies?" Without waiting for an answer, she continued. "Well, maybe not just this path. I think usually we go out through the floral theatre grounds instead of here into the forest."

"Ah. That would explain why I haven't met you before." He turned his attention back to Liesbeth. "Well, Sisters Zwart and Zwart, I will leave you to find your way back and I will treat myself to another ten minutes before returning to the mound of reports waiting on my desk." He replaced his hat, nodded and strolled away with his hands clasped behind his back. Liesbeth and Alida walked in the opposite direction, back toward their quarters.

Alida leaned close to whisper. "He seems so nice. Not at all high and mighty."

Liesbeth nodded. "Yes, I think he is nice. He always speaks gently to the patients and he takes the time to listen if one of them has a complaint or something to tell him."

Alida studied her sister as they walked along. "You like him, don't you?"

"Don't be silly. I don't even know him. I'm just agreeing with you. He seems nice, that's all."

Liesbeth caught the smile on Alida's face, but before her sister could say anything further, Liesbeth pointed out a new rose that had bloomed during the day and the conversation turned to the beauty of the garden.

———

"Why are you here?"

Liesbeth looked up at the patient whose dressing she was replacing. She rested his amputated leg on her forearm as she wound the bandage with her free hand. "What do you mean? I'm here to look after you." She smiled at him.

"No, I mean, you and the others here." He waved toward the doctor at the end of the room "You are Dutch, not French like the rest of us. Holland is neutral."

"True, but that doesn't stop the Dutch from caring about what goes on with our neighbours. Some of the patients here and most of the staff have some connection to the Netherlands. The Dutch Red Cross have sent ambulances to many of the war zones, but there isn't the money to pay for a whole hospital, so private initiatives fund this hospital and our wages."

He frowned. "I'm not Dutch. I'm French through and through."

"Not many patients are Dutch. Some are and some have one Dutch parent. But no, we are just here to look after the wounded, so most patients are in fact like yourself—French." She gave him another smile and finished the wrapping, laying down his leg and pulling the sheet back over him. The day was hot and no one felt like more than just a sheet for covering.

She straightened up. "There now. That's done until tomorrow."

"Thank you. You're much faster than some of them. You're good at what you do."

She dipped her head. "Thank you, sir. Relax now because it won't be long before you go for your therapy. I think today you are being measured for a leg as well."

That was the last of the dressing changes. Matron nodded and crooked her finger at Liesbeth from the end of the room. Liesbeth wound her way between the long rows of beds and around carts and tables to join her superior.

"Yes, Matron. Did you need me?"

Matron spoke quietly. "We'll be moving some patients around today. Go and see Sister MacIsaac for instructions. After everyone has been moved, I need you to go through and count every empty bed and report the number to Assistant Director Bos."

Liesbeth's eyes widened. "Is something happening?"

Matron frowned. "We need to be prepared." She dismissed Liesbeth with a curt nod and turned away to study her clipboard again.

Liesbeth moved into the next ward to join Sister MacIsaac. They had become good friends in the last month. "Sister, how can I help?"

MacIsaac's round face was shiny with perspiration. She blew air over her hot face. "Good, yes I need you." She drew Liesbeth to the side and went over the changes to the patient placement.

Sister MacIsaac bustled off and left Liesbeth to find Alida and a junior nurse to help with the reorganization.

Liesbeth gathered her two helpers close and pointed to the wooden chairs placed beside each patient's bed. "I want all of those chairs moved so that they are tucked in at the end of the bed instead of beside them. That will make room for a few more beds. I'll find a porter to bring over some beds from storage and start assembling them."

The work continued all afternoon. When all the beds that could be compressed into the ward were made up and patients moved in from other wards as directed by MacIsaac's plan, Liesbeth began a review of the supplies.

Finally Liesbeth helped Alida to push the last wooden crate, emblazoned with its distinctive red cross, into a corner, nestled under an ornate carved oval relief. She straightened and wrinkled her nose. "I can smell myself and it's not a pleasant fragrance."

Alida laughed. "There will be a line-up for the baths tonight, I think."

Liesbeth nodded. "We better take advantage of the chance when we get it. Given all these preparations, I think we'll be busy soon. We're finished here now, so go and get your supper."

Alida brushed dust off her apron. "What about you?"

Liesbeth pushed a strand of hair back under her cap. "Don't worry about me. I'll get something shortly. I'm going to have a very quick wash and then I need to do up a report for Sister MacIsaac."

Liesbeth tracked down MacIsaac in the kitchen after the patients had all been served their supper. "I have the report of empty beds ready."

MacIsaac held up her own bowl of steaming beef bourguignon. "Have some supper first and then you can take it up to Assistant Director Bos."

Liesbeth waved her hand. "No, I'm fine. I'll eat later."

The cook turned to Liesbeth "Are you going up? Can you take a plate of sandwiches up? I was going to send it up with one of the porters, but if you don't mind taking it, it'll save him the trip, and I really need him here."

"Yes, of course. Give it here." Liesbeth folded the page with her report and tucked it into her waistband, leaving her hands free to take the proffered tray laden with sandwiches and a small jug of buttermilk with a glass.

As she took the tray, she turned to MacIsaac. "So where exactly am I going?"

"You've never been up to the office?"

Liesbeth shook her head. "No, I've never had the need."

"Up to the third floor and second door on the left. Are you sure you can manage?"

"Quite sure. I'll come back to find you when I've given my report so we can see what else needs to be done."

MacIsaac shook her head. "I think we've done as much as we can do for this evening. Get something to eat and then we should try to get some sleep. It may be a short night. I've already sent anyone who could be spared to bed."

Liesbeth nodded. "All right. I'll just take this up, then"

It was quiet on the third floor, away from the patients. She stood for a moment at the top of the steps to catch her breath. The second door stood open and she heard him cough and papers shuffling.

"Hello? Assistant Director Bos?" She called out so that he wouldn't be startled.

She gazed around his splendid office. The crystal chandelier sparkled from the last of the sunlight pouring in through the floor-to-ceiling glass doors. She could see the veranda beyond the doors and wondered if he ever found time to step outside. There were arched mirrors on doors along one wall that possibly led to a closet or other room, reflecting the light across the wide space.

He stood up and walked around his desk to take the tray as Liesbeth came into the room. "They should have sent a porter with that. It's too heavy for you to carry up all those steps." He sounded annoyed.

She stepped back. "No, it was fine. They're busy." She started to turn to leave again when she recalled the real purpose of her trip to his office. "Oh, I have the report on total available beds for you." She fumbled, feeling now that it was unprofessional to pull a report of such importance out of her waistband. She unfolded it and stepped up to his desk to hand it over.

He waved his hand toward the chair in front of his desk. "Please, sit down for a moment." He skimmed the report, running his hand through his hair. "Hmm. Yes, it will have to do."

Liesbeth felt the sweat prickling under her arms, wondering if she should speak or wait until he spoke to her. He was reading through the short report again, his brow furrowed and lips pursed.

Feeling that her report had been inadequate, she bit her bottom lip. "Do you have questions, Sir?"

He looked up, almost as though he had forgotten she was there. "Questions? No, your report is clear and concise. It's not the report that is the issue. Unfortunately it is the number of available beds."

"Ah." There didn't seem to be much more that she could think of saying.

He took a sandwich and slid the plate closer to her. "Have you eaten?"

She held up her hand. "Oh no, thank you." She felt herself flush. She couldn't possibly sit here alone eating sandwiches with the assistant director.

He stopped eating and studied her. "I asked if you have eaten. I know that Cook will have finished with supper by now. You owe it to your job to eat and rest when you can. So eat."

She reached forward and took a sandwich. The bite went down in a lump and she held back a cough. She finished the sandwich, swallowing each piece, she felt, with loud gulps.

Bos leaned back in his chair, eating slowly, first looking out one of the tall windows beside his desk, then back at her. "You're one of the girls I met in the forest, aren't you?"

"Yes. My sister was the other girl."

"I recall. You've been here a while now, haven't you? I don't get to know the staff the way I should."

"We've been here since March, so more than four months already."

"And do you still walk in the forest?"

"When we can. The quiet times seem to have ended, though."

"True. And it will only get worse." He straightened up and brushed the crumbs from the desk onto the empty plate. He drained his glass of buttermilk and set it on the tray, along with the plate.

Liesbeth stood and leaned over to take the tray.

He shook his head. "Leave it. I have to go down shortly anyway. Thank you for bringing it, and staying to keep me company. You better go and get some rest now."

"All right. Good night, Sir."

"Good night, Sister Zwart. Tell me your first name again?"

"Liesbeth."

"Liesbeth. Yes. Good night, Liesbeth."

Liesbeth made her way down the steps. Along the corridor to her room, she took several deep breaths, her heart pounding as if she had been running. She paused and closed her eyes before entering the room. Alida was still awake, reading.

She looked up as her sister came in, and frowned. "What's wrong? You're all red."

"Shh, you'll wake the girls."

Alida kept staring at her. Her voice was soft but persistent. "You can't fool me, Lies. What's happened?"

Liesbeth undressed and slipped into bed. "Nothing, I tell you. I've just come down three flights of steps, that's all."

"Why were you on the third floor?"

"I had to deliver a report to Assistant Director Bos."

Alida smiled. "Aha, the lovely Mr. Bos. Or is it Max by now?"

"Don't talk nonsense, Ali. I'm going to sleep now, and by all accounts, you should too." Liesbeth turned her back to her sister and closed her eyes. She could feel the smile on her on face. *Don't be silly.*

He only wanted a distraction while he ate. Anyone would have done just as well as me.

She heard Alida close her book and the room settled. Liesbeth fell asleep to the sound of the warm summer breeze flapping the dark blue cambric curtains.

———

"Up! Everyone up! You're needed." It was Matron herself who called into the room before slamming the door again, her shoes tapping on the tile floor before she called to wake the girls in the next room.

Liesbeth lit her bedside candle. It was still dark outside although the fresh breeze coming in through the window told her dawn was not far off. All the candles were lit now and the girls hurried into their clothes. They took turns splashing some water on their faces at the grey marble-topped washstand. There was indoor plumbing and a proper toilet down the hall, but each room had a bowl and jug of water for quick washes.

Liesbeth straightened her white bib, tucking it into the white starched apron which fell full-length over her uniform skirt and turned to Alida. "Ready?"

Alida took once last glance at her cap in the mirror. "Ready."

The other girls followed close behind as Liesbeth and Alida hustled along the corridor. The sound of moaning throbbed through the hallway towards them. The louder noises of boots on tile, sharp voices, and the clink of metal-wheeled trolleys layered over the groaning to create a discordant symphony.

Sister MacIsaac was already there, working with a doctor as he examined the patients coming in and directing where they should go. His words were little more than grunts or barks. "Ward three, surgery. Ward one, this one can wait—put him in the therapy room."

MacIsaac expanded on the directions for the stretcher-bearers who were not familiar with the hospital. "Down that hall and first on the right, just there to the back of this ward, down that hall to the very end."

MacIsaac and the doctor worked as a team. There were no hesitations or questions between them, and Liesbeth was impressed by the unspoken understanding between them.

Matron pointed to Liesbeth. "Sister Zwart, quickly now, down to surgery!"

Orders flew up, down, and across the corridors as Liesbeth hurried along to the surgery.

She hustled down the hall, passing through the surgery waiting room. A row of stretchers lined the wall. She glanced at the first man in the line as she walked past. *He's hardly more than a bundle of filthy rags.* He had an abdominal injury dressed with a putrid thick pad and his leg was a pulverized mess of flesh, mud, and shreds of blue uniform fabric. She hurried on into the dressing room to layer the white surgery gown over her uniform.

The surgeon looked up from the patient on the table. "Ah, Sister, good that you are here. Come around this side to hand me the instruments."

Liesbeth took her place beside the doctor, placing equipment in his hand as he called for it. Across from her was another, more senior nurse who carefully swabbed the wound and picked out obvious bits that she dropped into an enamel bowl. Another doctor sat at the patient's head and administered anaesthetic. They were lucky here. They had enough equipment and medicines to do the job. She had heard horror stories of the surgeries that took place at the Casualty Stations, or 'CS's, where they may only have brandy to dull the pain of everything from cauterizing to actual amputations.

Hours later, after Liesbeth had lost count of the hours and the patients, they finally cleared the waiting room. She made her way to the kitchen and collapsed on a chair at the long dining table. Several of the other nurses were there as well. The worst of the rush was past and most patients had been settled into beds. "My legs are like rubber."

Alida rolled her shoulders. "I know what you mean. My back and shoulders feel like I'll never walk upright again. I've been bent over undressing, washing, and redressing so many bodies by now, I could do it in my sleep. In fact I think I have been doing it in my sleep these past couple of hours."

Cook put a plate of sandwiches on the table. "Eat up, ladies, while you can. There's hot cocoa coming."

Liesbeth bit into a sandwich layered with creamy goat cheese. "You're a lifesaver. I didn't realize until now that I'm starving."

Trudy Hoorn sighed as she accepted a mug of cocoa. "Alida, I don't know how you can say that you were 'undressing' them."

Alida raised her eyebrows. "What do you mean? You were doing the same thing."

Trudy shook her head. "No, I was peeling bits of vermin-infested rags off bodies. I could hardly call those things 'clothes' anymore."

Alida nodded. "Yes, you're right. I haven't seen it this bad before. Usually they get some kind of rinse-off and uniforms at the CS before we get them. I wonder what's going on that we're getting them straight in here now. What's changed?"

Hoorn put down her mug and stood up. "I don't know, but I sure hope it doesn't last. I feel like I'll have to burn this uniform after tonight."

The girls all finished their drinks and last bites of sandwich and rose to go back to work. The patients might be in bed, but everything had to be tidied up, sterilized, and replenished before the nurses could rest.

| | |

Autumn 1916 – Exploring Paris

L iesbeth pushed a limp strand of hair behind her ear. She knew she was a mess but didn't have the time to go and freshen up. It had been like this for weeks now. The Battle of the Somme they were calling it. *Battle for more space, I call it.* One more patient for dressing changes and then she could take a few minutes to get something to eat before meeting with her group of therapy patients. She pulled her watch from her waistband to confirm the time, then, tucking it back in, moved on to the next man, a British soldier. The smell of gangrene lay over him in a miasma of rotting flesh, but she set her face with a cheerful smile.

"All right, now. You know this will be tough, but you've been through worse." She gently peeled back the dressing from the stump of his leg.

He closed his eyes and sucked in his breath. "Yes, much worse. You wouldn't want to know."

"If it would help you to tell me, then I'm here to listen." Her voice was soft and gentle as she worked.

"The day before this happened, I was just sitting and talking to three of the lads. We hadn't eaten in two days and we finally got some rations, so we was just sitting there in our trench, eating. Next thing we know, Fritz starts up again and a shell lands right there on top of them. They was sitting close and I was a bit off because there wasn't room. It was awful. Gone. Bits of them everywhere."

Liesbeth tutted and shook her head. "You knew them well, I suppose."

"Yeah. One of them, Harry, we was together from training. I guess I got lucky just losing my leg, though God knows how I can be a farmer again with just the one leg."

"We'll do our best to get you walking again. Don't worry about that. Now, that's you done and you can just rest again."

She stood and saw Dr. Bos—Max—come into the ward at the end of the long room. She didn't smile in his direction, even though she saw that he was looking at her. *He's probably here to find Sister MacIsaac to pick up the latest daily report.* Just as she finished that thought, he nodded toward her in a 'come here' motion.

He smiled as she approached. "Do you have time for a short walk? It's stopped raining and I feel the need for some fresh air."

"I have about ten minutes before therapy."

"Good. Come, then. Do you feel like it? Or would you rather sit in the kitchen with a cup of tea?" His eyes were large and kind behind his round spectacles. His hat made him seem a little taller than his six-foot height.

"Oh, I'd rather the fresh air, if you're sure."

"Come, let's not waste a moment more." He led the way through a side exit and they were out on the grounds. He didn't offer her his arm, but they walked side-by-side, turning together to one of the broad pathways leading beneath tall horse chestnut trees. He bent down to pick up a dark, glossy nut and rubbed it against his sleeve before handing it to her.

She took it and held it to her nose to smell the earthy fragrance. "It's incredible to think that here it's so peaceful. Paris is almost normal with its markets and theatre, and yet, at the Somme, there is this unbelievable brutality."

Max sighed. "Yes, it's beyond belief to think about what man is capable of. Imagine if all that energy went into improving the world instead of destroying it."

Liesbeth was silent as they walked on, then pulled out her watch. "I'll need to turn back."

They turned to retrace their steps. When a golden leaf fluttered down and landed on Liesbeth's shoulder, Max picked it off and held it for a moment, studying it. "Liesbeth, these moments are better than refreshment for me. It's like sipping a cool drink. I've looked at the schedule and see you have a day off coming. Let's spend the day together. We'll go be tourists in Paris."

Lisbeth turned to look at him. "We've each been tourists in Paris. You've seen the galleries just as I have, I'm sure."

"I haven't been a tourist with you. There is a café in Montmartre that I would like to visit, and we can go up to see the Basilica of the Sacré-Cœur."

She chewed on her bottom lip before answering. She hadn't spent her days off with anyone other than Alida and some of the other girls before. "Alida usually has the same day off as me."

His face fell, the smile turning down before he caught it and smiled again. "Then we'll make a group of it, if you prefer."

"Let me talk to my sister first and then we'll see. Now, I really need to hurry back."

———

Liesbeth straightened her cap, tucking the stray wisps of hair back under the stiff, white cotton and reached behind her neck to ensure the long folds fell neatly down her back. She slipped into the ward where the doctor was already at work strapping an artificial arm around the chest of one of the patients. He was the same doctor who had arrived when she did.

Doctor deWit glanced over his shoulder. "Nice of you to join us."

Liesbeth flushed as a few chuckles went around the group. "I'm sorry, Doctor."

"Never mind, just don't let it happen again." He smiled to soften the words.

She bobbed her head and turned to the patients waiting for her. There were three others who already had their artificial arms strapped on and were practicing stretching out and flexing.

She smiled at the group. "Today you are going to start learning how to grasp with your hook, and we will start with a good old broom for that lesson." She motioned to them to follow her outside where she had simple brooms made from poles and branches. For the next hour she explained, demonstrated, and helped her patients learn how to grasp with the hook.

A man with a thick black moustache drooping over his top lip let the broom drop again and grunted. "I will never learn this, and my arm aches."

Liesbeth was the same height as him and she rested her hand on his good shoulder. "You will learn it, but it's certainly enough practice for today."

One of the others thrust his broom at her with his good hand, the hooked limb hanging at his side. "Thank God."

Liesbeth's voice was cheerful. "You've all done superbly for your first attempt. You'll be amazed to see how quickly you catch on over the next few weeks."

The three men returned to the therapy room to have the artificial limb removed again before being released for the afternoon. The doctor would take a look at each stump to see how much swelling had occurred or if there were any signs of excessive rubbing.

When all the patients had left, Dr. deWit leaned back in a chair and crossed his legs as he studied Liesbeth tidying up the room. "So what kept you today, Liesbeth? It's so unlike you to be late for anything."

"It was nothing." She kept her back to him as she worked.

His voice was curious. "Margaret tells me that you and Max Bos have been getting quite friendly."

She turned then to look at him. "Well, Pieter, you should know by now that Margaret has an active imagination." She gave a final glance around the room. "That's that." She nodded in farewell. "Doctor." She ignored his soft laugh as she left the room. She was comfortable with Dr. deWit. After all, they had travelled from Amsterdam together and had become friends. She was delighted that he had taken an interest in Sister MacIsaac. They were a good team and seemed so easy together. *Why can't I be so relaxed with Max, the way Margaret is with Pieter? What will I do? Should I just tell him that I always spend my time with Alida and leave it at that? But I like him. As long as we talk about work, I'm fine, and maybe if we go with a group it would be fun.*

Liesbeth walked down the corridor to study the latest staff schedule and saw that Margaret was off at the same time. If Margaret and Alida would both come, she'd manage. They could do the talking, if necessary. Liesbeth made her way to their room and was pleased to see her sister there, reading.

Alida closed her book and set it on the bedside table. "It's marvellous to have a break, isn't it?"

Liesbeth took her cap off and started to pull the pins out of her hair. She would comb it and re-braid it neatly again. Her mid-length hair was thin and continually slipped out of the pins. As she combed her hair in front of her mirror, Liesbeth focused on her sister. "Speaking of a break, assuming it doesn't get crazy again by then, what were you thinking of for our day off?"

"I hadn't really thought about it yet. Why? Is there something you'd like to do?"

Liesbeth took a breath. "Well, Max—I mean Assistant Director Bos." She stumbled and stopped.

"Max. Yes, well what did Max have to say? Has he finally asked you out properly? The two of you have taken enough walks around the grounds by now that you must know every inch of it."

"He was suggesting that we go to Montmartre. We could go up to Sacré-Cœur and have a meal somewhere in the area." Liesbeth turned to look at her sister. "I told him that we always spend our time off together. What do you think? Would you like it?"

"I won't be a gooseberry, making a third with you two lovebirds."

"Oh, Ali, don't be silly. We're hardly lovebirds." Liesbeth felt her face grow hot to even say the term. "I was hoping I could convince Margaret to come as well, and anyone else who might be off. Please."

"Ah. You need moral support. You're so silly, Lies. You are older than me and certainly more skilled than I am, so why can't you talk to a fellow without being so embarrassed?"

Liesbeth didn't answer. "What do you say? Will you come?"

Alida smiled. "Let's see what Margaret has to say. If she and Pieter both go, you don't need me. I won't make a fifth any more than I'll make a third, but if she's willing to go as the four of us, then it sounds nice. I can see that I need to find a beau."

Liesbeth smiled and nodded before turning back to finish tidying up her hair and cap. "Thank you, Ali."

It wasn't until the next day that Liesbeth saw Max again. She had just finished her morning rounds when he found her restocking the rolled bandages.

He looked stern in his dark suit, but his head was tilted a little as if uncertain of himself. "Did you give some thought to your day off?"

She nodded. "I spoke with both Alida and Margaret MacIsaac. They both have the same day off, and if you don't mind going with three girls, it sounds nice. I haven't spent much time in that area and I'd really love to see the basilica properly." Knowing that she wouldn't be alone with him had given her more courage than usual.

"Spending the day with three lovely ladies sounds perfect. I'll see you at the front entrance at ten o'clock then on Thursday." He nodded and turned to go up the wide staircase to his office.

———

The day was sunny and golden. The leaves fluttered down around them as they walked in a group along the Route de Suresnes. The road narrowed to a pathway through the woods and came out again at the end of the lake. It was a long walk which took them out at the gate at Porte Dauphine.

Liesbeth shook her head as they approached the train station. "I can never get used to taking a train underground. It seems unnatural somehow."

Max stepped in front of the women to lead the way down the steps into the station.

Margaret's voice echoed against the tile walls. "I think it's amazing. It's so fast to get from one place to another. There's nothing like this where I come from."

Alida linked her arm through Liesbeth's. "It is rather strange though, isn't it?"

Max bought four second-class tickets and they made their way down more steps to the platform level of line two and waited for the next train.

Margaret was studying the large map on the wall. "Do we need to change trains somewhere?"

Max had made a note in the little book he always carried. "No, this will take us right out to Anvers Station and from there we can walk to the basilica."

Alida left Liesbeth and went to join Margaret at the map.

Suddenly shy and at a loss for something to say, Liesbeth stared along the tracks into the dark tunnel.

Max took her hand and linked it through his arm. "Are you nervous?"

Startled, but not wanting to pull her arm away from him, she shook her head. "Oh no. I've taken the Metro before."

"Ah, you suddenly looked rather pale and I thought perhaps you were afraid of the trains."

"Oh no, not of the trains." She stopped then, aware of how that sounded.

He raised his eyebrows. "Of me, then?"

The rushing wind prevented her from answering as a train screeched and squealed into the station.

She used her free hand to hold her straw hat in place and glanced back to see the other two girls doing the same. Somehow Max's fedora seemed solidly clamped on his head and didn't move. The doors opened and several passengers alighted, then the four of them slipped in and found seats. Liesbeth pulled away her arm, smoothing her skirts before sitting. She glanced at her sister who gave her a small, secret smile. Alida had clearly seen her resting her hand on Max's arm.

As the train pulled away, Max told them about the various stations they were passing and a little about the history of the Metro.

"Imagine, they've had this system in place already for years. Of course it would be much more difficult to build such a thing in Amsterdam. Too much water."

Margaret shook her head. "I can't imagine Canada having a system like this. Pretty much everyone I know still uses horses out in the country, although I know that there are a lot of people now using motor cars."

They arrived at their station and blinked in the bright sunlight. Max shaded his eyes, then pointed the direction they should go. "There. We'll walk up along Rue de Steinkerque."

The narrow street was busy with shoppers and tourists. There were many soldiers in uniforms of all sorts wandering along, some with obvious injuries, some in groups clearly on leave.

Max put his hand against Liesbeth's back to propel her through the crowds. "Look, there."

Ahead of them, Le Funiculaire, the water-driven car system that carried people to the top of the Montmartre hill, stood waiting to load the next group.

"Shall we take that up, or do you ladies feel ambitious enough to walk up the three hundred steps?"

Alida clapped her hands like a child. "Oh yes, let's take the funicular up."

Liesbeth pulled out her purse as Max was reaching into his jacket. "We'll pay for these tickets, though."

He shook his head. "No, I invited you out for the day."

Liesbeth was firm. "You didn't plan to pay for all of us. No, I will pay for these tickets, and the girls can buy their own lunch."

He held up his hands in defeat. "All right, then. I won't argue."

They made their way into the line-up and watched the cars mount the hill and slide back down on the two sets of tracks. When it was their turn, they stepped into the car and climbed up to one of the top benches.

Alida patted the seat beside her. "Come and sit here, Margaret!"

Liesbeth slid in beside Margaret with Max taking his seat beside her. Slowly they ascended the hill to the basilica, with Alida chatting and pointing out the sights along the way. As they passed the car going down the hill, Alida waved to the other passengers. Liesbeth glanced at Max and saw him smiling at Alida's obvious delight. He caught Liesbeth's look. "Are you enjoying it?"

Liesbeth nodded. "I am, but probably not as much as my sister."

Alida turned toward her and smiled. "Be young for once, Liesbeth! You're always so serious."

Liesbeth felt her neck muscles tense. She was saved from having to respond when they arrived at the top and everyone stood to disembark. She lifted her long pleated skirt and stepped down onto the platform. "Oh, it is lovely." Liesbeth gazed up at the sparkling white stone of the cathedral. She didn't want Max to think she wasn't enjoying her outing, but she just couldn't chatter and bubble the way that Alida usually did.

Alida tugged at Margaret to look out over the city, while Liesbeth continued to gaze at the building itself. "It's so new-looking. It's, well, it's dazzling, isn't it?"

Max nodded. "Well, it *is* new, isn't it? It's just barely finished, and in fact it looks like they are still working on some of the stone walls."

Liesbeth bit her lip. "I think, rather than new, I mean *clean*. After all the rottenness of what we see every day, it just seems so pure, somehow."

Max tilted his head. "I see what you mean. It is a wonder, isn't it, that it could be so very white." He took her hand and tucked it into his arm again. "Come, let's walk around to the front."

They strolled along, Liesbeth glancing back once to see if Alida and Margaret were following. They were there, keeping back, but following. *So much for being here to help me with the conversation.*

The doors stood open and Max led Liesbeth inside.

Liesbeth stood with her head craned back to study the ornate ceiling with its spectacular gold and blue depiction of Christ. "Oh!"

Max's voice was a solemn whisper in the hush of the church. "It's magnificent, isn't it?"

"Yes, unbelievable."

They joined the circuit of people walking around the outer edge of the nave. Alida and Margaret came in and crossed between two pews to tuck in behind them.

Alida touched Liesbeth on the shoulder. Her giddiness was gone and her voice quiet. "Did you see the stained glass there?"

"And look at the beautiful mosaic." Margaret pointed behind them as they slowly made their way through the Chapel of Saint Vincent de Paul.

The four of them made the circuit and finally found their way back out into the autumn sunshine.

Alida's voice was still awed. "Well, that was really something, wasn't it?"

Margaret nodded. "You can't help but feel that there is something very magical about it. It's different than going to the Louvre, isn't it?"

Max turned to Margaret. "It's very different from the Louvre. It's somehow more accessible, not quite so overwhelming."

Liesbeth pointed down toward some gardens. "Let's walk there for a moment to let it all settle." Liesbeth found a bench amongst the bright pinks and reds of the dahlias. A bed of towering sunflowers made a bright backdrop for Max in his dark suit. Margaret and Alida wandered along a path through the garden, but Liesbeth wanted to just sit for a few moments.

Max sat beside her. "What are you thinking? Are you tired?"

She shook her head. "No, not tired. I just want to absorb it all."

He nodded and leaned back, stretching out his legs. They sat, not speaking for a few minutes in the warm sun. The air was pungent with the smell of leaves and flowers.

Liesbeth saw that he was watching her sister and Margaret. "I'm sorry I'm not full of conversation like Alida. It doesn't mean I'm not enjoying the day."

Max turned to her, his eyebrows raised. "Do you think I would prefer the company of someone who talks so much?" Before she could respond, he continued. "I find you restful. Just the company I need after the madness that we go through day after day."

She smiled then. "Thank you. I was worried that you might be bored."

He patted her hand. "Stop worrying. I knew from the first moment I saw you that you were different. I saw you the day you arrived and you stood apart from the group. It seemed to me that you were imposing but reflective. You didn't rush ahead to keep up with the group. You just stood and studied. I liked that."

Liesbeth smiled at him. "I noticed you too, standing in the window."

The two girls arrived back at the bench where Max and Liesbeth sat. Alida pointed to the long set of steps. "Shall we walk down instead of riding the Funicular? Are you able to do it, Liesbeth?"

Liesbeth stood up. "Yes of course I'm able. Heavens, I know I'm your older sister, but I'm not ancient. Come, the walk down will be fun."

They made their way down the steps, stopping often to admire the view where all of Paris lay spread out below them. As they reached the bottom, Margaret and Alida fell behind again while Max led the way through the narrow streets of Montmartre to the bistro that he had heard about.

Max stopped in front of the small eatery with its bright red-and-white striped awning. He waited until the girls had caught up again, then pointed to the small tables. "Inside or outside, ladies?"

Liesbeth shrugged. "It doesn't matter to me."

Alida was quick to point out a corner table under the awning. "Oh, outside, please. It's such a lovely day. Let's enjoy the good weather while we still have it."

Max glanced at Liesbeth, who smiled and nodded her agreement. They seated themselves with Alida and Margaret side-by-side with their backs to the open bistro. Liesbeth, facing the restaurant, could see that there were only a few people seated inside. Most people wanted to enjoy being outside in the mild fall sunshine.

The waiter brought them the printed paper menus and left them to make their selections while he hustled off to serve other customers.

Liesbeth couldn't decide. *Something substantial? The beef bourguignon? Perhaps it would be more expensive than Max had counted on. A salad instead? Maybe he'll think I don't like the menu.* "What are you having, Margaret?"

Margaret inhaled deeply. "I could smell the onion soup from the moment I sat down. I can't resist it."

Liesbeth was quick to agree. "That does sound good. Yes, I'll have the same."

Alida put her menu on top of the others. "I'm having the herring and potato salad. I don't think I've had herring since I left home."

Max ordered a *paté en croûte* along with a carafe of the *vin de table*.

The red house wine was strong and Liesbeth felt herself relaxing after a couple of sips. *I need to be careful I don't fall asleep.*

She listened as the two girls chatted together about people going by. Max added his comments once in a while, twisting in his seat to identify different uniforms of soldiers strolling past.

"I'm sorry?" Liesbeth realized that he had asked her something.

He was holding the basket with fresh rolls and thick slices of baguette. "Will you have some bread?"

"Oh. Yes, thank you, I will." She took a chunk of baguette and spread it with a thin layer of creamy butter. "Isn't it strange to think that only a hundred and fifty kilometers from here, people are shooting at each other, and yet here we sit, in this beautiful place, eating and drinking as if nothing is going on."

Alida frowned. "Oh Liesbeth. Don't we see and hear and smell enough of that every day? Let's enjoy this bit of peace without feeling guilty." She gestured to the passersby. "Everyone feels the same. It's not just us."

Max rested his hand on Liesbeth's arm. "I can understand what you mean. It isn't about feeling guilty or not, is it? It's just the amazement that there can be such disparate worlds existing in such close proximity."

Liesbeth looked at Max gratefully. "Yes, that's it exactly."

Their meals came and conversation slowed as they enjoyed the food and drink.

Margaret rested her spoon to take a sip of her wine. "Mmm. Isn't it wonderful to have the leisure to enjoy a meal instead of wolfing it down just as fast as we can?"

Alida nodded. "So nice. I have to say, though, that I'd still take the herring from the fish seller on the Zandvoort boulevard over these."

Max laughed. "It would be hard to compete with fish straight from the sea to those that need to be caught and brought here."

"Yes, I suppose it isn't a fair comparison. And I am really enjoying them."

They finished their meal, then took some time to stroll around the winding streets until they came to Rue du Mont Cenis.

Max consulted his notebook with a small sketch of streets. "If we follow this, we'll get to Place du Tertre."

Liesbeth peered over his arm to the sketch. "What is special about that?"

Max closed the book. "It's the heart of where artists work, including the famous Picasso."

Alida made a face. "Isn't he the fellow who paints blue and red people in all sorts of strange squares and shapes?"

Max smiled. "You're not an admirer, then?"

"No." Alida turned to her sister. "Remember we saw some of his work in an exhibit we went to a few months ago?"

Liesbeth nodded. "Yes, I do remember, and I agree. Neither of us thought much of his work. Give me Rembrandt any day, I'm afraid."

Max nodded. "That's all right. It would still be interesting to find the place where he works though, I think."

Liesbeth stopped to let Max go ahead since the walkway was too narrow to accommodate more than single file. "Oh yes, by all means."

They came to a small cobblestoned square. Small cafés and shops lined all four sides, while in the centre in the shade of the golden-leaved trees, several artists had their easels set up. Some were using pastels to quickly sketch portraits, while others displayed small water colours of Parisian street scenes.

Alida stopped and gazed around. "Oh, how lovely!"

Max pointed to an empty table amongst the cluster set up in front of the Hôtel du Tertre. "Are you ladies ready for a cup of tea already?"

Liesbeth was quick to answer for all of them. "Oh yes. Just to sit and watch is a pleasure."

After they ordered their tea, Max pulled out his notebook again and began to sketch. Liesbeth was dying to look over his shoulder to see his work, but didn't dare.

Alida stretched her neck a little but couldn't see the page. "I didn't know you were an artist. Will you show us?"

Max looked up and gave a small smile. "I wouldn't say I'm an artist, but I do enjoy capturing moments like this." He turned the small book around to show the girls.

Alida turned around to look at the scene behind her. "Oh, you've captured it perfectly. Look, Lies." She pointed out the horse and two-wheeled cart at rest in front of a building just off the square, with the dome of Sacré- Cœur rising in the background.

Liesbeth touched the page, then looked up at Max. "It's beautiful."

Margaret and Alida finished their tea and Margaret nudged her friend. "Come, Alida, let's wander around the square to see the artwork." They left Max still sketching and Liesbeth taking her time over her tea.

Although it was busy in the square, there was a hush that made it peaceful. Chirping birds argued over crumbs of bread on the stones. Piano music filtered through the air from an apartment on the second floor of the building next door. The melody was slow, as though picked out by a student wanting to be perfect in execution.

Liesbeth watched Max work, his long tapered fingers flicking the pencil across the page.

She had a sudden vision of her father's fingers. She was very young. It was a weekend, and her father was trying to teach her to play checkers but she wanted to stack the pieces up and knock them over, and he let her. His fingers picked up the pieces to hand them to her and she laughed. Her mother, who had been sitting nearby, knitting, spit out a 'shush!' and her father placed his large warm hand over her small one to stop the game. Silently, he had gathered the pieces up and put them back in their small wooden box.

Liesbeth blinked as she felt Max glancing at her and she leaned in to look at the progress of the drawing. "You don't mind me looking?"

He shook his head. "Not at all."

"You really are very talented."

"It's a good way to relax. You see here the way the light filtering through the trees makes the horses shine." He pointed his pencil tip to show her. "When I draw, I pay attention to these little details and that takes me out of myself." He rubbed the pencil lines to blur them, creating the sense of leaves on the trees beside the horse and cart. "There. A perfect moment captured for all time."

She nodded. "Yes. A perfect moment."

He carefully tore the page out of his book. "Would you like it?"

Liesbeth caught her breath. "I . . .I would love it."

He slid it over to her. "Then it's yours."

She studied it for a moment and then slid it back. "You must sign and date it."

He laughed and, with a flourish, signed and dated the small drawing before giving it back to her. It was small enough that Liesbeth could slip it into her purse without fear of damage. Little did Liesbeth know then, how many times in the future, she would draw upon this moment.

The waiter was hovering nearby and Max waved him over to hand him the payment for their tea. Max offered his arm to Liesbeth as they strolled away from the café. "We better find your sister and Margaret and think about heading back."

Liesbeth pointed them out amongst the myriad of colours: the light blue of French soldiers with flashes of startling red trousers here and there, the dresses of women in every shade of green, lilac, white, and pink. Liesbeth felt drab in her no-nonsense skirt of dark brown and her white blouse in comparison to the Parisian women. *Does he notice the difference as much as I do?*

Max steered Liesbeth across the square to meet up with the other two. "Are you two ready to go back?"

Alida sighed. "Back to reality. Yes, I suppose we better."

They wandered back through the narrow, winding streets of Montmartre to the train station and were soon back at Porte Dauphine. The girls pooled their money to pay for a taxi back.

Liesbeth was very aware of the heat of Max's arm tight against hers in the taxi going back. Her breath caught in her throat and she wondered if he was as conscious of their closeness as she was. To cover her embarrassment, she commented on the taxi. "Imagine all those taxis coming forward to transport men to the front a couple of years ago. It was truly heroic, wasn't it?"

The driver spoke up. "I was one of them, Mademoiselle."

Margaret twisted in her seat. "Were you? How brave!"

The few minutes of the drive back was filled with the Frenchman's description of that drive to the front. His words made it sound like pure chaos, yet the tremble in his voice showed he was proud to have been a part it.

The evening air was cool and filled with the spicy fragrance of decaying leaves, and Max and Liesbeth lingered for a moment, letting Alida and Margaret go in by themselves. Liesbeth pressed Max's arm. "Thank you so much for a wonderful day. It was magical to leave all this pain behind for a few hours."

Max tilted her chin with two fingers. "I've enjoyed it, too. Just what I had envisioned. May I kiss you?" His voice was so quiet, Liesbeth almost didn't hear him, but as he leaned in close, she closed her eyes.

He didn't wait for any further answer, but touched her lips with his own. Liesbeth's heart pounded, sounding loud to her. The warm, musky scent of him filled her as he kissed her.

He made a small bow to her. "I'll go to my office to see if there is anything urgent before turning in. Good night, Liesbeth." He hesitated. "*My* Liesbeth, yes?"

She reached up to touch his face tentatively. "Yes." *It won't last. He'll get bored, but he is lovely and I should enjoy this feeling while I can.*

IV

Winter 1916 – New Skills

The cold November rain found its way between Liesbeth's woollen hat and military overcoat as she threw all her strength into cranking the motor of her Ford ambulance again. She was still bent over, ready to go again, when it kicked and roared into life.

"Liesbeth!"

She turned and straightened as she saw Max in the grey-yellow combined light of pre-dawn and the one electric light that burned over the doorway. She gave him a triumphant grin as the engine settled into a steady rumble.

He strode over, the shoulders of his jacket already darkening with the rain. "Have you been called out?"

"Yes, it's a real scramble by the sound of it. All hands to the pump sort of thing."

"I can't get used to you driving an ambulance. I always worry about you."

Liesbeth smiled and shook her head. "I'm not going far right now. Only to the receiving post at La Chapelle." She didn't add that she loved her new duties as ambulance driver. It was exciting, and she felt the adrenalin coursing through her every time she got behind the wheel.

Her orderly, Rémi Liniger, came through the gloom with a bag slung over his shoulder. "Ready, Sister?"

Liesbeth nodded and touched Max's arm. "Go inside, you'll be soaked." She climbed in behind the wheel and set off, making her way along the Allée de la Reine Marguerite and right on to Allée de Longchamp. It was still dark as she drove through the rain-soaked forest, but bright enough for her to pick up speed when she turned on Avenue du Bois de Boulogne. The shiny roads were mostly deserted until they drew into the quarter of La Chapelle. Here there were dim lights to be seen behind windows as the working citizens began their day.

Liesbeth arrived at the yard of the freight station which had been turned into a receiving-post for the wounded. She braked to allow an ambulance rushing out of the yard the right of way. "I've never seen it this busy!"

Liniger sucked on a cigarette as he peered through the rain. "Crazy."

Liesbeth felt the blood pounding in her temple as she eased her way forward into the yard. Behind the huddle of smaller sheds and outbuildings, hundreds of ambulances were waiting to inch forward and receive their loads. The yard was a cacophony of shouting, gears clashing, and engines roaring. Beams of headlights crossed and criss-crossed through the driving rain in a dizzying spectacle. Motors pulled out and more pulled in behind her as she waited her turn.

A harassed-looking man waved them over "Quick, over here!"

Liesbeth pulled her ambulance up the incline into the enormous shed which had been set up for the loading of the wounded. The building was a good four hundred feet long and four hundred feet wide. Around the outer walls were rows of ambulances. Stretcher-bearers loaded the wounded into the car, and as soon as they loaded, it was waved away and another would take its place. The air was blue and stank of gasoline. At one end of the building was a series of small wooden buildings. Some were offices, one was an operating room, and others were filled with stretcher-horses where the wounded were laid until they could be taken away by ambulance. These huts were assigned colours which identified the hospital to which the patient would be sent.

As Liesbeth stayed with the vehicle, Liniger jumped out and went through to the large hut that served as the assignment area. When he came out, he waved his slip toward Liesbeth and pointed to the hut with the painted green stripe. The slip would have their hospital name, the names of the wounded, and the colour of the hut in which the men would be found. Liesbeth watched only Liniger, hardly noticing the festive-looking decorations of shrubs and evergreen boughs that had been set here and there in some well-meaning desire to soften the horror of the place. Liesbeth took her eyes off Liniger for a moment to watch as a train squealed into the siding that ran along the length of the building. On this night, a regiment of French Zouaves had been pressed into service to help the stretcher-bearers. They wore their classic red baggy trousers and short blue jackets. The dash of colour gave the scene somewhat of a carnival atmosphere.

As an opening cleared, Liesbeth backed her ambulance into the space by the green hut and jumped out to open the back of her vehicle. Liniger helped to carry one stretcher, followed closely by two Zouaves with the other. The wounded looked as if they had been rolled over and over in grey-white mud, their uniforms saturated and skin covered with the flaking dry powder.

Liniger climbed into the back with the wounded as one of the stretcher-bearers loaded their patient. He banged on the side of the ambulance to let them know the door was shut. Liniger shouted through to her. "Quick as you can, now."

Liesbeth ground the gears up and down as she navigated her way through the running stretcher-bearers, orderlies, and ambulances. Once she was out on the Boulevard Saint-Germain she was able to pick up speed. It was full daylight now and there was more traffic, but she was expert at moving around slow-moving vehicles and horses.

She called back over her shoulder. "How are you doing back there?"

Liniger was trained at providing basic medical attention, but if it was serious, Liesbeth herself would need to attend. Liniger was not an experienced driver, though, so almost always Liesbeth did the driving and Liniger would keep a firm hand on the patients to keep them stable during the drive to the hospital.

His voice came back to her without hesitation "We're good. Nothing that can't wait."

They arrived at the hospital where waiting porters carried in the wounded. Liesbeth squeezed the hand of one of the soldiers as he was carried past her. "You're in good hands now." She nodded to Liniger "We'll get some breakfast and then get back out."

"Sounds good. I'll be back in twenty minutes." He nodded and turned to go across the drive to the building fondly known as the 'farmhouse', where the male staff lived.

In the kitchen, Liesbeth shrugged off her big overcoat and hung it over a chair to dry by the massive stove for a few moments. As Cook put down a bowl of oatmeal and a cup of tea, Max came striding in.

His forehead was pulled together in a frown. "How are you?"

She brushed away his concern with a flap of her hand as she dug her spoon into the bowl. "I'm absolutely fine, but I can tell you this is a bad one. We'll all be busy for the next few days."

"Yes, we had notice. Some of us thought it would slow down for the winter."

She took a sip of her tea and sighed. "It's not quite winter yet."

"True. Well, I better get going. I just wanted to make sure you were all right."

"Yes, thank you." She smiled at him. She didn't know how to explain to him that, in the midst of the pain and death, she felt more alive than she ever had. *I can never say that out loud.*

The next three days and nights passed in a blur. Liesbeth was sent to small hospitals all over the city when Le Pré Catelan was filled to bursting. Even small private pensions and converted high schools were called upon. She met volunteer Americans, fellow Dutch, British,

French, and Canadians as they scrambled to transport the thousands and thousands of wounded arriving in Paris.

At last the stream of wounded became a trickle.

———

Liesbeth pulled the empty ambulance in front of her hospital and parked. She was stretching her neck when Matron met her in the foyer. "Go get a hot bath and some sleep."

Liesbeth closed her eyes. "I won't argue with that. Is it over, Matron?"

Matron Hoff lifted one shoulder. "It seems to be. For the time being, at any rate."

V

Summer 1917 – Boulogne-sur-Mer

Alida bit her thumbnail as she watched Liesbeth pack her small bag. "Aren't you afraid?"

Liesbeth stopped to consider the question. "No, strangely enough, I'm not." She continued to roll spare underwear and clean tunics into compact units.

"Have you told Max yet?"

"I haven't had a chance. I've only just been told, but he sees the orders that come in before most people, so he probably knows."

"How far away is Boulogne-sur-Mer, anyway?"

"I'm not really sure. Between two hundred and three hundred kilometers, I think."

"Will you be right at the front, then?"

Liesbeth pulled the straps of her bag through their buckles and tightened them. "No, it's well back." She looked at her sister and smiled. "Don't worry. I'll be completely safe."

Liesbeth picked up her bag and slung it over her shoulder. "Come, walk with me. It's time for you to go on duty anyway."

They walked together to the bottom of the main staircase and Alida pulled her sister in a quick hug. "Take care of yourself and write to let me know how it is."

Liesbeth watched her sister pass into the main ward, then pulled out her watch. She hesitated, hating to disturb Max. She took a breath, and leaving her bag against the wall, ran up the steps to the third floor. She tapped on his office door.

His voice was abrupt. "Come in."

He looked up from his papers and leaned back in the chair when he saw her. "What's going on?"

She stopped just inside the door. "I only have a minute. I thought you might have heard already."

"Heard what?" He stood and walked around the desk towards her.

"The Canadians are asking for extra nurses, so Matron is sending Margaret and me."

His brow furrowed. "Where to?"

"To Boulogne-sur-Mer."

"My God." He reached out and took her hand. "This wasn't what you signed up for."

"Well, it is, really. I signed up to be a nurse. Certainly I expected I'd be staying here with the Dutch ambulance team, but it was never a guarantee." Liesbeth was anxious to get away. Here, in this office, this man was Assistant Director Bos, not her special friend, Max. "I better go. I'll write to you tomorrow to let you know that all is well. I'll be with the number three, Canadian General Hospital."

Max leaned in to brush a kiss across her lips. "You are the most capable person I know, so you will have them sorted out and will be back here in no time."

Liesbeth wasn't sure if he was trying to comfort her or himself, but she smiled before whirling out of the office. She didn't ask him if he'd still be waiting if it turned out to be months.

———

Liesbeth bit her lip, then began writing:

Dear Max,

Margaret and I have been put into a new nurse's hostel here in Boulogne. The trip up was fine but slow as the train kept getting shunted off on various sidings to make way for other, higher priority trains. We met up with ten newly arrived VADs—we don't have them at Le Pré Catelan—but they're the Voluntary Aid Detachment nurses. Everyone just calls them VADs. My sense is that they aren't trained that well, so some people look down on them, but they seem willing enough to me. We all got a tour of the hospital (1040 beds). So many of the wounded have been gassed. It's quite dreadful to see. Margaret and I are being sent along with some others to the American No 11 General Hospital to learn the Carrel-Dakin method. It's supposed to be tremendously helpful to save amputees from infection. After that we'll be put on rotation.

Must close now as I've promised to write Ali and my parents as well.

Yours, Liesbeth

Liesbeth looked it over before sealing it into an envelope. She knew it was all work-related, but didn't know what sort of personal thing to say. She missed him, but those words didn't come easily to her. *It's fine as is.* She dashed off a postcard to Alida and another to her parents, then looked across at Margaret. "I'm going down to find the letterbox. Are you done with your letters?"

Margaret looked up. "Just give me another minute to finish this letter to Pieter." She finished the letter and tore the pages out of her notebook, then closed the envelope and stood. "Right, let's go and see what's what."

The streets were crowded even at eight o'clock at night. Soldiers were everywhere, standing in groups smoking or walking with purpose this way and that. Accents of every Allied nation could be heard. Liesbeth turned quickly at a burst of loud laughter from a group of Americans, healthy and oddly robust-looking. The girls had to step back as a nearly silent gang of Chinese labourers were marched past under the direction of a French officer.

Margaret put her letters into the letterbox and stood for a moment, watching. "It's a different world than Paris, isn't it?"

Liesbeth nodded. "It is. I'm tired and ready for bed. What about you?"

Margaret turned back towards the hostel. "Oh yes." She hooked her arm through Liesbeth's and they went back together.

———

By the weekend, Liesbeth and Margaret had been moved into quarters at the hospital. They worked long hours, but on Saturday evening they both had some time off.

Margaret fastened a clip into her hair and turned to Liesbeth. "Are you ready?"

Liesbeth studied herself in the mirror. Her dark hair was combed back with a few waves lying against her temples. "These waves will never hold. I don't know why you bothered fussing with my hair like this. I envy you with your natural curls." She turned away from the mirror to look at Margaret. "Honestly, I'd just as soon stay here and relax."

"Well, I'm not letting you. You must come with me. It'll be fun and you'll get to meet some of my fellow countrymen." Margaret reached out to grasp Liesbeth's hand. "Please?"

Liesbeth heaved an exaggerated sigh. "Oh, all right. Come on then, let's get going."

Margaret linked arms with Liesbeth and they walked the block to the canteen where a dance was being held. As they neared the building, the romantic sounds of *All the World Will Be Jealous of Me* came drifting through the windows.

Margaret quickened her pace. "Oh, I love this song. I hope there are some decent dancers here, otherwise you'll have to dance with me."

Liesbeth glanced at her friend to see if she was joking. "I'm just here to watch. You won't catch me dancing."

"Why not?"

"Would you dance with just anyone? Wouldn't Pieter mind?"

"No, of course he wouldn't mind. It's just a dance." Margaret sang along with the last of the song as she tugged Liesbeth into the hall.

Margaret led the way to a small round table close to the canteen counter where cold drinks could be purchased. "Look, there's Raymond." Margaret pointed to one of the Canadian stretcher-bearers they had met at the hospital. "Raymond! Over here!" Margaret caught his attention and he carried his drink over to their table.

Before he could sit down, Margaret took his drink from his hand and set it down. "Dance with me!"

Raymond grinned, singing along with the band as he took Margaret's hand and led her off for a waltz.

Liesbeth watched them whirl around the floor, the music drowned by people singing along with John McCormack's *Send Me Away With A Smile.* She herself didn't know the words, although she recognized it as something she had heard before. Liesbeth stepped up to the counter, bought two glasses of lemonade, and returned to the table as the dance was finishing.

Margaret and Raymond came back and sat down, Margaret fanning herself. "Oh, is this for me? Thank you, you're a lifesaver." She took the cold glass Liesbeth handed her.

Liesbeth took a sip from her own glass. "You're such a good dancer. You both are."

Margaret tapped Raymond on the arm. "He's a good leader. That makes all the difference."

Liesbeth thought of her own uncomfortable dancing experiences. *Perhaps that's why I always seem to stumble over my partners' feet. They weren't good leaders.*

Margaret and Raymond began chatting about home. They were from neighbouring towns in Nova Scotia. It didn't take long before they found people they knew in common.

Margaret was laughing. "And what about 'Square' Adams?" Margaret turned to Liesbeth. "There are so many people with the same name that almost everyone gets nicknames."

Liesbeth smiled. Margaret and Raymond danced a few times, then he drifted off to talk to other friends. Margaret danced with various men, some whom she knew and others she didn't. Two or three times someone asked Liesbeth to dance, but each time she flushed and shook her head. Soon, they stopped asking.

After two hours, Liesbeth was tired. "Margaret, I'm going back. I'm ready for bed."

Margaret drained her drink. "You're right. I am, too. It's been a lovely evening but five o'clock comes around pretty quickly and I'll be sorry if I don't go to bed as well."

The girls made their way through the throng and out onto the pavement. The air was cool in comparison to the hot, stuffy room. The street was quieter now.

As they walked along, Margaret tilted her head to look up at her friend. "Why is it that you can talk with such confidence to anyone about all things medical when we are at work, yet you clam right up when we are out on a social evening?"

Liesbeth's shoulders stiffened. She took a deep breath. Margaret was only saying the truth. "I don't know. I can never seem to find anything to say. At least nothing that I think people will be interested in."

"But that's silly. You're a bright person with all kinds of interesting experiences."

"We were never encouraged to talk at home. Or at least, I wasn't." A picture of her mother came to mind, the permanent furrow across her forehead. *Why* hadn't *she ever been encouraged to talk?*

Margaret was quiet for a moment, then shook her head. "But Alida is full of chat. How did that happen, then?"

"I'm not really sure. Somehow Ali always had the courage to just ignore my father's worried look and my mother's admonishments to hush. I, on the other hand, learned to play chess and was content to sit with my father for a quiet Sunday afternoon of strategic thinking. We just had different approaches, I suppose."

"And now that you are grown up? Do you speak with your parents more openly?"

"Not really. I think my parents got used to Alida being the spokesman. She can sit and prattle away and they seem content to listen. I suppose I never got into the habit of it. My mother is always rather serious and my father, well, who knows? He doesn't say much of anything, although when he does speak, we all pay attention." Now it was Liesbeth's turn to ask Margaret. "And how is it that you can talk to everyone? You can dance with complete strangers and make it look easy."

Margaret laughed. "I come from a family with five children. We learned to speak up often and loudly, or else you'd get lost in the crowd. As for the dancing, well, we often have Saturday night kitchen parties at our house or one of the neighbours'. Someone will have a fiddle or a mouth organ, maybe an accordion on a good night, and away we go. Everyone dances right there in the house with anyone who happens to be there. I suppose it's in the blood."

Liesbeth pictured the chaotic scene of clattering children and raucous musicians and compared it to her childhood home. *It's like life from a different planet.*

They walked a while without speaking, each with her own thoughts. As they approached the old Jesuit college that was now a hospital, a line of transports from the casualty clearing station was being processed.

Margaret nodded to the line. "We better get to bed. It looks like we have a busy day ahead of us."

VI

Autumn 1917 - Longuenesse

"Sister Zwart?"

Liesbeth looked up at the VAD who stood by the side of the bed. "Yes?"

"Matron is looking for you. Could you please go see her in her office when you are free?"

"Yes, certainly. Let me just finish up with this patient and then I'll come."

"I'll let her know. Thank you." The young woman turned and wove her way between the beds and up the stairs past what used to be a stage, then further up toward the matron's office on the second floor. Liesbeth turned back to finish bathing and rebinding the amputee's leg.

The British Corporal nodded and smiled a ghost of a smile. "Nice job, Sister."

"You relax now. You're scheduled for transport in the next couple of days and will be home before you know it." She patted his arm, then stood and followed the route the VAD had taken.

Liesbeth tapped on the open door, then stepped inside the office. "You wanted to see me, Matron?"

The head nurse sat back in her chair and removed her glasses. She pointed to a chair on the other side of the desk and rubbed the bridge of her nose as Liesbeth sat. Matron sighed and put her glasses back on. "You do very fine work, Sister."

Liesbeth wasn't sure where this was leading. "Thank you, Matron."

"You've been a great help to us. You and Sister MacIsaac, both. Especially when I had so many staff away either on leave or sick. I'm slowly getting back up to strength now and there are others whose need is now greater than mine."

Liesbeth sat silently, imagining she knew what was next as she waited for Matron to continue. *I'll be glad to get back to Paris and to Max.*

"I've had an urgent request for trained nurses to go to the CCS at Longuenesse."

"A Casualty Clearing Station?" Liesbeth blinked.

"Yes. They've had some losses there and they need help. It's critical."

Liesbeth swallowed. "Yes, of course. When do I leave?"

"I've already spoken to Sister MacIsaac. She's packing now. I know you haven't finished your shift, but I'll have a VAD step in for you so you can pack as well. There is an ambulance train going back that way"—Matron pulled out her watch—"in an hour. I have a porter standing by to drive you to the station."

Liesbeth stood and hoped she didn't look as shaky as she felt. "Very good, Matron."

Matron handed her the transfer papers that would take her to No. 4 CCS. "Thank you, Sister. They'll be very glad to have you there. You have a cool head and superior nursing skills."

Liesbeth grew hot at the compliment. "Yes, Matron. Thank you."

"You better hustle on now." Matron turned her attention back to the papers on her desk as Liesbeth left the office.

———

They had seats on the train since it was on its way back to the front. It was still crowded with troops, stretcher-bearers, nurses, and even a few doctors on their way to Longuenesse, but the troops were satisfied to sit on their kit bags and leave the seats to the nurses. It was a colourful scene. Most of the nurses were the Canadian 'Bluebirds' as they were called, wearing the bright blue uniform under the white aprons. These, combined with an array of Allied uniforms, made for a rainbow.

Margaret waved to a couple of nurses she knew, then turned back to Liesbeth. "My stomach is doing turns. Are you afraid?"

Liesbeth thought for a moment, then shook her head. "I think I'm more excited than afraid. It reminds me of when I first started driving the ambulance. I love trying new things."

"You're braver than I am. Could we have said we wouldn't go, do you think?"

Liesbeth shrugged. "I don't know. It didn't occur to me."

Margaret nodded. "I'm sure we'll be fine. Other girls have been working at the CCSs for ages with no trouble. I know no one is completely out of it, but I'm sure it's safe enough. I'll be fine when I get there and get working."

Liesbeth peered out the window. "You'll get your wish soon enough. It looks like we're there."

The train slowed and men got to their feet with groans and comments about 'getting back to it'. The cheerful storytelling of leave anecdotes faded, and a grim, heavy atmosphere pervaded the coach. The train pulled into the rail head and the doors were pushed open, spilling out the men. Liesbeth and Margaret waited until the crowd cleared, then made their way out to search for the Orderly Room where they would hand in their papers and receive their billets and assignments.

They wound their way through the maze of tented structures and large wooden huts.

Margaret's eyes were large as she took in the rows and clusters of facilities. "It's bigger than I expected."

The porter who was pointing out where they needed to go heard her comment. "Yes, we're quite proud of what we've got here.

The Aussies have their CCS down the way there and it isn't as tidy as ours." He nodded goodbye and turned into a hut as they continued on to the administrative tent.

After handing in their forms, Liesbeth and Margaret were assigned billets and told where to report for their assignments.

The Regimental Medical Officer was Dr. Cushing. He perched on the edge of his desk to talk to Liesbeth and Margaret. "We're very glad to have you here. We've had three of the sisters come down with scarlet fever and I've sent them to Boulogne to recover, despite their protests." He folded his arms across his chest. "You'll see everything here. A lot of sickness. Some infectious, some just the usual kind of thing that people get, but because the men are weak and run-down, it hits them harder. Sometimes they're kept with their units, but when the Corps moves, they aren't fit for the long marches. It's best they come here to recover. I'm afraid we see quite a bit of venereal disease, and then there's trench foot." He stood. "Are you ready to get to work?"

Liesbeth spoke for both of them. "Yes, Sir."

"Right. Sister Zwart, you'll be working in the amputations ward and Sister MacIsaac, you're in the infectious ward." Dr. Cushing led them out to where a sergeant was sitting at a desk. "Sergeant Michaels will show you to your wards."

———

Liesbeth scratched absently at her scalp, then, realizing what she was doing, slid her fingers through her hair, feeling for lice, before returning to her letter.

"Dear Alida,

Thank you for your letter – it was forwarded from No. —." Liesbeth knew by now that any reference to actual names or places would probably be blacked out, so she just left the information out.

"By now you will have received my note and know that we have been transferred to a CCS. I'm quite well and there's no need for worry." Liesbeth stopped and looked around.

"Margaret and I have comfortable billets here. It's under canvas, but there are electric lights and a wooden floor, so really very civilized, only rather chilly. It's amazing to me how clean and organized things are. I imagined that it would be all dirt and flies, but it isn't. I'm working with amputees, so I'm using the Carrel-Dakin training I took and it does seem to be very helpful. It gets rather messy and we are constantly changing the sheets, but the flushing of the wounds every few hours with Dakin's solution really makes a difference in keeping the sepsis at bay.

I think my biggest horror is all the lice. By the time patients get to Paris, most of the time they've been deloused, but here the little greybacks are rampant.

The other thing to get used to is the noise. There's no hiding the fact that we are closer to the front here than I've been before. It seems, from talking to some of the girls, that most nights when there is a moon, Fritz flies overhead on his air raids. Sometimes he drops his bombs here, despite our big red crosses and then all the nurses are moved into the chateau, with nine to a room. Luckily we haven't had that happen in our few nights here yet.

When the sisters who are posted here are well again, I'll be back. Try not to worry. Write soon and give me your news.

Love, Lies"

Liesbeth folded the letter and took out a fresh sheet to write to Max.

"Dear Max,

You will know by now that Margaret and I have been temporarily posted." Liesbeth paused and imagined Max reading her letter. He would run his hand across his hair as he did when he was worried. She smiled when she thought of him. What could she write that would let him know that she was thinking of him, yet not be embarrassing?

"Your counterparts here are doing a fairly good job managing things. We only have patients who are quite serious. The ones who are not so bad are kept back and dealt with at the frontline ambulance stations. The ones who are serious but can be moved get put on a train pretty quickly and sent forward (to you!) and that leaves us with those whose wounds threaten life and limb. We have an operating theatre with two beds that runs twenty-four hours a day. The surgeons work sixteen hours on and eight hours off, as do we all.

I often think of your efficient organization which ensures that we all have everything we need all the time. It isn't the same here, sadly. Supplies run short regularly. Right now, it seems to be syringes. We have been reusing them and treat them like gold.

Well Max, as I say, I think of you and know that we'll have lots to talk about when I next see you. Until then, take care.

Yours,

Liesbeth"

Liesbeth looked up at the night sky as she walked with an armload of clean sheets from the laundry back toward her ward. Planes had been back and forth several times and now she could hear them coming again, a buzzing sound that grew into a drone. The clouds were closing in over the moon and with every step, the light waned.

Boom.

The explosion threw Liesbeth to the ground and she lay stunned for a moment. She shook her head as she jumped up and ran to her ward, hardly hearing her own voice through the noise. She felt as if she'd been struck partially deaf. "Are you all right, boys?"

There were a lot of groans, followed by a chorus of "Don't bother about us" and "Yes, fine".

All the hospital lights were out, but the sky was full of searchlights and bursting fireworks from the anti-aircraft artillery. She raced through the ward and out again on her way to the next ward where the chest and abdomen injuries were kept. Running through the semi-darkness, she tumbled into a large bomb crater.

Liesbeth put her hands down on the ground to push herself up again. They sunk into soft, oily clay. *What is this?* She managed to clamber her way out of the five-foot deep hole and it was only when she pulled her handkerchief out of her pocket to give her hands a quick wipe that she realized her hands were covered in blood up to her wrists.

She refused to think of whose body had been down in the crater with her. There was no helping him now.

She hurried on to the next ward where she met up with the padre. He looked at the blood on her uniform. "Are you all right, Sister?"

She nodded. "Yes, fine, Padre. It's not my blood."

"You should go to the chateau and take cover."

She pushed past him and reached for the handle of a stretcher poking out from under a torn flap of canvas. "There are men here who need me." She tugged on the stretcher and the splintered handle came away in her hand, making her stumble backwards into the padre.

He leaned down and helped to pull the stretcher free, but the patient on it was dead.

Liesbeth tipped the stretcher to roll the body off. She grasped the one broken handle and the other good one on her end. "Come, Padre. Grab the other end."

Together, Liesbeth and the padre made their way through the ward, trading the broken stretcher for a whole one they came across. They found an orderly lying on the ground, one of his legs completely gone. They carried him to the surgery which had escaped damage and was in full operation already. An emergency generator had been started, providing enough light with which to work.

Liesbeth worked through, helping patients back into their beds. She re-dressed wounds that had opened. She carried and lifted bodies and body parts. It was full daylight by the time order was mostly restored. Margaret found her and they stepped outside into the autumn sunshine.

Liesbeth looked at Margaret. "Do I look as bad as you?"

Margaret looked down at herself. "Yes, I would say you do."

Liesbeth rubbed her hands against her once-white apron "I'm going to find some hot water to wash myself and my clothes."

Margaret nodded. "And then we'll find something to eat. I met up with Cook somewhere during the night and he was cursing because the bombs had put out his fire. He must have gotten everything up and running again because I saw oatmeal and tea going around the ward."

Suddenly Liesbeth's stomach was growling. "That sounds heavenly if I can stay awake long enough."

The two of them went off to beg some hot water from the kitchen as their first priority.

VII

November 1917

The CCS didn't suffer any further attacks during the six weeks that Liesbeth and Margaret spent there, but they were close enough to the front to hear the thunderous rumble of the guns and see the horizon lit up with bursting shells and the bright arcs of Verey lights.

One night in mid-November, the roar of the guns became a continuous din, and at one o'clock in the morning, the ambulances began to arrive. Liesbeth dressed quickly, although she was early for her shift. She stopped in at the reception marquee before going to her own ward. The wounded had overwhelmed the ward with dazed and bleeding men spilling out into the mud. The orderly officer was a new doctor who had only been on-site for three days. It was clear to Liesbeth the moment she walked in that he was out of his depth.

She stepped to his side. "Can I help you here, Doctor?"

He looked up from the tag he was reading, pinned to the chest of one of the wounded. "I'd be grateful, Sister."

Liesbeth nodded. "First, let's get the walking wounded over to that side, and have the stretchers on this side."

The officer nodded and Liesbeth went through the crowd, issuing orders. It was remarkably quiet inside the reception. The men were too exhausted or numb to complain or even groan.

When the chaos took on a more organized appearance, with orderlies moving patients to one location or the other, Liesbeth went back to the doctor's side. "Now, how about I take the walking wounded to the resuscitation tent for the time being? We'll get them looked after there with dressings and further assessment."

His forehead furrowed. "But it'll be jammed with the dying."

Liesbeth glanced around the reception. "You need the space here. It'll have to do for now. I'll have an orderly arrange it to keep the dying quite separate."

He wiped a hand across his brow, leaving a streak of blood. "You're right, of course."

Liesbeth touched his arm. "You continue to focus on the bad ones for pre-op and evacuation. Leave these others to me. When I know things are organized I'll have to check on my ward."

"Thank you again, Sister. I'll manage now. The duty sergeant, orderlies, and I will be able to handle things."

Liesbeth made her way back to the other side of the reception tent. "Now, gentlemen, only a few more steps and then we'll let you sit in peace while we get you the help you need. Can you follow me?"

Men who had sat down struggled to their feet again, some wrapped in blankets or coats, all with bandages or splints stiff with mud, blood, and dust. The labels listing their injuries gleamed through the grime like tiny windows. They shambled forward, stumbling behind Liesbeth with the help of their comrades.

An orderly had run ahead to make space for the incoming walking wounded.

Liesbeth gave a quick smile to the orderly in the resuscitation tent. He had pulled folding screens across the tent to separate the dying from the new arrivals. This ward was intended for the shocked, collapsed, and dying cases that were not yet able to withstand an operation. There were heated beds to help with the shock. Here also they were given blood transfusions that sometimes worked miracles on reviving patients enough to enable them to have the surgery they needed.

The orderly in charge of this unit, a nineteen-year-old corporal, was one of the kindest, most patient soldiers that Liesbeth had ever met. Together, he and Liesbeth settled the men on benches or on the floor to rest while nurses began to deal with the wounds.

Liesbeth watched him for a moment before leaving for her ward. He was of medium height with copper-coloured curls inherited from his Irish ancestors. He moved amongst the men asking questions and making small jokes that brought weak smiles to the dusty faces.

"Well done, Corporal Harrington. You're managing everything perfectly here."

"Thank you, Sister. I have to get back to the other side. My boys there need me, but I think everything here is under control and I'll come back around to check regularly."

Liesbeth allowed herself a smile as she hurried along the wooden walk to her own ward. *That young man should be recommended for a medal. He's been in that ward for months without relief. He's been the keeper of many a last message and farewell look or touch.*

"Sister Zwart." Liesbeth heard Matron calling her name.

Liesbeth dashed across the muddy road between two ambulances. "Matron?"

"You're to report to pre-op." Matron nodded towards the reception tent. "I heard of your help in organizing things. Good for you. Poor Dr. Stevens was thrown in at the deep end."

With that, Matron whirled away and Liesbeth retraced her steps to make her way to pre-op.

When she entered the ward, Margaret was already there, peeling off dried and caked-on dressings, washing wounds, and helping to prioritize the wounded.

"Do you want me anywhere in particular, Sister MacIsaac?"

"Start over by the door. Get them as cleaned up as you can and dress the less serious wounds. Just leave the major wounds for the surgeons. They've got all four tables working so they're putting them through as fast as possible."

Liesbeth moved from stretcher to stretcher, stripping off cloth, washing and dressing wounds and sometimes calling for the order-lies to move away the dead who had slipped away while awaiting their turn on the tables.

It was mid-afternoon before Liesbeth was able to take time off. She stripped off her uniform and filled a basin with water to give herself a quick wash before crawling under her blanket.

Margaret came in and refilled the basin. "I hear we're getting help."

Liesbeth opened her eyes again. "Oh?"

"Yes, the Aussies are sending down a couple of visiting teams."

Liesbeth sighed and turned over. "That's good." She didn't know if Margaret said anything further because she fell asleep immediately.

———

It was quiet outside. Liesbeth put her hand on Margaret's arm to stop her as they walked to the mess to get supper. "Listen."

Margaret stood still. "I don't hear anything."

"That's just it. I can hear a lark. Isn't it amazing that in all of this, they are still here?"

Margaret smiled and walked on. "It's a treat."

Liesbeth joined the line for supper behind the orderly from resuss. "Good evening, Corporal Harrington. How are things in your world?"

"Quieter now, thank goodness, Sister. We got through all the walking and have some space again."

"I hope you got some rest?"

"Oh yes. Don't worry about me. I've learned how to fall asleep in an instant and even an hour or two does me."

Liesbeth and Margaret received their plates of corned beef hash and joined Harrington at a table. From the next table over, there was a burst of laughter. Harrington nodded toward the group. "Those are the visiting Aussies. They always take a place by storm, don't they?"

Liesbeth glanced over at the newcomers. "It's good to get the help for the doctors."

Harrington nodded. "Oh yes, no question. They just seem so different from us Canadians, though. More confident, maybe."

Margaret raised her eyebrows. "Certainly louder, anyway."

Liesbeth finished eating and wrapped her fingers around her tin cup of tea, nursing the lukewarm drink. "Don't be bowled over by them, Corporal. I would choose your quiet Canadian ways anytime."

Harrington stood and picked up his plate and cup. "Well, once more into the fray. Have a good one, Sisters."

Liesbeth and Margaret finished their tea and went to start their shift.

———

The regular CCS nurses were fully recovered from their scarlet fever and returned to the CCS.

Liesbeth packed her bag. Margaret had gone off to say goodbye to various friends. Liesbeth had already shaken hands with the doctors and had her last meeting with Matron. *Who else should I visit before I leave?*

She gave one last tug to the strap around her bag and looked at her watch. She still had some time before catching the train. *I'll walk over and see if Harrington is on duty.*

A crisp wind made the flags and tent canvas flap. Liesbeth drew her cardigan tighter around herself and hustled to the resuscitation tent. The ward was warm in contrast and Liesbeth glanced around. The two nurses on duty both looked up from their work and Liesbeth nodded at them. One started to rise from her work table but Liesbeth shook her head and waved her back to her seat.

Liesbeth saw the boy then. He was mopping the wooden floor and as he moved between the beds, he sang. "*Kathleen Mavourneen, awake from thy slumbers. . .*"

Liesbeth moved closer but waited, listening as a patient took up the song and joined in, his voice scratchy. "*The blue mountains glow in the sun's golden light. . .*"

Corporal Harrington turned then and saw Liesbeth. He propped his mop against the wall and came to her. "You're off, then?"

Liesbeth smiled. "Yes. I'm sorry to have interrupted the song."

The orderly shook his head. "I hardly even realize I'm doing it. It seems to soothe the patients though, and if once in a while, someone joins in, I think it makes everyone feel a bit better."

Liesbeth put out her hand to shake his. "You're very good for the patients. I wish you well."

He grinned as he shook her hand. "If you're ever in Toronto, look me up, Sister."

She smiled. "I don't think that's likely, but thank you for the offer."

He tilted his head. "You never know what the future will bring."

"So true. I'll say goodbye, then, and let you get back to work."

Liesbeth went back to her billet to pick up her bag, humming the song to herself.

VIII

Winter 1917 - Paris

Margaret's head fell forward, then she jerked awake again as the train's brakes squealed. Across from her, Liesbeth smiled. Margaret shook her head and rolled her shoulders. "I'm so tired, I feel like I could sleep for a week."

Liesbeth nodded. "I know how you feel."

"You look as fresh as a daisy."

"I had a pretty good night last night."

Margaret shook her head. "I didn't. I think I'm just so excited to be seeing Pieter again that it took me forever to fall asleep."

Liesbeth smiled again, then looked out the window at the passing countryside. She could feel Margaret watching her, so she turned back again.

Margaret tilted her head. "Aren't you excited to see Max?"

"Yes, of course."

"It feels like there is a 'but' there."

"No, no 'but'." Liesbeth sighed. "Perhaps I'm just a little nervous. I'm not like you. You're so sure that Pieter will be as happy to see you as you are him."

Margaret frowned. "Why should you be nervous? You've been getting letters from Max. In fact, he was sending all those extra supplies. Poor Dr. Cushing was sad to see you go because he knows that his backdoor supply route is finished. The first time Max sent you those boxes of syringes, I thought the doctor was going to kiss you."

Liesbeth laughed. "I know. It was super of Max to send us those extras. And yes, he's been writing and there's nothing to make me think there is anything wrong. I'm just being me, I guess."

Margaret wouldn't let it go. "What does that mean?"

"I've never had a long-term relationship like this. I just always imagine that there are so many prettier, funnier, chattier girls around, so why would anyone want to be with me?" *There, I've said it out loud.*

Margaret pursed her lips. "So you think that, because Max likes you, there must be something wrong with him?"

"No, I'm not saying that. There's nothing wrong with him."

Margaret shook her head. "I give up. Liesbeth, yes, you are serious, but clearly that's what he likes about you. So stop analysing everything so much and just have some faith."

"Faith?"

"In him, in yourself." Margaret shook her head again and picked up the book that had fallen closed on her lap.

———

She saw him before he saw her. A porter had been sent to pick them up at the train station, and as they drove up the wide drive, Liesbeth saw Max standing by the kitchen door. He was smoking a cigar and talking to a nurse Liesbeth didn't recognize.

The driver pulled up and then Max saw her. He threw down the stub of his cigar and stepped up to open the door for her. As Liesbeth climbed out of the vehicle, she saw the nurse turn and disappear into the kitchen.

Max picked up her bag. "Liesbeth, Margaret! Welcome back. It's so good to see you both." Liesbeth was glad that he didn't lean in to kiss her. She longed to feel his lips on hers, but only when they were in private.

She reached out to take her bag from him. "It's great to be back. Let me just take my things to my room and then I'll come back to have a cup of tea and hear all the news."

Margaret came around to stand with them. "How wonderful to be back here. Where's Pieter, do you know?"

"I believe he's on shift in surgery at the moment."

Margaret's face fell. "Well, I'll catch up with him later, then." She picked up her bag and turned to head to her room.

Liesbeth nodded to Max. "I'll be down in about ten minutes. Will you have time for a cup of tea with me?"

Max gave her arm a gentle squeeze. "Definitely."

Liesbeth followed the walkway around to the entrance that would take her to her quarters as she thought about seeing Max with the other nurse. *He seems the same. Who was she? Should I ask him about her? I probably should not and by saying nothing he won't be on his guard. I'll just wait and see.*

She focused on putting away her few things, then hastened back to the kitchen.

Cook smiled and put a pot of steaming tea on the table where Max was already sitting. "Welcome back. We missed you girls. Will you have a sandwich as well?"

Margaret walked in at that moment and stopped to give the big French cook a hug. "Oh I've missed all this, especially your sandwiches!"

Cook glowed. "So that means 'yes'?"

Margaret grinned. "Oh yes, please. What about you, Liesbeth?"

Liesbeth nodded. "As long as it isn't jam. I feel like I've been living on jam sandwiches for weeks."

Cook wrinkled his nose. "You're in Paris now. I hope that even though we, too, are rationed these days, I can come up with something more than that."

As Cook made up a small plate of sandwiches for them, the girls talked with Max.

Margaret paced to the window, then came back to Max. "I can't believe it's starting to snow already. Has it been very busy here? Have you fellows been downtown lately?"

Max laughed and held up a hand. "Catch your breath. Yes, it's been busy, but seems to be getting better now, and as for going out, I can't speak for Pieter, but I have been keeping myself busy here."

Liesbeth watched Max as he answered Margaret's questions. *Busy with what, or should I say whom?*

He turned away from Margaret and smiled at Liesbeth. "And now, how are you doing? Did you have a good journey back?"

Liesbeth was caught by the warmth of his voice. "Yes, no problems at all. We were held up in Boulogne for a couple of hours, but we got out and stretched. We couldn't really go to see anyone because one never knows when the train will be ready to move on again, but it broke up the journey at least."

Max patted her arm and nodded. "Good. It isn't much weather for taking long walks, but perhaps after supper we can go out and get a bit of fresh air and catch up properly. What do you think?"

Liesbeth suddenly wanted that more than anything. "Oh yes, I'll wear my woollies."

"Good. I'll see you in the foyer at seven, then."

She watched him stride out of the kitchen. *I've been silly. Nothing's changed.*

Later, bundled up in her long, dark woollen coat, scarf wrapped around her neck and flat-topped hat secured to her head to protect her from falling snow, Liesbeth slipped her hand into the crook of Max's arm. He looked down at her, the snowflakes melting on his glasses, as they did on hers.

He took his free hand and laid it over her hand on his arm. "Are you warm enough?"

She nodded. "Yes, it's lovely and peaceful here. So quiet."

They walked on in silence for a moment, then Max shifted to put his arm around her as they walked.

Something inside Liesbeth loosened and she sighed. She could feel the tension leaving her shoulders and she pressed closer to Max. *I love him.* It came as a surprise to her.

He must have sensed her relaxing and when the path led them under a stand of trees, he stopped in its shadows and turned to her. Leaning over, he kissed her, the leather of his gloved hand cold as he rested his fingers against her cheek, the other hand pressing against her back.

He straightened up again, then laughed as he removed his glasses. "Steamy."

She nodded and took her own off to give them a polish with her handkerchief. She was glad for the moment to catch her breath.

He put his glasses back on as she continued to wipe hers. "Did you miss me as much as I've missed you?"

She answered without looking at him. "That's hard to answer. I know that I did miss you."

When she replaced her glasses, she looked up at him. "I know that I never said so in my letters, but I certainly thought about you a lot."

He nodded. "Yes, it's not something that goes into a letter that will be read by censors. I understand."

They began walking again, he with his arm around her.

He rubbed her shoulder through the heavy coat. "I missed this. Just this quiet walking together and talking of work or the day. I always enjoy your thoughtful conversation."

They turned back as the wind started to blow the snow. At times, the eddying snow made Liesbeth feel as though they were alone in an alien world. She felt safe and secure tucked in against Max's side.

She took a deep breath. "I didn't recognize the nurse you were talking to earlier. She must be new."

He was silent for a moment. "I can't think who you mean."

Her heart beat faster. "You and she were deep in conversation when we drove up this afternoon."

He laughed. "Apparently seeing you put all others out of my mind because I can't recall who I was talking to."

Liesbeth swallowed. "Oh well, I'm sure I'll meet her soon enough."

He walked her to her entry into the building and kissed her good night before turning to walk along to his own quarters. She watched him disappear into the snow storm. *Why didn't you want to talk about her?*

IX

Spring 1918 – Spanish Influenza

Sister Albrecht, the new nurse, was flirty. It grated on Liesbeth's nerves because she couldn't make up her mind if she was flirtier with Max than the other men, or if that was just in her imagination.

She watched them together now. Sister Albrecht touched Max's arm and laughed. Liesbeth couldn't hear the conversation from the other side of the long ward but Max was enjoying it. She could tell. He smiled and nodded, putting his hands in his pockets, seeming to relax in a way Liesbeth had rarely seen.

Liesbeth walked over to where Margaret was loading a cart with clean linen. "Sister Albrecht spends a lot of time talking to Max, doesn't she?"

Margaret looked toward Max and the nurse. "No more than she talks to anyone else. If she put as much energy into her work as she does chatting, she'd be marvellous." Margaret turned back to look at Liesbeth. "You're not jealous, I hope."

Liesbeth stiffened. "Shouldn't I be?"

"Not at all. Don't start imagining things. You know Max only has eyes for you."

Liesbeth nodded and went back to work.

———

Renny deGroot

Now it was spring. The snow was melting and the patients could be taken outside more often for short walks. This morning, Liesbeth had led a small chain of men on a walk around the grounds. Blind patients, each with his left hand on the shoulder of the man in front, shuffled through the gardens and trees to build up their confidence. They inched along, Liesbeth describing clues for them to listen to, to smell, and to feel as they learned to navigate the world using their other senses.

Afterward, Margaret and Liesbeth were alone in the therapy room, tidying up.

Liesbeth folded a blanket, but her mind was already thinking ahead to her day off. "We're off together. Alida has already informed me that she has a date with one of the Aussie ambulance drivers. They are going on a picnic, apparently. Do you already have plans?" The days of them automatically spending their time off was past. Usually Margaret and Pieter tried to work the schedule to be off together.

Margaret hesitated as she lined chairs against the wall. She turned and, swivelling her head to ensure no one else was within hearing, she moved closer to Liesbeth. "Pieter and I are going away. Overnight."

"Oh." Liesbeth raised her eyebrows as she studied Margaret. "That sounds nice. Where are you going?"

"Pieter knows of a small inn in the country."

"But that sounds lovely. Don't you want to go?"

Margaret looked at Liesbeth. She bit her bit her bottom lip and blushed. "We're going to share a room. As husband and wife."

Liesbeth felt her own face flush. "Ah. Are you comfortable with that?"

Margaret grasped Liesbeth's hand. "You won't tell anyone, will you?"

Liesbeth patted Margaret's hand. "No, of course not."

"Not even Alida?"

"Definitely not. Although, she probably won't be as shocked as—"

"As you?"

"I was going to say 'As you may think'."

Margaret straightened her shoulders. "Well, to answer your question, I can't wait." She sat down on one of the chairs and Liesbeth sat down beside her. "I love Pieter so much and everyone says the war is almost done. You know, we're getting married as soon as it's over. Why wait?"

Liesbeth lifted one shoulder. "Well, if you're happy with it, that's all that matters."

Margaret rested her hand on Liesbeth's arm. "Lies, you're my best friend, aside from Pieter, of course." She smiled. "You're a thinker. I love that and I don't want you to think less of me."

Liesbeth took Margaret's hand in both of hers. "Margaret, I don't and won't think any less of you. It's a mad world. If nothing else, I think we've all come to realize that over the past few years. You're quite right that it must be over soon. With the Russians out of it now and the Americans in it, this awful stalemate must be broken." She pressed Margaret's hand. "Go and have fun."

Margaret bit her lip. "There's something else."

Liesbeth smiled. "What is it? You want me to do a shift for you?"

Margaret held Liesbeth's hand tighter. "No. I've had a letter from Janice at the CCS."

Liesbeth felt a chill slide down her spine. "And?"

"I'm afraid there's bad news about that Corporal Harrington you grew so fond of."

Liesbeth blinked and waited for Margaret to continue.

"Apparently he went down the line with an ambulance to pick up some wounded from the main dressing station."

Liesbeth imagined the young man, singing as he worked.

"I'm sorry Liesbeth. They were hit and he didn't survive."

Liesbeth sighed and pulled her hand away from Margaret. She reached for another blanket and stood, hugging it. "That's sad. He was a kind young man."

"Yes, he was."

Liesbeth reached out and squeezed Margaret's arm. "Go and enjoy your time with Pieter. You're absolutely right to do so."

———

A warm April breeze caught Liesbeth's hair and flipped a strand into her eyes. She brushed it back behind her ear. "My God, it's good to get outside in the fresh air for a few moments."

Max nodded. "I know. It seems never-ending. A month ago, I thought I could start to work on wind-down plans. So much for that idea."

"The Boche are going all-out again. It's almost impossible to keep up, especially with four of the sisters out with the flu."

Max looked down at Liesbeth, his square forehead furrowed. "Are *you* feeling all right?"

She smiled at him. "Oh yes, just tired, as we all are. I'm sure it will get better again once the usual spring flu cases are done and we get back up to full strength. So many people have no resistance after the long, hard winter, but I'm fine. The short walks that you always pull me out for are keeping me healthy."

"Then I won't feel guilty for taking you away from your work."

Liesbeth consulted her watch and sighed. "I said 'short walks'. I do have to get back now." They turned and went back toward the main building. As they made their way up the walkway, Alida came out, tears in her eyes.

Liesbeth dropped Max's arm and rushed towards her sister. "Ali, what is it? What's happened?"

"It's Martina. Martina Van Egmond." Alida gulped and dabbed at her eyes as Liesbeth held her hand.

"What about her?" Sister Van Egmond was one of the nurses who was sick with the flu.

Alida could hardly get the words out. "She died."

Liesbeth just stared. "What?"

Alida threw her arms around Liesbeth's neck. "Just now. A few minutes ago."

Liesbeth automatically hugged her sister, then pushed back. "I checked on her this morning. She seemed a bit better."

"I know. I saw her too, and then, just now, she took a turn for the worst." Alida was getting herself back under control. She wiped her eyes with her handkerchief. "I know we see death every day, every hour, but it's different when it's your friend."

Max squeezed Alida's arm. "I'm going back in. I'm sorry about Sister Van Egmond."

Liesbeth nodded to him. She knew he was leaving them alone to grieve together for a few moments. She turned back to her sister. "It's heartbreaking, Ali. I know the two of you had really become close friends. She would want you to carry on, though."

"I know. I'll be all right. You go in. I just want to walk for a few moments on my own."

Liesbeth leaned in and kissed her sister's forehead. "All right, little one."

Liesbeth went back inside and detoured past Martina's bed on her way back to work. The orderlies had already removed her body and were changing the sheets. Liesbeth wouldn't go to the morgue. She would remember Martina Van Egmond as she was when she was alive.

X

Spring 1918 (continued) – a New War

Margaret was back from her holiday with Pieter. She and Liesbeth strolled together arm-in-arm in the sunshine during a lunch break.

Liesbeth breathed in the fragrant spring air. "This time of the year is the best. Everything is full of the promise of new life."

Margaret was quiet, lost in her own thoughts.

Liesbeth couldn't wait any longer. "So, Margaret, was it all that you had hoped for?"

Her friend came out of her reverie. "Oh, Lies, it was the most magical time of my life. Pieter is so wonderful. Gentle, understanding, and loving."

Liesbeth stopped and looked at Margaret's shining face before resuming the stroll. "You certainly look happy."

"I don't have words to describe how I feel. Full. Somehow just full of happiness and of love."

"I think those words tell the whole story."

Margaret rhapsodized about the inn, the meals they ate, and the wonderful countryside. "Somehow it still seemed relatively untouched by it all. Of course the food was scarce and people had that usual haunted, hungry look. There were some officers with their wives there, wounded men, missing limbs, that sort of thing. But despite those things, you could almost forget about the war for a little while."

"It sounds wonderful."

"It was, and it just made me wish the whole damn thing was over and done with so Pieter and I can get on with our lives. I can't wait to be married and start a family."

"What about your job?"

"I think I've lived a lifetime of nursing already and won't miss it that much."

Liesbeth thought about that. "I'm not sure I could give it up so easily."

"When you're married, you'll be expected to."

"I know. Well, unlike you, Max and I are a long way from that still, so I won't worry about it yet."

They turned back and Margaret gestured toward the building. "The hospital looks so beautiful from here in the grove, doesn't it? We'll have to come back some day in the future when it reverts back to being a restaurant and spa."

Liesbeth laughed. "I doubt if we'll be able to afford it. Besides, I think when we leave here, I will have walked those marble halls quite enough to last me a long time."

"Perhaps you're right."

As they neared the entrance, Liesbeth tapped Margaret's shoulder. "Where is your beloved Pieter, by the way? I was setting up for the physiotherapy session and usually he's there before me, reviewing all the charts, but he wasn't there."

Margaret tilted her head. "Really?"

"I know. It surprised me too. He hasn't been sent on a consultation to another hospital, has he?"

"Well, you have me curious now. I'll have to see what he's up to."

"I'll leave you to it while I get to work. If I see Pieter, I'll tell him to find you later and give you a full report about his absence this morning."

Margaret laughed. "You do that."

———

Liesbeth was working with an arm amputee when a doctor came in to help out. He picked up the charts and walked over to Liesbeth. "Sister, may I speak with you for a moment?"

"Certainly, Doctor."

"Dr. deWit has been taken ill and I'll be taking over the physio sessions until he recovers. Can you take me through these notes to bring me up-to-date, please?"

The hair on the back of Liesbeth's neck rose. *Margaret's Pieter ill?* "Certainly, Doctor."

When the afternoon session was complete and the room once again tidy, Liesbeth hurried to find Margaret where she had just finished running a small training session on the irrigation of wounds.

Liesbeth could tell by the smile on Margaret's face that she hadn't heard the news yet.

The smile faded as Margaret saw Liesbeth. "Liesbeth, what is it? Is something wrong?"

"It's probably nothing to worry about, but Pieter is sick. He's taken to his bed and Dr. Smit has taken over the physio until Pieter is better again."

Margaret's eyes widened. "Sick?"

So many people were down with the Spanish Flu now that the word 'sick' had become synonymous with that illness. The patients fighting the flu numbered almost as many as those struck down by the war.

Margaret stood with the irrigation equipment still in her hand, her face draining of all colour, blinking back tears. Liesbeth took the implements from her. "You go and find him. I'll finish up here, but Margaret, be careful. We don't need both of you coming down with it. Get a mask, for God's sake."

Margaret nodded and hurried off.

———

Even as the stream of incoming battle-wounded slowed, the beds once again filled to bursting. Wards were set up to isolate the victims of the Spanish Flu, and they too were full with extra beds crammed into corners and aisles.

The fever kept Pieter moaning and hallucinating. At one point he thought he was at the inn with Margaret. Liesbeth watched as Margaret grasped his hand and he muttered in his delirium about going down in time for the breakfast, and then, "Am I hurting you?"

Margaret blushed, but her voice was steady. "No, my love. You've never hurt me."

Liesbeth turned away from Margaret and Pieter. They were in a world of their own, despite the moaning men in the beds on either side.

Death stalked the wards and touched down arbitrarily. Men with horrific wounds survived and began to recover, physically. Some of them cried out that they wished to die. And in the flu ward, people died with neither rhyme nor reason. Men who had been strong and healthy a few days previously succumbed, while in the curtained-off women's ward, petite, frail nurses pulled through.

When Liesbeth could take time away from her work, she sat with Margaret by Pieter's side. She was there for his last moments.

Margaret held Pieter's hand as he choked and gasped for air. "Pieter, don't leave me."

Liesbeth stood and pulled a screen in place to give them privacy. She tucked in the sheet around the patient in the next bed and heard Margaret sobbing, imploring God to leave him with her a while longer. And then, the awful struggle for air stopped and Pieter was quiet. Liesbeth went back around the screen. Margaret was slumped over, her forehead on her crossed arms on Pieter's chest.

Liesbeth stepped forward, first lifting Pieter's wrist to check for a pulse, then, swallowing to master the lump in her throat, she bent down to rest her hand on the back of Margaret's neck. "It's over, Margaret. Come with me now and lie down for a bit."

In a daze, Margaret rose. She stroked Pieter's face one last time, then Liesbeth led her away.

XI

Autumn 1918 – At last

Everyone knew it was just about over, yet the killing continued. The stream of patients had slowed, but not stopped.

Margaret was packing and Liesbeth handed her the items from her locker as Margaret rolled and stuffed them into her bag. "It won't be the same here without you."

"I feel that I'm leaving you all a little in the lurch, but I just can't manage any longer. I thought the work would help, but it doesn't." Her eyes filled with tears.

"I know. I understand."

"Every corner, every tree just reminds me of Pieter and what I lost. I actually wished that I would get the damned flu as well."

"Well, I'm glad you didn't. It's bad enough that you're going back to Canada instead of Holland."

Margaret sat on her bed. "When my mom told me that my dad was sick, it was as good a reason to leave here as any. I couldn't have made a new life in the Netherlands without Pieter. You know that."

"Yes, I know that. Still, I'll miss you."

"Perhaps you and Max will come to Canada someday."

Liesbeth smiled. "Perhaps."

Margaret stood again. "Help me tighten the straps on this now. A driver will take me to the station in an hour, which gives me plenty of time to go around and say good-bye to everyone."

Liesbeth helped to carry Margaret's bags down and they set them in the kitchen beside the door, ready to go. "I'll say goodbye now because I need to get to the ward."

Margaret gave Liesbeth a hug. "Goodbye, Lies. Look after yourself and that man of yours. Enjoy every minute together, because—" Her voice broke. "You never know."

Liesbeth wasn't given to great displays of affection and she hugged Margaret quickly, then stood back. "I'll be looking for your first letter to know you got home safe, and then I'll write back."

Margaret nodded. "I'm glad that I'm escorting some patients home from England. I'll feel like I'm not running away, but still being useful."

"You have no need at all to feel guilty. You've been here longer than most nurses and you've given everything you have to the job."

Margaret nodded. "Yes, everything I had."

Liesbeth gave Margaret's arm one last squeeze, then went off to work, leaving Margaret to make her farewells.

———

It was much later when Liesbeth and Alida were together in their room.

Liesbeth sat beside her sister on Alida's bed. "Don't cry now. We've seen other nurses come and go."

"But not Margaret. She is such a friend. We've been through so much together."

"Yes, it's true. Other than you, I've never had such a friend. I'll miss her too."

Alida looked at Liesbeth in surprise. "I'm glad to hear you say that. You're usually so . . ." She frowned. "Strong."

Liesbeth considered this. "I think the war has changed us all in ways that maybe we don't even understand ourselves."

Alida nodded. "I know that I'm worn out by it all. Losing Martina, then Pieter, and now Margaret going home. So much loss. You're becoming more emotional and sometimes I think I'm less."

Liesbeth smiled and wiped a tear from her sister's cheek. "I don't think you need to worry about that."

"I mean that sometimes I feel afraid to get too attached to someone. That lovely American sergeant keeps asking me out but I won't go other than in a group. I just don't want to fall in love, you know?"

"Yes, I understand what you're saying, but surely by now you can relax your guard a little. The war is almost over."

"And look what happened to Pieter. Margaret was devastated."

"You need to take a chance though, Ali."

They both burst out laughing. "We've changed places, Lies. I was always the impulsive one and now I'm the one being so careful."

"I don't think I can be accused of being impulsive."

Alida stood up to prepare for bed. "No, probably not. You're right, though. I'm going to make an effort to let the old me come out to play a little more."

Liesbeth got ready for bed as well. She lay in the dark, thinking about their conversation. *She's right. I am more open than I used to be. Does Max see it?* She fell asleep imagining herself taking the initiative to kiss Max before he kissed her next time they were alone.

XII

November 1918

At eleven a.m. on the eleventh of November, the church bells began ringing. Liesbeth peered out into the fog that clung to the trees and bushes outside the Pré Catelan but could see little. The swell of noise grew as the horns of trucks joined the church bells.

Inside the hospital, nurses and patients alike shouted, "Hurrah hurrah!" and "Is it true?"

Liesbeth was passing the bottom of the wide main staircase when Max came bounding down from his office. She called up when he was still only halfway down. "Well? Is it? Is it over?"

He reached her and swept her into a hug. "It is. At five o'clock this morning, in General Foch's railway carriage, it was agreed that all fighting would stop. It's over."

Liesbeth's eyes burned and her voice caught. "Thank God."

Liesbeth circulated through the wards, stopping to talk to patients everywhere. "Yes, it's true. It's really over." She patted a young Scot on the shoulder as he cried.

"Why couldn't it be over last week?"

Liesbeth adjusted the frame holding the stump of his amputated leg. "I know." There was really nothing else to say.

An hour later, after the first frenzy was over and the patients were settling back, exhausted from their excitement, Liesbeth made her way up to Max's office.

He was back at work, but pushed it aside to come and perch on the edge of his desk as she entered. She took his hand. "Max, will you be able to get away later this afternoon so we can go downtown?"

"We'll make time. This is the biggest event of our lives."

She released his hand to pull him into a hug. She touched his lips with hers, enjoying the feel of his hard chest pressed against her. He responded, his tongue probing her mouth.

She pulled back with a gasp. "Oh." Her heart pounded and she felt a hot slippery sensation in her groin that she had never before experienced.

I want this man. I want to make love with him. It was a shock to realize it. Liesbeth stepped back and took a few deep breaths.

He stood and straightened his jacket. "When can you get away?"

She lifted the watch pinned to her bodice, took another deep breath and hoped that her voice wouldn't tremble. "Give me an hour and I'll meet you in the kitchen."

He nodded. "Three o'clock, then. Now let me get back to work." He gave her a smile.

She went back down and searched for Alida. "Max and I are going into town at three o'clock. Do you want to come along?"

"I'm off in a few moments and I'm meeting Frank at the front gate. He just sent me a note."

"Ah, your young American."

Alida shrugged. "He's fun to be with."

"I'm not criticizing. I'm glad you're seeing him. Just don't make plans to be swept off to America."

Alida shook her head. "Don't worry. I can't wait to just go home again. It's been so long. It was fine going to England a couple of times on leave, but home is all I want now. Dutch voices and food. Clean Dutch homes. All of it."

"It won't be long now. Go and have fun with the celebrations. Perhaps we'll see you there."

"We'll be down around the Arc de Triomphe."

"I'm not sure where we'll be. I'll leave it to Max. I just want to be part of the excitement."

When Max and Liesbeth did make their way to the heart of the city, Liesbeth realized how futile it would be to search for her sister. Every street was packed with people.

Max tugged on her hand to pull her out of the way of two Jeeps pushing through the crowd, horns blaring, and American soldiers waving their flag as they inched forward. The sea of humanity closed in behind as the vehicles passed, only to part again for a horse-drawn bus. The three horses pacing abreast tossed their heads, nostrils flaring as they pushed through the people. The vehicle was forced to stop every minute or two as the crush of people blocked the route. When it stopped, soldiers leaned out to pull willing girls toward them for a kiss.

Liesbeth pointed to a group of men standing on the sidewalk. "Look, Max."

He turned and they watched as bottles of wine were passed hand-to-hand around a group of soldiers in uniforms of various Allied countries. As soon as one bottle was finished, a new one was uncorked and they started the round again.

Max shook his head. "Luckily everyone is in a good mood."

They were carried along the Champs Élysées with the masses of singing, waving, crying people. Every café and bar was bursting with crowds of people inhaling glasses of wine and beer.

After half an hour of being pushed along, Liesbeth pulled Max to a stop, her back pressed against the wall of a shop. "I don't think I can go any further. I feel like I can't breathe."

A man stopped beside them and offered Max a cigarette. "*Vive la France!*"

Max took the cigarette and nodded with a smile. "*Merci. Vive la France.*"

The man grinned and went on, leaving Max and Liesbeth to watch the pandemonium as Max smoked. When he finished, Max pulled Liesbeth's arm through his, holding his other hand firmly down on hers to keep her close.

He dipped his head toward the route back home, raising his eyebrows, and she nodded. The noise of trucks and trumpets, shouts and singing was too raucous to allow for conversation. They turned and began to edge their way back toward the Metro station.

Alida went home before Liesbeth. It didn't take long to start shipping patients out. If they were stable enough to move, they were sent by train and ship to England, and from there to America. The local French patients were transferred to more established hospitals and convalescent homes. The need for such a large staff lessened.

Liesbeth's thoughts flashed back to Margaret as she helped Alida pack her cases. "The trip home will be so much easier."

Alida smiled. "Do you remember how it took five days to get here? And now it will just take one to get home."

"What about Frank? Did you see him again to say goodbye?"

"Yes, he'll be around for a while longer. He may come for a visit to the Netherlands, but we both know our friendship has run its course."

"Your heart isn't broken?"

Alida snorted. "Not at all. They are like a different breed of people altogether aren't they, these Americans? It's been fun, but no. He's just too foreign."

Liesbeth considered Margaret again. "Was he so different from Margaret? She was from North America as well."

"In some ways they are similar. They're both so confident, which in a man comes across as brash. But, no. Having known both, there's definitely something different about Canadians. More English, I suppose."

Liesbeth nodded. "Yes, Margaret had more reserve than some of the Americans I've met. I wonder if most Canadians are more like Margaret or more like Frank."

Alida tightened the last strap. "Perhaps one day you'll go over to see for yourself. I, for one, think I've had quite enough of travel to last me a lifetime."

Liesbeth carried one of her sister's bags. "Travel safe and get my room ready for me. I won't be long behind you."

There were two cars waiting to take the four nurses to the station for the trip home to the Netherlands. Liesbeth and Alida shared one last hug.

Alida turned to Max, who had come to say goodbye. "Take care of my sister, Max, and I'll see you at home."

Liesbeth could hear Max's words in Alida's ear, despite how quiet he was. "Soften the way for me with your parents."

Alida smiled and nodded.

In a roar of diesel engines, the cars disappeared along the circular drive and turned out of sight.

Max took Liesbeth's arm and tucked it into his. "Let's walk for a few moments."

Liesbeth shivered. "It's getting so empty here. That should be a good thing, but somehow it's unsettling."

"Not long now and we can close the doors behind us and let this beautiful building revert to being a place of happiness."

The Netherlands

XIII

Summer 1919 – A New Beginning

The wedding was to be held in Zandvoort aan Zee, Liesbeth's hometown. They would go first to the town hall, then walk over to the church for the religious ceremony. The church was the old one in the centre of old Zandvoort, and the reception would be a small lunch to be held in the restaurant of the Hotel Grand Café on the Kerkplein just a few steps away.

Alida handed Liesbeth her small bouquet of flowers, white daisies with three sprigs of freesias. "Can you believe that Papa arranged for Mr. Van deWerf to drive us in his carriage?"

"I can't, and furthermore, it's silly. I'm perfectly able to walk."

"Oh Lies, it's your wedding. Don't be so practical today. Enjoy it, and let Papa be proud to be able to do what he can for you."

Liesbeth touched her sister's face. "You're right, of course. We'll look like royalty in our carriage. Let's go and enjoy it."

Her father was waiting at the door when the two girls came from their room. Liesbeth saw him study her simple white dress with its lace v-necked bodice "You're lovely, Liesbeth."

She took his proffered arm and let him hand her up into the open carriage, and then Alida beside her. Her mother came out and sat across from her and finally her father climbed in and they set off to the church.

The neighbours all came out to wave and wish them well. The girls were already somewhat of a novelty after going off to war, and now this grand parade to the wedding made them seem even more so.

Liesbeth was embarrassed by all the show, and chose to study her mother during the short drive. *She's lost so much weight. I wonder if she's ill or is it, as she tells me, just from the rationing during the war.*

Liesbeth had tried to talk to Alida about their mother, but for some reason Ali was reluctant to discuss the changes. "It's the rationing. They had lots of fish, but not much in the way of potatoes and vegetables for the whole of last year."

Liesbeth had put the worry to the back of her mind. She was at a new job at a small residence for elderly people, and preparing for the wedding had taken up the rest of her time. The job was just temporary. Once she was married, she would be moving to Amsterdam with Max.

Liesbeth came out of her reverie as they arrived in front of the town hall with its distinctive butterfly-shaped façade and water sculpture. She saw her father hand the carriage-owner some money and again she felt bad. Her father worked at a shop and didn't have money to spare.

They climbed the stone stairs and Alida fussed with Liesbeth's veil for a moment until their father joined them. Liesbeth had agreed to the veil but had refused a fancy wedding gown. The simple dress could be reused in future with only small alterations.

Alida stepped back to allow her father to take her place, but not before she squeezed Liesbeth's hand. "You look beautiful."

Liesbeth smiled. "Go with Mama now and get her seated. We're right behind you."

As Liesbeth walked down the short aisle on her father's arm, she looked through her veil to Max. He was handsome in his dark grey suit. His face was flushed and he smiled the whole way down the aisle.

Her father took her to Max's side, then stepped away to sit beside his wife.

There weren't many spectators.. Max's cousin and mother had come, along with one aunt. A few friends from Amsterdam were there, and a few of the nurses and one doctor with whom they had worked in Paris had also come.

The civil service, followed by the religious one, were both over quickly, and before Liesbeth knew it, she was married and they were walking to the lunch.

Max held her arm in his. "Well, Mrs. Bos, how do you feel?"

Liesbeth considered the question. "Just the same, really. It hasn't sunk in yet. You'll have to ask me later."

They enjoyed their lunch, then their out-of-town guests left to catch the tram back to Amsterdam. Liesbeth and Max would stay at the hotel where the reception was held and would go back to Amsterdam in the morning to start their new life.

Now they were alone in their room.

Liesbeth set the veil down on the dressing table. "Why didn't I give that to Alida to take home for me?"

Max took his jacket off and hung it in the wardrobe. "Too many things on your mind, I suppose. Never mind, it won't be a burden to carry in the morning."

"No, but I'll feel silly carrying it." Liesbeth knew she was chattering to keep her mind off other things. She hung her shawl in the wardrobe beside Max's jacket.

Max turned to her and held open his arms. "Never mind those things now."

"It's still daylight out." Liesbeth couldn't relax in his embrace.

Max released her and walked over to draw the curtains closed, even though they were up on the second floor without any chance of anyone looking in. The room was dim in the filtered light. "There. We can imagine it is evening."

She blinked in the soft light. "Max." She didn't know what she wanted to say.

He took his glasses off, then removed hers, setting them on the dressing table. "I know. Don't be frightened."

"It's not that I'm frightened." She was a nurse. She understood what was about to happen. She just didn't know if she would measure up.

He held her and stroked her back as he kissed her neck.

She took a deep breath. "I may not be any good at this."

He unfastened the back of her dress. "It isn't a test. It's just you and I getting to know each other."

The silky fabric slid off her shoulders and she stepped away from him and out of her dress. He looked deep into her eyes as he pushed the braces off his own shoulders and removed his shirt. She stood, frozen in her new champagne-coloured slip. She could feel her nipples harden and was embarrassed.

He continued only to look into her eyes as he undid his trousers, then turned away as he took them off and lay them on top of his shirt on the back of a chair. He turned back and pulled her into an embrace.

She fought the urge to squirm away as his caresses became more urgent. Now his hand moved away from her back to her bodice. She closed her eyes and tried to relax as his hand cupped her breast. He exhaled, moaning. Still, she stood, frozen, her arms straight by her side. She remembered the sensations she had felt in his office on Armistice Day and tried to bring them back. *I'm no good at this.*

He pulled away and moved to the bed. He pushed back the duvet. "Come and lie down with me."

She did as he asked, then closed her eyes, feeling his hand on her leg. He pushed her slip up and found her garter. She felt him fumbling to undo the stocking and opened her eyes again. "I better do it."

She sat up as he lay back with his head propped on his hand, watching her. She undid her stocking and rolled it down and off, then the other. She took a deep breath. *Now what?* "Shall I put my nightdress on?"

There was a dressing room attached to the room and she could go there to get changed.

He smiled. "Yes, why not."

She nodded and went to her case and pulled out the new soft cotton nightgown, embroidered with tiny white and green flowers. He was still lying on the bed, watching her, and she went into the other room to strip off her remaining clothes and took her time pulling on the nightgown until she knew she couldn't delay any further. She came back into the bedroom to find he had undressed and was lying with the duvet pulled up to his waist. She thought he was probably completely naked, but perhaps not. She would find out soon.

She sat down on her side of the bed with her back to him and then, taking another breath, pulled her feet up off the floor and slipped in under the duvet. She rolled over to face him and he stretched out an arm to pull her close.

He took her hand with his free one. "Touch me."

He guided her hand under the duvet to rest on his hip. Yes, he was naked.

Liesbeth had touched so many men in the past few years that it shouldn't have been such a shock, but this . . .this was different. There was no room to be objective here. This was her man. He was touching her now as well and that was completely different. He pushed up the fabric of her gown and pushed himself closer to her. She felt his swollen member pressing against her belly now, his skin against hers. She closed her eyes again and let her hand move against his buttocks.

He murmured. "Mmm. Don't be nervous. Yes, touch me. Your skin is so soft."

He left off touching her then and came back to take her hand. He guided it to his penis and curled her hand around it, slowly moving her hand up and down. She felt him grow even harder.

He left her hand on him and he went back to touching her. His finger found her opening and slid inside. She gasped at the shock of it.

"Are you all right? Am I hurting you?"

"No. No, I'm fine."

It all seemed to happen quickly then. He rolled over on top of her, then instead of his finger, it was his penis pushing, probing, thrusting. A sharp pain and she bit her lip to prevent herself from gasping again. He was lost then. She knew he was trying to be gentle but his body took over and he thrust again and again until, with a groan, he was finished.

They lay side-by-side, facing each other. His forehead was wrinkled as he looked at her and she smiled. "Don't look so worried."

"It wasn't much fun for you."

She loved him then with a wave of emotion she had never felt before. "It'll get better. I expected it to hurt, so I was probably tenser than I should have been."

He touched her face, brushing aside a tendril of hair from her forehead. "I love you, Liesbeth. I feel that you and I will make such a good partnership."

"I love you too, Max. Perhaps I don't always show it, but I love being with you. It's a bit of a mystery why you picked me out of all those lovely nurses, but I'm glad you did."

"I picked you because you're the girl for me."

She smiled. "I'm still getting used to that thought."

He stretched. "Shall we get up and go for a walk by the sea before finding a very quiet place for supper? Or would you prefer just to stay here in the room and read?"

"No, let's go for a walk. I'll have plenty of time for reading, but I won't be by the sea for a while."

They rose to get dressed. Liesbeth still felt uncomfortable seeing him naked, but she knew that would wear off. She went into the dressing room and poured some water into the basin to wash herself off. The water was pink and the cloth stained when she was done, but bloodstained water seemed so normal to her that she hardly noticed. She dressed and joined Max for a stroll along the boulevard, enjoying the fresh sea air. *Now I can relax. The hard part is done.* For the first time since she had come home from Paris, she felt free.

XIV

Winter 1919 - Adjusting

L iesbeth was restless. She was in their apartment on the second floor of a building in an old part of Amsterdam. It was on a quiet street a block away from the Royal Palace. She looked around the flat once again and couldn't see anything left to clean or tidy. It was already spotless. She wandered across to the windows and looked through the smear of rain and snow trailing down the glass.

This time last year I was racing through the streets of Paris with my ambulance.

She knew she shouldn't long for the war, and she didn't, at least not for the death and horror of it. She did miss the excitement, though. She could admit that to herself. She turned away from the dreary sight and went back to her newspaper. At last the bill had been passed that gave women the right to vote. It wouldn't be exercised until 1922 when the next general election would be held, but at least it was coming.

She closed the newspaper again. She had read it cover-to-cover already. Liesbeth went to the bookcase and pulled out her writing case. She smoothed the paper and started a letter to her sister.

Dear Ali,

I'm so pleased that you are enjoying the job in Zandvoort. I loved it too when I was there, so if I had to give it up, I'm glad that the place went to you, especially now that it is a permanent job.

I stay busy with keeping the flat nice, and of course the daily shopping is always an adventure, just trying to find enough of the foods we would like to have. In hindsight, I have no idea how Cook managed to feed us all at the Catelan all those years! It wasn't something I thought much about back then.

Liesbeth paused. She struggled to think of some news to give her sister.

How is Mam doing? She looked so frail when I saw her a couple of months ago. What exactly is wrong with her?

Well Alida, write to me and give me all your stories. Tell me about your patients with all their foibles.

Of course I know Max sends his greetings to you all. We enjoy our quiet evenings here together. He tells me about his work at the office and I can picture exactly how it goes. Of course I often feel that I could go in and straighten out some of his problems, but alas, those days are gone now that I am an old married woman. In response to the question in your last letter, yes, I would love to have a baby, but so far no sign.

Love, Lies

Liesbeth decided she would venture out to the baker to get the bread and could post her letter at the same time. She took her umbrella and basket, and went out onto the street. She turned up along Zwartehandsteeg, and at the corner where it crossed Blaueustraat, she saw a few women standing under their collection of black umbrellas, listening to someone speaking.

Liesbeth joined the group, and saw a tall woman wearing a long men's oilskin coat standing in the drizzle. The woman spoke with passion, shaking her fist in the air. "We have the vote now, but it won't make much of a difference unless we educate ourselves to understand the issues and formulate our own solutions."

Liesbeth took one of the papers being handed out by an assistant and read the headline. 'IFWW Wants You'. She read on to discover that the letters stood for the International Federation of Working Women. *Well, that leaves me out of it.*

Liesbeth listened to the strident voice of the woman for a couple more minutes, then turned away to do her shopping. She crumpled the paper and stuffed it into her coat pocket.

She made her way to the baker and stepped in out of the wet weather and inhaled the delicious fragrance of fresh baking. "This is always such a refuge."

The baker smiled at her. "Mrs. Bos, good morning. You're a little bit late today, but we still have some nice rolls left."

Liesbeth looked at the scanty offering and chose two rolls made from a dark rye. She would have to bake her own loaves, but that was all right. It would give her something to do with the afternoon and was cheaper anyway.

The rain had stopped by the time she left the baker, and she took the long way home just to enjoy the walk. When she got home again, she pulled the paper out of her pocket and tossed it on the table, meaning to use it to light the fire later.

It was almost dark when Max came home. The smell of baking greeted him. "Mmm. Something smells good."

She kissed him and took his dripping coat. "I've been busy all afternoon. Fresh apple cake for dessert. I haven't had a chance to get the fire going yet, though, so why don't you do that while I pour you a glass of sherry to take the chill from your bones."

Max walked into the kitchen a moment later, brandishing the flyer. "What's this?"

"Oh nothing. Someone was handing them out on the street corner."

He read out loud. "International Federation of Working Women. What nonsense. I hope you don't intend to get involved with them."

Liesbeth looked at him and could feel herself getting hot. Her shoulders tensed. "Why not?"

"They are like a trade union. They are disruptive to the idea of family."

"It didn't sound like that to me. It just sounded like they were looking for fairness for women and children who are working. Shorter hours. That sort of thing."

Max glared at her. "So you are thinking of getting involved."

"No, I wasn't thinking that at all. But what would be wrong if I did want to? I used to be a working woman. I have some experience that might be useful."

"I don't like the idea at all. Isn't it enough that women have the vote now? You can have your say during the election. All this other business is one step away from Bolshevik thinking."

Liesbeth didn't like to argue. She gritted her teeth and handed the glass to her husband. "Forget about it, Max. I have no plans to join the group."

He gave her another glance, then took his drink into the living room. She could hear him crumple the paper and put it into the fireplace.

She took a sip of her own drink and followed him into the living room. "Why would it bother you if I was interested? I thought you respected my abilities."

He applied the bellows to the fire and, when the fire was burning steadily, got off his knees and came to sit beside her on the sofa.

His tone was softer. "I do respect your abilities. What you did back in Paris was amazing. You were never afraid, you were always kind and thoughtful. But that was then and there. Here you are my wife, and I hope that soon you'll be busy giving all that love and kindness to our growing family."

She tilted her head. "I want that too, Max. Unfortunately there is no child yet, and meanwhile there are days that I'm, quite frankly, bored."

The frown was back on Max's face. Liesbeth hated confrontation. This was the closest they had come to a disagreement.

He took a breath, making an effort to smooth his face, and reached for her hand. "If you aren't satisfied with being a housewife, then perhaps there is some volunteer work you could do at the OLVG. I know it's a Roman Catholic hospital, but there is a Ladies' Auxilliary that I hear does some fine work. Why don't you check there?"

Rolling bandages? She knew he was making an effort. "That's a great idea, Max. I'll do that."

The trouble passed, and they enjoyed their drink in front of the crackling fire with Max bringing Liesbeth up-to-date on his day before sitting down to supper.

———

The next day Liesbeth went to the hospital and asked if the matron would have a few moments of time for her.

"Thank you for meeting with me, Matron."

"You indicated that you are a nurse?"

"I am, or I suppose I should say I was." Liesbeth went on to describe her history. She showed the matron her demobilization papers from Paris.

Matron frowned. "But these are for Sister Zwart."

Liesbeth sat up straight. "Yes, that was my maiden name. I'm married now."

"Ah. You should have said that at the beginning. We don't employ married women."

Liesbeth had known that, but thought she would give her credentials first in case that would help her case. "I see. Matron, I wonder if there would be any volunteer positions within the nursing cadre, or even in the laboratory."

Matron shook her head. "Mrs. Bos, we have a waiting list of qualified nurses as it is. If you are looking for volunteer work, you should be seeing the head of the Ladies' Auxilliary. They do fundraising projects, visiting the sick, and that sort of thing."

Liesbeth stood. "Thank you, Matron, for your time. I'll go and see her."

"Down the hall on the left. Mrs. Van Hout."

Liesbeth gritted her teeth as she walked down the hall. *All that experience good for nothing now, just because I'm married.*

She found the office and saw a frumpy woman of about sixty years old seated behind a desk. "Mrs. Van Hout?"

The woman looked up. "Yes?"

"My name is Mrs. Bos. I would be interested in discussing volunteer work with you, if you have some time."

The woman waved her hand imperiously at the chair across from her. "What did you have in mind?"

"I'm a nurse by training and experience." Liesbeth went on to describe her background again.

XV

Spring 1920 – Volunteering

Liesbeth sat beside the man in his thirties who was complaining about the pain from his appendectomy.

She patted his hand. "I can only imagine. Now what will you do when you go home? Do you have someone or should I put your name on the list to apply for a domestic to come in and help you?"

He took her hand in both of his, almost in a caress. Liesbeth coughed, pulling her hand away to reach for her handkerchief.

He scowled. "I don't want to pay for someone to come and help me. Can't you do that?"

"No, I'm afraid not. That isn't an option."

"My sister might come."

Liesbeth raised her eyebrows. "Ah, I didn't realize you had a sister. Does she live here in Amsterdam?"

"Yes, but we don't really get along."

What a surprise. "Perhaps I could send her a note for you. Shall I get some paper?"

He tried to shift his position and groaned. "I'm not up to it today. Maybe tomorrow."

Liesbeth stood. "I'll let you rest for now and I'll have someone come to see you tomorrow to get that note written. Does she even know that you are in hospital?"

He shrugged. "I don't know. I didn't tell her."

Liesbeth resisted patting him again in case he made a grab for her hand. "No matter. We'll find her." She forced her face into a smile and left the room.

She walked down the hall and put her head into Mrs. Van Hout's office. "Could you get someone to meet with Mr. deJong again tomorrow? It seems he has a sister in Amsterdam who may be able to come to help him when he goes home. Otherwise I suppose he'll have to get his name on the list for a domestic. I'm surprised it is standard procedure to get that sort of help for an appendectomy, though. I expected that he would be capable of managing by himself when he leaves here."

Her supervisor frowned. "An appendix removal is no small thing, Mrs. Bos. I'm sure he's in quite a bit of pain and will be in need of help when he goes home."

Liesbeth sniffed. "Yes, I didn't mean to infer that he isn't.."

"You're finished for the day?"

Liesbeth nodded. "Yes, I'll be going now."

"Very well. We'll see you next week, then."

Liesbeth nodded, but Mrs. Van Hout had already turned away from her.

She took the long way home, enjoying the walk in the April sunshine. She took the route through the flower market and inhaled deeply. The smell of flowers took her back to the Bois de Boulogne. It was more intense here, surrounded by freshly cut hyacinths and narcissi, but still, if she closed her eyes she could imagine the grounds outside the hospital with the trees and gardens budding with new spring growth. She sat down on a bench beside the Prinsgracht Canal with her back to the bustle of the market and closed her eyes for a moment.

What do that awful Mr. deJong and Mrs. Van Hout know about pain and suffering? The spring air took her back to her first days in Paris. Men there had joked with her as she tended the stumps of their amputated limbs or their fire-scarred faces. *People here have no idea.*

She had tried to talk to Max about it. *"People with the smallest ailments make such a production about it. I want to tell them stories about some of the patients we had. About how they learned to eat with a hook instead of a hand, or walk on a wooden leg."*

Max just shook his head. *"What can you say? You can't compare those injuries to what people have here. For these patients, they feel their own misery. There's no point in saying that it could be far worse. This is one of the reasons that the Netherlands remained neutral, so that her citizens wouldn't experience that kind of suffering."*

Liesbeth bit her lip. *"You're right of course, but don't you sometimes feel that we are living in a completely different world here?"*

He had smiled and put his arm around her. *"This is the real world, Lies. That other one was the alien world. It's time to forget about it."*

"I'm having a hard time forgetting, I suppose."

"Perhaps working in the hospital is not a good thing for you."

Liesbeth sighed. *"Perhaps not."*

Yet, here she was. She continued going in but knew in her heart that she couldn't go on for much longer. She felt so disconnected from things, as though she were waiting for something. *Waiting for what?*

———

Weeks later, she was again at the hospital. Today she would be visiting an elderly woman who had no relatives to visit her. She could hear the thin voice calling out as she stepped through the door.

"Sister! Sister, please help me."

Liesbeth went quickly to the bedside. "What is it, Mrs. Visser? Are you in pain?"

The thin fingers clenched Liesbeth's wrist, and she bent down to hear the old woman's urgent whisper. "I need a bedpan. Please help me. I've been calling for a long time but no one comes."

The woman in the next bed spoke up. "She has been calling, but they're on their lunch break. They won't interrupt that, I can assure you."

Liesbeth disengaged her wrist from Mrs. Visser's grasp. "Hang on just a little longer and I'll go and get someone to help you."

Tears trickled down the creases of the elderly face. "Please hurry."

Liesbeth went out into the hallway only to find it completely deserted. She knew the nurses must have a break room somewhere, but to go in search of that would take too long. Instead she went into the water closet and found several bedpans stacked on the shelf there. She snatched one up and hurried back to Mrs. Visser.

She dragged the screen that separated the patient beds in place to give the old woman some privacy and then drew back the sheet and blanket. "Now then Mrs. Visser, you've done this before. When I say so, you lift yourself and we'll get this bedpan under you. Ready now? And now."

Liesbeth supported the frail body with one arm as she slid the bedpan under Mrs. Visser. Liesbeth draped the sheet back across the woman, then turned away. "Mrs. Visser, I'm going to find someone to help you when you're all done."

The woman's voice was still choked with tears. "Thank you, dear. Now I don't care how long it takes for someone to come. I feel quite sick from holding on so long."

Liesbeth gave her head a small shake and pursed her lips as she left the room. She heard the sound of laughter and so found the break room where three nurses were just finishing their lunch.

They looked up as Liesbeth marched into the room. Liesbeth's voice quavered. "Mrs. Visser has apparently been calling for some time for a bedpan."

One nurse detached herself from the group. "Yes, Mrs. Bos. I'll come now."

"You needn't rush now. I've put her on the pan, but she might be finished by now."

"You did what?" The nurse scowled at Liesbeth.

"The poor woman was about to explode and it was faster to help her than to come and search for you."

The nurse stopped in front of Liesbeth, her face flushed and arms folded across her chest. "Mrs. Bos, you are a *volunteer*." She made it sound like Liesbeth was some sort of criminal. "A volunteer's purpose is to converse with patients, or perhaps read to them. That is all. Leave the medical care to those employed for the purpose."

Liesbeth's heart pounded and sweat prickled under her arms. "Sister, I understand my role here, and while I wouldn't call providing a bedpan to a patient in urgent need medical care as such, I can assure you that I am quite capable of offering at least that small service. I believe you know that I am a fully trained nurse."

"Yes, I know your background. You're the one who went off to participate in the war."

Liesbeth twitched as though she had been slapped. "You make it sound as though I did something wrong."

The nurse shrugged, then set off for Mrs. Visser's room, calling back over her shoulder. "Most of us believed we should be neutral."

Liesbeth stood in the wake of the nurse. *Good God.* She wanted to cry out, *But I helped people!* Instead she swiveled and stumbled to the door, her eyes blurred with tears.

She didn't know whether or not to talk to Max about the incident, and in the end gave him an abbreviated version, focused on the nurse's reaction.

"Do people make comments when they find out that you were in Paris during the war?"

"It's probably different for a man."

"So you mean 'no'."

"Liesbeth, I've told you before that you should just let it be."

"Yes, I know you have. I'm sure you're right. It's not like I go around discussing it all the time, yet somehow it seems that it's a mark against me."

"That woman was just annoyed because you were doing the job she should have been doing."

"Yes, perhaps."

Liesbeth left it at that, although the incident continued to haunt her. The next day she went back to the hospital and gave notice that she would no longer be able to continue. She wondered who was more relieved, Mrs. Van Hout or herself.

She found a letter waiting for her when she got home. She delayed the pleasure of opening it by peeling and cutting the vegetables first. She made herself a cup of tea and only then sat down with her letter. First, she studied the stamp and postmark. She admired the careful handwriting and noticed from the return address that Margaret had moved since her last letter.

My Dear Liesbeth,

How long it's been since my last letter to you. You are such a trusty correspondent and it always takes me ages to write back to you. My apologies. It doesn't mean that I'm not thinking of you.

You may have noticed that I have moved. This is a boarding house where most of the residents are nurses like myself. It's better than the last one where there were some rough sort of characters living. This place reminds me a little of our own rooms back at Pré Catelan—not so much the rooms, because here I have one of my own, of course, but it's good fun when we are all together in the lounge in the evening. The other three girls living here are nice for the most part, and even the woman who runs it is quite decent. It's sad—she is a widow who lost her husband, Vince, in the big Halifax explosion of 1917, when so much of the city was destroyed. Remember we talked about that when it happened? I always thought Nova Scotia was safe, being so far away from all that horror that we were experiencing in France, and yet thousands and thousands were killed or injured. You can still see the devastation. I think Mrs. Coleman is very glad to be in Antigonish instead of constantly being reminded of the tragedy in Halifax. So, that's the new address. I think I'll be staying put here for the foreseeable future. I don't get home an awful lot, but when I get a few days off in a row, I do go. My mother has moved in with her sister now that Daddy has died, and that seems to be working out fine.

I thought I was done with nursing, but in fact I like the work. It's rather nice to be able to apply all that experience here. I am working exclusively with the war veterans, so we all speak the same language, so to speak. It's interesting to see the men when they are somewhat more healed than anything we ever saw over there. Sometimes I see an injury where I think 'what a pig's ear they made of this job' and know that if he had been with us, he'd be in better shape now. I can't help but think of Pieter (all the time) but I can think now of all the good work he did and the happy times we had together, instead of just feeling the pain of losing him. I suppose, like these other veterans, I'm healing, in spite of myself.

I hope you and Max are doing fine. Are you settling back in to life at home? You told me you are volunteering at a hospital. That's super. Are you enjoying it?

That's all the news from me. Do let me know how you are managing. I had a letter from Alida last week, so she's next on my list to write to. Stay well and give me all your news.

Love,

Margaret

Liesbeth read the letter through again, stopping to think about each of Margaret's points. She could picture the room full of girls chatting in the evening over hot chocolate, comparing notes on patients and staff alike. She sighed as she imagined Margaret at work, tut-tutting over a poorly healed amputation or an infected wound.

Liesbeth folded the letter and put it in her writing case, to be answered at leisure. In the meantime, she had supper to make.

Over supper, Liesbeth told Max about her letter from Margaret. "I wonder what Canada is like."

Max pushed his empty plate away. "Big and cold, I imagine."

Liesbeth laughed. "It's not always winter there."

Max laughed as well. "I'm sure you're right, but that's how I picture it."

"Could you ever see yourself living in a country like that?"

"No, never. The past years were enough for me. I'm glad to be here in Amsterdam. It's my home, you and I together here in the Netherlands. I know this is where I belong and I'm happy with that." Max paused for a moment. "Aren't you?"

She took his hand across the table. "Yes, of course I am. Margaret's letter just had my imagination going."

He nodded and stood up. "Let me help you with the dishes."

They worked together to tidy the kitchen, Max talking about his day and Liesbeth listening.

XVI

Autumn 1920 – A New Life

Liesbeth felt strange sleeping in her old room in Zandvoort again. Alida slept in their mother's old room so she could be closer to her father in case he called out in the night.

Liesbeth bolted up in the pre-dawn light and groped for the pot under the bed, vomiting into it. *Dear God I hope this sickness passes quickly.* She decided she might as well get up now. Perhaps some dry toast would help.

She tried not to make too much noise in the tiny kitchen as she boiled the kettle and put a slice of bread under the grill, but she heard her sister's door open.

Alida yawned. "Are you making a pot of tea?"

Liesbeth nodded. "I can if you'll have some with me."

"I will. I need something to warm me up. You're up early."

Liesbeth grimaced. "I wasn't feeling the best, so thought I might as well get up."

"Oh?"

Liesbeth added more bread to the grill, then turned to face her sister. "Yes. I'm pretty sure this is it. The morning sickness, the tenderness. I have the classic signs."

Alida hugged her sister. "Oh, Lies. That would be so wonderful. Papa needs something to look forward to. After Mama died, he just seems to have lost all will to go on. A grandchild is just what he needs."

"Don't say anything yet. I'll make an appointment once I get back home. Max doesn't even know yet."

"I'm sure another few days won't matter, but make an appointment as soon as you can, will you? I'm worried about Papa."

Liesbeth handed Alida a cup of tea and set the plate of toast down between them. "I wouldn't have imagined that Papa would take Mama's passing so hard. They always seemed so distant somehow."

"I think they were much closer than they showed to the world."

Liesbeth thought about that for a moment. "But we weren't the world, and I couldn't see that they were close. She was always so, I don't know, I don't like to say sour, but serious, perhaps. Especially after Mama moved to a separate bedroom, it seemed like Papa was always trying to avoid her."

Alida shook her head. "That was because of her headaches. You know she got those terrible migraine headaches so often. Well, Papa was just doing what he could to try to make life easier for her. He tried to keep us quiet and he accommodated her temper because he knew what was behind it."

Liesbeth nibbled on a piece of toast, then put it back on the plate. "How odd. I didn't realize she was suffering so much. I somehow just thought she was bad-tempered and that poor Papa was the one to be pitied."

Again Alida shook her head. "No, she was really sick a lot of the time. I actually think those headaches wore down her resistance, and combined with the poor nutrition during the war, she just didn't have the energy to fight when she got cancer." Alida drained her tea. "I better get dressed. Will you come to visit your old workmates this afternoon? We can walk home together along the beach and get some fresh fish for supper tonight."

"I will. I'll come around three o'clock. How nice that you have tomorrow off so the three of us can go together to Haarlem for the day. There's a lovely baby shop there that we might stop into. Just to look, you know?"

Alida smiled. "Just to look. Certainly. We'll settle Papa at a café and do some shopping on our own. It'll be a wonderful way to spend our last day of your holiday here."

Alida went to get dressed, leaving Liesbeth to set the remaining toast aside. She would warm it up again in the oven when her father rose. Maybe by then she would be able to eat as well.

Liesbeth had enjoyed the train ride back to Amsterdam. The wait at Haarlem hadn't been long, and overall the trip was fast and easy. It was cold and windy on this November day, but not raining, so even the walk home was fine. She had brought some pickled eel and fresh halibut back for Max.

The halibut was baked to perfection and the green beans and boiled potatoes were ready by the time Max walked in.

He swept Liesbeth into a hug. "I've missed you."

She wrapped her arms around his neck as he held her. She wasn't usually given to physical displays of affection like this, but she had missed him too. "It's only been five days."

"That's four days too long."

She broke away from him first. "Supper is ready. Hang up your coat and you can tell me all the news while we eat."

"It smells wonderful. I was longing for your proper cooking again. Having soup and bread or eating at the café just isn't the same."

Max spoke about his work. There was a new secretary who seemed like she would be efficient, and so far, everyone liked her. He asked her all about her father and Alida and listened as she told him about her father missing her mother.

"It doesn't surprise me."

"You didn't see them together very often. They always seemed to barely tolerate each other."

He smiled at her. "Sweetheart, you might seem cool toward me in the eyes of other people, but I know you love me."

She tilted her head. "That's different."

"How so?"

"Would you want me to drape myself all over you in front of other people?"

"No, of course not. I'm simply saying that appearances can be deceiving."

Liesbeth was bursting to share her news with Max. "I have an appointment with the doctor tomorrow."

He looked up from his dinner. "Oh? You didn't catch something while you were away, did you?"

"I don't think this can be caught."

He frowned. "What is it?"

"I think I may be pregnant."

Max set his knife and fork down, tossed his napkin on the table beside his half-eaten supper and stood up. By the time he'd come around the table to her, Liesbeth had also stood up.

He enfolded her in his arms. "Oh, Liesbeth. My dreams are all coming true. Are you certain?"

She was surprised to hear the thickness in his voice. "I'm quite certain, but women have been wrong before, so we'll wait until we hear from the doctor before counting it as a fact."

He released her and looked in her eyes. "If you're certain, I'm certain. You aren't often wrong."

She touched his face, swallowing the lump in her throat as his eyes filled with tears. "We'll celebrate when we have it confirmed, but yes, I do think that we can expect a little one to disrupt our peaceful evenings sometime around June."

He kissed her forehead. "All right. We'll wait to celebrate."

"Finish your supper before it gets cold."

He went back to his plate, but kept looking up at her, his eyes shining.

———

When Max arrived home later in the week, carrying a huge bouquet of flowers, Liesbeth only had to smile and nod before he dropped the flowers on the table to sweep her in his arms. He kissed her long and soft, then pushed back to gaze at her in wonder.

"My darling, you must tell me what I can do to help and make it as easy as possible for you."

She patted his arm, laughing. "You can treat me normally. I feel sick in the mornings, but it should pass soon, and then we just carry on as usual. I'm not an invalid."

"All right, but you must look after yourself. No visiting at the hospital. None of that sort of thing."

"You know I gave that up. Don't worry. The baby and you. Those are my concerns now."

He nodded.

Liesbeth rubbed her stomach. "There's really nothing more to do. Now we just have to be patient, and get things ready."

———

Liesbeth thought that she would have a thousand things to keep her busy in preparation for the baby's arrival. Instead, she found that once they had transformed Max's office into a nursery, most of the work was done.

Max always looked excited when he walked through the door in the evening. He touched the growing swell of her belly. "How are you both today?"

"We're both fine. We're resting up today because tomorrow we're meeting with your mother to go shopping."

"That sounds like fun for you."

Liesbeth didn't say that she really didn't enjoy shopping. "I'm sure it will be, although it seems like there are fewer and fewer places to shop these days."

"I'm sure there are places enough."

Liesbeth laughed. "Yes, I'm sure."

Max picked up the ball of wool that Liesbeth had been working with. "What are you knitting this week?"

"A sweater with matching booties." She held up the pattern drawn out on a piece of paper. "Alida sent me the pattern."

"You're very industrious."

She smiled. "It helps pass the time. It sounds like your mother has made some little outfits as well."

"I know she's very excited."

"I'll be glad to have her help."

Max squeezed her hand. "You miss your mother, don't you?"

Liesbeth frowned. "I suppose I do, but quite honestly, I don't think I would have turned to her just because I'm pregnant. We weren't close in that way."

He shook his head. "I thought all women wanted their mothers at this time."

"I suppose I'm not all women."

He smiled. "No, you're one of a kind."

———

Liesbeth surprised herself by enjoying the day with her mother-in-law. They sat together drinking tea in Mrs. Bos's flat after shopping. "Thank you for going with me to get the layette sorted out. Between what you've given me of Max's old things and these new pieces, I'm all set."

Max's mother nodded. "I knew I saved it all for good reason. Will your sister come to help you when the baby is born?"

Liesbeth frowned. "Oh, I don't think so. She has a job. She may come for a day or two just to see the new baby, but that's it."

"Oh. Well, you know that I'm just a tram ride away."

"Thank you, Mother. I think that we'll be fine, though. I know what to expect. I am a nurse, after all."

Her mother-in-law smiled. "Yes, I know you were, but knowing what to expect and actually experiencing it are two different things."

Liesbeth winced at the use of 'were'. *Is that it, then? I used to be a nurse and now I'll be a mother. I can't be both, I suppose.* "I appreciate your offer of help and I'll certainly come calling if I need it."

"Send Max. That's easier."

Liesbeth smiled. "Yes. I'll send Max if need be."

XVII

Spring 1921 - Family

The day was warm and Liesbeth felt as though she were suffocating. Max's mother was planning to come to spend the afternoon with her, but Liesbeth wished she wasn't. There was nothing that needed to be done. All was ready for the arrival of the baby, the room freshly painted in a pale buttery yellow, tiny clothes folded away into the chest of drawers, and the old rocking cradle set up in their room next to the bed.

Liesbeth paced to their room and stood looking down at the richly stained oak contrasting against the white cotton blanket of the cradle. Max had spent several evenings patiently sanding off the old paint from the cradle, then staining it. She had to admit it was a lovely piece now, hardly resembling the chipped old thing he had found in the second hand shop.

The bell tinkled at street level and Liesbeth went to the window and waved. She went out and down the two steps to the small landing to tug on the rope attached to the front door. The front door latch lifted and her mother-in-law let herself in.

"Mother." Liesbeth leaned in to receive her kisses.

Marion Bos tut-tutted and rested the back of her hand on Liesbeth's forehead. "You look flushed. Do you feel all right?"

Liesbeth frowned and turned away. "I'm fine. Just hot in this unseasonable weather."

Marion paused before removing her hat. "It's lovely outside. Everything is in bloom. Shall we go for a walk to get out of this stuffy flat? Perhaps you need some bread or something?"

Liesbeth waved her hand at the deep basket perched on the windowsill. "No. I've had the baker come by already and we just did the usual routine of sending the money and order down in the basket for him to send my bread back up."

Marion wrinkled her nose. "I never trust them to give me the freshest bread. I always prefer to go to the shop."

"I know. I agree, but I feel like a walrus and hate climbing up and down those stairs if I don't have to."

Marion laughed. "A walrus? What do you know about such a creature?"

Liesbeth smiled in spite of herself. "A cow, then."

Marion took off her hat and hung it on the rack beside the door. "Go and sit down by the window and I'll get you a glass of cool water."

Liesbeth sighed but went obediently to the sitting room. She pushed open the window as far as it would go and dropped into the chair, leaning her elbows on the casement.

Marion carried in a tray with two tall glasses of water. "You're impatient for the waiting to be done. I remember going through this phase with Max."

Liesbeth took a sip of water, then put the glass down on the small round table that separated her from her mother-in-law. "I'm so used to being busy. Being clumsy and tired all the time is annoying."

"You'll be busier than you can imagine in another two weeks."

Liesbeth shook her head. "I really can't see how I'll be that busy. The child will sleep for the most part. At least in the beginning."

Marion smiled. "You'll be surprised."

Liesbeth watched the street life below as Marion pulled out her sewing. She was cross-stitching a small pattern of ducks on a white bib. They sat without speaking, the sounds of the city enjoying a spring day swirling around them.

Liesbeth's eye caught sight of a young woman in a stylish green suit with a pert matching hat. Her auburn hair caught the sun, flaming out and making her stand out from the crowd. She saw men turn and glance at the woman as they passed her. The sight made her think of the new woman working in Max's office, even though Liesbeth had never seen her.

She turned to her mother-in-law. "Does Max talk to you much about his work?"

"Not a lot. When he comes to see me he usually talks about you, and these days, about the coming baby. He's very excited."

Liesbeth nodded. "Yes, he is."

Marion glanced up. Something in Liesbeth's voice must have caught her attention. "Why do you ask?"

Liesbeth looked back out the window but the woman with the red hair had disappeared from view. "No reason."

Marion threaded her needle into the fabric so that it wouldn't dangle and laid the bib down on her lap. "Something must be behind the question. Are you worried about Max's job?"

Liesbeth's breath caught in her throat when she saw the frown on Marion's forehead. She stretched over to touch the older woman's hand. "I didn't mean to worry you. No, there's absolutely nothing. Max seems very happy with his job. He likes the work and he likes the people."

Marion tilted her head to study Liesbeth. "Well that's good then, isn't it?"

"Yes of course. It's wonderful."

Marion resumed her embroidery, shaking her head.

Liesbeth tried to imagine what the young woman in Max's office might look like. He hadn't said much about her appearance. He only spoke of how efficient she was, and once in awhile he repeated something she had said when it seemed especially clever or interesting. *Yes, Max definitely likes the people he works with and maybe one person more than others.*

———

Their daughter arrived just as the dawn was breaking. When the midwife placed the tiny bundle in her arms, Liesbeth felt the moment burn inside her. She was conscious of the birds outside the window, their many voices creating a symphony to welcome the new baby. The warm spring breeze carried in the sounds of the city just waking up with the clop-clop-clop of a horse and dray making its way along the street below. She kissed the baby's head, the downy dark hair tickling her nose.

Marion smoothed down the clean sheets over Liesbeth's legs. "Can I let Max in now? Are you ready?"

Liesbeth tore her gaze away from the child, feeling a fissure in the world that had, for a moment, consisted of her and the baby alone. She smiled and reached out to touch Marion's hand. "Thank you for being here with me. I was so glad to have you."

Marion squeezed Liesbeth's hand. "Where else would I have been?"

"Yes, go and get Max. I'm sure he's dying to meet his daughter."

Max must have been hovering just outside. When his mother opened the bedroom door, he almost fell into the room.

Marion patted him on the arm before she left them alone together. "Don't tire her out."

Liesbeth angled the baby toward him so he could see past the towel that wrapped the little girl. "Here she is. Safe and sound."

Max sat in the chair beside the bed. "She's beautiful. Like her mother."

Liesbeth grimaced. "Yes, *she's* beautiful."

Max stroked the baby's cheek and let her grasp his finger in her waving fist. "Johanna Marion. Welcome, little Hanna." He looked at Liesbeth. "May I hold her?"

Liesbeth felt a second of hesitation. "Yes, of course." She placed the bundle in his waiting arms and marvelled at how natural he was as he shifted to support the child's head in the crook of his arm.

She watched as he kissed the tiny nose. "You look like you've done this before."

He glanced at Liesbeth. "I'm glad it looks like that, but I can honestly say that I don't ever remember holding a baby in all my adult years."

He crooned and kissed her forehead before handing her back to Liesbeth.

"Liesbeth." He took off his glasses and, taking out the clean white handkerchief he always carried, wiped his eyes.

"Max, everything is fine. We're both fine." Liesbeth's heart contracted to see her strong husband so emotional.

He blew his nose and put his glasses back on. "Yes, I know that. I love you both so much. I have everything I want in life now."

Liesbeth was at a loss to know how to respond. "And I love you."

Max smiled. "I'll leave you both to rest now. I feel that I need to go out for a walk. Tell the world my happy news. My mother will be here if you need anything."

"All right. I'll see you in a while."

After Liesbeth fed her baby for the first time and was listening to the snuffling beside her, she heard the front door close. Max had gone. *Who are you rushing off to talk to?*

XVIII

Autumn 1921 – Taking Stock

The October sun sparkled on the sea as Liesbeth and Alida walked along the boulevard in Zandvoort.

Liesbeth pushed the pram toward a bench. "Let's just sit for a bit. I want to let the good sea air wash over me."

They sat side-by-side, watching the waves churn, the water a deep green-blue frothing white as it broke on the beach.

Liesbeth could sense her sister studying her, so she turned to smile at Alida. "Why are you looking so perplexed?"

Alida's brow wrinkled. "Why are you so quiet?"

"I'm always quiet. You should know that by now."

"Not with me."

Liesbeth leaned over to pull the blanket up further under the baby's chin.

"Don't fuss with Hanna. She's perfectly fine. Let her sleep. Liesbeth, talk to me."

Liesbeth leaned back again. "There is nothing at all wrong. You're imagining things."

"I know things look fine to an outsider. You have a kind and successful husband. A perfect child." Alida smiled at the sleeping face of her niece before turning back to her sister. "But I know you too well. There's something. What is it? Are you worried about Papa?"

Liesbeth grasped the explanation eagerly. "He does seem very frail these days. I know you look after him so well, but he seems to be failing."

Alida nodded. "Yes, even though I'm with him every day, even I can see that he isn't well. There isn't anything to do about it, though. He's simply getting old and he misses Mam."

"I know you do everything possible for him. I wasn't criticizing. You probably spend more time than you should caring for him. You hardly seem to have your own social life anymore, Ali."

"Oh, don't worry about me. I have my work which I love, and I really don't mind being with Papa. We enjoy our quiet evenings together."

Liesbeth sighed. "Yes, you have your work."

"Ah, there it is."

"What do you mean?"

"You miss working, don't you?"

Liesbeth glanced at her sister, feeling her face flush. "You *do* know me too well."

"But that's only natural after what we've been through. Even I feel impatient at times."

"You? Why?"

"Because my friends here seem to live in a different world from me. All they talk about is getting married and having families. The idea of wanting to work and wanting to, well, I don't know, want *more* is quite foreign to them. That's a big part of why my social life has just faded away. I don't seem to have anything in common with them anymore."

Liesbeth bit her bottom lip. "So you can imagine how I feel. It's like a dream when I remember how busy and important we were in Paris."

"And being a wife and a mother isn't enough to fill the space?"

Liesbeth hesitated. "Don't get me wrong. My heart is fuller than it ever has been. I love Hanna and Max more than I ever imagined I could love. It's different though, isn't it?"

"Yes, I imagine it's different." Alida nodded. "When I talk to other women my age, I feel so radical. They act like I'm a suffragette. In other words, like I'm not quite feminine enough. When I try to tell them that women are just as capable of good ideas and hard work as any man, it's like I'm telling rude jokes or something. It's just not the 'done' thing, you know? Of course they agree with me, but at the same time, I feel that they wish I would just keep these thoughts to myself."

Liesbeth nodded. "When I read the newspapers, I sometimes think we should have gone to England after the war."

"Why?"

"Because people over there understood. Women came out of the shadows and refused to go back. Of course, there's been all sorts of bother because they didn't want to give up those jobs that they got during the war. I don't know what the answer is because of course the men needed their jobs back, but still, there must be some way to make it work without women having to just settle at being at home all the time." Liesbeth shook her head, her brow wrinkled.

Alida tilted her head. "But Max understands, doesn't he? He saw you at your best and knows how capable you are."

"He saw me and yes, he values my ability, but that efficiency must be spent on the household now. That's his thinking."

"I suppose he's like every other husband, then. But to be fair, what else could he think or do? He couldn't have you working at his office or something. Especially now that you have Hanna."

"No, I'm sure not. There *are* women who work with him, of course. Single women."

Alida reached for her sister's hand. "But you are happy, aren't you, Lies?"

Liesbeth squeezed the hand and stood. "Yes, of course I am. Just once in a while I get restless, I suppose. Speaking of restless, let's walk on and then we'll head back to the house. It's almost time to feed both Hanna and Papa."

Alida laughed. "Our children."

"I'm glad I came for a few days' visit. It's like a tonic being here."

"And Max didn't give you an argument when you said you wanted to come?" Alida looked sharply at her.

"No, not at all. He goes to his mother's for meals and I think she's glad for his company."

As they turned for home Alida rested one hand on the handle of the pram beside Liesbeth's. "I like Max's mother. She seems nice."

"Oh yes, she is. She's been really good with Hanna. I've grown quite fond of her, actually. Don't get me wrong Ali, I know I have a good life. Good Lord, if anyone knows it, we do, you and I. Life could be so much worse."

Her sister gave Liesbeth one last look before turning the topic to some local gossip as they made their way back to the house.

XIX

Autumn 1921 (continued)

Max was clearly pleased to have Liesbeth and Hannah back at home. He came in carrying a bunch of sunflowers. "Here are my girls, safe at home again."

Liesbeth gave him a hug and then turned back to the dinner she was preparing. "Don't wake Hannah. She'll probably be awake soon anyway, so let her just sleep until she wakes by herself."

"Not even a peek?"

"Not even a peek."

"I'll pour us both a glass of sherry, then. Can you come and sit for a few minutes without spoiling the meal?"

Liesbeth turned down the gas on the stove. "Just for a minute."

They sat together and sipped their drinks as Liesbeth told Max about their few days away.

Max wanted to know everything. "And how is your father?"

"He's getting old."

"Yes. He's in his seventies now. That's a good age."

"Yes, I suppose it is."

Max asked how Hannah enjoyed the seaside. "Did she paddle her toes in the water?"

"I did dangle her in a couple of times, but the water was quite cold and she pulled her fat little feet out as soon as the water splashed up against her."

"But she didn't cry?"

"Oh, no. I think she was more surprised than upset."

"I think she's a brave little thing. She'll be good with new experiences. You'll see."

"Yes, she seems to take things in her stride."

At that moment, Hannah cried out. Max set his glass down. "I'll go."

Liesbeth returned to the kitchen to continue with the supper. She could hear Max talking to Hannah and she smiled. She called out to him, "She probably needs changing. I'll be there in a moment."

"I'll do it."

Liesbeth felt her eyes widen and waited a moment before looking into the baby's room where Max was just finished the diaper changing. "Now there's a surprise."

Max picked Hannah up. "I've changed her before."

"Only when I'm not here."

He kissed the baby's nose, who giggled and pulled his glasses askew. "I've missed my little princess."

———

It was late and Max turned the lights off in the living room. Liesbeth had just stopped in to check on Hannah, asleep in her crib in her own room, and now she and Max were both in their bedroom. He reached for her, pulling her close.

With one hand he took his glasses off, setting them on the dressing table, then he removed her glasses, setting them beside his. "Hannah's not the only one I've missed."

He kissed her, his lips gentle on hers. His hands began to trail up and down her back. She stiffened in his arms.

"What is it, Liesbeth? It's been six months since Hannah was born. I miss you. I long for you." His voice was thick.

Liesbeth could feel the baby fat around her abdomen pressing against Max's firm body. She pressed away from him as far as she could despite the strong circle of his arms. She resisted as he tried to pull her tight against him again.

"Liesbeth, don't you want me, too?"

She felt her heavy breasts wedged against him. *I'm just a big lump. He can't see me like this.* "Max, I'm so tired after the journey. What I'm longing for most is a good night's sleep my own bed again."

She could hear that he was trying to sound lighthearted. "Well, let's get you into your own bed then." He released her and reached to unbutton the top button of her blouse.

Liesbeth reached for her nightgown on the bed. "I need to visit the washroom before bed." She took the gown and, as she had done every night since Hannah had been born, she went and changed in the other room.

Max was still awake when she returned and flung back the covers to invite her into bed. "I've warmed up the bed for you."

She climbed in and turned her back to him. "It's nice to be home. I can't believe how tired I am."

Liesbeth felt Max lay his hand on her hip. "Liesbeth, won't you turn over?"

She bit her bottom lip, then turned. She knew she was being foolish. He didn't care about how she looked, yet her heart pounded when she felt his hands sliding under her nightgown.

Over time she had grown to enjoy the feelings that sex brought. It wasn't so much the physical act, although even that did bring moments of real pleasure. It was the intimacy that she enjoyed, so now she breathed deeply, trying to relax. His hand was warm against her skin. He stroked her leg, then tugged at the cotton gown to drag it up over her hips. She knew she was stiff and unyielding, and willed herself to relax as his lips found hers while his hand continued to caress her. He broke away from her to unbutton his own pajama shirt, then Liesbeth could feel him push the bottoms off, kicking at the pants until they were in a ball at the bottom of the bed.

"Do you want to take off your gown?" His voice was husky.

She pulled him toward her. "No, it's chilly. I'll leave it." She couldn't be naked in front of him.

He nibbled at her neck. Both hands were under her gown now as he nudged her onto her back. He pushed her gown up to reveal her breasts and she felt her face heating. Max didn't seem to notice. Instead, he licked her nipples. "I've missed you so much."

He positioned himself above her, leaning on his elbows. Liesbeth forgot about how her body was shaped as she felt him begin to probe her. Despite herself, her hips rose to meet him. For a short time she once again felt fused to him. Her heart pounded and she was engulfed by the heat of their two bodies throbbing together.

When Max had collapsed beside her again, he turned on his side to look at her. "I needed that."

She enjoyed a moment of deep contentment, then yanked her gown back down. She slanted her eyes toward him to see if he had been looking at her baby-thickened body. The contentment disappeared.

She turned her head to look at him. "I think men have greater needs than women in that department."

His brows furrowed. "You don't need me?"

"I didn't mean that. I need you. Of course I do." She paused. "I love the feeling of closeness I get being with you like this."

He was sleepy now and Liesbeth could tell he wasn't really listening. He shifted away from her as if to turn over, but just before he did, he leaned in to kiss her. "I love you."

She tugged again at her gown and whispered to his back. "I love you, too."

Liesbeth turned over as well but didn't fall asleep right away. It was often like this. She listened to him breathing. She strained to hear in case Hannah was restless, but all was quiet. Her mind wouldn't settle and so her body wouldn't relax. She found herself continuing the conversation with Max. *I love the feeling of closeness, but I don't trust it. I know that you want something that I can't give you or be for you.*

The Max in her mind asked her: *What is it that you can't be?*

I can't be that witty elegant woman from your office that you keep talking about.

XX

Spring 1922 - Sisters Alone

In the spring of 1922, Liesbeth's father died.

Max held Liesbeth, rubbing her back. "He had a good long life, Lies."

She stepped back, pulling away from him. "Did he?"

Max frowned. "I think seventy-three is not a bad age."

She turned and looked out the window, staring down at the people passing along the sidewalk. She shook her head and turned back to him. "Yes, you're right, of course, especially when we think of all the young men who didn't even make it to twenty-three, let alone seventy-three."

The frown cleared from Max's brow. "We'll go together for the funeral and then you should stay on for a while to help Alida. What will she do now, do you think? She won't stay in the house, will she?"

"No, it's meant for a family. I think she knows a couple of girls with whom she can share a place."

"Yes, that sounds ideal."

She nodded. "It does, doesn't it?"

Hannah toddled over and Max bent down to swoop the child up into his arms. "You're going to visit Tante Alida, little one. I'll miss you."

Liesbeth watched them for a moment. "You won't mind us being away for a couple of weeks?"

"I'll mind, of course I will. I'll manage, though."

"Will you go and stay with your mother?"

He shook his head. "No, I'll stay here, but I'm sure she will enjoy cooking me supper once in a while."

"And I suppose some of your friends will also invite you to dine with them."

He kissed Hannah on the nose and she giggled. "Oh, don't worry about me. I'm more capable than I look."

She smiled. "You never look anything *but* capable. I'm sure you'll be fine."

———

Max went to catch the tram right after her father's funeral was finished.

Alida hugged him first. "Thank you for coming, Max. I'm sure it isn't easy taking a day off from work."

Max patted her arm. "Of course I'd come. I was fond of your father."

Max turned and gave Liesbeth a quick embrace, then bent over the baby carriage to tickle Hannah under the chin. "Look after Mama for me and I'll see you in two weeks." He straightened as the tram came into view. He squeezed Liesbeth's hand. "Let me know how you get on here. If you need to stay longer, just let me know."

Liesbeth nodded. "I will. I'll write in a couple of days."

Liesbeth and Alida watched him mount the tram and waved as it pulled away with a screech. They turned to walk back to the house, Liesbeth pushing the carriage. Hannah was sitting up and bouncing, trying to peer around the hood. Alida reached across and pushed the hood down partway and the child rewarded her with a smile.

Alida smiled in return, then turned to study her sister as they walked along side by side in the warm April sun. "You're very lucky, Lies, with your beautiful little girl and your very nice husband." She paused. Liesbeth didn't respond. "Why do you seem so down?"

Liesbeth glanced at Alida. "Our father just died, for goodness sake. How could I be anything other than down?"

Alida shook her head. "Liesbeth, he was my father, too. I'm sad as well, but I can tell you that he didn't fight it. He was glad to go. Does that make it easier?"

Liesbeth swallowed, feeling the lump in her throat. She was saved from having to answer as they turned into their own small yard. She parked the carriage beside the front door and unbuckled her daughter's harness.

Alida went in first. "Shall I make some tea?"

Liesbeth walked along the narrow hallway to her old bedroom. "Yes, that would be good. I'm just going to put Hannah down for a nap, if she'll cooperate. I know she's tired."

She lay the child down in the old crib that had once been her own. It was amazing that her parents had stored it all these years. Alida had given it a fresh coat of paint to brighten it up for whenever her small niece might come for a visit.

When she came back to the living room, Alida had the pot of tea ready. The old pot, covered with the tea cozy with the top that snapped together, sat on the small round table between two wing chairs. The furniture was faded but solid. The room was cozy.

"Can you take any of this furniture with you to the new place?"

Alida glanced around. "Not much, I'm afraid. I have a bedroom to furnish, but other than that, the other two girls have already got everything pretty much set up."

"What will you do with it all?"

"What will *we* do with it all, you mean."

Liesbeth smiled. "Yes, that's what I meant to say."

Alida snapped open the cozy and took out the pot to pour the tea. Liesbeth looked at the familiar things and tears burned her eyes.

As Alida handed her sister the cup, she noticed the welling tears. "Oh, Lies. I wish you would tell me what's going on with you. Just as you know that Hannah is tired, I know you so well. It isn't like you to be this upset over Papa. You were so stoic at Mama's funeral. Both Papa and I had to lean on you to get us through it."

Liesbeth took a sip of her tea, making an audible gulp as she swallowed. Liesbeth bit her lip. "I wish I could explain it to you." She set her cup down and took a deep breath. "I'm sure that Max is seeing someone."

Alida's tea spilled into her saucer as she plunked her cup down. "No. I just don't believe it."

Liesbeth closed her eyes, her lips pressed together.

Alida reached over and took her sister's hand in hers. "You must have that wrong, Lies. Tell me everything. Tell me why you think that."

Liesbeth slipped her hand away from her sister's to pull her handkerchief from her pocket. "There's a woman in his office. I think I've said something about her before."

Alida nodded. "Go on."

"It's as you said about knowing me, or me knowing Hannah. Well, I also know him. It's in the sparkle he gets in his eye when he mentions her name."

Alida raised her eyebrows. "A sparkle in his eye?"

"You know. His voice lifts when he talks about her."

"And is that what you are going by? The way his eye sparkles or his voice lifts?"

"I know what she's like. She always has the newest clothes and is tall and slim with that perfect wavy blonde hair."

Alida smiled. "Lies, you could have that perfect wavy hair, too, if you cut it shorter and spent some time with curling papers."

Liesbeth frowned. "It's nice that you think this is amusing."

Alida reached across again and patted Liesbeth's arm. "It's not amusing. Not at all. I just can't believe that it's as serious as you seem to believe."

"He's perfectly content that I should stay here with you for weeks. It will give him just the freedom he's been hoping for."

Alida shook her head. "No. You're reading everything the wrong way. I'm sure of it. He just knows that I can't pack up this house on my own, and he's being agreeable to not make a fuss over you staying here to help me."

Liesbeth dabbed at her eyes, then picked up her tea again. "I'm not reading this wrong. I just feel it. I am not giving him what he needs in our marriage."

Looking sideways at her sister, Alida was silent for a moment. She took a deep breath. "You mean sex?"

Liesbeth felt herself flush. "I don't satisfy him."

There was a silence between them.

Liesbeth glanced over to her sister and then away again. "I'm sorry. I shouldn't be burdening you with these private things. Especially not now, after everything you've gone through with Papa."

Alida smiled, gazing off into the distance. "I'm not completely without experience, you know." She turned to look at Liesbeth. "Do you remember my American soldier?"

"Yes, I remember him. I was afraid you'd run off to America with him."

"No. Both of us knew that wouldn't happen, but life was so frantic then, wasn't it? There were no rules that one could count on, and so it seemed right to seize the moments as they came along."

"Yes, I suspected that the two of you were . . . close."

"Well, there you are. But still, I'm rather out of my depth with this, so I'm not sure what to say to you, other than it always seems to me that Max loves you and dotes on Hannah."

"Oh yes, there's no question he adores Hannah."

Alida picked up her empty cup. "Lies, I think you are making too much of these suspicions. You need to just remember all that you have together and draw confidence from that. You two went through so much together in Paris, and now you have this new life together with Hannah. You need to stop second-guessing every move he makes and just, well, just be happy."

Liesbeth picked up her cup also and stood up. "Yes, I'm sure you're right. Let's make a start while Hannah's napping. We'll go through Papa's closet and see what can be given to the poor box and what must absolutely be thrown out."

XXI

Summer 1922 - A New Friend

The summer of 1922 was proving to be hot. Liesbeth took Hannah out each day, once in a while with a picnic lunch to eat in one of the many parks. Max would join them, although he wasn't fond of eating outside. Today they met in Vondelpark to eat the cheese sandwiches Liesbeth had packed. It was a tram ride away for Liesbeth, but it was close to Max's office.

Max flapped his hand at the pigeons that hopped closer to his bench, and Hannah clapped her hands as they flew a short way off. "I don't know why you like eating out here."

Liesbeth gave a hard biscuit to Hannah to gum while she ate her own sandwich. "Because it's so much cooler and fresher out here."

"I find it hot. How you can sit there on the ground is beyond me."

"It's actually quite relaxing." Liesbeth knew she was just being contrary because, in fact, sitting on the blanket on the hard ground was not comfortable. Her back ached from sitting with her legs stretched out in front of her.

Max finished his lunch and swept the crumbs from his trousers. "Perhaps I should be taking lunch to the office with me on these days when you want to come and eat amongst the pigeons."

Liesbeth frowned. "You'd miss the break if you ate at the office, though."

"I would. I like to take some time away to come back refreshed."

"Yes, I know." She was quiet for a moment, dabbing at Hannah's chin with a white napkin. "Do you remember how we used to take a short walk whenever we could, just so you could take a break from the work in Paris?"

"Yes, it's the same now. I like the break, but I don't like sharing my lunch with the birds and flies."

"I'm sorry, Max. The flat just seems to stifle me on these warm days."

"I think I should take my lunch to eat at my desk, and then I'll just take a short walk afterwards. That would probably suit both of us."

"Won't you feel strange sitting there on your own, eating your lunch?"

He shrugged. "Oh, I won't be alone. There are others who do that."

"Oh. I didn't realize. All right then, if you don't mind."

———

They began the new routine, Liesbeth packing a lunch once or twice a week for Max to take with him to the office.

Liesbeth set off with Hannah in the carriage. The picnic was packed in a basket stowed under the carriage, along with a book. She walked across the Torensluis and on to the Herengracht to find a spot by the canal under the cool shade of the plane trees. It was busier than she expected and she finally selected a spot near a woman wearing the white apron of a nurse's uniform, also eating lunch in the warm summer day.

Liesbeth laid out the blanket and set Hannah down while she unpacked the lunch things. She turned away from the child for only a moment, digging around in the basket to find a spoon for Hannah's applesauce.

"Your little one is escaping!"

Liesbeth's heart thumped. She jumped up as she saw Hannah crawling as fast as she could in the direction of the canal to pursue a waddling duck.

She swooped the little girl up in her arms "Hannah! No! You stay with Mama."

She sat back down on the blanket and put the little girl down between her own legs to keep her more contained. She looked over to the nurse who had shouted the warning. "Thank you. She's as slippery as an eel these days."

The nurse laughed. "I can see that. She's a lovely little thing."

Liesbeth smiled. "Would you like some fresh strawberries to finish off your lunch?"

The woman stood up and carried her towel over to sit down opposite Liesbeth. "There, we'll pin her between us to prevent further escapes."

Liesbeth held the bowl of strawberries out to her new friend. "Would you like some sugar to dip it in?"

The woman bit the top off the berry. "Oh no. It's delicious just as is. These must be the last of the season."

"Yes, I'm sure they are. I was lucky to find any. I'm Liesbeth Bos and this is Hannah."

"I'm Jo Steen."

"You must work around here."

"Yes, I'm with the OLG hospital. I start work at two o'clock so I sometimes come and spend some time outside first."

"I understand. The fresh air helps get you through the coming hours with the smells and sights that are not so fresh."

Jo laughed, her teeth white against the dark tan of her round face. "You *do* understand."

Liesbeth felt herself smiling along with Jo. "I did some volunteer work at OLG for a short while. I was once a nurse myself."

"Ah, where did you work?"

"In Paris."

"Paris? You aren't French?"

"No. It was during the war."

Jo's hand went to her mouth. "Oh. How brave of you. You must have been through some truly atrocious times."

Liesbeth looked down at her daughter for a moment. "Yes, certainly. At the same time, it wasn't all wretched."

Jo tilted her head. "I imagine that when you were able to help some of those poor boys, you had great satisfaction."

"Absolutely. Although even that was bittersweet at times because if they became very well, they went back to fight again."

Jo put her hand on her heart. "And did you see many like that?"

Liesbeth shrugged. "Not so many. Most of the patients I worked with were missing limbs."

"Oh, my. You must have some marvellous stories to tell. I have to get to work myself, but I would love to meet up with you again some time. Do you come this way often?"

Liesbeth smiled. "It would be lovely to talk to you again. I'll be back again on Friday if the weather cooperates. Perhaps I'll see you then."

Liesbeth pulled Hannah on her lap as Jo walked away. "I think we've made a friend, Hannah. Isn't that nice?"

———

Liesbeth was humming when Max got home. She turned away from the stove to give him a quick kiss before going back to flip the fish over in the fry pan.

He gave her another small kiss on the back of her damp neck. "You seem very cheerful."

"I made a new friend today."

"Did you? And who is that?"

"She's a nurse at OLG called Jo Steen." Liesbeth went on to relate how she had met Jo.

Max listened as he hung up his jacket and loosened his tie. "She sounds nice. Have you arranged to see her again?"

Liesbeth was glad to hear the approval in Max's voice. "Nothing specific but I'm sure we will look for each other again when Hannah and I go back to the park."

"I'm glad. You need more friends."

For a second, it crossed Liesbeth's mind that Max was happy because it would free him up a little bit. *Don't be silly.* "You don't mind, then?" Her voice sounded a little bit harsh even in her own ears.

He tilted his head to look at her, his forehead wrinkled. "Why would I mind?"

She turned away from him again, feeling the clench in her jaw. "You didn't want me joining any women's groups. You minded about that."

She felt him behind her and he pulled her around to face him. "Liesbeth, that was a whole different thing. You know that."

She breathed deep and exhaled. "Yes, I do. I'm sorry. Go and sit down. Supper will be ready in a few minutes."

As she dished out the supper, Liesbeth could hear Max chatting with Hannah. She giggled and gurgled responses as if they were having a real conversation. Liesbeth smiled to hear it. *Yes, I do have a good life.* Yet, as she carried in the plates, she wondered what Jo might be doing at this moment.

XXII

Summer 1922 - Mail

The July weather continued warm, but Liesbeth didn't mind as much. She met Jo in the park again on a hot but breezy day.

Liesbeth handed Hannah to Jo while she snapped the plaid blanket out and let it float to the ground. "Can you believe it? Seven women elected now. It's wonderful, isn't it?"

Jo nodded as she settled herself on the blanket. "The thrill of casting my vote was really something. I thought afterwards that I wish someone had taken a photo. I would have paid to have one of my first vote."

Liesbeth laughed. "I'm surprised there wasn't some enterprising person out to make some money doing just that. I went with Max to cast my vote. He seemed to think I might be nervous or need instruction."

"Still, it's nice he didn't try to talk you out of it. I heard there was more than one husband who did that."

Liesbeth snorted. "He'd know better than to try that."

"I also heard that husbands were trying to go in with their wives to make sure they voted the right way."

"Meaning their way."

"Exactly."

"No, I have to say that Max didn't try any of that."

They chatted about the results of the general election and what the changes might mean.

Jo brushed the crumbs from her lap. "I have to get going. We have a staff meeting before my shift starts."

Liesbeth felt a sudden lump in her throat. "I remember those meetings. Often there would be discussion about a new procedure or something to be on the lookout for. I didn't mind those meetings."

Jo laughed. "I suspect they were more interesting during wartime than the ones I attend."

"Perhaps you're right. It was always intense. It seemed like everything was important."

"I'm sure my meetings are important in their own way as well. And with that, I'll be going."

Liesbeth watched her friend walk away, her steps filled with purpose. Liesbeth played with Hannah, handing her a soft red ball and taking it back from her again and again, the child giggling each time. "It's a good thing I'm not working, isn't it? I couldn't leave you with someone else each day." *Could I?*

———

There was a postcard lying on the floor with the other mail. Liesbeth frowned. *Who do we know that has gone on a holiday?* She teased herself by not turning it over. It was from Italy. She carried the mail up and left it on the kitchen table while she took a cool facecloth to wipe down Hannah before laying her into the crib for a nap. At last she couldn't wait any longer and turned the card over to read the message.

Hello Max,

Rome is beautiful! Wish you were here!

She couldn't make out the signature which was a flattened scrawl.

Who in the world could it be from? Liesbeth thought back to their evening conversations and couldn't recall any mention of a friend going to Italy for vacation.

Liesbeth set the card aside to begin preparing supper, but she kept returning to the card. She stood by the window, peering in the bright afternoon light. The name definitely started with an R. It was a fairly short name, but it was so flat, it seemed almost to be a straight line. It was one of those confident signatures where the writer seemed too busy to bother defining their name with precision. *Roel perhaps?* She knew Max had a cousin Roel. Perhaps it was from him.

When Max arrived home, she waited until he had removed his jacket and lifted Hannah out of her playpen. "We have a mystery here today."

He looked at her over the soft blonde curls of Hannah's head. "Oh?"

Liesbeth waved the card in front of him. "A card from Italy."

Max blinked and set Hannah down. "Italy?"

"I can't make out the signature, though."

Max took the card from her without looking at the scene on the front, immediately flipping it over.

Liesbeth's brow creased as she saw his cheeks turn pink. "Can you make out the signature? Is it Roel?"

Max looked up at her. "Roel?"

Liesbeth's heart beat faster. "Yes, you know, your cousin Roel."

"Ah, no. I don't think so."

"Well then, who?"

He looked back down at the card. "I think it might be Rosa Brouwer." He put the card down and picked up the newspaper, opening it up as if caught by an interesting article.

"Miss Brouwer, the woman from work?"

He folded the paper again, frowning as if he was being drawn away from something important. "Yes, her."

"Why would she be sending you a card?"

Max picked up the card and carried it along with the paper into the living room. He tossed the card into the fireplace where it lay with the bright scene of Rome facing up against the blackened grate.

Liesbeth followed him and watched as he sat down in his chair, ready to open the paper again. She saw him throw a quick glance at the card. *He forgot there was no fire.* Liesbeth was sure he was wishing he had done something else with it, but he wouldn't go back to pick it out now. "Well?"

"Well, what?"

"She must be a special friend if she has your home address and sends you messages."

"She's just a colleague, but she likes playing little pranks. This is her idea of a joke, or probably she sent one to everyone in the office. That's her way. She's friendly. Now that's an end to it. It's just a silly card."

Max snapped open the paper and Liesbeth was left to stare at the advertisements of the day.

They didn't speak again about the card or Rosa Brouwer. As they sat together in silence, Liesbeth with a book and Max with a business journal, Liesbeth imagined Rosa. *How does she know Max's home address? Has she been here? Oh God. Have they been here together when I was away?* Her stomach churned at the thought.

Her eyes kept travelling to the card in the grate, wondering if it would sit there for the next few months until the weather was cold enough to light a fire.

The next morning after Max had gone to work, Liesbeth went back to the fireplace grate, drawn to the card, needing to read the message again. She stood staring down at the empty grate, feeling sick.

The flat felt too small, the furniture oversized and brooding. She fed and dressed Hannah quickly. When she stepped outside, she sucked in the morning air as though surfacing from a swim in a murky pond.

Liesbeth pushed the baby carriage through the throng of early morning shoppers, not stopping at any of the shops.

She barely glanced up when the baker called out a greeting. "No bread this morning?"

"No, not today, thank you."

"The apple tarts will be ready in about thirty minutes."

She didn't answer as she continued walking, too lost in thought to carry on a conversation. What could it mean? A card from a woman that said 'wish you were here'.

I knew it. I knew that he would tire of me with my untidy hair and heavy legs. I knew I couldn't keep his interest. How could I compete against a beautiful professional woman?

Liesbeth had never seen this Rosa Brouwer but she knew she must be lovely. She had seen her type before. Liesbeth knew she was just as she described to Alida. Her hair was sure to always be in a neat coif, curvy calves showing beneath tailored skirts, red lips.

Liesbeth found herself in Dam Square and sat down on one of the stone benches. Hannah was content to watch the pigeons waddling past, pecking and chipping at the cobblestones in search of a crumb.

So now what?

Liesbeth sat oblivious to the people going past until Hannah got restless. The baby began to cry and Liesbeth got up to move on, pushing the baby along narrow streets past stalls selling flowers and shops selling cheese or pickled herring.

"Lies! Liesbeth!"

Liesbeth turned to see her mother-in-law hurrying after her. "I'm sorry, Marion. I didn't hear you."

The older woman had to stop and catch her breath. "I've been chasing you since you crossed Spuistraat!"

Liesbeth flushed. "I wasn't trying to ignore you, honestly."

Marion eyed Liesbeth with a frown. "What are you so lost in thought about?"

Liesbeth forced herself to smile. "Nothing special. I was just wondering what I should make for supper tonight."

"That doesn't sound like you. You are usually so organized."

Liesbeth hoped her mother-in-law wouldn't want to come home with her, because she would see that there was a piece of smoked ham sitting under the tea towel, ready to be sliced.

Hannah was reaching up her arms to be picked up and Liesbeth bent over to unstrap the child from her carriage. "You want Oma to hold you, don't you?"

Marion set her shopping basket on the ground and took her granddaughter into her arms. "Hello, little one."

Liesbeth picked up the basket and put it into the carriage. "Where were you going? I'll walk there with you."

As they strolled along, Liesbeth was happy to stay quiet as Marion chatted and cooed to Hannah.

They arrived at the butcher shop that Marion had been heading to and Liesbeth took Hannah back to set her down in the carriage. "I'll leave you here, Marion."

"I thought you were looking for something for supper? You can't get a better butcher than here."

Liesbeth sighed and went into the shop.

Marion pointed out the display of fresh chicken. "You can't go wrong with a bit of baked chicken."

Helplessly, Liesbeth selected two pieces to purchase. It was beyond her to think of any explanations as to why she wouldn't shop here. *The ham will last until tomorrow.*

When they left the shop, Marion put her hand on Liesbeth's arm. "Will you come home with me for a visit? A cup of tea or chilled buttermilk perhaps?"

"No, Marion, I'll go straight home, I think. Thank you, though."

"Something's wrong. I can see it in your face. Is it Max? Is he all right?"

Liesbeth leaned in to kiss Marion first on one cheek, then the other, then back again in the usual Dutch way. "Nothing's wrong. Max is absolutely fine. Perhaps I'm just feeling a little tired."

Marion only squeezed her arm and then leaned over to kiss Hannah. "Well, go home and have a little rest, then. If you need me to help out in any way, you know you only need to ask."

Liesbeth felt tears pricking. "You're good to me. Thank you."

She knew that Marion was still watching as she and Hannah turned and walked away, the unwanted chicken stowed beneath the carriage.

She did go straight home. Her feet felt like lead and for a few moments she wished she had asked Marion to take Hannah. When she opened the front door, the mail was again lying on the floor. She closed her eyes before bending down to pick it up.

"Ah, Hannah, a letter from your Tante Margaret all the way from Canada."

Just seeing the Canadian stamp and the tidy handwriting of her good friend made Liesbeth smile for the first time that day. She gathered up Hannah and the package of chicken, the precious letter slipped into her waistband to avoid both the messy bundle and the little girl's grasping fingers. She hustled up to the flat. Just as she had done the day before with the post card, she laid the letter on the table, delaying the joy of opening it, savouring the knowledge that it was there waiting for her.

When she had washed Hannah's face and hands with a cool wet cloth, she set her down in the playpen with her favourite blocks. Liesbeth washed and dried her own hands, then couldn't wait any longer. She slit the envelope open and flattened the thin blue paper.

'Dear Lies,

How are you enjoying the summer? I imagine you out every day, walking and playing with your lovely little girl. You must send me a description now that she is growing a little bit older. Is she getting your fine, silky hair?'

Liesbeth turned to look at Hannah. No, thank goodness. Liesbeth smiled at Margaret's kind way of describing Lies's very fine, unmanageable hair. She went back to the letter.

'I imagine you and Max spending evenings delighting in the life you've made together, so far from where you met and so full of hope with the new child.

Life is full of very different adventures for me. I enjoy the hospital and my colleagues. The nurses are nice, although I believe that I am getting tired of living in residence here. Of course it is convenient, and I don't mind the rules since I have no desire to go out and spend nights at late-night dances or what have you, but I feel that I never have any quiet time alone. The doctors are nice also. There is one who seems quite friendly, but I've made it very clear that I'm not interested in anything more than a working relationship. You can understand, I'm sure. There is just no comparison to what I've had before, I'm afraid. Perhaps there never will be.

I go home routinely to visit the family and they are all getting on with their lives. I have both a nephew and a niece now, and while I enjoy seeing them, I don't long for a baby of my own. When I go home on a few days off, I get back into helping with farm chores as there just aren't enough hired hands to get everything done. It's good for me, I'm sure, I just wish there weren't so many insects to plague us. First the blackflies and now the mosquitoes and deer flies. I suppose I should be happy they aren't lice! I've seen enough of them to last a lifetime.

I'm meeting so many more people from Europe these days. Canada is crying out for immigrants. Have you seen any of the articles or advertisements to lure people here? I've heard that they've been in various newspapers in Holland, Belgium, and France. I'll bet they don't mention the mosquitoes. Could I tempt you and Max to come here?

There's all my news. It's your turn to write. I hear from Alida regularly. She's a wonderful correspondent and we've begun a bit of a stamp collection together. She is focusing on North America and I focus on Europe, so I go about hounding people for their stamps as they are sure to be useful either to my collection or hers.

Lots of love,
Margaret'

Liesbeth left the letter on the table as she went on with the day's chores around the flat. *Max will want to read it.*

She returned to the letter and re-read it two more times during the afternoon and then, after more consideration, she folded it carefully, replacing it into the envelope. She slid it into the drawer under her nightdresses where she knew Max would never look.

XXIII

Summer 1922 (continued) Brooding

Liesbeth was dusting, sliding the soft cloth across each picture hanging on the living room wall. She stopped to study the small sketch, framed in dark oak. She could still envision Max on that day in Paris when he had created this. She closed her eyes and could see his face as he studied the scene of the busy square. She almost heard the scrape of his pencil drawing in the detail of the horse and cart and the softer whisper of his finger blurring the lead to soften the tree branches and leaves. She remained standing with her eyes closed, the dust cloth hanging from her hand. She could hear again the distant melody being picked out on the piano and could smell the baking bread from the kitchen of the café.

She opened her eyes and looked at the picture. *I was so happy that day.*

She resumed her dusting until she heard Hannah waking from her nap. She put away her cloth and polish and went into the child's room.

Hannah stood in her crib. She grinned a big toothy smile and reached out her arms to Liesbeth. "Mama!"

Liesbeth lifted her daughter out and held her close, enjoying the smell of baby sweat and talcum powder. "Hello sweetheart. Did you have a good sleep?"

The child wriggled to be put down and Liesbeth kissed the soft curls one last time before setting the toddler down to run. "Oh, Hannah. Even you can't wait to leave me."

Liesbeth followed Hannah into the living room and through to the kitchen. "Come, little one. We'll have a glass of milk and then I'll get you cleaned up for a walk."

Liesbeth sat Hannah on her lap with a bottle while she herself had a glass of milk. Usually she put the little girl into her high chair, but today she enjoyed the comfort of keeping her close.

"What am I going to do, Hannah?"

The girl craned around, holding tight to her bottle, to peer up into Liesbeth's face.

"Your father doesn't love me anymore. He can't, can he? He has someone new."

Hannah's blue eyes were fixed on her and Liesbeth felt a lump in her throat. "I'm sorry, Hannah. I shouldn't be talking like this to you. Who knows how much you can understand. This is Mama's problem and I mustn't inflict it on you." Liesbeth swallowed the last of her milk, coughing as it almost choked her.

When Hannah had finished her bottle, Liesbeth got her dressed to go out for a walk. She strode along Spuistraat and then crossed at Raadhuisstraat to take her to the Singel canal. Turning left, she slowed down and walked along the water. Usually she took the time to chat to Hannah about the canal boats, geese, or other sights along the walk, but today she didn't see and didn't talk. She was too busy repeating an argument with herself:

Maybe it really is nothing, as he said.

Why did he take away the postcard, then? Why didn't he just tear it in half immediately and throw it in the bin?

He was just flustered.

Max doesn't get flustered.

Liesbeth quickened her step. Her heart was pounding and sweat trickled down her back. She took a deep breath and slowed her pace.

Calm down.

She had walked further than she realized and now turned left into the narrow laneway of Vliegendesteeg to move away from the canal. The lane smelled damp. The dark walls almost scraped the baby carriage on either side. Hannah reached out her arms.

"No, Hannah, don't touch. The walls are dirty." She could hear panic in her own voice.

Liesbeth moved as quickly as she could. Her heart throbbed and her hands were slippery with sweat on the handlebar of the carriage. The walls were closing in on her; pressing against her and her baby.

When she emerged from the dank street, she breathed a sigh of relief. She shook her head as her heartbeat slowed again. *How silly.*

Her spirits lifted as she decided to head to the serene gardens of the Begijnhof. When she reached the small courtyard inside the ancient brick walls, she took Hannah out of the carriage to let her explore. Liesbeth sat on a low stone wall as Hannah wandered around, bringing her mother pebbles and feathers.

Liesbeth took an acorn from Hannah. "Thank you. Just don't put anything in your mouth."

The sun filtered through the leafy trees. She felt safe. *I wish I could just stay here. We could live here like the nuns.* She smiled at her own thoughts. *Sure. I go crazy at home. I'd last a week here.*

At last she stood up and brushed off her skirt. "Come, Hannah. It's time to go home."

As she left the sanctuary of the enclosed church and old homes, Liesbeth found herself thinking again of the woman, Rosa Brouwer. *How dare she go after another woman's husband?*

She imagined the woman chatting with Max at the office, perhaps leaning low over him to discuss some paperwork, her perfume intoxicating him. Liesbeth's jaw ached and she realized her teeth were clenched.

But Max should just walk away. He must like it. He wants her to moon over him. Yes, he's just as much at fault as Rosa. Of course he is.

"Mama, Mama." Hannah was pointing to some chocolate on display in a shop window.

Liesbeth blinked, and looked at her daughter. "No, Hannah. Not today, sweetheart."

Hannah turned to watch the shop window retreat, her bottom lip quivering.

Liesbeth kept walking. "We don't always get what we want, Hannah. I'm sorry but it's true."

The child turned to face forward again, distracted by a small dog trotting past.

Liesbeth smiled. If only every disappointment could be resolved so easily.

They walked on. She had gone further than she had intended and now her back ached. Her blouse was damp under the arms. Several strands of hair had come loose and stuck to her forehead and temple. She'd have to have a wash when she got home before starting on the supper. *I feel worse than when I worked a twelve-hour shift.*

She came to the corner of Paleisstraat and saw a new billboard had been erected. She stopped to study it, her eyes widening. On the poster was a beautiful scene showing a golden field of grain in the background with a young farmer in a white shirt standing in front of a set of strong looking horses. To the side was a young wife holding a baby and a basket of vegetables. In large letters was the word 'Canada'.

Liesbeth crouched beside Hannah as an excuse to linger in front of the sign. "What do you think of that, Hannah? That's where Tante Margaret lives. Wouldn't it be nice if Papa could be convinced to go there?"

Liesbeth read the proclamation on the poster. 'Free Information About Canada can be Obtained at the Holland Emigration Central.' She repeated the address in the Hague several times to herself without really thinking about why she was bothering. *Paulownastraat 8, Paulownastraat 8.*

When she got home and had settled Hannah in the playpen with her favourite toys, Liesbeth pulled out Margaret's letter and wrote the address down on the back before tucking it back into the drawer out of sight.

———

It was after supper and Liesbeth had put Hannah to bed. Max was reading a trade journal and looked up as she came back into the room. He closed the magazine and set it on the small table beside his chair. "You got her settled quickly."

"Yes, she was tired. We went for a long walk today and then she spent some time exploring."

"That sounds nice. Where did you go?"

"The Begijnhof."

"That is quite a walk, but it's a very peaceful spot. I haven't been there in a long time."

"It's a good place for thinking."

Max's brow wrinkled. He didn't ask her what she wanted to think about. He glanced over at his journal.

Liesbeth spoke before he could begin reading again. "I saw a new billboard today."

Max lifted his magazine back to his lap. "Oh yes? There are so many up these days, I don't even notice or pay any attention to them."

"This one caught my eye."

Max seemed to stifle a sigh. "Why is that?"

Liesbeth bit her bottom lip and then went on. "It was about emigrating to Canada. There was a lovely scene on it."

Max opened the journal and found his page again. "I'm sure it's a beautiful country."

Liesbeth frowned. "Max."

He looked up.

"Max, sometimes I think it would be good to have a complete change. You and I and Hannah. We could go somewhere else."

His eyebrows pulled together. "We have a good home here. I have a good job, which in these days, not everyone can say. We aren't going anywhere."

"I think you could have a good job in Canada too."

He closed his journal with a slap. "You're being ridiculous, Lies. This is our home. My mother lives here, as does your sister."

"Other people leave their mothers and sisters."

"We aren't other people. Now that's an end to it." He stood up and went to look out the window.

Liesbeth felt the blood in her face. "You won't even discuss the possibility. Is it because you couldn't bear to leave *her* behind?"

He spun around to face her. "I knew it. I knew this Rosa nonsense was still simmering in your mind. I told you before and I'll tell you again: there is absolutely nothing going on between her and me. I've told her she created a storm with her silly card and she's quite sorry about it all. She'll tell you herself if that's what it takes. I'll bring her home one evening."

Liesbeth was standing now too. "I don't want to meet her. I don't care what she has to say. I say that there is something keeping you here that is more than just because your aging mother lives around the corner."

Max's face was beet red. "My mother is important to me and is the grandmother to our daughter. I'm sorry that your family doesn't mean more to you, but I can't just walk away from mine so easily. Besides that, I just don't want to leave Holland. I've told you that before. This is my home and I like it here."

Liesbeth could feel herself shaking. "We once were partners."

"You once had more sense."

Liesbeth didn't want him to see her tears. She turned and went to the bedroom, hearing him open his journal again as she left.

XXIV

Autumn 1922 – A Chill in the Air

It took little more than a week before Liesbeth found the courage to write a letter to the address in the Hague. She was just curious, nothing more. She knew that Max wouldn't be budged, so if she was going to pursue anything, she would have to do it alone and of course that was unthinkable. Leave Max? No, that wasn't possible. So when she wrote the letter asking for more information, it was simply because she was curious.

The thick envelope arrived ten days later. In it was a pamphlet that described in great detail the opportunities for farmers. Liesbeth could see that they were ideally looking for young men who had experience in agriculture.

Liesbeth gave Hannah a hard crust of bread to gnaw on while she looked at all the pages that had been sent. "Well, Hannah, I don't think you need to worry anymore because it doesn't look like they would take you and me anyway."

Hannah laughed and drooled over the crust.

Liesbeth sat with her elbows on the table. She rubbed her temple with her left hand while she turned the pages with her right. "Hmm. There are exceptions to the agriculture requirements for people categorized as domestics. That's what I do here, but would I go across the world to do that over there?"

Hannah finished the crust and started to slap her hand on her tray.

Liesbeth looked up. "Yes, all right. Let me put all this away. It was just a silly dream anyway."

She put all the papers back into the envelope and added it to Margaret's letter in her dresser drawer.

———

The papers were out of sight but not out of Liesbeth's mind. When Hannah went down for her nap that afternoon, she took them out again and read it all through once again.

I should throw it all away. There's no point in keeping it.

As a distraction she decided to respond to Margaret's letter.

'Dear Margaret,

I was so pleased to receive your last letter. I'll be honest with you, I've been feeling a little out of sorts lately. I don't know how to really explain it.'

Liesbeth chewed on her lip, hesitating to commit her thoughts to writing.

'Hannah is a delight, of course, and no, luckily she has her Tante Alida's lovely hair instead of mine.

All right, I'll be honest with you and trust that you will keep it to yourself. I've tried to talk to Ali but she just thinks I'm overreacting. Margaret, I'm sure that Max has a fancy woman. I won't go into all the explanations about how I know, but I know. When I received your letter, you gave me food for thought. Perhaps a new start is exactly what I need. Accordingly, I wrote away for the information about emigrating to Canada. I'm sorry to say that after I received it and read everything thoroughly, I can see that I wouldn't be welcome without my husband.

I should have known that a woman gives up her life once she becomes a wife and that's true whether here in Holland or there in Canada. I sense that it is worse here because women are, for the most part, quite content with it. There were so few of us who went through those experiences which now makes me unfit for this role that I feel quite alone.

So, there you are, Margaret. I must grit my teeth and settle to the job of being a wife. Surely it can't be any worse than the tedium of a night shift on the infectious diseases ward?

I'm sorry for such a melancholy letter.

Love and greetings from both Hannah and myself,

Liesbeth'

Before she could change her mind, Liesbeth prepared the letter to mail. When Hannah awoke from her nap, Liesbeth got her ready for another walk.

Liesbeth waved the thin envelope in front of the child. "We have a letter to post off to your Tante Margaret in Canada."

Hannah reached for it, but Liesbeth slipped it into her purse. "Sorry, sweetheart, but this letter has a long way to go and I'd like it to get there in one piece."

Liesbeth wondered what Margaret would think of it all. *She'll probably think I'm imagining things, just as Alida does.*

When she pushed the letter into the postbox, she sighed and looked down at Hannah in her carriage. "Hannah, I wish I knew what to do now."

They strolled down to the square in front of the palace and sat down to watch the pigeons fluttering and pecking. Liesbeth felt weary. Her head throbbed and she felt as though she were coming down with something. Her thoughts bounced from one idea to another. At one moment it was *I must just settle in and be happy. If I make an effort, Max will come back to me.* And then she would flush and her teeth ground together. *After what he's done, I couldn't possibly have sex with him again. I must leave. Perhaps back to Zandvoort.* And then despair weighed down her shoulders. *How can I live? He'll have to give me money, I suppose. Will he even let us go? He'll want Hannah near.* And then her heart began racing. *Oh my God. What if he wants Hannah to live with him and his woman? Never. Never.*

She stood, panting. "We'll walk on, Hannah. Mama needs to move."

Hannah bounced and reached out her arms, wanting to get out of the carriage.

Liesbeth pointed toward a garden where a large yellow butterfly paused on an orange chrysanthemum. "Look, Hannah. How pretty."

Hannah was distracted for a moment and Liesbeth walked on, still talking. "I know you want to get out. You'll soon be too big for the carriage, won't you?" Her daughter was growing out of her baby-hood. *If I'm going to do something, I should do it soon. It will just get harder as time goes by.*

———

The days turned into weeks. Liesbeth's thoughts continued to whirl without leading to any conclusion. Things were strained between them, but Max and Liesbeth skirted around any real discussions. Evenings were the worst, when the hours between supper and bed-time stretched. At night they slept in the same bed as always, but Max made no move to pull her close.

Liesbeth found that Max was inviting his mother to come over more often, but she didn't mind. A third person made things easier.

One evening she came over, pulling a small doll from her basket. "Look Hannah, here's a new lady to add to your family."

Hannah clapped her hands and ran across the living room. "Oma!"

Liesbeth smiled. "Marion, you spoil her."

"I make these from little scraps and wool. It's nothing." Marion crouched down to give her granddaughter a hug and handed her the doll. "Besides, I think I get as much fun out of giving her the doll as she gets out of receiving it."

Max watched his daughter's excitement with the small gift. "Little things mean so much at that age."

His mother smiled at her son. "At every age, Max."

He frowned. "Perhaps you're right."

Liesbeth went back to the kitchen. *What about the big things? Like betrayal.* She wondered how her mother-in-law would react if she knew what her son had been up to.

Over supper, Marion kept the conversation going. "Max, how is work going for you? Is it stressful?"

Liesbeth froze. Max's work was a subject they had avoided for weeks now.

Max glanced at Liesbeth, then turned to his mother. "It's fine, Mama. Why would you think it is stressful?"

Marion seemed oblivious to Liesbeth's silence. "Well, one reads so many conflicting reports in the papers these days. In one article they say that the country is going into a depression, and then the next report talks about how exports are up."

Max's shoulders relaxed. "It does seem like a conflict, but both reports are true. The banking business is struggling. They are fiddling too much with the gold standard. Exports are up, though, especially as Germany tries to rebuild."

Marion shook her head and went back to eating. "It's too confusing for me."

Max nodded. "It can be confusing, but it's nothing for you to worry over."

Liesbeth felt a flash of anger. "Because she's a woman?"

Max tilted his head. "Because I'm here to ensure that my mother is always looked after."

Marion looked from Max to Liesbeth, a puzzled frown wrinkling her forehead. She patted Max's hand. "I'm glad of that. We are all glad to have Papa looking after us, aren't we Hannah?" She smiled at the child and Hannah grinned back.

———

They were in bed and the lights were turned off. Max spoke quietly in the dark. "Liesbeth, you're like a bear with a sore tooth these days.

I don't know what to say or do to bring things back to the way they were."

Liesbeth lay on her back, bile in her throat. She plumped her pillow to prop herself up further. "I don't know either, Max."

"It's all so silly. I know that you still don't believe me that there was nothing going on between Rosa and me, but I thought with time you would just let it go."

Liesbeth wheeled around to sit on the edge of the bed, her back to Max. "Let it go? Can you be serious?"

He touched her back and Liesbeth flinched away. His hand burned her.

Max sighed. "Tell me what I can do. I don't understand why you are so quick to think I would look at another woman. I thought you understood that you and Hannah are everything I want."

She stood and picked up her dressing gown. "There's nothing you can do to make up for it." She headed for the door.

"Make up for it? There was no *it*."

For the space of a heartbeat, Liesbeth paused. *Can that be true?* She caught her image in the full-length mirror, frozen in the act of leaving. As if she were looking at someone other than herself, she saw the shapeless cotton nightdress and tired dressing gown. She saw her long hair in its untidy braid draped over one shoulder. Superimposed over that image she saw the Rosa of her imagination in silky bone-coloured lingerie.

Liesbeth left the room, closing the door behind her.

XXV

Autumn 1922 - Opening Doors

Liesbeth fashioned a bed for herself in Hannah's room. Max tried to argue her out of it, but at last threw up his hands. "Fine. If you want to be silly, go ahead and be uncomfortable. One of these days, you'll come to your senses and then we can talk this through and go back to normal."

Liesbeth knew that things would never go back to what they had been. She felt out of control and didn't know what to do about it, but she knew she couldn't do nothing.

I wonder if I could talk to Jo Steen about it all. She dismissed the thought as quickly as it had come. *I'm not a talker.*

The plans spun through her mind in a kaleidoscope of images. Living here, living there. With Alida. On her own. With Max but in continued separate rooms. She was no further ahead ten days later when a letter from Margaret arrived.

As usual, when Liesbeth looked down and saw the postman slip the mail through the letter slot, she took Hannah's hand to go down and get it. Hannah wanted to climb down the steps on her own, so it was a slow trip.

"Good girl. Two more steps now. Big jump. Very good, here we are."

Liesbeth picked up the mail and saw the Canadian stamp. "Oh, Hannah, here's a letter from Tante Margaret. Come, let's go back up to open it."

Hannah was ready to climb all the way up again, but Liesbeth scooped her up. "No, sweetheart. I'll carry you up."

She ignored the child's cries of protest as Liesbeth hurried up the stairs. She hustled in and dug out a hard biscuit to give to her daughter. "Here now. This will make up for Mama spoiling your fun."

Hannah sat on the floor and Liesbeth tore at the envelope. She flattened out the tissue-thin paper to read.

'Dear Liesbeth,

Oh my dear friend. I was so shocked to read your letter. How can it be? Are you quite sure that you got the facts right? I would have sworn that Max was true-blue. Well, it goes to show that one never knows what goes on behind the doors of someone else's home. I'm so very sorry.

So now that we have that out of the way, let us be practical. Here is what I did: I have spoken to both Matron and the Chief Administrative Officer (Mr. MacLeod) of the hospital where I work in Antigonish. It isn't a large hospital, but they have broken ground to double the size from what it is now (expected to open in four years). Even as it is, they have trouble getting and keeping quali-fied nurses. So, they would love to have you. The problem is that nurses aren't on the list for the big recruitment program right now, so if you were willing to come as a domestic, Mr. MacLeod believes he could write a letter to support your application, despite hav-ing a child. So, after having ascertained that you will come to a job (and Matron stressed that indeed you will have to help out with domestic work until you could be trained and certified to the current Canadian standard—you and I both know that won't take long!) I spoke with a wonderful woman who lives nearby about child-minding when you are on shift. Of course, if I'm home and you are working, I would look after Hannah, because naturally you and I would find a small place to share. Mrs. Lewiski would be *happy for the work. She is a widow with a very small pension, so would be glad for the money.*

There you have it, Liesbeth. If you are very, very sure that you want to leave your old life, there is one waiting here for you. You must really think it through, though, and not be hasty. Having said that, of course I will be anxiously waiting to hear your thoughts on it all.

Love,

Margaret

P.S. – Wouldn't you talk it all over with Alida?'

Liesbeth's eyes had been burning since the first line of the letter. Now the tears rolled down her cheeks. She put her head on her arm on the kitchen table and cried.

A moment later, she felt Hannah's small hand patting her knee. "Mama?"

Liesbeth looked up and pulled her handkerchief from her pocket. She wiped her eyes and blew her nose. She lifted Hannah onto her lap and hugged her. "Don't worry, Hannah. Mama's all right. Mama will be just fine."

She set Hannah back down and went into the bedroom to retrieve the package she had received from Emigration Central and studied every page once again. Included in the package were various forms to be completed for application. She spread them out on the kitchen table.

Liesbeth read parts out loud. "I need a passport which, of course, I have, but it needs to be specially stamped with 'For the trip to and stay in Canada'. Oh, and of course I will need to get you added to my passport, Hannah."

Hannah tilted her head at her mother and Liesbeth smiled. "Don't mind me, I'm just talking to myself."

Hannah went back to playing, crooning and gurgling in a language all her own to her doll family.

Liesbeth continued down the checklist. "We'll need some money to keep us going until I start to get paid. I think the bigger problem will be to get our passage there, but it seems like the Canadian government might pay for some or all of it."

Liesbeth stacked all the papers and returned them to their hiding place in her drawer. *I better write back to Margaret first of all and get any help I can in the way of letters of support or job offers.*

"I'll just write this letter to Tante Margaret and then we'll go out, all right Hannah?"

Hannah stood and rested against Liesbeth's knee. "Out."

Liesbeth leaned over and kissed the top of the child's head. "Yes, sweetheart. Give me a few minutes and then we'll go."

Hannah went back to her toys and Liesbeth took a deep breath. *Am I really going to do this?* Her heart was racing, her stomach queasy. *Adrenalin.* She gnawed her top lip. *Yes. I am going to do this.*

She began writing.

'Dear Margaret,

What a champion you are. Not only do you not *lecture me about being a good wife, you jump right in to help me. I can't tell you how grateful I am.*

I have been thinking of little else these many weeks. I wish that things were different. I wish that I felt the way I did when I was in Paris and falling in love with Max, but the truth is, I don't. Your careful plans have filled me with excitement. I still am not sure that they will come to fruition, but I would certainly like to proceed until I'm told it can't happen.

Let us start with getting the letter that your very kind Mr. MacLeod has offered to write for me. Once I receive that, I can proceed with my application. I understand that the Canadian Government often offers financial support for the passage, so I will work on finding out what those requirements are.

I want to have as many of these details worked out before I need to reveal anything to Max. I don't think he can stop me, but he may try, so the less time he has to wear me down in that way, the better. I have read in the literature from the emigration department that one should go to Canada in the spring. April is six months away, so that is my target departure.

I promise that I will talk to Alida.

Thank you again, my friend, for your moral and practical support. I look forward to seeing you again!

Love,

Liesbeth'

She sealed and stamped the envelope and put it in her bag, then turned her attention to Hannah. She scooped the girl up in her arms and danced across the room. Hannah laughed.

"Yes, Mama's feeling a little silly." Liesbeth set the child down to fasten on her shoes.

Outside their apartment door, Liesbeth nodded to her daughter. "All right, Hannah, let's see you go down the stairs. You need to be a big strong girl, able to do all these kinds of things for yourself when we go to Canada."

Liesbeth held the two small hands in her own and helped support her daughter's wobbling little legs to climb down. Halfway down, Hannah looked up into her mother's face.

Liesbeth smiled. "Take your time, sweetheart. You're doing fine."

When they reached the bottom, Hannah stood beside the carriage where it was stored under the steps and waited to be lifted in.

"Shall we leave that behind and walk today?"

Hannah clapped her hands.

"Come, then." Liesbeth held out her hand and again grasped Hannah's in hers and they made their way along the sidewalk.

When they reached the postbox, Liesbeth took one last deep breath before pushing the letter in. She looked down at Hannah. "That's it. No turning back now."

There was a small park across the way and Liesbeth picked up Hannah to cross the road. She sat on a low bench while Hannah wandered around the grassy enclave.

This time next year I won't have time to sit and watch my daughter. Am I doing the right thing?

Liesbeth's stomach churned. The excitement of writing and sending the letter was wearing off. *What have I done?*

Stop. Stop doubting. Liesbeth straightened her back. "Come, Hannah. Time to go home. I have all sorts of chores to do."

She and her daughter made their way back toward home.

XXVI

Autumn 1922 - Revelations

Two weeks later, Liesbeth and Hannah were getting ready for a trip to Zandvoort to visit Alida. It was Alida's birthday, which provided the excuse Liesbeth needed to take the trip.

Max had been quick to agree. When he said good-bye to Liesbeth that morning, he'd pulled her into a quick hug. Liesbeth stiffened. They hadn't had physical contact for weeks now.

He released and kissed her, the three ritual kisses on the cheeks, as he would have given any friend or family member. His face was flushed. "I hope you have a good trip. Give my regards to Alida."

She nodded. "I will. Thank you."

He turned away, and then, with his hand already on the door-knob, he turned to face her again. "Liesbeth, I hope that you can talk things out with your sister and come back in a better mood. We can't go on like this."

She nodded again. "Yes. I am planning to have a nice heart-to-heart with her. You're right that we can't go on like this."

He smiled and tears pricked Liesbeth's eyes.

He turned away and left without another word.

She stood for a moment, remembering how she felt when he'd asked her to marry him. She hadn't been surprised, of course. From the moment he had said that she was 'his Liesbeth', she had felt the progression of the relationship as a series of expected milestones. She had walked toward the marriage, not really thinking about it and what it would mean to her life.

He should have fallen in love with Alida. She would have been better for him.

Liesbeth packed up the few clothes and toys that they needed for the trip and headed out, one hand holding Hannah's and the other clutching their bag. They would take the train to Haarlem and from there change to the train to Zandvoort. It was an easy trip these days, but this was the first time she had done it with Hannah walking. Liesbeth had Hannah secured by a harness to prevent her from suddenly slipping out of her reach.

They waited for the tram that would take them down to the central station. She looked down at Hannah. "Now you be sure to stay right beside Mama at all times, all right Hannah?"

The child smiled up at her mother, blue eyes shining in the sun.

The tram and then the trains were not crowded. Liesbeth found a seat for both of them and Hannah knelt on the seat to watch the changing scenes roll past.

Liesbeth talked about points of interest as they appeared. "Look, Hannah. Do you see the windmill turning?" And then, "Look at how strong the horses are to pull such a heavy barge."

Hannah would twist to smile at her mother, then gaze back out the window.

Liesbeth leaned close to her daughter and enjoyed the fragrance of her soft hair. "Oh, Hannah. We are going to see such wonders in Canada. Just you wait."

When they arrived at the small station in Zandvoort Aan Zee, Alida was waiting to greet them. Alida picked lifted Hannah over her head. "Oh my! I won't be able to do this much longer. You'll be far too heavy."

Liesbeth smiled when the little girl laughed and grabbed at her aunt's hat. "Careful. She'll have your hat off and tossed away before you know it."

Alida lowered the child, grasping one of the small hands in hers. Liesbeth took Hannah's other hand, lifting the suitcase, and they set off through the village square toward the rooms Alida had rented for them.

"It's strange not going home to stay anymore."

Alida nodded. "Yes, it took me a while to get used to it as well, but now that I live in residence, I quite like it. I have my own room and we can use the small kitchen there for simple meals."

Liesbeth bit her lip. "The landlady of the pension where Hannah and I are staying won't mind if she makes a little noise?"

"No, she's very friendly and has grandchildren. She's looking forward to meeting you both. It's like a little self-contained flat. You'll love it."

Liesbeth had never stayed alone before. It would be strange. No parents. No sister. Not even a husband.

Alida stopped in front of a door on the Haltestraat and set down the case. "Here we are." Before she could knock, the door opened and a short, plump woman greeted them with a big smile.

She bent over and tickled Hannah under the chin. "Welcome, little one." The woman straightened. "Welcome to both of you. I'm Mrs. Akkerman."

Liesbeth shook the warm hand and relaxed, realizing she had been clenching her teeth. She relinquished her suitcase to Mrs. Akkerman at the woman's insistence. "Thank you."

Lisbeth picked up Hannah and followed her landlady up the narrow staircase to the second floor, Alida huffing and puffing behind her.

Liesbeth set Hannah down. "Oh, it's lovely."

Mrs. Akkerman led the way through the small suite. "The toilet is down the hall, but here you have a hotplate and sink. You see you can open this screen if you want to have baby sleeping in the evening while you sit up later." Mrs. Akkerman unfolded a three-panel linen screen that would act as a room divider.

Liesbeth felt Alida squeeze her hand. "It's all right?"

Liesbeth smiled. "It's super."

Alida nodded. "It's too bad you've only come for three nights."

Mrs. Akkerman handed Liesbeth a set of keys. "One for your room and one for the front door, but mind, I put the lock on the front door at ten o'clock."

Liesbeth laughed. "Heavens. If I'm not in by ten o'clock, I deserve to get locked out."

"Even though you have your own hotplate, you know that breakfast is included in the price? I serve from seven o'clock until nine."

"That's wonderful. I'll be spoiled and never want to leave."

Mrs Akkerman smiled. "Will oatmeal be good for the little one?"

"Perfect."

Alida closed the door behind Mrs. Akkerman. "I'm glad you like it. One of my colleagues rents it sometimes for her brother."

Together, they unpacked Liesbeth's overnight bag. When they finished, Alida poked around the small kitchen cabinet. "There's some tea here. Shall I make some?"

Liesbeth gave Hannah a doll to play with, then came over to join Alida. "Yes, that sounds lovely. I'll be sure to buy some to replace Mrs. Akkerman's supply."

Alida filled the kettle and turned on the stove to boil the water. She sat down at the small two-person table and looked up at Liesbeth. "So, are you going to tell me what's brought you here?"

"What do you mean? It's your birthday. Do I need any other reason to bring Hannah to visit her aunt?"

Alida pushed out the other chair and Liesbeth sat down. "Lies, you've been fretting for months now. I can read between the lines of your letters and I can see it in your face."

Liesbeth blinked, her lips pursed. "Let me get the tea first."

Alida nodded and remained quiet, watching Hannah play while Liesbeth stood up again and fussed with cups, strainer, and teaspoons.

Liesbeth set the things on the table. "There's even a bowl of sugar here."

"Yes, it's a nice spot."

Liesbeth set down the teapot and resumed her seat.

Alida gently shook the pot to stir the leaves, then set the strainer on her own cup and poured out the tea. "Steeped enough for you?"

Liesbeth nodded. "Yes, fine. I see you still remember Mama's lesson."

Alida raised her eyebrows.

"A good hostess always takes the first cup of tea and the last cup of coffee."

Alida nodded. "I do it so automatically, I forgot that I learned that from her."

"Mama didn't like having people over. I wonder how she learned that rule."

"From Oma, I suppose."

"Yes. I suppose we learn more from our parents than we realize."

Alida sat back holding her cup and saucer. "Well?"

Liesbeth stared into her cup as she stirred it. "Something I know I picked up from our mother was the problem of really talking about things. You told me she was the way she was because she had such bad migraines, and somehow I didn't even realize that. I just knew she was always silent and fierce-looking."

Alida nodded. "You built a big wall around yourself. You became the fierce, silent one, but without the headaches, luckily."

Liesbeth set down her spoon and took a sip of tea. When she put the cup down again, she sighed. "It's hard now to change a habit of a lifetime."

"It's just me, your sister. You can talk to me, surely."

Liesbeth twisted around to take her purse from where it was hanging on the back of her chair. She pulled out Margaret's last letter and handed it over to her sister. "Read this first and then we'll talk."

Alida glanced at the envelope. "From Margaret. What can she possibly be saying that has you so serious?" She put a hand to her mouth. "She's not sick, is she?"

Liesbeth shook her head. "No, no. Just read it and then we'll talk."

Liesbeth left Alida to read the letter while she crossed over to Hannah. She crouched down. "Everything all right, Hannah?"

Hannah had a doll in each hand. "Yes, Mama. Shopping." She bounced the two dolls side-by-side on the floor.

Liesbeth stroked her daughter's cheek. "Very good."

Alida called her. "Liesbeth, I don't understand this at all. Are you seriously trying to tell me that you are moving?"

Liesbeth went back to the table. "Yes. As you can see, Margaret is prepared to help me. Yes, Ali. I'm going to emigrate to Canada."

Alida waved the thin blue paper in the air. "This is madness."

Liesbeth motioned for Alida to lower her voice. "Let's not upset Hannah."

Alida's eyes were large. "She'll be pretty darned upset if you go through with this crazy scheme."

"Why crazy?"

Alida shook her head, leaning her elbows on the table. "I . . . I can't even describe how crazy. Liesbeth, have you said anything to Max about this?"

Liesbeth back was stiff, her chin raised. "I started out by asking him if he would consider the move, together as a family, for a fresh start."

"And of course he wasn't interested. Why would he be? He's happy. He has a good job here and his mother a few minutes away."

"Not to mention his floozy."

Alida sat back and closed her eyes, then looked at Liesbeth. "His floozy?"

"His mistress. Whatever you want to call her."

Alida took a deep breath. "I know you've mentioned your suspicions before, but are you now certain? Do you have some sort of proof?"

Liesbeth folded her arms across her chest. "I have all the evidence I need in his behaviour, and of course, the letter she sent him from Italy."

Alida's eyes widened. "Letter?"

Liesbeth nodded. "I forgot. I didn't tell you about that yet."

"She sent him a letter? Did you read it? What did it say?"

Liesbeth frowned. "Yes, I read it. Actually it was a postcard, so naturally I read it. And it wasn't so much what it said as the fact of her sending it."

Alida's voice was breathless. "So? What did it say?"

"Some nonsense about wishing he were there with her."

Alida took Liesbeth's hand. "Lies, are you sure it wasn't just some silly thing? I think it's not uncommon to just write that on a card to friends and it doesn't mean anything at all."

Liesbeth pulled her hand away. "You sound just like Max. Of course he said exactly that, but I know. I just know."

Alida bit her lip. "Oh Lies, I think you're being rash. Max loves you. It's just too horrible to think of you and Hannah moving to the other side of the world, especially just because of one postcard."

Liesbeth shook her head. "It isn't just one card. Max just isn't the same as he was when we first met. He doesn't respect me as he did. We aren't equals anymore."

Liesbeth turned her head and blinked back tears. She heard Alida rise from her chair and then her sister's arms were around her. She stood to receive the comfort, then felt Hannah's small hand tugging at her skirt. Liesbeth stepped back and lifted her daughter.

"Mama?" Hannah tapped Liesbeth's cheek.

Liesbeth smiled through the tears. "It's nothing, Hannah. Mama got some dust in her eyes."

She set the child back down. "Go and play now while Tante Alida and I talk some more."

Liesbeth sat back at the table and watched as Alida filled the kettle again and set it to boil.

Alida resumed her seat. "I'm sorry you're feeling this way. I thought you and Max were solid and that I would be the spinster aunt visiting you in your happy home, surrounded by children."

Liesbeth turned the conversation. "Why aren't you seeing anyone, Ali? Why aren't you the one with the happy home and children? I always thought that's how it would be."

Alida tilted her head. "I'll be honest, I thought so too at one time."

"Is it because you see what the reality of marriage is and don't want it for yourself?"

Alida shrugged. "I'm not anti-marriage. I just haven't found anyone I like well enough to give up what I have."

"I agree with you. Don't be in a hurry to give it up."

The kettle whistled, and now Liesbeth stood to refill the pot and rinse out the cups. She heard the rustle of paper and saw that Alida had picked up Margaret's letter again to read it a second time.

Liesbeth filled their tea cups in silence as Alida studied the letter.

Alida put the letter down and took a sip of tea. "So now what happens?"

Liesbeth felt queasy and she put down her cup and pushed it to the side. "I have all the information and forms from the emigration people. What I don't have is all the money I need."

"You have your inheritance from Papa still, don't you?"

"I have most of it, but I need more if I have to pay for everything myself."

"You don't imagine that Max will pay your way, do you?"

"No. I'm hoping that I qualify for some financial support from the Canadian government."

"Is that likely?"

"It's possible. They are actively recruiting for people to immigrate there." Liesbeth stood. "Let's go for a walk. We'll take Hannah to the beach and I can tell you all the plans." Now that the first hurdle of telling Alida was overcome, Liesbeth felt better.

Alida stood. "All right, then. Let's figure this out."

XXVII

Autumn 1922 - More Revelations

By the time Liesbeth arrived back in Amsterdam, she was firmly settled on her plans. Several times Alida had tried to convince her to change her mind, pressed her to at least postpone the plans for a year to see if things changed between her and Max, but Liesbeth was determined. The time was right and Max wouldn't change no matter how long she gave him. Liesbeth was convinced of that. Reluctantly, Alida had given her support, even with an offer of money, if it was necessary.

Liesbeth climbed the steps to their flat behind Hannah. "That's good, Hannah. Take your time now."

Liesbeth's heart flip-flopped when the door opened and Max was standing at the top of the landing. "Oh, I didn't expect you to be home from work already."

He climbed down to meet them and scooped up Hannah. "I took a half-holiday so I could be home when you got here."

They went inside and Liesbeth carried her bag straight into Hannah's room.

Max stood holding Hannah as the child wiggled her fingers in his hair and under his chin, trying to tickle him. "Liesbeth, why don't you bring your things into our room? Please."

Liesbeth hesitated, then turned and carried the bag into their room. *I don't want to argue.*

Max set Hannah down and followed Liesbeth into the room. "I'm glad you're home. I think we need to talk."

Liesbeth set her case on the bed and unpacked. This to laundry. That to the dresser. The suitcase up on top of the wardrobe. She turned and saw that Max was leaning against the doorframe, watching her.

Liesbeth forced a smile. "I'd love a glass of cool water."

He turned and then looked back. "You wouldn't rather have a sherry?"

Liesbeth frowned and looked at her watch. "At three o'clock in the afternoon? No, I don't think so."

Max nodded and went into the kitchen to pour her water. He took out a small crystal glass and poured himself a sherry.

Liesbeth could feel her heart beating faster. *Something's wrong.* She took the glass he gave her and sat down at the table. "What is it, Max? Why are you home in the middle of the afternoon?" *He's lost his job.*

Max took a sip of his sherry and set the glass on the table. He went into the living room where he had his desk and removed an envelope from one of the cubbyholes. Returning, he set the envelope in front of her without a word.

Liesbeth could see without picking it up that it was from the Emigration Society. The envelope had been opened and she pulled out the letter. Without reading it, she looked over at Max, who sat across from her, sipping his drink.

"You opened my mail."

He nodded. "I did."

She opened the folded letter and read it.

Dear Mrs. Bos,

Further to your enquiry for information, we wanted to follow up with you to notify you that we have received a letter from one

Mr. MacLeod of Antigonish, Nova Scotia. Mr. MacLeod informs us that he will guarantee you a job as a domestic in St. Martha's Hospital of that town, at the rate of twenty dollars a month.

Given this information, we are pleased to inform you that the Canadian Government is prepared to advance you fifty percent of your passage money upon your agreement to sign a one-year contract.

Please provide us a letter to confirm your agreement to a one-year contract, a doctor's certificate of health for both yourself and your child, and a letter of reference to confirm that your previous experience qualifies you to fulfill the role of a domestic in a hospital. Please also confirm that you have sufficient funds to cover your travel costs and initial living costs. After receipt of these confirmations and documents, we will proceed with your application for Emigration to Canada.

Regards

Liesbeth set the letter down on the table. Her face was hot and her pulse raced.

She looked up at Max. His face was white and his nostrils flared.

He unclenched his jaw. "Well? What do you have to say? Tell me this is some absurd mistake."

She took a breath and raised her chin. "No, it isn't a mistake."

Max jumped up, shoving his chair away. "God almighty. What are you thinking?"

Hannah crept back into the kitchen, her eyes filled with tears. "Papa?"

He closed his eyes, then turned to his daughter. "It's all right, Hannah. No one is angry with you. Papa just needs to talk to Mama, so you go back to your toys, all right now?" He patted her on the head and sent her back into the living room with a gentle push.

Liesbeth took the moment to gulp down several swallows of her water.

Max turned back to Liesbeth, his voice lower now. "I asked you what you can possibly be thinking."

Liesbeth squared her shoulders. She was grateful that she didn't feel any tears pricking. "I'm thinking that you and I are a mistake, Max. I'm not the wife you need or want, if you are honest."

He pulled his chair back and sat down again. "How can you say that? I have tried in every way I can think of to let you know that you are the one I want."

Liesbeth shook her head. "I know all that you've said, but I'm not convinced. Whether you admit it to me or not, you are attracted to Miss Brouwer."

Max shifted in his chair. "You're using this imaginary relationship with Rosa as an excuse to leave me."

Liesbeth's head throbbed. "I asked you to come along. A fresh start. You aren't interested, so I conclude that you have too much to keep you interested right here."

Max stood up and looked down at Liesbeth. He studied her in silence, shaking his head. He heaved a deep sigh. "Liesbeth, my life, *our* life is here. This is home. I have no interest in leaving it to go halfway across the world to a foreign place."

Liesbeth looked up at him, her arms folded across her chest. "And I think we need a fresh start, and if you aren't interested, then you force me to go without you."

"I will not beg you to stay. If you don't want to be with me, then you go. You know my feelings and my mind. I don't want you to, but if you feel it's necessary, so be it." He waggled his finger at her. "But, if you go, you go alone. Hannah stays here and my mother can help me look after her."

Max turned and walked away, leaving Liesbeth stunned. She felt her gorge rise. She hadn't considered that he would take this position. Her head was pounding now. She stood and refilled her glass, gulping down the cool water. She took several deep breaths.

She set down her glass and followed him into the living room, where Max sat in his chair with Hannah on his lap, reading to her.

Max looked up at Liesbeth. "I did some shopping and bought a nice chicken to roast."

Liesbeth clenched her teeth and forced herself to relax again. She needed to be sure of her ground before she continued the discussion. It was unthinkable to leave without Hannah. "Yes, all right. I'll go and get supper started, then."

Max smiled and kissed the top of Hannah's head before continuing to read.

XXVIII

Winter 1922 - No Turning Back

It was more than a month later. The November sleet smeared against the window and Liesbeth shivered. She longed for the next few months to hurry past. Every day seemed endless with them hardly even speaking. Max didn't ask her what she was planning. Liesbeth imagined that he thought she'd given up her plan.

She lingered in the kitchen with a second cup of tea after Max had gone to work. Liesbeth was meeting a man today who had been recommended to her by Jo Steen. Marty Lenaerts occasionally provided legal services to the hospital where Jo worked. Jo had told Liesbeth that Marty could give her guidance on her rights.

Liesbeth finished the last of her tea with a gulp. She lifted Hannah off her chair and carried her into their shared room to get her dressed. "Now, sweetheart, you look as pretty as a picture and I hope you'll behave just as nicely when we meet with Mr. Lenaerts."

The child trotted off to find her favourite doll while Liesbeth got dressed. *What shall I wear? My Sunday suit?* In the end, she dressed in her everyday clothes. She pinned her grey felt hat on and hoped she wouldn't look too bedraggled when she arrived at Mr. Lenaerts's office. Liesbeth blessed the raincoat Max had bought her last year as she belted it. The dark red colour was modern and did a good job of keeping her warm and dry. *I'll be glad of it in Canada.*

She bundled Hannah into her wool coat. "Mama's going to carry you, Hannah, but you can help me hold the umbrella."

The two of them set off, catching the tram before they were too wet. They arrived at the office tucked into an old building not far from the central train station.

Liesbeth's voice was hushed as she gave her name to the man at the desk. "I'm here to see Mr. Lenaerts. I have an appointment. I'm Mrs. Bos."

The secretary looked at the appointment book and nodded. He frowned as he pointed her to a seat. "Mr. Lenaerts will be with you shortly."

Liesbeth bit her lip and held Hannah a little tighter on her lap. *He knows I'm leaving my husband.*

Liesbeth was hot and felt flushed by the time the secretary came to her. "Mr. Lenaerts can see you now."

Hannah was already fussy after the ten-minute wait. "Out, Mama." She tugged Liesbeth toward the door.

"No, Hannah, we have to go in and see this man."

Liesbeth grasped Hannah by the hand and they went into the inner office. The secretary closed the door with a loud click, enclosing her in the room.

The tall ginger-haired man leaned across the desk to shake her hand. "Please take your coats off and relax."

He opened his drawer and took out a paper bag. "Can the little one have a cookie?"

Liesbeth smiled. "I'm sure she'd love that."

He leaned over and held out the open bag in front of Hannah. "And what is your name?"

Her little fist dove into the bag, pulling out a home-baked cookie. "Hannah."

Liesbeth gave the child a stern look. "What do you say, Hannah?"

"Thank you."

Mr. Lenaerts sat back and returned the bag to his desk. "You're welcome. Now, can I give you this book to look at while your mama and I have a quiet talk?"

Hannah nodded, nibbling the cookie to make it last.

He set a picture book in front of her and glanced at Liesbeth. "She's not the first child to visit."

Liesbeth could feel herself relaxing. Her heart wasn't racing and she was cooling down now that she had removed her coat. "Thank you, Mr. Lenaerts."

"Please call me Marty and I'll call you Liesbeth, all right?"

Liesbeth nodded.

"Jo mentioned that you are considering some big life changes and you'd like to understand what your legal position is."

"Yes, that's right. I'm emigrating to Canada. My husband will not be going."

"I see." He waited for Liesbeth to continue.

"I did ask him, but he has too many interests here."

Marty nodded. "I must be blunt in order to best advise you. Is there a case of adultery to be made?"

Liesbeth swallowed and felt the heat rise in her face. "I believe so."

"But you don't know for certain? He hasn't admitted it?"

"He hasn't admitted it."

"It will be very difficult to get a divorce, then. The best we can do is to proceed with a separation from bed and board. After five years of being separated, you or he can move for a divorce."

"To be honest, I have no intention to go for a divorce. I really only care about"—she glanced over to Hannah—"understanding my rights where she is concerned."

"Ah, yes. Is he planning to put up a fight there?"

"So he has threatened."

Marty frowned. "Yes, child custody is a problem. As you may know, a wife does not have equal rights with her husband. If he truly chooses to insist, than indeed, the law will be with him, I'm afraid."

Liesbeth put her hand in front of her mouth. "Oh, my Lord. That's it, then. An end to my plans."

Marty shook his head. "Not necessarily. We have a system of mediation here where you can both tell your side to a judge and have him decide."

Liesbeth held up her hands. "What would be the point? A judge is sure to side with him."

Marty folded his hands on his desk and leaned forward. "I know this is very difficult for you, especially in front of the little one. Can you tell me if there were any specific reasons why you want to leave?"

Liesbeth shook her head, her eyes swimming. "I can't explain it."

"Beatings?"

Again, she shook her head.

"Other"—he hesitated—"reasons in the bedroom?"

"No, nothing."

He sat back with his head tilted.

She knew he was waiting for some explanation. "I just know in my heart about him and this woman in his office."

Marty nodded.

"And then, it's just that—" She stopped, uncertain of how to go on.

Marty raised his eyebrows. "Just that?"

"Just that he doesn't treat me the way he used to treat me."

Marty picked up his pen to make notes. "Very good. Tell me more about that. How does he treat you now compared to the way he used to?"

Liesbeth took a deep breath. "We used to be equals when we worked together during the war. But now he makes decisions for me and tells me that I can't join a political party. Things like that."

Marty put the pen back down and swivelled his chair to look out the window for a moment.

When he turned back, he nodded. "I think the best thing you can do is talk to him and try to convince him to let you take her. I have to tell you that I don't think you'll get very far, otherwise. I know it isn't what you hoped to hear, but it's my honest opinion."

Liesbeth felt the sweat trickle down her back. "I see."

There was nothing further to be said. Liesbeth rose and put her coat back on. She buttoned Hannah back into her coat.

Marty stood and held out his hand. "Let me know if there is anything else I can do. I'm willing to arrange for mediation if you want to try it."

"Thank you. I'll think about everything you've said. How much money do I owe you?" Liesbeth prayed that it wouldn't be much.

Marty shook his head. "Nothing."

She stiffened her back. "That can't be. I pay my way."

Marty smiled. "You can thank Jo. She agreed to go out for supper with me in exchange for this meeting."

"Well then, I will thank her. That's very kind of you."

He ushered her to the door and Liesbeth stepped outside, holding Hannah's hand.

Liesbeth looked down at Hannah. "At least the rain has stopped. That's the best I can say about this morning, Hannah. We might as well walk home since it's dry."

Hannah pulled her hand away to skip along the sidewalk in front of her mother.

Liesbeth watched her daughter as they made their way towards home. *She's independent. Just as I was when I was young.*

The weight of her disappointment dragged at her feet. Her shoulders were slumped and she felt more like forty-eight than twenty-eight years old.

What can I do? Liesbeth saw the years stretch ahead, feeling her life a drudgery to be endured. Max wouldn't just let her go. Why should he? She had made a commitment and she would have to just live with it.

She made supper as usual but was silent as they ate, barely registering as Hannah chattered to Max.

"Man give Hanna cookie, Papa."

Liesbeth looked up and felt herself flush as Max frowned at her. She turned to Hannah. "Eat up now, Hannah."

She helped her daughter finish eating. Liesbeth felt Max watching her. She turned to him as she lifted up the child. "I'll put Hannah to bed and then we'll talk."

He nodded and went into the living room to read the paper.

Liesbeth lingered after she put Hannah to bed, sitting by her side and stroking the soft curls as the little girl fell asleep.

Liesbeth went back to the kitchen to wash the supper dishes. She was startled when Max came into the kitchen and took the drying towel off the hook.

She shook her head. "You don't need to do that."

He lifted a shoulder. "I want to."

They worked without speaking for a few moments, finishing the clean up quickly.

Max hung the towel back and then leaned against the countertop with his arms folded as she continued to wipe down the sink. "Well? Are you going to tell me about this man who gave Hannah a cookie today?"

She hung the dishcloth over the sink edge and dried her hands. Taking a deep breath she looked up at him. "I went to see a lawyer today."

Max's face paled. "Oh, Liesbeth. Why?"

Liesbeth slipped past him and went into the living room. She walked to the front window and stood looking out for a moment, the tears burning her eyes. She felt him close behind her.

She turned to face him. "You know why. I want to go to Canada and I can't go without Hannah."

Max shook his head, then took off his glasses and pressed his closed eyes with the fingers of his left hand. He put his glasses back on. "How is it possible that you are so unhappy?"

Liesbeth looked up at the ceiling to keep her tears from falling. "I need more."

"More than what I can give you."

She looked at him. "Yes."

Max turned and gripped the mantelpiece above the fireplace. "I'm sorry I'm such a disappointment to you." There was a silence and then he continued, his voice more in control. "What did the lawyer say?"

She sniffed and bit her lip. "He felt that my position for taking Hannah away was not strong."

Max sighed and nodded. He turned again to look at her, then went and collapsed into his easy chair. Leaning his arms on his knees, he stared at the floor.

Liesbeth could hardly hear his words. "I'm not a cruel man, Liesbeth."

She sat on the sofa across from him. "I know that. I didn't say you were."

"I feel that I must be a monster for you to want to leave so badly."

She shook her head, and removed her glasses to wipe at the tears flowing down her cheeks. "You're not a monster."

"No. I'm not a monster, and so I won't separate a child from her mother."

"What are you saying, Max?"

He looked up. "If you really feel you need to leave, then do so. I won't prevent you from taking Hannah. God knows how I'll manage without both of you, but I won't keep you here if you really insist on going."

She leaned toward him to take his hand, but he pulled away. "Thank you, Max."

"I won't let her forget me, though. I will write to her and I expect you to allow her to write to me when she is able."

"Yes, of course. You're her father and always will be."

"And Liesbeth?"

"Yes?"

"I don't intend to give you a divorce, so I hope that wasn't your expectation."

Liesbeth frowned. "I hadn't thought about it. I don't have any intention of remarrying, so it's fine."

Max nodded.

Liesbeth tilted her head. "I'm surprised, though. I would have thought that you would want the freedom for another relationship."

Max sighed. "Liesbeth, I've told you and told you. There is no one else I want to be with. You are my wife and will remain so. Perhaps you'll get this out of your system and we can rebuild our marriage."

Liesbeth pursed her lips, but didn't respond. She rose and went to prepare for bed, feeling exhausted but optimistic for the first time in weeks.

Part Two: The New World

I

June 1923 - Beginning Again

Her first view of the New World was finally here. She stood on the deck of the Rotterdam IV along with most of the other passengers, all of them craning their necks to get a glimpse of their new world. She held Hannah in her arms so she could also see, but the toddler was tired and rested her head on Liesbeth's shoulder, uninterested.

Liesbeth kissed her child's blonde curls. "Look, Hannah. Do you see where we will be living from now on? Well, we aren't quite there yet. From here, we'll take the train."

Hannah lifted her head and gazed out to where her mother was pointing. "Papa?"

Liesbeth turned away from the sight and carried Hannah to a quiet spot before setting her down. "Oh, sweetheart. You know Papa is back in Holland. He stayed there. This is an adventure just for you and me."

Hannah's bottom lip pushed out and trembled. "Home."

Liesbeth led the child by the hand and they went back to their cabin to check one last time that everything had been packed up and put away. "Nova Scotia will be our home from now on." Liesbeth sat on the narrow bunk and drew Hannah onto her lap. They sat, quietly cuddling for a few moments and Hannah fell into a doze in Liesbeth's arms.

Poor Hannah. First the whole confusion and tiring days travelling from Rotterdam to Gravesend, where they were inspected. From there they took a train to London's Victoria Station, then another transfer. This time they travelled by motorized omnibus to Euston Station and finally took the train to Liverpool. They spent the night in a filthy dormitory where Liesbeth lay awake all night to ensure nothing happened to their belongings. Finally, they had a more thorough medical examination before they were allowed to board the ship. Liesbeth was sure that it was partially due to the exhaustion from those first days that led to her daughter's initial seasickness from which she never really recovered during the twelve days of the sea crossing. *She'll be better once we get settled.*

The engines took on a different note, grinding and pulsing as they slowed. The loudspeakers began to blare instructions to the passengers about disembarkation. The noise woke Hannah up. She blinked and looked around in confusion.

"Well, Hannah. I think it's time for us to say good-bye to our little cabin." She stood and steadied Hannah on her stout little legs. "Can you walk by yourself?"

When Hannah nodded, Liesbeth strapped the harness on her daughter, buckling the white leather chest piece firmly over the little girl's cotton coat. She wrapped the straps around her own wrist. Now that Hannah was tethered, Liesbeth picked up her large carpet bag and basket. Between these two, she had everything they needed for the first couple of days, just in case her trunks went astray between Halifax and Antigonish. Liesbeth had no concept of how far it would be, but she knew she had to change trains in Truro, so anything could happen.

Mother and daughter made their way up to the main deck and joined the long line of passengers preparing to leave the ship. Some were already making their way along the pier into a large building. Here and there Liesbeth could see officials in uniforms, directing people.

The woman standing next to Liesbeth, holding a baby in one arm and a toddler by the other hand, frowned at the scene. "It looks like chaos."

Liesbeth moved a step forward with the rest of the line. "They've done this many times. They must have a system by now."

The other woman grunted. "Maybe."

The husband who held the hand of their third child turned to his wife. "Give it a chance, Eke."

Liesbeth glanced at the woman's wrinkled brow. *He wanted to come and she didn't. This is how it would have been if Max had agreed to come with us. He would have been miserable and I would always be trying to convince him it was wonderful.* She was glad she didn't have to deal with that. She and Hannah were in the adventure together and would make the most of all the opportunities this new life would give her.

She smiled at the woman as they moved again. "I think it's going to be great. Where will you be going?"

The woman sighed. "After this, we have days more to travel. We're going to Ontario. We have a place on a farm somewhere north of Toronto."

Liesbeth nodded. "There is lots of land here. You'll make a go of it, I'm sure."

The husband twisted around. "That's what I've been telling her. I am working as a labourer for the first year, but it will give us a chance to look around to buy our own place."

The line funnelled down the gangplank and Liesbeth lost sight of the family. She didn't envy them their long trip still ahead. She was glad she was staying in Nova Scotia. The country was so vast and most of the people she had met during the ocean voyage were travelling onwards to Quebec, Ontario, and even as far as Saskatchewan.

When Liesbeth began walking along the pier towards the building, she stumbled. Her legs were rubbery after the long journey on the rolling sea. Hannah sat down and began to cry.

Afraid that her daughter would be stepped on by the moving crowd, Liesbeth flung her carpet bag over her shoulder and quickly scooped up Hannah. "Don't cry, honey. I know it feels strange, but your legs will get used to being on land soon."

The tiny arms clung around Liesbeth's neck. Liesbeth felt weighed down with her bag, basket, and now her daughter, but somehow she walked on. "I remember getting off the boat in France. We were all wobbling and bumping into each other, even Tante Alida." Liesbeth kept up a stream of prattle to distract her daughter.

Hannah's words were muffled against Liesbeth's neck. "Tante Ali."

Liesbeth sighed. "I know, Hannah. I miss her too, but we'll be seeing your Tante Margaret soon and that will make up for it."

The child snuffled in response. Liesbeth knew that the name meant nothing to Hanna.

"I know you don't know her yet. You'll like her, though, I promise. She worked with us, with Tante Alida and me, when we were in France together."

Liesbeth rubbed Hannah's back. "Papa was there too. You remember those stories, don't you? How we all worked together in a hospital?"

She could feel Hannah nodding against her shoulder. "Well, just like then, Mama will be working with Tante Margaret in a hospital again."

"Why?"

"I'm a good nurse and think I can help people."

Liesbeth tried to shift her daughter's weight and the carpet bag slipped down her arm. They stepped through the double doors of the building into a large hall with rows of benches. "Can you try to walk on your own again, sweetheart?"

For an instant, Hannah clung tighter, then her natural independence got the better of her. She nodded and Liesbeth stooped down to set her back on her feet.

Liesbeth listened to the shouted instructions and read the signs, then made her way to the group of benches behind the large sign for names beginning with the letters A to C. She settled on a bench. Hannah stood at her knee, her eyes large as she gazed around at all the activity.

Finally, her name was called, and Liesbeth wove her way through the milling crowd to the long table at the front. Hannah was at eye-level with the table, her chin just clearing it.

The man in a dark blue uniform smiled at the child. "Hello."

Hannah looked up at her mother, not understanding the English word.

Liesbeth translated and told her daughter how to repeat the greeting. "Say 'Hello'."

Hannah stepped behind her mother's skirts and peered at the man silently.

Liesbeth handed over their travel papers, including their Form 30A and medical examination papers. The man studied each form and report, glancing up at Liesbeth once in a while. *Dear God, don't let there be a problem.*

Finally he finished the review. "You are married but your husband did not accompany you? Am I reading that right?"

Liesbeth felt herself flush. "Yes, that's correct."

He frowned. "So you're not a widow but you aren't divorced?"

She felt sweat forming under her arms. "No, I'm not a widow and no, I'm not divorced."

He sniffed. "Don't expect any financial help here. You have to make your own way."

She nodded. "I understand that. I don't expect the government to help me." She pointed to the letter from the hospital. "I have a job."

He leaned back in his chair. "And you think you'll be able to live on that wage?"

Liesbeth blinked. "Yes, I do."

He nodded at Hannah. "Your room and board will take up most of your money."

She swallowed. "I'll be sharing a place with a friend, so I feel confident I can manage."

He shook his head but stamped the form. "Good luck." He handed all her papers back and pointed to a door halfway down the long side of the hall. "Exit there."

With that, she and Hannah were free to go. She lifted her cases and took Hannah by the hand, leading the child through the seething crowd.

To leave the building, she had to show their stamped papers. Before stepping away, she asked the uniformed guard where she could make the final arrangements to ship her trunks.

He pointed toward another building. "Over there."

Liesbeth blessed the fact that she spoke English. *How do people manage otherwise?* She overheard fragments of conversations between family members. *Where do we go now? What did he just say? Why is he shaking his head?* People were asking those who spoke some English to please come and translate. Liesbeth kept walking. Her instinct was to stop and help, but she would never get away at that rate.

She joined another line of people, all trying to get their trunks and suitcases separated from all the luggage that had been unloaded from the ship to have it shipped or delivered. Again she had to show papers. Again there were line-ups.

She pulled out a sandwich from her basket and gave half to Hannah and ate the other half herself. It had been hours since they had last eaten. At long last, it was all arranged. The trunks would be delivered to the train station. If possible, they would be on the same train as her, but if not, they would go as soon as space was available. They were all well-marked with Margaret's address in Antigonish. There were buses to take passengers who had passed all the steps and inspections to the train station. She had to show their papers again to get on the bus, and then she felt secure to put them away in her purse. After this last bus, they would be on their own. They would be free to take the train to Antigonish.

Halifax was a major Canadian city, but it looked small to Liesbeth's eyes. The train station was not even the size of the station in Haarlem, let alone Amsterdam or Rotterdam.

She easily found the ticket booth and purchased the ticket that would take her right through to Antigonish. She could carry Hannah as she didn't need a ticket for her.

The man in the booth handed her the ticket. "You'll be changing trains in Truro, which will take you to Antigonish. You have half an hour to do it, so lots of time."

"Thank you. I understand."

Their train wasn't scheduled to leave for more than an hour, so Liesbeth found the lounge where she could buy a cup of tea. She found a seat at a small table in a corner and sank down with Hannah on her lap. "Oh, Hannah, isn't it so nice just to sit quietly for a little while?"

Hannah leaned back, resting against her mother with her eyes closed.

Liesbeth made her tea and a glass of milk for Hannah last as long as possible, but the station lounge was busy, and as soon as her cup was empty, she felt compelled to leave. They went out to the platform for the hour-long wait for their train. Liesbeth found some wooden packing cases at the end of the platform and spread her jacket on top of them to sit upon. Hannah had found her second wind and wanted to wander.

"No, Hannah, I won't take your harness off. Stay close to Mama, please."

Liesbeth was grateful when a girl of about ten years old came to play with Hannah.

The parents came over to Liesbeth. "You came off the Rotterdam as well, didn't you?"

Liesbeth nodded. "Where are you going from here?"

The husband spoke the strange name with difficulty. "Tatamagouche."

The wife nodded. "My brother lives there. He's been here since before the war and now owns his own dairy farm. We're so glad to come. My husband's been out of work for so long."

Liesbeth smiled at them both. "Do you speak English?"

The man responded with a heavy accent. "I have been taking lessons, along with the children."

The girl looked up from her game with Hannah. "Have, not *haf*, Papa."

Liesbeth nodded. "You'll do fine, I'm sure."

"My brother is coming to Truro to pick us up from the train station. Where are you going?"

"Antigonish. I have a friend there who has gotten me a job in the hospital there."

The woman glanced around. "You have no husband with you?"

Liesbeth stiffened. "No, Hannah and I are on our own." She didn't elaborate. Let them think she was a widow if they wanted to.

They whiled away the time comparing notes on where they were from and speculation about what lay ahead of them. When the train arrived, groaning and belching into the station, the crowd surged forward to find places. They were separated in the crowd, and although Liesbeth was pleased to have made friends with them, she wasn't sorry to be parted from them before they began to ask too many questions about her history.

As the train got underway, Liesbeth thought about her situation. *Even here, a separated woman is a freak. Perhaps I should say I'm a widow.* Liesbeth shook her head at the thought. *No, I'm not going to lie. I'll just hold my head up. Why do I care what everyone thinks? I'm here to start a new, productive life and I'll prove through my work what I'm worth.*

The trip to Truro wasn't long and before she knew it, Liesbeth was picking up Hannah and her cases again, struggling to get off the train.

She used the public toilet, found that her trunks had indeed been offloaded and were waiting for the next train, and joined the rest of the smaller crowd waiting to travel further east. All around her, she heard English and French. Her fellow Hollanders had melted away in other directions.

When she spoke to Hannah in Dutch, she noticed the curious glances around her. "We're almost there now, Hannah."

The bright tone of Liesbeth's voice must have been infectious because Hannah smiled up at her mother.

They found a seat by the window, and as the train huffed its way through the darkening countryside, Liesbeth pointed to interesting sights. "Oh, Hannah, look at that big animal!"

"Horse, Mama?"

Liesbeth turned to the man sitting beside her and pointed. "Sir, please, can you tell me what that animal is?"

He peered beyond Liesbeth's shoulder. "That's a moose, madam. They're quite common here."

Liesbeth repeated the word for Hannah. "It was a moose. Not a horse, but sort of a deer."

Hannah wrinkled her forehead.

Liesbeth kissed the wrinkles. "We'll see lots of new and interesting things here. Some things we'll like the Dutch versions better, but I know that we'll also like many things here better."

Hannah didn't respond but kept staring out of the window as the trees and rivers flowed past in a blur.

Liesbeth's stomach began to flutter. Every fifteen minutes or so, the train would begin to slow. *Are we here? Is this it?* She would strain to hear as the conductor came through the car shouting the name of the upcoming station.

"Glengarry! Station stop Glengarry!"

Liesbeth would sit back again and they would watch the hustle of passengers stepping down at the small round-roofed station, then with great gasps of smoke, the train would start again.

"Stellarton! Next stop Stellarton Station!"

This was a bigger station and several people stepped down here with only a couple of people getting on. The train was now half-empty. The man who had identified the moose was gone and there were no passengers sitting close enough for Liesbeth to easily ask how far it was to Antigonish.

Her heart leaped when she heard the conductor shout: "Merigomish! Coming next is Merigomish!"

Did he say Antigonish?

The conductor came back through the car as the train screeched to a stop. Liesbeth reached out to touch him, poised and ready to gather everything and clamber out. "Excuse me, did you say this is Antigonish?"

"No, Ma'am. This is Merigomish. You still have half a dozen stops to go. Antigonish is after Brierly Brook."

"Ah. Thank you."

She settled back again, the flutters in her stomach making her queasy.

By now darkness had fallen and their solitary faces reflected back at Liesbeth from the train window. Here and there lights twinkled for an instant from the passing forest. She held Hannah closer, tethering the child to her more than the harness ever did. And then finally it came.

"Antigonish. Next station is Antigonish."

Liesbeth shifted Hannah over to the seat beside her while she stood up. "This is our stop, sweetheart."

Liesbeth slung the carpet bag over her shoulder again, scooped up Hannah, feeling her back protest, and lifted the basket. She moved to the door as the train was still slowing down and had to put the basket down between her feet while she grasped a handle to keep her balance in the swaying train. Another woman was getting off here as well.

"Shall I carry the basket for you? You have your hands full."

Liesbeth smiled at her. "Thank you. I appreciate the help."

With a squeal of metal on metal, the train stopped and the other woman led the way off the train. For an instant, Liesbeth wondered what she would do if the lady hustled off with her basket, but before the thought was completely formed, the lady turned back to her. "I'll just set this down there by the ticket booth, shall I?"

Liesbeth nodded. "Thank you again."

"It's no trouble. Good evening."

Liesbeth waited and watched as her trunks were unloaded. She approached the porter with Margaret's address. "Can the trunks be delivered?"

"Yes, but not tonight. We'll get them out to you tomorrow morning."

"That's fine. Can you give me directions to this house?"

He took the paper from her hand. "Thirty-two Elm St. No one is coming to pick you up?"

She shook her head. "My friend didn't know what train I'd be on, so we agreed I'd make my own way there. Are there buses or taxis?"

The porter smiled and shook his head. "You aren't in Halifax here, Ma'am."

The station master walked over to join them. "Problem, Angus?"

"This lady and her little one need to get to Thirty-two Elm St."

The ginger-haired station master stroked his mustache for a moment. "You and the princess look all done in, Missus."

"Our ship from the Netherlands just arrived today, so yes, it's been a long day and a long journey."

He bent down and picked up her basket. "Come. I'll run you up in my auto."

Liesbeth only hesitated for an instant. "Thank you. You're very kind." She grasped her bag in one hand and Hannah's small hand in the other and followed him outside.

Her first impression was that they were in the middle of farmland. Around the station were pens for sheep or cattle. Beyond that was just the darkness of farm fields. "My goodness, it's so dark here."

The station master led them to his auto which had an odd large white sign attached to the passenger side windscreen that read: 'Keep to the Right'. He put the basket on the rear seat while she climbed into the car and settled Hannah onto her lap. There was no conversation over the roar of the engine, but Liesbeth was content to look around at her first glimpse of the town in which she planned to make her life. It was evident that the station was on the outskirts of town and as soon as they crossed a small river, they were immersed in a community full of lights and houses. In only a few moments they arrived at the house and, as the engine quieted, the front door flew open.

"Liesbeth!"

"Oh, Margaret. I can't tell you how good it is to see you!"

Margaret took Liesbeth's bag and basket from the station master. "Thank you, Donald, for delivering them to me. There's a strawberry tart in it for you if you come in for a moment."

Donald dipped his head in thanks. "As tempting as that is, I've left Angus on his own there and I better get back to the station. I'll take you up on that offer another time, though."

Margaret nodded. "That sounds just fine."

As the car roared to life again, Margaret led the way into the house. She set the bags down in the front hall and turned back to face Liesbeth and Hannah.

"Welcome home."

11

November 1923 – Getting Settled

*D*ear Alida,
  You asked me how long it would be before I start my transition
to nursing. I wish I knew the answer to that. I had expected it before
now, and yet I continue to work simply in the role of 'domestic'.
In Paris, we would have called this job 'porter'. I clean bedpans,
change bedding, wash floors, beds, tables, etc. When I ask about
moving into a nursing position, I'm told to be patient. I'm told that
there will be classes starting early next year for new nurses and I
can sit in on some of the lectures. It's a start, I suppose. I know that
Margaret feels badly to see me washing the floor when she is tend-
ing to a patient, but I smile and carry on.

   On the bright side of things, Hannah has really settled into her
crèche and enjoys being with the other children. Again on the positive side, because I am just a domestic, it was easier to request that I
only work day shift. Clearly when I do take on nursing duties I'll have
to be prepared to go into rotation and then Margaret and I will have
to devise a new schedule to include her friend a few doors away who
will take Hannah when need be.

   Margaret is such a treasure. She loves Hannah like her own, and
Hannah loves her, which has helped to make things easier here.

Between us all we are teaching Hannah English and she picks it up so easily. The young mind is so flexible!

So you see, there are good things here. Sadly there are also things that I didn't expect. There is a high rate of unemployment here, just as at home, so I'm not quite sure why the Canadian government would continue to actively recruit immigration when their own citizens are finding it hard to get steady work. Never mind. I'm working so I'm happy with that.

Well Alida, I'm so tired by this time of night I haven't the energy to write long letters. I do enclose a 'letter' from Hannah where she has drawn a picture of the house for you. It is a continual pleasure for her after living her life in our small flat in Amsterdam. She hides in rooms and calls out for us to find her, which luckily we always do.

Love,

Liesbeth

Liesbeth reread her letter and hoped that it sounded cheerful and positive. She tugged her cardigan closer around herself. The wind was howling in a way she had never heard in Amsterdam. The windows let a draft in and Margaret had said that they should try stuffing newspapers around the frames. She shivered and rose to look in on Hannah.

She pulled the quilt higher over her daughter and the child opened her eyes, blinking.

Liesbeth stroked the soft baby-down cheek. "Shh. Go back to sleep."

Hannah closed her eyes and was snoring again in a moment.

Liesbeth felt a lump in her throat as she watched her daughter sleep. *Did I do the right thing in coming here, so far from all that you knew?*

She heard the front door close. One was always required to slam the door as it had swollen a little over the years, and stuck. A yank to open it and a slam to close it again.

She closed the bedroom door and went down the hall to the kitchen where Margaret was shaking her umbrella over the sink. Margaret looked up. "I didn't wake her, did I?"

Liesbeth shook her head. "No, it's fine."

"What a rotten night out there. The sleet is just bordering on snow. I wouldn't be surprised if it snowed overnight."

Liesbeth set a kettle on the stove to boil. "Tea? Or would you rather I make cocoa?"

"No, tea is good, thank you." Margaret sat down at the kitchen table. "Did you see that they posted a notice about the nurses' training?"

"I did."

"So what do you think? Will you sign up for the courses?"

"I suppose I'll have to. I can't do this . . . this drudgery for ever."

Margaret flushed. "I wish it were different. I don't understand why they aren't just having you sit some tests and then let you work as a proper nurse."

Liesbeth sat down and sighed. "I suppose that the government brought me over as a domestic and perhaps there would be some problems if I were upgraded."

"Hmm. It seems unlikely."

"Perhaps it's because they can pay me so much less in this way, and yet they know that I do more than a strict domestic would do. They know that I care about the patients and will spend time talking to them. They know that I'll notice if something isn't right and go find a nurse. These things they know, so they get a domestic-plus in me."

Margaret nodded. "Yes, that's probably true. I'm sorry. It's not what we expected. Are you sorry you came?"

Liesbeth took Margaret's hand. "No not at all, and I don't mean to sound ungrateful. You got me away from an intolerable situation, and here I am having this great adventure and working. It isn't yet the job I am looking forward to doing, but that time will come. So, no, I'm not at all sorry."

Margaret smiled. "Well that's all right, then."

The kettle boiled and Liesbeth made the tea. She set out some scones, butter, and jam.

Margaret's eyes widened. "You baked scones?"

"I did. I found your recipe and I tried them. They won't be as good as yours, but they are my first real attempt at Canadian baking."

Margaret spread a thick layer of butter on one and took a bite. "Mmm. They're very good. We'll make a Canadian out of you yet."

Liesbeth took one as well. "Now if I only had a good piece of Gouda cheese to go with it, I'd be happy."

Margaret laughed. "Scones and Gouda cheese. No, I don't think so. But I tell you what, there's a Dutch family who own a dairy farm out on the way to Cape George and they make their own version of Gouda that they sell. I think, on the weekend, if the weather cooperates, I can convince Donald to take us for a drive. What do you think?"

"I think Gouda can only be Gouda if it comes from Gouda. Having said that, I'd love to go for a drive, and if the cheese is anything like Dutch cheese, I'll love it."

"Right. I'll talk to Donald tomorrow and if he isn't working, we'll make a date."

"He likes you. I think he'll agree."

Margaret shook her head. "We went to school together. We've known each other forever. We're nothing more than friends."

"Yes, all right." Liesbeth smiled at Margaret and rinsed off their cups and plates before saying good night.

————

Saturday was a dry, frosty day. The cold bit Liesbeth's nose as she stood outside with Margaret and Hannah, waiting for Donald to pick them up.

She bent over Hannah. "Are you warm enough?"

The child jumped up and down, flapping her arms. "I can warm myself if I'm cold."

Margaret laughed. "Is that what you learned in school?"

Hannah nodded. "Ellen showed me. She doesn't have a warm coat, so that's what she does."

Liesbeth and Margaret shared a glance. Poverty nibbled at the edges of their lives every day in subtle ways.

Donald drove up in his black Ford. The big car, known as the 'Doctor's Coupe', felt warm after standing out in the crisp morning air.

Liesbeth had spoken to Donald several times since the night of her arrival when he'd driven her to her new home. "Thank you for taking us out today, Donald."

He threw a quick glance to the back seat. "My pleasure. I haven't been out Cape George way in a long time."

Margaret wiped the steam off the window that formed from their warm breath. "You didn't have to work today, did you?"

He shook his head. "No. That comes from being the boss. I usually have the weekends off unless there's a problem."

They motored along, and Liesbeth pointed out the hospital as they went past. "See Hannah? That's where Mama and Tante Margaret work."

Once they were past the hospital, Margaret and Donald took turns talking about the scenery. Both of them knew people who lived along the route and had stories to tell. They often fell to laughing about certain people, although Liesbeth was usually at a loss to understand why. *Maybe it's the language difference. Maybe I just don't understand the Canadian humour.*

It was almost lunchtime when they pulled into a large, tidy farmyard. A man and woman came out to greet them.

Margaret introduced Liesbeth and Hannah. "Adriaan and Gertrude Dekker, this is my friend, Liesbeth, and her daughter, Hannah."

Liesbeth shook hands. Adriaan's hand scraped Liesbeth's palm, the calluses hard and skin cracked. Gertrude's was also bony and rough. Liesbeth knew they were in their mid-fifties but they looked older.

In Dutch, Gertrude welcomed Liesbeth, then bent down to look Hannah in the face. "What a lovely girl you are. Will you come in and have a cookie?"

Hannah grinned at hearing her own language again. "Oh, yes please."

Gertrude took the child's hand and let the way into the white rambling farm house. The kitchen smelled of baking. The big cast iron stove had a kettle whistling softly on the back plate.

Donald and Adriaan were talking about farming and market prices. Adriaan led him to an alcove off the kitchen to show him some advertisements for a spring auction.

Gertrude gestured to the kitchen table as she handed Hannah the promised cookie. "Please sit. I'll make some tea. Unless you'd prefer coffee?"

Liesbeth shook her head. "Tea would be wonderful."

Margaret stood beside Gertrude at the long wooden counter. "What can I do to help?"

"You can slice up some bread there. We'll just lay out some lunch."

Liesbeth protested. "Don't go to any trouble, please."

Gertrude laughed. "You're in Nova Scotia now. You can't get away without having a lunch, no matter what time of day or evening you visit."

Gertrude kept up a steady stream of conversation, switching between Dutch and English, often within the same sentence. "We came over before the war. We count our blessings every day. It's hard, but we're working for ourselves here instead of a landlord as we did when we were in North Holland."

Liesbeth felt comfortable sitting in the kitchen. All around her were things that reminded her of home. "I love the Delft tiles that you have on the wall."

Gertrude glanced at them. "They've been in my family for a long time. I couldn't leave them behind."

The men came back and joined Liesbeth at the table as Gertrude and Margaret set out food and tea. Liesbeth breathed in the fragrance of the fresh bread. "It's so home-like and welcoming here."

"It's different than when people visit in Holland, isn't it? It all seems so much more formal there with small cookies and the nice dishes. Here it's plain but plenty."

Adriaan pushed the beechwood cutting board along to Liesbeth as well as a wedge of pale, creamy cheese and the Dutch-style cheese slicer. "Try it. It's impossible to make it taste the same. The food the cows eat is different and the water is different, so naturally it can't taste exactly like a Gouda or Edam, but we brought our own moulds and our recipe so it's as close as we can get to the original."

Liesbeth sliced off a piece, giving half to Hannah, then savoured the aroma and taste for herself. Both Adriaan and Gertrude seemed to hold their breath until Liesbeth smiled. "Delicious."

"*Lekker.*" Hannah smacked her lips.

Margaret took a slice as well and layered it on top of a slice of warm bread and butter. "How big a chunk can we buy from you?"

Adriaan looked at Gertrude, who thought for a moment. "If you want a young cheese, we have a small wheel you can take, but if you are looking for anything older, you could get a quarter only. I'll have more medium ready in about two more weeks, and old, well, you'll have to wait until Christmas for that."

Liesbeth nodded. "A wheel of young will be perfect."

They enjoyed their lunch, then Adriaan stood. "I'm afraid I have to get back to work. Our boys are both away today helping one of our neighbours to build a shed, so I need to get ready for the afternoon milking on my own." He looked down at Hannah, who was fidgeting. "Shall I take the little one with me?"

Liesbeth furrowed her brows. "I'm afraid she might be in the way."

"Nonsense, I'm used to having children around. I'll keep her out of harm's way."

Liesbeth looked at Hannah. "Do you want to go and see the cows?"

Hannah leaped off her chair. "Let's go!" She held her hand out to Adriaan.

When they had left, Liesbeth asked Gertrude about their family. "So you have two teenage sons, is that right?"

"Yes, Joseph is fifteen and Jimmy is seventeen. Both good boys. Jimmy works with his dad full-time now, but Joseph is in his last year of school. It'll be easier when he's finished as well. Adriaan would like to buy the land behind here and clear it."

Margaret reached over to touch Gertrude's arm. "How's your neighbour, Riley, doing now? I heard his wife died a few months ago. He has two young children, doesn't he?"

Gertrude nodded. "Yes, it was very sad. She had tuberculosis. It's left him with his daughter, who's eight, and a son who's eleven. It's been very difficult for him, but his sister has come up from Halifax to help look after them for a while."

Donald spoke up. "Can't she stay on? I know Riley McKenna and he wouldn't be much good with kiddies on his own."

Gertrude shrugged. "I don't go over there often, but I suspect they don't get along that well. She's good with the children, although they seem pretty quiet and would probably get along with just about anyone, but Riley and her? Well, they seem to snap at each other a lot."

Margaret grimaced. "They're probably too much the same."

Gertrude nodded. "I suspect you're right."

Liesbeth insisted on washing the dishes while Gertrude dried and put them away. Margaret and Donald sat on, having another cup of tea and chatting.

Gertrude leaned in toward Liesbeth. "These two seem to really be getting along well."

Liesbeth glanced at Margaret before responding. "I think so too, but if you say anything to Margaret, she'll tell you they are just friends."

Gertrude nodded. "She had a sweetheart once. Did you know him?"

Liesbeth nodded. "I did. He was a doctor at the hospital we both worked in. He was wonderful and the two of them were just made for each other."

"The problem with being made for someone is the difficulty of finding another as well-suited."

Liesbeth nodded. "Yes, I can't imagine her with anyone else, but who knows? As they say, time heals all wounds."

Gertrude took a breath. "And what about you? You obviously have wounds also."

Liesbeth hesitated. "My situation is different from Margaret's."

Gertrude didn't prod for more as Liesbeth dried her hands. "There now, that's done."

Margaret stood up. "We should be going. Let's go look at those cheeses."

In the end, they selected a half-wheel of young cheese, and planned to come back at Christmas for some of the older type. They had Gertrude cut a wedge off their half and wrap it separately as a gift to Donald for driving them.

Margaret went back to join Donald while Liesbeth and Gertrude went out to the barn.

Liesbeth could hear Hannah chattering away as they entered. Gertrude turned and pointed to her husband and the child at the far end. "Look, he's showing her how to milk."

Hannah turned her attention away from Adriaan as she heard her mother. "Mama, I'm going to have a cow."

Liesbeth laughed. "Hannah, we can't keep a cow in town. It wouldn't be fair."

Hannah frowned. "Mama, I know that."

Adriaan came to the rescue. "I've promised that when our next female calf is born it can be hers to name and whenever she comes to visit, she can talk to her and eventually learn to milk her."

Liesbeth took Hannah's hand and nodded to Adriaan. "That is very kind. Thank you."

Adriaan smiled. "We would have loved to have a little girl. I think we'll take you as our niece, Hannah. What do you say? Can I be your Oom Adriaan, and Gertrude can be like an aunt? She can be your Tante Gertrude?"

Hannah nodded, her face serious. "I don't have any other uncles. You are my only *oom*."

Adriaan stood up from his stool. "Well, that makes me feel even more special." He turned to Liesbeth. "You must think of this as a second home. You're a long way from the Netherlands, and you need some people who understand your culture without explaining everything."

Liesbeth nodded. "We'd like that. But for now, we need to get on our way. Donald and Margaret are waiting."

They all walked around to the front of the house where Margaret was already waiting in the car, out of the wind, while Donald smoked a cigarette.

Liesbeth quickened her pace. "I'm sorry we took so long." She turned to shake hands with Gertrude and Adriaan, but Gertrude leaned forward and kissed her Dutch-style: once, twice, and a third time.

Liesbeth was taken aback. These people were so friendly to her, even though a few hours ago she had been a stranger to them.

Adriaan lifted Hannah and carried her the rest of the way to the car. "Good-bye for now. We'll see you again soon."

Liesbeth nodded. "Around Christmas." A thought suddenly struck her. "Do you celebrate Sinterklaas?" The traditional Dutch gift exchange with poems took place on December fifth or sixth.

Gertrude shook her head. "No, when we came to Canada we told the boys that we were Canadian now and would celebrate as they do."

"Yes, that makes sense."

Liesbeth climbed into the back seat with Hannah, and they drove off, waving to Adriaan and Gertrude.

Margaret twisted around to look at them as they vanished. "They're so nice, aren't they?"

"Yes. I'm glad to have met them. I can imagine we'll become friends, although they are rather far away."

Donald spoke over his shoulder. "Margaret tells me that you know how to drive. You drove ambulances during the war, is that right?"

Liesbeth smiled. "It seems so long ago, but yes, that's right."

"Have you driven since then?"

"No, there was no need in the Netherlands. You can get anywhere easily by tram or train."

"How about I take you out in this baby and you can reacquaint yourself with driving?"

Liesbeth was quiet for a moment. "That's a very kind offer, but since I can't imagine having the money to buy my own car for many years, I'm not sure there's any point."

Donald chuckled. "The point would be that if I knew you were a good driver, I'd lend you the car once in a while if you wanted to drive out here."

Margaret clapped her hands. "Donald, that would be champion."

Liesbeth shook her head. "I couldn't ask you to do that."

"Damn it!" Donald honked the horn several times as a team of oxen lumbered toward them. He slowed down until the farmer managed to get the plodding beasts to the other side of the road. Donald glanced in his rear-view mirror at Hannah. "Sorry. That's something you'd have to watch for. We're all still getting used to driving on the right-hand side. You probably know that we only switched over to the right in April."

Margaret's voice was sympathetic. "Poor animals. If we humans are still having to think about staying on the right side, how are they supposed to remember when they've been trained all their lives to go along on the left?"

Donald grunted. "You know the newspapers are calling this 'The Year of Cheap Beef' because so many oxen are being killed when cars run into them on the wrong side of the road? Anyway, I had been about to say that I'm offering my car to you, assuming you can convince me that you can drive here on these crazy roads. You haven't asked. I'm offering."

Margaret turned again to look at Liesbeth, her eyes sparkling. "Liesbeth can drive through anything. Remember driving all the way out to the Casualty Clearing Station? You told me how there was hardly a road to even speak of, just mud and holes."

Liesbeth looked out the window, seeing some of those far-away scenes in her mind. "That's true. If I could drive there, I'm quite sure I can drive here." She leaned toward Donald. "I would certainly pay for any gasoline I use. Donald, I'd be so grateful to use your car once in a while. It's a very generous offer."

Donald nodded. "That's settled, then. Next week we'll find some time and you can take your first driving orientation."

Liesbeth was content to be quiet for the rest of the drive. Hannah was nodding off beside her, leaving Liesbeth to her own thoughts. She pictured the farmer with his stick striking the hips of the oxen as he tried to steer them to the other side of the road. They, poor beasts, were expected to overcome a lifetime of training and habit. Could some of them do it? Or was it a matter of time before all the older animals would die from being hit by automobiles or simply sent to slaughter because it was too much trouble for the owners to try to overcome their old ways?

III

June 1924 – Changing Lives

*D*ear Alida,
    I've told you before about the bitter cold and all the snow. It truly seemed endless and went well into the beginning of April. I thought longingly of the snowdrops and crocuses that were surely in bloom in the Netherlands while here it was still a frozen moon-like world. The walk to the hospital takes an hour unless a kindly person stops to offer a lift.

We had a small respite from nature between the days of melting snow and mud and the sudden and vicious appearance of blackflies. It's a constant battle between man and nature here.

I was surprised to read in your last letter that you and Max got together at Christmas. Do you keep in regular touch then? It seems so strange to me. You can't sit and talk about Hannah and me for a whole evening, so what do you find in common?

You will probably know that Max sent money to buy Hannah a gift for Sinterklaas/Christmas and I must say that I was very glad for it. She got a new winter coat since her Dutch one was completely inadequate and I had money left over to buy some nice treats for ourselves and to share. Now that Hannah is more than three years old, she is really becoming an independent lady and goes off with other children sledding. I miss the baby that she was. Perhaps you'll consider coming for a vacation one day to see for yourself what a little lady she's growing into.

You asked about the nursing classes and, yes, I have indeed finally been put into two classes. At first I felt it would be a waste of my time, but in fact I'm enjoying it. There are new methods of infection fighting with which I haven't kept up. There is a heavy focus also on working with TB patients. What a dreadful disease. As I say, I'm happy to take the classes because I feel that perhaps, at long last, I am moving back in the direction I want to go. Matron has made it clear to me, though, that I will work out my one-year contract as a domestic and then they will see what happens.

Well Ali, that's all my news. I look forward (I can't tell you how much!) to your news. It sounds to me that you are becoming a little less satisfied with your job in Zandvoort. Are you thinking of a change?

As always, I enclose a letter from Hannah. You can see that she is starting to learn her letters. Only in English, of course. It's all we speak at home anymore.

Love from both of us,

Liesbeth

Liesbeth put the letter aside to post in the morning. She picked up her sister's last letter from the table and re-read it, then sat back in her chair, holding the flimsy paper.

There were questions there that Liesbeth hadn't answered. One especially: Alida had asked if she were now happy.

Liesbeth had always prided herself on being a woman of action. When she wasn't able to work as a nurse anymore, she had felt that something was missing from her life and she took the steps that would lead her to filling that need.

She should be happy, but she felt a fissure of darkness within herself that she couldn't identify. Liesbeth sighed and folded the letter to add it to her others. Perhaps when she was working fully as a nurse instead of a drudge, she'd be able to answer Ali's question. For now, she would leave it alone.

People spend far too much time and effort analysing themselves. With that thought, she put it out of her mind and set up the ironing board to tackle the stack of sheets and uniforms while Hannah was out playing.

———

The sun was warm, and all memory of the snow gone in the explosion of life. The farm fields were green, the trees all in leaf, and the biting, itching flies swarming.

Liesbeth and Margaret sat at the kitchen table as Hannah tried again.

Hannah's small brow was wrinkled. "Please, Mama?"

Liesbeth shook her head. "Hannah, we aren't even Roman Catholic. It's bad enough that we aren't going to church regularly and when we do, it's Anglican. Your Oma and Opa would have been shocked if they knew."

Hannah tried again. "Ellen is going and I want to go too."

Margaret picked up the latest copy of the weekly newspaper, *The Casket*, to read the article about the upcoming stop in Antigonish of the Papal delegate. "He isn't even getting off the train. There won't be a mass or anything, Liesbeth. What harm can there be in letting Hannah go and wave along with her friend?"

Liesbeth threw up her hands. "All right, all right. You've worn me down."

Hannah threw her arms around Liesbeth's neck as she sat at the kitchen table. "Thank you, Mama."

"Thank your Tante Margaret. She's always on your side."

Hannah went to the other side of the table and hugged Margaret as well. "Thank you for being on my side."

Margaret looked toward Liesbeth. "Shall we all walk over to Ellen's house to drop Hannah off? It's such a fine day."

"Yes, all right. Hannah, go and put your shoes on."

"I want to wear my Sunday shoes."

"Absolutely not."

Hannah knew better than to keep arguing. She slipped away to her room to pick a ribbon for her hair.

Margaret smiled at Liesbeth. "It's just an outing for her. Her friend is going, so she wants to go. It doesn't mean she's embracing Catholicism."

Liesbeth nodded. "I know. I just feel that we are losing our identity. She doesn't seem like a Dutch child at all."

Margaret shrugged. "She isn't. She's Canadian."

Liesbeth tilted her head. "Yes, I suppose that's true."

"What did you expect would happen?"

"I hadn't really thought it through, I suppose. Of course it's for the best that she fit in and just be Canadian."

"I would have thought so."

"You're right. I'm making a fuss over nothing."

They walked together to the house of Hannah's friend, enjoying the sun and fragrance of blossoming plants. Mrs. MacDonald promised to drop Hannah off again later, so Liesbeth and Margaret had a free couple of hours.

As they turned away from the MacDonald home, Liesbeth had a sudden thought. "You didn't want to go see this Papal fellow, did you?"

Margaret laughed. "No, I can live with hearing all about it from Hannah. Let's walk along Main and get a cup of tea. I'll treat you to a biscuit to go with it."

The women linked arms and walked along. Liesbeth enjoyed the rare moment of leisure. They stopped and chatted with others who were out strolling as well. With Liesbeth's height, she could look along the street and see people before Margaret noticed them.

Now Liesbeth pressed Margaret's arm. "I see Donald up ahead. Perhaps I should leave you with him and I'll go back home. I promised myself that I'd darn Hannah's stockings today."

Margaret shook her head. "No, don't leave. Not yet. I promised you a cup of tea and a biscuit. Donald can join us if he wants to, but don't you leave."

"All right. If you're sure."

"You and Gertrude are always trying to match-make. You know I'm not interested."

Liesbeth glanced down at the pink flush on her friend's face, despite her protests.

Donald had seen them coming and was leaning against the wall of the post office, waiting for them. "Hello, ladies. Isn't this a fine day?"

Liesbeth slipped her arm away from Margaret. Her friend didn't seem to notice. Margaret stepped forward and she and Donald walked side-by-side as Liesbeth hung back.

They had only gone a few steps before Margaret turned back toward Liesbeth. "Come, Lies. Don't disappear on me."

Liesbeth caught up again and they walked three abreast. "Donald, will you join us for a cup of tea?"

Donald glanced at Margaret and raised his eyebrows.

Margaret smiled. "Yes, do join us."

He smiled. "I will, then. I was just out for a walk with nowhere special in mind."

They walked together to the tea room on Main and Acadia and found a seat near the front window so they could watch people passing by.

As they sat sipping tea, Margaret nodded out the window. "I'm reminded of the Place du Tertre in Paris, Liesbeth. Do you remember?"

Liesbeth nodded. "Yes, of course I do."

Margaret told Donald of the day in Paris when they went to see Sacré- Cœur, after which they had found their way to the small cobblestoned square full of artists. As she listened to Margaret speaking, Liesbeth thought about Max. *What would he think about this place?*

Donald was quiet for a moment. "I was in Paris a few times, too. My buddies and I went there on leave, but I don't remember ever going to that place." He laughed. "We were more interested in finding the closest place for cheap wine."

Liesbeth had never discussed the war with Donald. "Where were you for the most part?"

"I was in Belgium, mainly."

"Passchendaele?"

He nodded. "I'm proud of what we accomplished, of course, but it isn't a time I think of very often. At least I try not to."

Liesbeth shook her head. "No, I can understand that."

He seemed to shake off the mood. "It sounds like you ladies have some nice memories to look back on, though."

Liesbeth smiled. "They were very intense days."

Margaret's eyes were hooded. "We had some good days, memories I don't ever want to forget. We also had miserable days." She shook her head. "I'm sorry I brought it up now."

Liesbeth patted Margaret's hand. Neither mentioned her lost love.

Liesbeth drained her tea, then rose. "Listen you two, it's a lovely day and you should enjoy it. I absolutely must get back to do some mending, though."

Donald rose as well. "It seems a shame to spend this day inside."

Liesbeth pushed him down again. "You relax. I've had a lovely walk out and enjoyed my treat. Thank you, Margaret. I'll see you later."

Liesbeth left them lingering at the table and headed home. She was a fast walker and enjoyed the brisk pace more than the saunter she and Margaret had taken earlier.

A car coming toward her tooted the horn, slowing as it approached.

Liesbeth shaded her eyes and saw Gertrude rolling down the window. "Hello!"

Gertrude called out to her as Adriaan stopped the vehicle. "We haven't seen you for so long. When are you coming out for a visit?"

Another car drove up behind Adriaan and he started to pull away as Gertrude waved.

Liesbeth waved and called after them. "Yes, soon. I promise."

True to his word, Donald had taken Liesbeth for two driving lessons soon after their first visit to the farm, then she had borrowed the car to drive out to the farm herself, gripping the wheel as they drove through a snow storm, fearful of a sudden cart or careless driver coming the wrong way down the road. Nothing had happened, and they made it out and back in one piece, but Liesbeth had been exhausted afterwards. She remembered declaring to Margaret that she would never do that again. The best thing about that drive had been meeting the Dekkers' neighbour, Riley McKenna. He seemed nice.

Now that the snow was only a bad memory, Liesbeth felt more able to try the drive again. *Maybe next week.*

IV

October 1925 – Relationships

The construction for the new addition to increase the number of beds at St. Martha's was almost complete. A grand opening was planned for early in the new year. Liesbeth couldn't wait. She was now working as a trained nurse and more aware of how small and inconvenient the hospital was. Supplies were crammed into every available space, and patients were crowded as close as if they were back at Le Pré Catelan in 1917. On top of that, the constant sound and dirt from construction was a nuisance.

Matron walked past as Liesbeth reached up to a high shelf for more towels. The sound of hammering echoed through the corridor.

Matron shook her head. "I'll be so glad for some peace and quiet."

Liesbeth smiled. "I was just thinking the same thing."

Matron sighed. "It'll be grand when it's done, though."

Liesbeth nodded. "Yes, I'm sure it will."

Liesbeth worked steadily through her shift, but her mind was on the coming evening. Riley McKenna had sent a message through Donald to say that he would be in the neighbourhood and would like to drop by. The question kept worming its way into her mind despite her best effort to concentrate on her work. *Why?*

She had had this conversation with herself already, but it just kept repeating itself. *He must know that Donald likes Margaret, and by now it seems that Margaret is starting to like Donald as more than a friend as well. So, he wouldn't be moving in on Margaret. When I met Riley over at Gertrude and Adriaan's farm, did I give any message that I might be interested in him? Surely not.*

Liesbeth bit her lip and focused on changing the intravenous fluids for her patient, but when she finished her shift, she spent the long walk home fretting about the visit. *Maybe he really will just be in the area and is coming by for a cup of tea for no other reason than to be friendly. I probably read far too much into these simple things.*

When she, Margaret, and Hannah were having supper, Liesbeth couldn't stop herself from expressing her worry to Margaret. "Why exactly is Riley coming here this evening?"

Margaret tilted her head. "I don't really know. I didn't ask. If someone wants to drop by, they're always welcome, aren't they?"

"Yes, of course. It's just so unusual that I wondered if there was a specific reason."

"Donald didn't say there was anything. I can't imagine what it would be, but I'm sure there's nothing nefarious about it."

Hannah kicked the table leg. "I don't like Mr. McKenna."

Liesbeth put her hand on Hannah's leg to stop the kicking. "Hannah, don't talk nonsense. You don't even know him."

"I do know him. I heard Jimmy and Joseph talking about him."

Margaret and Liesbeth exchanged a glance. Liesbeth frowned at Hannah. "Little pitchers have big ears. You probably didn't understand what they were talking about and came to the wrong idea."

Hannah shook her head. "I'm not wrong. He beats his children."

Liesbeth tut-tutted. "Hannah, his children are living with their aunt in Halifax, so there you are. You got it wrong somehow."

Hannah wrinkled her brow. "I did not. They are coming back because their aunt doesn't want them anymore. When we went to the farm last time and Jimmy and Joseph were teaching me how to milk Lissy, that's what they were talking about."

Margaret lifted a shoulder. "They could be coming back. They've stayed with her for a long time. I can't think the rest of it is right, though."

Liesbeth shook her head. "I'm sure not."

They tidied up the supper dishes and went to the sitting room, Liesbeth with her knitting and Margaret with a book. It was dark outside when Riley knocked on the front door. Liesbeth continued knitting, so Margaret rose to answer the door.

Liesbeth could hear their voices and didn't know if she was pleased or yet more worried when she heard Donald's voice as well.

They came into the small sitting room, filling the space.

Liesbeth stood up to welcome the visitors. Hannah bounded forward when she saw Donald there.

He bent down and scooped her up in a hug. "Oh, you're almost too big for this now."

She shrieked and giggled. "You're big and strong. You can still lift me."

He set her down again and she slipped back to her mother's side without acknowledging Riley's presence.

Liesbeth frowned at her. "Hannah, don't be rude. Please shake Mr. McKenna's hand."

Hannah stood firmly beside her mother until Liesbeth stepped forward herself to shake first Donald's hand and then Riley McKenna's. "Good evening. Please excuse my daughter. She can be shy with new people."

Riley McKenna was the same height as Liesbeth but stocky. His hair was thinning, although he would only have been in his early forties. Tonight his mousy brown hair was slicked back with oil, giving it a streaky appearance.

Margaret offered tea to their guests and went off to the kitchen to put the kettle on.

Liesbeth smiled at Donald. "We don't often have visitors in the middle of the week."

Donald rubbed his hands together. "Riley brought a few sheep in to be shipped down to Halifax tomorrow morning. When he was asking me where he could clean up after he penned them up for the night at the station, I offered my house, and then it seemed like a great chance to come along for a cup of tea and one of Margaret's teacakes."

Margaret came back in carrying a tray of cups and saucers. "You're very welcome, and Donald, you know you don't need a reason to come by."

He stood to take the tray from her hands. "I don't want to become a nuisance."

Margaret snorted. "What nonsense."

Riley took the opportunity of Donald and Margaret's conversation to sit in the chair closest to Liesbeth.

Hannah eyed him. Liesbeth kissed her daughter's forehead. "Hannah, it's almost time for you to be in bed, so why don't you go to your room and get ready?. I'll be there in a few moments to read you a story."

"Tante Margaret is making me cocoa."

"Ah. Well then, sit here beside me and be as quiet as a mouse, all right?"

Hannah nodded.

Riley nodded toward Hannah. "She's a pretty little thing."

Liesbeth smiled. "Thank you. You may not think that when she's been busy at the farm, playing in the straw or milking her cow, Lissy."

He didn't smile, his brown eyes very serious-looking. "Farming is a good life, a healthy life for children. Better than the city."

Liesbeth took the opening. "Did I hear that your children are coming home to live?"

Riley blinked as though surprised she should know this much about his life. "Yes."

He's worse than I am at making conversation.

Liesbeth felt sorry for him as the sound of Donald and Margaret's easy conversation carried to them. Liesbeth turned to Donald.

"I wonder if I can borrow your car one more time before the winter sets in, Donald. Hannah's been anxious to see Lissy again."

Donald laughed. "I hope that Gertrude and Adriaan offer some motivation for going out as well, and it isn't only the cow that you visit."

Liesbeth felt herself blush. "Yes, of course."

Margaret laughed as she set down the pot of tea and handed a mug of cocoa to Hannah. "He's only teasing you, Lies."

Riley leaned forward. "When will you come? I would like to show you my place too. You've never been there."

Liesbeth's breath caught. Did he think that she had been fishing for an invitation? "We never seem to have much time when we visit as it is. I'm not sure there would be time."

Riley frowned. "Leave earlier."

Liesbeth nodded. "Yes, perhaps we could do that." She turned to Margaret. "What do you think, Margaret? Would you have the time to give an extra hour to a day out?" *Please don't tell me you won't come along.*

"Why not? Donald, what do you say? Will you come along so Liesbeth can really enjoy a drive to see the fall colours?"

Donald closed his eyes as if he were reading his diary. "How about next Sunday? If you want to go to early mass, we could leave by ten o'clock."

Liesbeth stood to get the tea that Margaret was pouring, taking a cup for herself and one for Riley. She nodded. "That would be nice. Thank you so much. I'll admit that I don't drive often enough to really be comfortable with it. When I think about how I navigated my way through the Paris traffic in my ambulance, I chide myself at being nervous on these big Canadian roads, but still, the truth is I prefer you to drive."

Donald slapped his knee. "That's settled then. And we'll pop into Riley's to get the grand tour. Work for you, Riley?"

Riley nodded, turning to Liesbeth. "You drove an ambulance in the war?"

Liesbeth smiled. "It's hard to imagine now, but yes, I did."

"So you could probably drive a tractor."

There was a moment's silence. Liesbeth swallowed. "Well, possibly. I don't think I'm in a hurry to find out. I'm quite content with the job I have."

His face reddened. "Yes. I didn't mean anything by it. I was just saying."

She felt her heart beat faster. She hadn't meant to embarrass him. "Do you have a tractor? That's very modern."

He frowned. "No, I have my oxen. They'll do for me right now, but I've been looking at the catalogues."

Donald nodded. "It's good to modernize when you can afford it. I think the new machinery will help productivity. There's no harm in thinking ahead."

Riley sat back, his spine a little less rigid. "That's it. Just thinking ahead."

Liesbeth rose and held her hand out to Hannah. "It's past time for this young lady to be in bed."

Riley stood as well. "I'll be going now." He hesitated as if he wanted to say more, then dipped his head toward the group.

Margaret scrambled to her feet. "Let me see you out. Thank you for dropping in. It's always nice to have a chat with people you don't see often."

Riley turned before leaving the room. "I'll see you all on Sunday, then."

Donald also rose. "I should probably go too."

Margaret touched his arm. "Are you sure?"

He smiled down at her. "I'll see you on Sunday morning right after mass." He nodded at Liesbeth and Hannah. "Good night, ladies."

Hannah waved, then tugged on Liesbeth's hand. "You promised to read me a story."

"Come, then. Let's get you washed and tucked in."

After Liesbeth had read *Oom Pim: Vroolijk ABC*, a book in Dutch that Alida had sent for Hannah's birthday, she came back to join Margaret in the kitchen.

Liesbeth picked up the tea towel to dry the cups that Margaret had washed. "I feel a little sorry for Riley."

Margaret raised her eyebrows. "Why?"

"He just seems so awkward. I know how that feels."

"You aren't awkward."

Liesbeth bit her bottom lip. "I can be. I know I can. Working as a nurse has helped, but I'm certainly not like you, who can talk to anyone and everyone."

Margaret chuckled. "No, you're not like me, but that's because you're usually more serious than I am, that's all."

"I think Riley is serious too. I think that's the thing that sets him apart, perhaps."

"He doesn't know how to laugh?"

"I think he's shy."

"Maybe. Perhaps we'll see a whole different side of him when we go for a visit on Sunday."

Liesbeth hung up the towel. "I'm so glad you and Donald are coming along. I would never have gone there to visit on my own."

"Are *you* still so shy?"

"That's not it. I just wouldn't want him to get the wrong idea. I'm certainly not looking for a man in my life."

"Would it be so bad to have a man in your life?"

Liesbeth sat at the table and looked at Margaret. "Good question. I'll ask you the same thing. Would it be so bad?"

Margaret sat down and slid the salt shaker back and forth. "No, it probably wouldn't be so bad."

Liesbeth rested her hand on Margaret's arm. "Donald isn't Pieter deWit, but he seems like a very nice man."

Margaret blinked a few times, her eyes shiny. "No one will ever be Pieter."

Liesbeth nodded. "I know, but the question is, can you love Donald in spite of him not being Pieter?"

Margaret leaned against the hard back of the kitchen chair. "I think I could love him *because* he isn't like Pieter. If he were similar, I'd constantly be comparing."

"You could love him, or do love him?"

Margaret smiled. "Look at you, asking me all these questions about my feelings. You never used to do that."

Liesbeth smiled as well. "You've wrought great changes in me."

"In answer to your question, I think I can say that I do love Donald."

"Enough?"

"Enough to make a life together, I think. I'll confess that having Hannah around has made me realize that I would love to have a child or children of my own. With that realization comes the next thought, which is that I better hurry up with it because time is passing."

Liesbeth sighed. "It's surprising how fast the time goes, isn't it? You'll make an amazing mother, Margaret MacIsaac."

Margaret laughed and stood. "One step at a time. I think I better get married first. I'm for bed. Are you going?"

Liesbeth waved her hand. "You go. I'll turn off the lights. I just want to sit for a few more minutes."

When Liesbeth was alone, she realized that things would change. Margaret would only have to hint to Donald that she was ready to think about marriage and he'd propose in a moment. *What will happen to Hannah and me? Where will we go?*

She considered some of the women she knew and tried to imagine sharing a house with them, and couldn't think of anyone suitable. Many of the nurses were nuns, so they were out of the question. There were a couple of younger girls, recent graduates of the nursing school in Glace Bay. They were giddy and liked to take a drink, so they wouldn't suit.

Liesbeth shook her head. *Don't worry about it now. Something will come up.*

———

The day cooperated again for a drive in the country on Sunday. This time they packed some scones and an apple pie that Margaret had baked so they could contribute to the lunch they knew Gertrude would have ready.

Liesbeth pointed out different trees as they drove. "Look, Hannah, look at the brilliant red colour there."

Hannah was dazzled by the colours. "I like the orange ones."

Liesbeth leaned forward so Margaret and Donald could hear over the sound of the engine. "It's just unbelievable. So spectacular. I don't remember it so bright last autumn."

Donald explained. "We've had ideal conditions this year with the cool nights and sunny days. Last year was wetter and the colours don't develop as well then."

"I can't say that I'm looking forward to the long, snowy winter again, but I must admit that this kind of send-off to summer eases the pain a little."

Margaret nodded. "The changes of the seasons are really wonderful if you can embrace them. Even the winter."

Liesbeth sat back again to look at something Hannah was pointing at. *Embrace the changes. That's what I always think, too.* "Maybe this winter I'll get a pair of skates."

Hannah grinned at her. "Yay, Mama. That will be fun."

They took their time to get to the farm, turning down a small road at Antigonish Landing to get close to the sun-sparkled water. They stopped the car and walked along the canal for a few moments.

Hannah skipped ahead, then ran back to join them as Margaret, Liesbeth, and Donald walked abreast. She reached for Liesbeth's hand and turned up her face, the sun glowing on her cheeks. "Mama, I wish Papa was here. Is he ever coming?"

Liesbeth's step faltered. "No, Hannah. He lives in Holland. You know that. We've talked about it before."

They walked on, Margaret and Donald quickening their pace to get ahead of Liesbeth and Hannah.

Hannah looked up again. "But why not?"

Liesbeth's heart was racing. "Why are you asking about him now? You're happy here, aren't you?"

Hannah nodded. "I want him to be happy too, and he can't be happy without us."

Liesbeth smiled. "I'm not sure about that, Hannah. I'm sure he misses you very much, but he has Oma and his job which help keep him from being lonely."

They turned and walked back to the car. Hannah was quiet for a few moments, and then she spoke again. "All my friends have their papas at home. Only I don't."

Liesbeth felt a lump in her throat. "I'm sorry for that." She struggled to find comforting words as they climbed back into the car and settled instead for distracting Hannah by pointing out a large bald eagle floating on the wind current.

At the farm, Hannah went off to the barn to find Jimmy. Liesbeth called after her. "Don't get in the way now."

Hannah threw a frown in her mother's direction, but didn't respond.

Margaret laughed when she saw the look. "I think that was to tell you that she's never in the way."

"Yes, I'm sure that's what she thinks."

Donald went ahead to greet Adriaan, who had come out of the house to meet them.

Margaret slipped her hand through Liesbeth's arm. "Are you all right?"

Liesbeth nodded. "I didn't realize she still thinks about Max so much."

Margaret shrugged. "Maybe it's less about Max himself, and more about not having a man around the house. You know Donald adores her and would be happy to step in once in a while if you think she needs a father figure."

Liesbeth nodded and they followed Donald and Adriaan into the house.

Margaret nudged Donald before he sat down at the kitchen table. "Why don't you and Adriaan go and make sure that the kids aren't getting into mischief?"

Donald lifted his eyebrows and Margaret nodded toward the back door.

Donald poked Adriaan. "It looks like the girls want to have a chin-wag. Come on. You and I are sent to the barn."

Adriaan grinned. "My favourite place."

Gertrude filled the kettle and set out the three teacups. "Liesbeth, you look a little glum for such a fine day."

Liesbeth sighed. "It's a beautiful day and I am really enjoying the unbelievable sights of the trees in colour."

Gertrude glanced at Margaret, then turned back to Liesbeth. "What is it, then?"

Liesbeth was quiet so Margaret explained. "Hannah is missing having a man around the house. I didn't want to say anything before, but I overheard her friend, Ellen, asking her once why her father wasn't with the family."

Liesbeth felt a stinging in her eyes. "What did Hannah say?"

Margaret shrugged. "Something about her dad's job being too important for him to leave it."

Gertrude poured out the tea. "I never want to pry, but now that we're talking about it, why, in fact, isn't he with you?"

Liesbeth stiffened her shoulders. "It was my choice to come. Don't get me wrong, he's a good man but he had no interest in leaving his home and mother."

Gertrude sniffed. "Hmm. A mama's boy."

Liesbeth bit her lip. "He isn't, really. He just felt responsible for her. He didn't want to leave her alone in her elder years."

Margaret nodded. "He is a good and responsible man. I knew him and I can understand that he would find it hard to leave."

Gertrude turned back to Liesbeth. "So why did you want to come here so much?"

The words to explain slid out. "A married woman doesn't work in the Netherlands, and I felt that nursing was an important part of who I am."

Gertrude pursed her lips. "Caring for strangers was more important than caring for your husband?"

Liesbeth blinked at the rebuke. "He didn't need me as much as patients do."

Gertrude seemed to soften. "Well yes, patients are lucky to have women like both of you. Where would we all be without that kind of care?"

Margaret patted Liesbeth's hand. "So let's imagine that Hannah is just missing having a man around, versus Max per se. Will I talk to Donald about spending some time with her?"

Liesbeth smiled. "Maybe. If he came over a little more in the evenings, it might be a good thing for everyone."

Gertrude rose to put the kettle on again and to slice up the pie Margaret had brought. "There may be another option."

Liesbeth looked at her. "What do you mean?"

"Riley has been over here more often than ever before these last few weeks. He seems always to be asking about you. I think he's fond of you."

Liesbeth could feel her face heat. "I can't see myself taking up with another man. For one thing, I'm not divorced, so what would be the point?"

Gertrude lifted a shoulder. "I don't know. I suspect that Riley is just looking for some companionship. He has his children back with him now, and I think it's hard on him. I could be wrong, but perhaps he could be a sort of father for Hannah, and you can be a sort of mother for his children."

They could hear the voices of the men as they came back into the house, followed by the bubbling laughter of Hannah and the boys.

Adriaan came into the kitchen. "Is it safe to come in?"

Margaret flicked her towel at him. "Don't be silly. Of course you can come in."

They all crowded around the long pine table as Gertrude and the other two women set out a cold ham, potato salad, fresh baked bread, and beetroot pickles, along with two big pots of tea. The pie, scones, and squares all waited on the kitchen counter for after lunch.

The lunch was noisy with laughter. The boys teased Hannah to make her giggle. Liesbeth's spirits lifted and she leaned close to Margaret. "I remember you talking about meals like this years ago. I had a hard time imagining it, since my family was so very different, and now here I am enjoying it."

Margaret passed the butter in front of Liesbeth to Adriaan. "This is pretty tame compared to what my family used to be like."

"Even though your mother was from Amsterdam? I would have thought she would have been a quieting influence."

Donald overheard them. "Your mother is worse than anyone else, isn't she Margaret?"

Margaret smiled. "She loves to laugh. I suspect that there are many Dutch people who do, Liesbeth."

Liesbeth stiffened. "I'm sure there are."

Margaret went on. "I think it's more to do with coming from a larger family versus a small one. We kids always encouraged each other in bad behaviour."

Donald nodded at Margaret. "Did you ever tell Liesbeth the story about the time you and your brother knocked over the pot?"

Liesbeth tilted her head. "I don't remember that story."

Margaret laughed. "Oh, you'd remember it if I had told it."

Joseph called from the end of the table. "Tell us!"

Margaret lifted a shoulder. "I'm not sure it's appropriate for meal-time conversation."

Gertrude joined in. "Now you have to tell us. Go on."

Margaret began. "Oh well, you asked for it. So, you all know that I am one of seven children, right?"

There were nods around the table.

"So we lived in a typical one-and-a-half storey house out toward Cape George at the time. It was the usual kind with a large round grate in the ceiling above the woodstove so the heat would go up to heat the second floor. We didn't get much company and we kids had to make our own entertainment. All of us children were crammed into two bedrooms. The larger one was for the four boys with two bunk beds and the smaller was for us three girls with two more bunk beds. The spare bed was for any cousins or other visitors. Anyway, the grate spanned the landing and went partially into my brothers' room. So on this day, it was a cold, rotten day, and we were upstairs playing in my brothers' room, probably roughhousing. My mother had already shouted up to us to settle down a couple of times, but we were still at it. We also hadn't yet emptied the potty under the bed, which was one of our daily chores."

Jimmy started chuckling.

Margaret nodded. "You can see what's coming. Well, somehow the darned, rather full thing toppled over, spilling its contents through the grate and onto the woodstove below."

Gertrude shook and put a hand to her mouth. "Oh, no."

Margaret nodded. "Oh, yes. Well, you can imagine the shriek from my mother below. And the steam rising off the hot woodstove. And the smell. Oh yes, let's not forget the smell."

Adriaan laughed. "I can well imagine."

Margaret continued. "The worst of it was that even after it was all cleaned up by seven chastised children, it continued to absolutely reek in the house, and didn't the head of the Women's Auxilliary from the church choose that afternoon to drop by with her husband. My mother was too proud to say what had happened. I mean, who wants to explain that her rambunctious children did something so awful? So they sat there drinking tea and visiting, ignoring the stench coming off the woodstove until, when the woman was leaving, she apparently took a moment to say to my mother that whatever she was cooking might have gone off and she should be careful about consuming it."

Liesbeth joined in the laughter around the table. She compared the silence of the house where she had grown up and the Sunday afternoon chess games with her father to the story she had just heard. *Which is better?*

She glanced at Hannah, laughing with the others, and saw how she looked up to the two young men who were like adopted brothers to her now. She was growing up, more able to laugh and talk to people than her mother had. *That's a good thing.*

———

They decided to pack up their things to drive to Riley McKenna's farm, even though they could easily have walked it. This way they would have a short visit before heading back to town.

It was a very different farmyard from the Dekkers'. There were pieces of broken equipment lying beside the laneway, and a general air of neglect in stark contrast to the well-maintained place they had just left.

Margaret looked around as Donald parked in front of the house. "It looks like he could use a good tidy-up around here."

Donald nodded. "I suppose it comes from not enough time to do everything. He's on his own, don't forget."

Margaret frowned. "And do you suppose that having a wife would make him more apt to put things away? I doubt if it's Gertrude who is out in the farmyard putting broken pieces of machinery away."

Donald patted Margaret's knee as Riley came out of the house. "Don't be hard on him. He's gone through a lot this past couple of years."

Margaret nodded. "I know. Don't worry, I won't make any horrible comments."

They all climbed out and Riley shook hands all around, although ignoring Hannah. "Welcome. Come in."

Liesbeth took Hannah's hand as the child hung back. "Are your children here, Riley?"

He nodded. "Yes, they're in making the tea."

He led the way into the old farmhouse. It had been white with green shutters, but the boards wanted fresh paint. They stepped directly into the kitchen through the front door. The faded linoleum floor was grimy-looking, as were the two children who stood at the counter, slicing bread and laying out oatmeal cookies on a plate.

Liesbeth pulled Hannah toward the children. "Please don't go to so much trouble. We just finished a huge lunch with Gertrude and Adriaan."

The boy turned to look at his father, while the girl continued her work without acknowledging Liesbeth.

Margaret came over as well and rested her hand on the girl's shoulder. "Oh, I agree. Please, no food. We're stuffed."

Riley's voice was gruff. "You heard them. Stop that now and just bring over the tea."

Margaret took a tea towel and laid it over the loaf. "It's Dorothy, isn't it?"

The girl, who was about ten, finally looked at Margaret. "I'm called Dodie."

Liesbeth smiled at the boy, who looked about twelve. "My name is Mrs. Bos and this is Hannah. What's your name?"

"Gerard."

Riley and Donald had sat down at the kitchen table covered by a red oilcloth, scratched and scorched from years of use.

Margaret reached out to carry the cups. "Can I help you with this, Dodie?"

The girl's eyes grew large and she threw a quick look at her father. "I can do it."

Liesbeth let go of Hannah's hand and picked up the milk and sugar. "If we all take something, it'll be only one trip. You know what they say. Many hands—"

Hannah piped up to finish. "Make light work."

Liesbeth handed the sugar bowl to Hannah. "That's exactly right. You take this over to the table, then we can carry everything else."

Hannah carried the sugar over and pulled up a chair closer to where Donald sat, whispering to him. "May I sit beside you?"

Donald glanced around, clearly counting the chairs. "How about you sit on my lap?"

Hannah beamed and clambered up onto his knees.

Liesbeth and Margaret sat down. Liesbeth pushed out the chair beside her own and nodded toward Dodie. "Come and sit beside me here and tell me about yourself. I think you were living in Halifax for a while. Did you like that?"

The two McKenna children hovered beside their chairs until their father nodded. They slid into their chairs without speaking. Dodie's arms hung at her sides.

Riley growled at his daughter. "Mrs. Bos asked you a question. Answer her, for goodness sake. She'll think you're both dummies at this rate."

Liesbeth's eyes widened. "Oh heavens, the children are shy. I understand that. I was exactly the same at their ages."

Dodie's voice was barely above a whisper. "I liked living with my aunt. I miss her."

Margaret's eyes were shiny as she looked at the girl. "You've been through some hard times. I can imagine that you do miss your aunt. I'm sure you miss your Mama, too."

Dodie looked down and a large tear slid down her cheek.

Riley grunted. "Enough of that now. We're managing, aren't we?"

Without hesitation, both children responded together. "Yes, Papa."

They had their tea, then Riley offered to show them around. "It isn't as grand as the Dekkers' place, of course, but we have a good herd of milkers here."

Margaret nodded at the table. "Why don't you folks take the tour? I've been here before, and I'll help Dodie tidy up."

Riley shrugged. "She's able to do it on her own, but if you prefer to stay here, that's fine."

Hannah loved barns and farm animals, yet she slid off Donald's knee and stood beside Margaret. "I'll stay with Tante Margaret."

Liesbeth smiled at Hannah. "Are you sure? I think Tante Margaret and Dodie can manage without your help."

Margaret jumped in. "Let her stay if she likes. Perhaps when we're finished, Dodie can show Hannah her room."

Dodie flushed and didn't respond but carried the saucers to the sink.

Liesbeth nodded. "Very well, Hannah, if you're sure."

Hannah nodded. "Yes, please."

Riley led the way for Donald and Liesbeth. They toured around the barn, then looked out over the fields. He pointed to the distant forest. "I own some acres of forest, so I've been bringing in logs all summer."

Liesbeth shaded her eyes to look at the mixed dark greens of the spruce and pine, along with the red and gold leaves and white slashes of birch trunks. "It's so beautiful here."

Riley tilted his head to look at her, then back toward the forest. "I never think of it as beautiful. I just think about how much I can get for firewood or timber at the sawmill."

Liesbeth smiled. "I have a different perspective, I suppose. A stand of trees like that would be protected as parkland in the Netherlands."

"How do you heat your homes over there, then?"

"Coal, usually."

Donald nodded. "Coal is big here, too. Cape Breton has some of the finest coal mines around."

Riley turned and they went back into the house. Liesbeth called for Hannah and she came downstairs, followed by both Margaret and Dodie. "I was with Dodie in her room."

Liesbeth stroked Hannah's hair. "That's nice. How kind of Dodie. We'll have to have her visit with us so you can return the favour. What do you think?"

Hannah nodded and turned to the older girl. "Will you come?"

Dodie shrugged and looked at her father.

Riley looked at Liesbeth. "I'm sure Dodie would like to have a new friend. Tell us when would be convenient and we'll come for a visit."

Liesbeth cast her eyes up the steps but could see no sign of the boy. "And of course you'll bring Gerard as well."

Riley nodded. "That would be good."

They looked at the calendar hanging on the wall and set a date for a few weeks in the future for the three McKennas to come for supper.

Donald looked at his watch. "It's time for us to head back."

Liesbeth shook Riley's hand. "Thank you for the tea and the tour."

Riley let his eyes fall to the floor. "It isn't much, not like the Dekkers' place. Not like what you're probably used to."

Liesbeth felt her heart swell. "It's a fine place. You have every right to be proud. I'm sure it isn't easy keeping a place like this operating and to look after two children on your own as well."

Riley looked up again and his brown eyes pierced her. "Thank you. It isn't easy."

Liesbeth heard a small voice and noticed that Gerard was now sitting halfway down the steps. She didn't know if Riley heard his son say, "I help too." If he did, he didn't acknowledge it.

Once they were on the road again, Margaret heaved a great sigh. "What a sad place that house is."

Donald nodded. "It was never cheerful even when his wife was around, but now it's downright gloomy."

Liesbeth pursed her lips. "It must be very hard for him. If he just had some help to brighten the place up, it would probably help."

Margaret nodded. "Probably, but he's such a rough sort of character that people don't always take to him."

"He's serious, there's no question there, but I suppose he doesn't have a lot of time for socializing."

Hannah patted Liesbeth's knee. "Dodie hardly says anything. Tante Margaret had to do all the talking. And me. I talked."

Liesbeth laughed. "Yes, I imagine you did."

Margaret twisted to look back at Hannah. "You're right, Hannah. The girl is so much older than Hannah, yet she hardly had two words to say for herself. Even when we went to her room, she just stood there with her arms hanging by her sides and let us look at whatever we liked."

Liesbeth looked back at Hannah. "Did she have any nice dolls that you liked?"

Hannah shook her head. "She didn't have any dolls. She didn't have anything except her Sunday dress hanging on a hook."

Margaret and Liesbeth exchanged a glance, then Margaret turned back to the front. Liesbeth took Hannah's hand between both of hers. "Well, perhaps she's too old for dolls now. Perhaps she's more of a reader."

Hannah seemed to consider this. "No, I don't think so. I didn't see any books in the house."

Liesbeth blinked and realized Hannah was right. "When they come to our house, you mustn't brag and make her feel sad that she doesn't have as many nice things as you do."

Hannah was quiet for some time, watching the passing scenery in the darkening evening. "Mama, may I give her something when she comes to visit?"

Liesbeth frowned. "What are you thinking of?"

Hannah looked up at her mother. "Maybe Mama Bear."

Liesbeth raised her eyebrows. "You would give away Mama Bear? I thought you love her with her soft fur. She's so cuddly."

Hannah nodded. "I do love her. And she is cuddly. That's why Dodie needs her. She has no one to cuddle her."

Liesbeth looked over Hannah's head and out the window, the lump in her throat making it impossible to respond for a moment. "That would be a very kind thing for you to do, and if you really want to, of course you may. You can think about it until they come to visit and if you change your mind, I wouldn't blame you."

Hannah nodded and leaned against her mother, falling asleep before long.

V

June 1926 – Life moves on

*D*ear Alida,
   The big wedding is almost upon us. This time next week, Margaret and Donald will be married. Once in a while, I see Margaret looking thoughtful and I know she's thinking about the wedding that she dreamt of all those years ago. Donald and Pieter are very different people, but I believe Margaret will be happy. I have given them your gift and I know that Margaret just loves the piece of Belgian lace. She plans to have it on her dining table whenever the table isn't in use. Unlike in Holland, no one here has a sturdy tafelkleed to cover the table. Here they would consider that a rug and it would go on the floor!

   I could tell that you were surprised about my friendship with this man Riley McKenna. I feel rather sorry for him and I feel even sorrier for the two children. His daughter, Dodie, is a mouse of a child. Hannah positively overpowers her when they are together even though Dodie is eleven and, of course, Hannah is only six now. The boy, Gerard, is more robust, but still timid a lot of the time. I don't really know why. I don't think he's a good student but he seems to be a good worker on the farm. I don't suppose he'll continue with school when he reaches sixteen and even now I believe he misses more school than he should, but Riley keeps him home if there are big jobs to do, like during the spring planting. So I feel sorry and have gone there a few times now to give the house a good spring cleaning, and at Christmas to do some baking. I think Dodie is very pleased when I'm there, although she doesn't say so. I told you about Hannah giving Dodie her teddy bear, didn't I? Dodie cried when she received it.

We are moving into our new abode day after tomorrow. That's why I'm getting this letter out to you today. For one thing I can now give you the new address, but I think also I will be rather busy over the next few weeks. The good news is that the house is closer to work. It's on the other side of the railroad tracks, which means it's further away from downtown, but I'm happy that it's closer to the hospital. Of course, Hannah and I both have bicycles now, so it's easier to get around at the moment, but once the snow comes, I will be especially happy that I live closer. The house is rather run-down, but belongs to a friend of Donald. The owner has built a new home in Antigonish Landing for his growing family and this one has been for sale for some time. I am able to rent it for quite a good price in exchange for looking after it. We are starting with a one-year lease. It needs more than paint, I'm afraid, but Donald, Riley, and Margaret have all said they would help to make it livable. It has no running water, so that will take some getting used to, I'm afraid.

I am amazed to hear that you have gotten a job in Amsterdam. I thought you enjoyed your work in Zandvoort. I suppose it's a lonely place for a young woman and it has so many memories of Mam and Papa that, indeed, it may be time for a change. How good Max was to help you to get the position. Tell me, do you ever see Max with that floozy of his?

Hannah is standing by my side with a folded-up letter for you. She will put it in the envelope herself and she insists that I not read it so I make no guarantees as to its content or legibility.

Love from your sister and niece,
Liesbeth

Liesbeth held open the envelope for Hannah to put in her letter. "Why am I not allowed to read it? Is there a secret in it?"

Hannah frowned. "No. Not a secret, but . . ." She struggled to find a word.

"But it's private?"

Hannah smiled. "Yes. It's private."

Liesbeth sealed the envelope. "Very well. That's allowed."

When Hannah was in bed and Liesbeth alone with a mug of cocoa, she looked around the living room. It was stacked with boxes, some that would go to Donald's house and a few that would go to Liesbeth's house on Adam Street. She didn't have many belongings, but Margaret was giving her some of the furniture, as Donald already had a complete household.

It will be strange without Margaret. This is the first time that Hannah and I will be living alone. How do I feel about that?

As soon as she asked herself that question, she chuckled. *Imagine me even wondering about my feelings.*

She thought about the house they were moving to. It was more of a shack, and the idea of having to use the outhouse was decidedly unpleasant. She could afford it, though, so she would have to make it work. Her thoughts moved back to her question. *How do I feel?* She closed her eyes. *I feel down. That's the truth of it, Liesbeth Bos. I have what I wanted but I don't feel happy. It seems like I am going down in my standard of living, and what's worse, I'm dragging my daughter down with me.*

The new expansion was now open at the hospital and she was on shift work. Without Margaret in the house, Hannah would need more hours of care outside the home unless she could find someone who would come to the house on Adam Street.

I'm tired. I know it will all work out.

Margaret and Donald were visiting Donald's sister for supper, so Liesbeth drained her cup, rinsed it, and went to bed.

———

The next few days were chaotic. Before moving Liesbeth's belongings into the house, they had a work party go in to clean, paint, and replace some floor and wallboards.

Liesbeth thanked Riley as he packed up his tools. "I really appreciate you helping me like this."

He nodded. "You've helped me. That's how it works. Now I can help you."

Liesbeth smiled. "Yes. The place already feels so much better with the yellow paint on the kitchen walls and the good scrubbing that Margaret and I gave the rooms today."

Riley tugged his cap in place. "I'll come back on Sunday afternoon to finish sealing around that back window."

Liesbeth shook her head. "I think Donald said he would do that. He's so much closer by than you are. I can't ask you to keep coming all the way into town like this. You have enough to do on the farm."

Riley furrowed his forehead. "I told him I'd do it. Unless you don't want me here."

"No, of course that's not it. I just don't want to take you away from your own work."

"I can manage."

Liesbeth shrugged. "Then thank you. I appreciate it."

With the fresh paint and the furniture in place, the house didn't look quite as bad. It was a small square box with two tiny bedrooms, but it was their own.

Liesbeth helped Hannah unpack her clothes into the white-painted dresser. "What do you think, Hannah? Just you and me here now."

"I miss Tante Margaret."

"I know. It will be strange without her, but we'll see her very often. She's promised us that. She'll come here, and we'll go to her house. Sometimes when I'm working and she isn't, perhaps you can even go there for an overnight visit."

Hannah nodded but didn't say anything.

"We have two whole days before I have to go back to work and we're going to spend it making everything look nice here. I'm going to make curtains for the front window with that pretty flowered fabric that we got from Tante Gertrude."

Hannah continued to pull her things out of the box, silently laying them on the bed for Liesbeth to fold into the dresser.

Liesbeth stifled a sigh. "And Hannah, we have the wedding to look forward to. Won't that be fun? Tante Margaret told me that they have hired a fiddle player for dancing after supper. What do you think of that?"

Hannah brightened up then, looking up from her box. "Will Dodie be there too?"

"Yes, I think so. Now here's an idea, perhaps we'll ask Dodie to stay overnight here on that night. She can share your bed."

Hannah smiled and Liesbeth was surprised again at the friendship that had grown between her young daughter and the older girl.

"You'd like that, wouldn't you?"

Hannah nodded. "After we dance."

Liesbeth laughed. "Yes, after you dance. I'll send a note to Mr. McKenna and ask him if that's acceptable. If he agrees, then he can bring her bag here first and we'll all go over together."

A frown flickered across Hannah's face, but then she smiled. "I can wear my new ribbon, right, Mama?"

"Yes, indeed. That's why we got it, especially for the wedding."

———

Liesbeth held Hannah's hand as she sat and watched Margaret walk down the aisle. The child swivelled her head to watch Margaret and then back up to gaze at the circular paintings on the ceiling of Saint Ninian's Cathedral.

Liesbeth leaned in close to her daughter. "Isn't Tante Margaret pretty?"

Hannah nodded, eyes wide.

Liesbeth wanted to capture the scene exactly so she could write to Alida about it later, the way the sun slanted through the tall windows to make the dust motes dance, and the sight of all the friends and family dressed up in their finery. She listened as the Reverand Blase Campbell performed the ceremony, finally pronouncing Margaret Mary MacIsaac and Donald James Sutherland as man and wife.

Liesbeth and Hannah followed the procession out into the late June afternoon. They joined Riley and Dodie to watch as people crowded around to kiss the bride and shake the groom's hand.

Riley folded his arms across his chest. "I'll wait until the reception."

Hannah tugged on Liesbeth's hand. "Please, can Dodie and I go to kiss Tante Margaret?"

Liesbeth nodded. "Go on, but be patient. Don't push in front of others."

Liesbeth waited until the crowd began to thin. She watched the two girls reach Margaret's side. "I'll go and have a word with Margaret and then bring the girls back here."

Liesbeth made her way forward to take her turn to greet the couple. She reached out her hands to grasp Margaret's. "You look so beautiful. I wish you every happiness, Margaret."

Margaret squeezed her hands. "Thank you. I'm so glad you're here with me."

Liesbeth turned to Donald. "Congratulations, Donald. You look after her, now."

Donald leaned forward and kissed Liesbeth. "I think we'll look after each other."

Liesbeth nodded and moved away, grasping the shoulders of the two girls. "Come now, let's make room for others."

They rejoined Riley and stood chatting and watching until the wedding party climbed into the sparkling Master Blue Buick belonging to Margaret's uncle.

Riley grunted. "Nice car. Great for some."

Liesbeth shaded her eyes to watch them turn the corner on to Main Street. "Yes, it's a lovely car for a lovely couple."

"I have my car here. Do you want a lift to the house?"

Liesbeth touched his arm. "You go ahead. I would enjoy a walk. They'll be busy taking photos for awhile anyway."

Riley nodded. "Dodie, are you coming with me?"

Liesbeth saw Hannah take Dodie's hand. "I don't mind if she comes with me."

Dodie looked at him. "May I walk with Hannah and Mrs. Bos, Daddy?"

Riley shrugged. "Suit yourself."

———

The reception was held in Donald's house. Supper was followed by bagpipes, fiddles and phonograph music. Liesbeth watched the dancing but was content to chat with people, when the noise allowed for it. Gertrude and Adriaan were there and danced together beautifully. *Max and I hardly ever danced.*

Liesbeth was happy for Margaret. She had been solitary for too long. Liesbeth felt that Pieter would not have wanted Margaret to be alone in life. She was meant to be cheerful.

At last Liesbeth was ready to leave. Hannah had danced to exhaustion, and they had enjoyed cake and ice cream. They said their goodbyes, then climbed into Riley's car.

Liesbeth settled into the front seat. "I'm very grateful for the drive, Riley."

"You're not in the mood for a walk now, eh?"

She laughed. "No, indeed."

Riley parked and Hannah and Dodie scampered into the house, still in high spirits after the day. Liesbeth turned to shake hands with Riley and bid him good night, but was surprised to see him turn off the vehicle and walk to the door.

Liesbeth had no choice but to follow him through her own front door. She hesitated to offer him anything. "It's quite late, Riley. You'll want to get on the road, I'm sure."

He shook his head. "I'd love a cup of tea, if there's one going."

Liesbeth went into the kitchen to put the kettle on. "Of course."

As she took the cups and saucers out of the cupboard, she felt his presence in the doorway. The hair on the back of her neck rose.

She continued to hold a cup in her hand as she turned to him. "You go and relax in the living room. I'll bring it through when the kettle is boiled."

Instead of following her suggestion, he sat down at the kitchen table. "This is fine for me."

The kitchen was small and she felt crowded, but she was power-less to move him. She set the cups down and stood at the stove waiting, feeling his eyes studying her all the while.

When the water boiled and she had filled the teapot, she set it down and joined him at the table. "You don't mind Dodie staying here tonight?"

He shook his head. "No, I don't care. If Donald doesn't mind bringing her home tomorrow, it's fine with me."

Liesbeth nodded. "Donald and Margaret are going to see her mother to pick up some of the wedding gifts left there anyway, so they'll be going right past your place. I know they don't mind drop-ping Dodie off."

Liesbeth saw Riley's hand move as if to reach out to her. She lifted her cup of tea and held the saucer in one hand and the cup in the other as she took small sips. She took as long as she could to drink her cup and still he sat on.

At last she stood. "I really need to get those girls to bed, Riley. It's been a lovely but long and tiring day. Thank you so much for picking us up and delivering us back home again."

He looked up at her from his seat. "I don't mind waiting until you've got the girls in bed, although I'm sure they're big enough to get themselves to bed."

She shook her head. "I'm afraid I'm quite worn out with all the excitement as well. Once I know those two are settled, I'm going to bed myself."

He stood then and moved slowly to the front door, lifting his Sunday hat from the coat hook by the door. "I'll say good night, then."

He turned toward her and Liesbeth put out her hand to shake his again. "Good night, Riley."

———

Days later, the memory of that evening still made Liesbeth uneasy. Although she hadn't gone into great detail about her life in the Netherlands, she had been clear that she was still a married woman. She thought that was enough to ensure he didn't develop any expectations of her other than friendship. *I'm probably overreacting.*

She glanced at her watch. She called out the back door. "Hannah! Hannah, time to go."

Liesbeth smiled at the answering cry from beyond the thicket of alder bushes. "Coming, Mama."

Imagine me shouting out the door like an old fishwife. Mama would be appalled.

They had a routine now that would last as long as the weather permitted. Liesbeth had a small seat to carry Hannah behind her on her bicycle. She would pedal to the next street over where Mrs. Grant looked after Hannah while Liesbeth worked. It was not so bad on the afternoon shift like today, especially since school was now finished for the summer. It was more miserable on the night shift when Liesbeth took a sleepy-eyed Hannah from her bed to Mrs.Grant's. There was a small lounge settee where Hannah would lie down and fall asleep again, to be picked up early in the morning. Liesbeth hoped she could find a reliable woman to come in and mind Hannah at home by the time the fall came. Her plan was to have Hannah move in to Liesbeth's room and rent out Hannah's room for very little money in exchange for the child-minding duties.

After she dropped Hannah off, she cycled back along the road to St. Martha's. She hadn't told Hannah about her plans. She knew that the child was used to having her own room and wouldn't really like to share her mother's bed. She certainly couldn't explain that even a small rental income would really help the household budget. Although she was paid now as a full nurse, it was a blow to have all the expenses for maintaining a house fall solely on her shoulders. She had never had much left over at the end of the month, but there had usually been something to put toward new shoes for Hannah or other unexpected expenses. Now she lived from one paycheque to the next. *How did we manage everything on Max's pay? He must have been paid more than I realized.*

Liesbeth parked her bicycle, straightened her uniform and cap, and went to work.

VI

July 1928 – Unsettling Thoughts

*D*ear Alida,
In winter, I spend days imagining how wonderful it will be to welcome back the summer, and certainly for the first few weeks of spring and summer there is indeed a great celebration. Now though, the summer is hot and humid, the insects thrive, and the humidity makes one's uniform stick. You can imagine what my hair looks like, glued against my scalp.

As you know from my previous complaints, my house is drafty and the wind positively howls through on winter nights. We had to lay towels down by both doors to keep the snow from creating a drift in the hallway and kitchen and now we have no relief from the mosquitoes that find their way in through all those same cracks and crevices.

On the positive side of things, Peggy is working out wonderfully. As one of Mrs. Grant's nieces, she had already met Hannah and, luckily, Hannah adores her. That made the sacrifice of her room much easier to bear, and Hannah and I try not to kick each other or snore too much. It takes some getting used to, to share a bed again. We've worked out an arrangement that Peggy gets her room and board in exchange for the child-minding and cleaning. When I don't need her, Peggy often goes to spend time with her aunt, so that gives me some time on my own with Hannah.

I was surprised to hear that you had received a letter from Hannah which hadn't come through me. I appreciate that you let me know that she is writing to you through Margaret's letters but don't know what to make of it. Of course I won't ask what she's writing to you about, but should I be concerned? Is there something that I'm doing that I need to reconsider? I agree with you that her printing is quite exceptional, isn't it? When I see the penmanship of other children, even older, I'm surprised at how poor it tends to be. Of course, I work with Hannah, just as Mama did with us. One doesn't leave these things to chance.

I know you always want to hear a word of our friends, the McKennas. Quite frankly, I have attempted to reduce my visits with Riley as I do feel that he is building expectations which I won't be able to fulfill. You have expressed surprise that I seem to spend so much more time considering the feelings of others than I ever have. I hope that I wasn't such a brute as to ride roughshod over everyone, but I think perhaps you are right that I do spend more time thinking about it. The exercise seems to help me understand myself better. I know that I would enjoy spending time with Riley, not just for my own pleasure (I enjoy his serious consideration of matters), but I think that Hannah would benefit from a father figure. I have concluded, though, that rather than disappoint either Hannah or Riley, I will spend less time with the family. The sad thing about that decision is that I do miss Dodie. Gerard is now a big boy and out working on the farm, so I don't see a lot of him when I do go there, although I believe he could use some softer influences. I will, of course, continue to be friends, and when Margaret and Donald arrange a visit either to the Dekkers or Riley, Hannah and I are usually very happy to go along.

And while we are on the topic of men, I was completely surprised to hear that you and Max had taken his mother out to supper to celebrate her sixtieth birthday. I know you told me a while ago that there is no sign of the wonderful Rosa Brouwer but still I supposed that she was in the background somewhere. If Max asks *you to accompany him for his mother's birthday, then perhaps that woman is truly gone from his life. I know that you have hinted to me that she was never really in his life, but I can't believe that.*

As I have no letter to include from Hannah (she and Peggy are busy baking strawberry tarts), I will close now.

Love from your sister,

Liesbeth

Liesbeth went into the kitchen to see how the baking was coming along. "Peggy, give me a job so I can help."

Peggy smiled and pointed to a bowl of strawberries to be hulled. The sixteen-year-old girl seemed older than her years in many ways.

"Where did you learn to bake so wonderfully?"

Peggy continued to roll out the pastry while watching and correcting as Hannah worked her own smaller piece. "As you know, I'm the middle of five children, Mrs. Bos."

Liesbeth nodded. They didn't often have time to chat, but this much she knew.

"The other four are boys, so naturally I had to learn all the domestic skills while the boys learned how to fish, trap, and that sort of thing. Of course, when they each reach sixteen they go into the mines."

Liesbeth stopped hulling and looked at Peggy. "Oh, my. That's a hard job. And all of them are interested in that?"

Peggy tilted her head. "Interested or not, that's what has to happen."

Liesbeth smiled. "But surely if one of them is particularly bright and wants to continue with school, it could be arranged?"

Peggy gave a short, sharp laugh. "They know they are for the mines from the time they can crawl, Mrs. Bos. Some might work above-ground with steel, but in our family, it's the mines."

"But the mines seem to offer such an uncertain future these days."

Peggy nodded. "It's been hard on the family and hard on the whole town these last years with the strikes."

Liesbeth bit her lip. "That was all going on when I was so new to the country, I didn't really pay a lot of attention. It's all sorted now, isn't it?"

Peggy used a sharp knife to trim the layer of pastry to the right size. "The strikes are over, but I don't think things will ever be the same again."

Liesbeth frowned. "Why not?"

Peggy sighed and stopped what she was doing. "The miners had to take pay cuts and worked short hours for so long that it's taken the heart out of everyone. I don't know how to explain it, but Sydney Mines, where I'm from, went through so much, it's like everyone is just exhausted. Our family didn't have enough money coming in to look after everyone, but the boys really helped out. They went fishing and did things like that. Some families had it worse. It's why I'm here now, though, instead of at home helping Mama."

Liesbeth furrowed her head. "I don't understand."

"I'm one less mouth to feed, and I help my aunt with her work at the boarding house. Making beds, doing some mending; I bring in a bit of money there that I can send home."

Liesbeth felt her face get hot. This child was carrying such a load on her thin shoulders. "You're a good daughter."

Peggy laughed. "I don't mind. In fact, I love being here. The town is bigger and of course, I love Hannah." She bent over and planted a kiss on Hannah's head.

Liesbeth finished hulling the strawberries and washed her hands. She stepped outside and left the two girls to finish their baking. She went and sat on an old swing that had been fastened to the big maple tree in the front yard. *What sort of a future do Peggy or her brothers see for themselves?*

She tried to imagine it as though she were Peggy. It appeared bleak to her. The most she could hope for would be to make a good marriage, probably to a miner or fisherman. There would be an inevitable large family unless nature intervened, which in these Catholic families would bring a different kind of heartache. And yet Peggy always seemed so cheerful. Liesbeth closed her eyes and immersed herself in an imaginary visit to the small house in Sydney Mines. Probably one or more of them would play the fiddle. There would be loud conversation at the table, and in those lean years, supper would consist of bread and not much more.

Liesbeth opened her eyes and looked out toward the distant hills of Cape George. There was a strength and an extraordinary way of finding joy in every situation in these people. She herself didn't have that ability. She was strong and could make the best of something, but to be happy and find true joy when the windows were letting in a draft or she had to slog through two feet of snow, no. She didn't have the ability to laugh at those trials. She was surprised to realize this about herself. She would have pitted her own internal resources against anyone. She had come to this country to find a new beginning, so clearly she was resourceful. Now she understood that there was an attitude part to it all that she hadn't considered before. With a shock, she wondered what Hannah thought of her. *Does she think me sour? Do I always frown?*

Liesbeth had to walk. She strode down to Bay Street and turned right, walking past the hospital and out into the rural landscape. *What must I do? I can't turn into someone like Margaret. Wonderful Margaret who survived the death of her fiancé and still managed to laugh and see the world with hope.*

Liesbeth moved to the verge when she heard a horse and carriage coming up behind her. She didn't recognize the farmer and his wife as they trotted past her, but the couple both waved as they went by. Liesbeth raised her hand to return the greeting. *There it is. That automatic greeting, which I probably wouldn't do unless I knew the people.*

Liesbeth took a deep breath. *From now on, I will greet people, whether I know them or not.* She walked for a further ten minutes, then decided she should turn back. She had left without saying anything and Peggy and Hannah might be worried.

She continued to think as she walked back about little things she could do. *I need to pay more attention to how I'm behaving.*

She knew she couldn't turn herself into a different person, but if she could just be more aware about herself, she would already be more positive.

She stopped suddenly as a thought struck her. *I want to inspire Hannah. I don't want her to think about me as I did about Mama.*

Liesbeth felt like running back to the house. She didn't, but she walked briskly with her head held high, a smile on her face.

———

They were motoring to visit both the Dekkers and the McKennas. Donald and Margaret were singing *Farewell to Nova Scotia*. Hannah had learned the words to the chorus and joined in with gusto. "*When I am far away on the briny ocean tossed . . .*"

Liesbeth joined in as well. "*Will you ever heave a sigh or a wish for me?*"

Margaret dissolved into laughter as Hannah put her hands over her ears. "Mama, you can't sing."

Liesbeth felt hurt, but joined in the laughter at the pinched look on her daughter's face.

Margaret shook her head. "She's right, Lies. You can't carry a tune in a bucket."

Donald cut in. "Everyone can and should sing. I don't care how tuneful it is. You sing, Liesbeth, and never mind these two prima donnas."

Liesbeth patted her daughter's knee. "All right, I won't sing any-more at the moment. I'll practice a bit by myself before I join in again. How's that?"

Hannah nodded. "A lot of practice, Mama."

Donald started up again and they began the song from the begin-ning while Liesbeth was content to listen and sing along in her mind.

When they had finished singing a few more songs, including *Ain't She Sweet*, they were quiet for a few minutes before Hannah piped up. "Mama can't sing, but she can whistle, can't you, Mama?"

Margaret looked back at them. "I had forgotten that. Yes, Hannah, your Mama is a great whistler."

Liesbeth looked at Hannah. "I haven't whistled for ages. I didn't even know that you knew I could do that."

Hannah nodded. "I remember."

Donald caught Liesbeth's eyes in the rear-view mirror. "Come on, give us a tune."

Liesbeth felt her arm pits prickling. "Oh, I can't just start up. I don't even know if I can anymore."

Margaret nodded. "It's something you used to do when you weren't thinking about it." She turned to her husband. "I remember hearing it like something magical slipping around the sounds of pain on the wards."

Liesbeth smiled. "Yes, I know I used to whistle a lot as I was pulling off bandages or whatever because it distracted the patients. They would try to identify what I was whistling." Liesbeth wet her lips, and began.

Margaret clapped her hands and began to sing along with Liesbeth. "*It's a long, long way to Tipperary, it's a long way from home.*"

Margaret stopped singing and let the whistling fill the car. Liesbeth did the whole song, and when she finished, Hannah and Margaret both clapped while Donald nodded. "Well done. Well done indeed."

Liesbeth laughed. "My lips are cramped."

Hannah nodded and leaned forward to tap Margaret's shoulder. "See how good she is? I knew it."

Margaret nodded. "She certainly is, and we must hear more of that."

Liesbeth felt a lump in her throat at the smile on Hannah's face.

They arrived at the Dekkers' farm. Hannah jumped out of the car and ran off to visit Lissy, her cow.

Liesbeth and Margaret stood in the kitchen as Gertrude made a pitcher of lemonade. Adriaan watched Hannah through the window running toward the barn. "She's going to wonder why Lissy is so fat."

Donald looked over Adriaan's shoulder. "Ah, she's with calf?"

Adriaan nodded and turned to Liesbeth. "I'm not sure what to do here. My kids had their pet cows as well, but they are farm children. They understand that the pet is only a pet for so long."

Liesbeth blinked, trying to understand what Adriaan was getting to. "Yes?"

Adriaan sighed. "Lissy is starting to get older now. Another year and she'll be sent to market. So do I let Hannah have the new calf as a pet, or will the whole thing be too difficult every time for her to become friends with the animal only to have it 'end badly', shall we say. What do you advise?"

Liesbeth's eyes widened. "Lissy will be slaughtered for meat in another year? That's what you're saying?"

"Yes. Cows can live for much longer, but a dairy cow usually only goes for four or five years before they're sent to market."

Liesbeth's stomach turned. Although she was a nurse and quite strong when it came to human suffering, the idea that her daughter's pet would be slaughtered was difficult to think about.

She turned back to Adriaan. "No, don't let her get attached to another one. Lissy's calf will just grow nameless as part of the herd. We don't need to tell her about Lissy yet, though, do we?"

Adriaan shook his head. "No, of course not. We'll leave it until we have to say something."

Gertrude nodded to the barn. "Adriaan, go and get the children. I have the lemonade ready and we have some oatcakes to go with it."

Adriaan and Donald headed out for the barn while the three women carried the jug, glasses, and plate of oatcakes out to the wide veranda. They seated themselves and took in the warm summer day.

Liesbeth looked at the other two women. "Whatever shall I do about Hannah and Lissy?"

Margaret shook her head. "I wouldn't worry about it until you need to."

Gertrude was quiet, then looked at Liesbeth over her glass. "What about giving her a kitten? We constantly have too many barn cats to count and would be glad to find a home for one of the kittens. That way, all her attention would be on her own pet at home, and the hardship of saying good-bye to the cow would be lessened."

Liesbeth frowned. "A pet in the house. I've never had pets. Do they cost a lot to feed? Will it get fleas?"

Gertrude smiled. "They can be very clean and they aren't terribly expensive. A bit of milk or water and some scraps of fish."

Liesbeth glanced at Margaret. "What do you think?"

Margaret nodded. "I think it's a great idea. Just the answer."

Hannah and the men were coming across the yard to the veranda. "Don't say anything yet. Give me time to think about it."

Gertrude nodded and they turned their talk to other things.

After a visit and purchasing another piece of cheese, since Liesbeth couldn't manage without it, the four of them piled in the car and drove the short hop to Riley McKenna's home. They were all in good spirits, so it was with some dismay that Liesbeth saw the frown on Riley's face as they knocked on the kitchen door.

Liesbeth looked past Riley into the house. "Is something wrong?"

Riley ushered them into the kitchen. "No. Why?"

Liesbeth studied him. "You just look, I'm not sure, worried?"

"You mean I'm not laughing and joking around like I'm sure they do down at the Dekkers? Those fellas are always clowning around."

Margaret's smile was tight. "I'm not sure they would agree with that description, Riley."

He snorted. "No, probably not, but I know them."

Donald rubbed his hands together. "Something smells nice here. Has Dodie been baking or have you taken up baking yourself, Riley?"

Riley went to the bottom of the steps and shouted up. "Dodie, come down."

Liesbeth caught the glance between Donald and Margaret. Riley was clearly miffed about something.

Dodie shuffled into the kitchen, her hair drooping down her back in a limp plait.

Riley nodded toward the oven. "That bread done? Company wants something to eat."

Hannah had bounced over to her friend when Dodie came into the room, but stood quietly beside her as the older girl lifted a tray of fresh rolls out of the oven. Hannah closed the oven door for Dodie and looked at her. "Are you all right Dodie? You seem sick."

Dodie cast a glance at her father. "I'm fine."

Hannah crossed her arms as she watched her friend break apart the rolls and set some on a plate. "Can we go to your room?"

Dodie looked again at her father. "Can we, Papa?"

Riley frowned. "You haven't made the tea yet."

Liesbeth stood. "Let me make it. The girls probably have lots to catch up on."

Riley nodded and the two girls disappeared up the stairs.

Liesbeth filled the kettle, and Margaret put the rolls and butter on the table. As Liesbeth brought out cups and saucers, she saw Margaret standing back, watching Riley.

Liesbeth knew Margaret thought that Riley was sour, but Liesbeth thought he just came across as gruff. He had a hard life and it made him serious.

They chatted over their tea and rolls. Donald always seemed to be current with matters of farming and local gossip and made up for Riley's taciturn mood.

Liesbeth looked out the window but saw no sign of the boy. "Where's Gerard? Is he out working in the barn?"

Riley shrugged. "Teenage boys go their own way. He doesn't have any chores until the evening milking, so he's off somewhere. The two of them were away down to the pond for awhile but she came back on her own."

Liesbeth frowned. "You mean Dodie?"

Riley looked at her with a puzzled look on his face. "Yes, of course Dodie."

Liesbeth felt herself flush. "Dodie's done a lovely job on these rolls. You must be glad the two of them are old enough to really contribute now."

Riley nodded. "It helps."

Liesbeth stifled a sigh. It was hard work keeping up the conversation with Riley today. She wondered why Dodie and Riley both seemed in bad spirits.

After an hour, Margaret stood and cleared off the table. "We really need to get going."

Liesbeth rose as well and went to the bottom of the steps. "Hannah, we're going now."

Hannah came down while Dodie stood at the top of the steps and watched them with large, liquid eyes.

Liesbeth held out her arms. "Come and give me a hug, Dodie. I've missed having you over, but since Peggy has taken over Hannah's room, we don't have the space for sleepovers anymore."

Dodie came down and fell into Liesbeth's arms. "I miss you, too." The child's voice was little more than a whisper.

Margaret watched from the doorway. "Perhaps you and Hannah can both come for an overnight visit to our house. I miss the sound of children and we have a spare room."

Riley cut off any reply from Dodie. "Dodie's too big for that kind of thing now. Her place is here."

Liesbeth felt the girl's hand tremble in her own. She turned to smile at Dodie before releasing her hand. "I'll see if I can get him to change his mind."

Dodie shook her head. "You won't." The child turned and scurried up the steps again.

When the four of them were back in the car and on the way home, Liesbeth looked at Hannah, who was staring out the window. "Dodie seemed quieter than usual Hannah. Is she all right?"

Hannah looked at her mother, as if considering her reply. "Gerard hit her."

Margaret turned at Hannah's words.

Liesbeth looked at Hannah. "On purpose or was it an accident?"

Hannah eyes filled with tears. "On purpose. They were out at the pond and Gerard told Dodie to go in and get a wooden boat he had floated."

Liesbeth prompted her. "And she didn't want to go in the pond?"

"No. So when she wouldn't go in, he hit her across the back of her head. Hard. She fell down."

Margaret shook her head.

Liesbeth took Hannah's hand. "That's very mean. Did she tell her father? Is that why Gerard wasn't around, because he was being punished?"

Hannah shook her head. "She told him, but then he hit her too."

Liesbeth gasped. "Hannah, that can't be right."

Hannah jutted out her chin. "It is. He said that next time Dodie will do what she's told the first time."

Liesbeth shook her head. "Hannah, it may be that Dodie is exaggerating." Liesbeth didn't want to suggest that her friend was lying.

Hannah pulled her hand away from Liesbeth and turned back to look out the window again. "She's not."

The rest of the trip home was done in silence.

VII

January 1929 – Correspondence

*D*ear Alida,

Thank you so much for the money you sent over for Christmas, along with the dress for Hannah. She felt like a princess wearing it to a New Year's Eve party at Donald and Margaret's house. The organdy fabric and all those ruffles and bows were indeed the hit of the evening. I felt a little bit sorry for Dodie, who was wearing her Sunday best, which is now too small for her. I have suggested to Riley that I sew something for the girl if he will only buy some fabric, but so far he has not taken me up on the offer. I may have to do it without him, because the dresses she wears will soon be indecent on her, poor thing. I don't know what's happened to the aunt in Halifax, but she seems to have completely given up on helping the little family.

I must tell you that Max also sent money for gifts for Hannah, so she also had new boots (not to be worn with the new dress, by any means!) so between the practical and the wonderful, Hannah was delighted with her Christmas.

We baked and made ornaments from popcorn, berries, and paper. It was altogether a very festive time. I gave Peggy a little bit of money to take home with her and was given a big hug and a few tears in exchange, which I felt was a very good trade.

I can admit to you that I was very glad for a few days off. I feel tired. Am I getting too old for all the work? What happened to the excitement and satisfaction I felt with the nursing in Paris?

I have the drawing that Max made of Place du Tertre that long-ago day in Paris. Do you remember it? It's one of the few non-essential things that I brought with me. I study it now and can almost hear the birds twittering and the piano. Do you recall that someone was practicing the piano, and the notes fell through the square like rain-drops? Such a long time ago. A lifetime ago.

You have clearly received more letters from Hannah. What does such a young child find to say to her aunt so far away? I'm pleased though, as I want the two of you to have a relationship. As you must know, she and Dodie now have a 'date' to go to Donald and Margaret's every couple of months. I wasn't able to convince Riley that it was a good thing for his daughter, but somehow Donald did, so that's nice—probably offering to do the pick-up and delivery of the girl helped. I think they all enjoy the evening, and I have to admit, having a night all on my own is not a bad thing for me either, although by morning I am missing Hannah and can't wait to get her home again.

About work—yes, it's tiring, but of course I still enjoy it. We are seeing so many cases of TB these days, though, that it's hard to keep up. We know that so many people just don't get the treatment they need because they can't afford it. Out in Western Canada, Saskatchewan is providing free care for TB patients, but not so here. It's frustrating, but we carry on.

And what about you? You're enjoying the work by the sound of it, and imagine Max joining you to help with the hospital picnic. What did you have to do to convince him of that? He's not a terribly jolly person usually! I'm glad, though. He can be a very kind and caring man. I always knew that, and even now, he was very generous in his gift to Hannah at Christmas. She used to ask about him and seemed to long for her Papa, but she doesn't mention him at all anymore. I suppose she's gotten used to not having him around.

Perhaps Donald helps to fill that space in her life. I had once thought that Riley might, but she seems to have set her mind against him, although of course we still visit occasionally.

As to the house, well, it's all I can afford so we stay on here. Luckily the owners seem satisfied with the arrangement. I am heartily sick of running outside, though. I think longingly of the indoor plumbing of Amsterdam!

Well my sister, keep well.

Love,

Liesbeth

Liesbeth called out to Hannah: "I'm about to seal the letter to your Tante Alida. Do you want to put anything in?"

Hannah came into the kitchen. "No thank you."

Liesbeth sealed the thin envelope. "Why do you always put your letters in with Tante Margaret's and not mine?"

Hannah scuffed the floor with her toe. "Tante Margaret doesn't always complain about the extra postage when it weighs more. I can sometimes put in a picture I draw or . . . other things."

Liesbeth pursed her lips. "Do I always complain? I didn't think I was doing that. I'm sorry if I made you feel like you couldn't add what you wanted to."

Hannah shrugged and turned to go back to her book.

Liesbeth shook her head. *Did I really do that?*

———

The days stretched into weeks, with the winter blowing drifts through the cracks in the wall and under the doors. Some days, as Liesbeth pushed through the wind and snow on her way to work she felt fatigued beyond understanding. She would talk to herself as she peered through the white swirling world. 'You've worked longer hours and in more challenging conditions that this. Come now, perk up.' The lectures rarely helped. She would get to work, or get home, sodden and depressed.

The good thing was that Hannah was able to stay at home with Peggy. She did walk to school on her own now but she didn't seem to mind it. She would join up with other girls on the way and usually had some tidbits of news to chatter about at supper or breakfast.

Since Hannah was able to see Dodie at Margaret's house, Liesbeth felt less inclined to arrange a visit with Riley. She wasn't sure what had really happened with Dodie during that summer visit, but Hannah's explanation had, nevertheless, left her uneasy. Her communication with Riley for the past few months had all taken place at Margaret's house, with one visit to her own home.

She had other things to think about anyway. While her wages had not been cut back, as so many other workers' had been, they hadn't risen either. It seemed that her money just wouldn't stretch to cover everything these days. The coal to heat the drafty house ate up a big part of her wages. She had puzzled herself dizzy trying to figure out a solution. She couldn't use less; they all walked around wearing heavy cardigans and socks already. The only way would be to trade in Peggy for a full-paying tenant, but that wasn't feasible. Hannah was too young to be left on her own, especially at night, and one couldn't expect tenants to arrange their lives around guaranteeing to be in the house overnight every time Liesbeth had to work.

Liesbeth glanced out a window. It was early March, but it was snowing again. She was so busy staring out the window even as she walked, that she almost bumped into a man coming the other way.

Liesbeth turned as the man coughed. "Oh, I'm so sorry. I didn't see you there."

The man, shorter than Liesbeth but with a smile that made him seem taller, looked out the window. "Never-ending, isn't it?"

Liesbeth nodded. "You're so right. Can I help you? You look lost."

He set down his toolbox and stuck out his hand. "Jerome Arsenault. I'm here to look at the boiler, but I think I took a wrong turn, Sister."

Liesbeth shook the proffered hand. "Liesbeth Bos." She pointed down the hall. "Turn left there and you'll see the steps to go down to the boiler room."

He nodded and lifted his tools. "Not far wrong, then." He tipped his cap and nodded his thanks before moving past her down the hallway.

Liesbeth glanced over her shoulder and flushed to see that he had also turned, catching each other's eye. She heard his chuckle as she hastened away.

The shift was busy. It was three o'clock before Liesbeth knew it. She felt cheerful as she stepped outside and saw that the snow had stopped. In fact, the sun was shining. She squinted in the blinding sparkle and let her eyes adjust after the gloom of the hospital corridors.

The door opened behind her and the plumber stood beside her. "Now that's a pretty sight."

Liesbeth turned her head to look at him, wondering in which direction he was looking, but he stood gazing at her.

Liesbeth felt herself get hot and pulled her scarf around her neck and mouth. "It's nice to see the sun. Good day, Mr. Arsenault."

"Good day, Sister. Perhaps I'll see you tomorrow."

"You weren't able to finish the job?"

"No, I need a part. I'll be back tomorrow."

As they stood there, a motor pulled up. Liesbeth recognized Riley. She lowered her scarf as Riley leaned across to open the door from the inside. He called out to her. "Jump in. I'll drive you home."

She climbed in. "I won't argue. Thank you. What brings you to town?"

Before putting the car into gear, he looked past her to where Mr. Arsenault stood. "Who's he?"

Liesbeth glanced back. "Mr. Arsenault. He's repairing the boiler."

"Seems friendly."

Liesbeth laughed. "I hardly know. We've only exchanged five words in total."

Riley nodded and got the car going.

Liesbeth asked again. "So how do you happen to be just here when I need a ride home?"

He looked at her. "I just happened by. I wasn't hanging around waiting for you."

Liesbeth caught her breath. "No, of course not. I didn't mean to imply anything."

Riley nodded. "I had to meet with the bank manager."

Liesbeth didn't pry further. "How's the road out to your place? Is it difficult to get through?"

Riley shook his head. "No, not really. Most of the time I use the sleigh, but today I wanted to pick up some supplies, so the motor was easier."

They were at Liesbeth's house. She smiled at the dour man. "Will you stop for a cup of tea?"

"If you don't mind."

"Not at all. It's great to see you again."

He parked and they went in. Peggy was still at her aunt's house. She would be home a few minutes before Hannah usually arrived home. Sometimes Peggy would walk partway to meet the child and they would walk together.

Liesbeth got the stove going again, using the bellows to get the coal flaring up before she added more. Riley took the bellows from her. "I'll do it for you."

"Thank you. It's an art I haven't quite gotten the feel for, even after all this time."

By the time Liesbeth came back into the sitting room with the tea, the house was already feeling warmer.

He took a cup from her and sat on the sofa. "It's a cozy little house."

Liesbeth grimaced. "Do you think so?"

Riley tilted his head. "You don't?"

Liesbeth shrugged. "I prefer the house on Elm Street. That was cozy."

He nodded. "My house could be. I never put the effort into it. I'm not really sure what to do with it. I think it needs a woman's touch."

Liesbeth smiled. "Dodie is quickly becoming a woman. You should let her make some suggestions."

He snorted. "Dodie doesn't have any useful suggestions."

Liesbeth took a breath. "I don't think you give her enough credit. She really is growing into a young lady, Riley." She paused. "My offer to help make her a new dress or two still stands. She really should have something more suitable."

Riley's face darkened. "I know how to look after my own."

"Of course you do. It's just that, as you said, some things are best with a woman's touch."

Riley shook his head. "There's no money for fancy clothes right now."

Liesbeth had suspected as much. "If I got some fabric, would it be all right if I made something for her?"

His eyebrows pulled together. "We don't take handouts."

"I understand. I'm just thinking of some material that Margaret showed me a while ago that she had to spare. If she still had it, I think it would make a fine new skirt for Dodie."

"Why wouldn't you use it for Hannah?"

"Hannah just got some new clothes for Christmas and she doesn't need anything more at the moment."

Riley sighed. "If you want to, then fine. I thought you weren't interested in us anymore."

Liesbeth swallowed. "I never meant to give that impression. The winter just makes visiting so difficult. We're friends, Riley. If I can do anything to help out, of course I will."

At that moment Hannah came bounding in through the door, followed by Peggy. Liesbeth stood up to give Hannah a hug. "You're all rosy."

Hannah glanced past her mother at Riley. She mumbled a greeting, then turned back to her mother. "Peggy and I are going skating, Mama. Will you come with us?"

Liesbeth had gotten an old pair of skates from a neighbor and had gone out a few times over the winter. She smiled at her daughter. "Why not?"

She held up her hands to Riley. "It looks like I'm going skating, Riley."

He stood and carried his cup back to the kitchen. "I have to get on anyway. Maybe we'll see you one of these days at the farm."

She nodded. "Yes, absolutely. As soon as the weather is consistently better, I'll either borrow Donald's car or we'll make a trip all together again."

After he left, Peggy handed Liesbeth the mail. "I forgot to give you this letter, Mrs. Bos."

Liesbeth looked at the envelope. "Another letter from your Tante Alida. What a good writer she is, Hannah. We'll save it until we come back from our skating."

When they returned, Peggy and Hannah worked on the beef stew for supper while Liesbeth opened the letter from her sister.

Dear Lies,

It seemed to me from your last letter that you were a little annoyed that Max and I are friends. Are you? You know that I met him the same time as you did, and I always felt rather sorry that it hasn't worked out for the two of you. I have to tell you, Liesbeth, that after spending considerable time talking to him, I just will not believe that there was ever anything between that Rosa woman and Max. There. I had to get that off my chest because I think you've been unfair to Max. It's six years now since you've gone away to make your fortune, as they say, in Canada. From what I read in the papers here, the promise has not turned out to be quite what many people thought it would be, but perhaps for you, it is. I just wanted to say that I will continue to be friends with Max, if you don't mind! I mean that honestly. If you really do mind, then I shall say good-bye to him. So you can let me know. A sister is always a sister and must come foremost.

Love,

Alida

Liesbeth rested the letter in her lap. Her stomach felt a bit queasy. Ali was right. She had been snippy whenever she mentioned her sister's friendship with Max. It was an automatic response that came from somewhere deep inside of her.

Do I mind? And if I do, what does that mean? What in the world do I say?

She lifted the letter again and reread it. *I'll show it to Margaret. What a jumble of ideas in this one short letter. So strange. What brought this on?*

Hannah came in to show her a potato. "It has a face, Mama. I hate to peel it."

Liesbeth folded the letter back into the envelope and took the potato. "You're right, it does have a face. A bit like a man with a moustache, isn't it?" She handed the potato back and smiled at Hannah. "You still have to peel it. The man wouldn't want us to go hungry."

Hannah went back to the kitchen. Liesbeth could hear her chatting to Peggy. Liesbeth listened to the child's voice with its Maritime singsong cadence. She leaned back against the sofa and closed her eyes. Alida was right in her claim that the promise hadn't delivered. She had heard of people who went home again after their first year or a couple of years. They hoped for so much but they were still struggling after years of hard work. *Like me. So what to do?*

VIII

June 1929 – Friendships Tested

The warm summer morning enticed Liesbeth and Hannah to cycle downtown. The school year was almost over, and Hannah was full of the energy of a young colt. The two of them cycled down Main Street and turned right on Acadia. There was a boot repair shop there, and Liesbeth wanted her boots re-soled. They were hopelessly out of fashion, but they were comfortable and, if they could last another year or two, it would help. They also needed to stop at Whidden's Flour shop on the way back, but they were in no rush. Liesbeth had promised they would stop for ice cream, so they left their bicycles outside the repair shop and sauntered along, stopping to look in shop windows.

They stopped in front of a store that sold dishes and Hannah pointed out the pattern she liked best. "When I get married, I'll get those."

Liesbeth smiled. "Let's hope that's a long time from now."

A shadow blocked the sunlight, and Liesbeth turned to see who was behind them. "Oh, hello, Mr. Arsenault. How are you today?"

He removed his cap and smoothed back his thick greying hair. "I'm hot. I already miss the winter."

Liesbeth gasped in mock horror. "Don't say that. The fine weather has been a long time coming."

Jerome Arsenault nodded to Hannah. "And who is this lovely lady?"

Before Liesbeth could respond, Hannah held out her hand to shake his. "I'm Hannah." She looked up at her mother. "This is my Mama."

Jerome raised his eyebrows. "Your Mama. Ah ha." He glanced up the street.

Hannah seemed to guess what he was wondering. "My Papa lives in Holland still."

Liesbeth put her arm around Hannah's shoulder. "Thank you, Hannah. I'm sure that's more than Mr. Arsenault wanted to know."

Hannah shook her head. "No, I don't think so."

Jerome let out a hearty laugh. "She's a cheeky thing."

Liesbeth stepped away from the window. "Let's move on, Hannah. Mr. Arsenault, you have a lovely day."

Instead of letting them walk away he fell into step on the other side of Hannah. "I've been busy all over town fixing the damage left by the winter. Broken pipes, that sort of thing."

Liesbeth nodded, not sure why he was walking with them.

Hannah took the burden of conversation away from Liesbeth as she asked about his work and what buildings he had seen from the inside. She had an avid curiosity about the homes of others.

"What about the big McPherson house on College?"

He shook his head. "No, not that one. I do businesses more than houses. That's how I met your mother first. I fixed the boiler at the hospital. Now that the good weather is here, I have to go back and do a big maintenance job on it."

"So it doesn't break down next winter?"

He patted Hannah on the shoulder. "Exactly."

At that moment, Liesbeth saw Riley driving his big chestnut mare toward them at a fair clip. Liesbeth waved, dropping her hand limply by her side when he went right past without acknowledging her.

Jerome slanted his eyes to her. "Looks like your friend didn't see you." Then he went on talking to Hannah about his work.

When they reached the booth beside the hardware store that sold ice cream, Liesbeth and Hannah stopped. Liesbeth waved toward the booth. "This is our destination."

Jerome folded his arms and studied the blackboard displaying the offerings. "I can't remember when I last had an ice cream. It sounds like just the ticket on a day like this." He stepped up to the booth. "I'm buying three cups." He turned to Hannah. "What flavour will you have?"

Hannah looked at her mother. Liesbeth protested. "Mr. Arsenault, please don't. We can afford to get our own."

Jerome Arsenault grinned. "Of course you can, but it would give me a treat to treat you two ladies."

Liesbeth sighed and nodded to Hannah.

They walked back and found a bench on the other side of the street in the shade. Liesbeth and Hannah sat down to enjoy their ice cream while Jerome walked on to talk to a man he knew.

Hannah watched him. "He seems nice, Mama."

Liesbeth licked her ice cream. "He treated us. Of course he's nice."

Hannah shook her head. "I wouldn't like him just because of that."

Liesbeth swallowed. "I'm glad. You're right. He does seem nice."

When he came back to them, his ice cream was gone, while Liesbeth and Hannah still lingered over theirs. He stood with his hands in his pockets. "I suppose I better get back to the errands I'm meant to be doing."

Hannah wiped her mouth on the back of her hand. "Thank you for the ice cream, Mr. Arsenault." She thought for a moment. "I have a girl in my class called Janey Arsenault. Are you her father?"

He shook his head. "She's my niece. I live with them. Shall I tell her hello for you, Hannah?"

Hannah shrugged. "Sure."

Liesbeth finished off her ice cream and stood up to shake Jerome's hand. "Thank you again. We enjoyed that immensely."

He nodded once more to both of them and strode away.

Liesbeth brushed down her skirt and pulled her handkerchief from her pocket. She spat on it and wiped Hannah's cheeks. Hannah tried to squirm away. "Mama, don't."

Liesbeth continued to rub until her daughter's cheeks were clean and ruddy. "We can't have you walking around town looking like a ruffian."

As they set off back toward the flour shop, Hannah took Liesbeth's hand. "Why do you think Mr. McKenna didn't say hello when you waved at him?"

"He didn't see me, I suppose."

"He did. I saw him look right at us."

"Then he must have been too busy and was afraid that if he slowed down, we'd keep him talking instead of going about his business."

"I don't think Mr. Arsenault would drive by someone without waving back."

"Perhaps not. We don't know. He's very friendly today, but we know nothing about him."

Hannah nodded. "I like Janey. She sat two seats ahead of me in class, Arsenault, Baxter, and then Bos. She has really long hair in two braids."

The rest of the day continued picture-perfect, the kind of day Liesbeth knew would fix in her memory. The green, blue, and white of the land, sky, and clouds. The ice cream. The conversations.

She went to bed, slipping in beside Hannah, and enjoyed the little-girl smell. It wouldn't be long before Hannah outgrew that particular childhood fragrance, but at the moment it was a warm and comforting end to a nice day.

———

The big old maple tree in Margaret's front yard creaked and whispered in the summer breeze, and Liesbeth and Margaret sat out on the veranda, enjoying the afternoon. Margaret handed Liesbeth a glass of iced tea. "Did you ever hear back after you told Alida that you had no problem with her and Max being friends?"

"I heard from her, but she hardly mentioned it. She just thanked me and said it was good to know I didn't mind. Margaret, what do you really think? You get letters from her as well. Does she say more to you than she does to me?"

Margaret shook her head. "She really doesn't. I know she sees him regularly—probably I hear more about that than you do—but she doesn't say anything about how she feels about it."

Liesbeth mused. "I know it should be nothing to do with me, but it just seems rather odd to me."

Margaret shrugged. "I don't really think that there's a great passion there. I think they are just friends, as Ali has said."

"So why ask me if I mind?"

"Perhaps you made too many snide remarks?"

Liesbeth sighed. "You're probably right. It was probably just her way to ask me to stop making those sorts of comments."

"I suspect that's probably it."

Liesbeth changed the subject by nodding to Margaret's swelling belly. "How are you feeling?"

"I'm fine now that I'm past the morning sickness." She folded her hands and rested them on the bulge.

"And Donald is getting excited?"

Margaret's smile was radiant. "He's hopping. He's finished the cradle already and I'm still three months away from being due."

Liesbeth recalled the time leading up to Hannah's birth. "Max was excited, but ever so quietly. You'd have to really know him to even realize it."

Margaret laughed. "Not Donald. There's nothing subtle about him. He's found a kindred soul in his sister. Helen's been going through all her old baby things and we've had a great time sorting out what can be used now, or what's for later."

"You're saying that Donald has been participating in that kind of thing?"

"Oh, yes. You should see the little outfits in his big hands."

Liesbeth smiled. "That's nice."

Margaret's curls bobbed. "Yes. It's very nice."

They sat without speaking for a few moments, then Margaret recalled something. "Speaking of children, I meant to tell you that Dodie was wearing the new skirt you made for her the last time she came to visit. That was very kind of you, Lies. It looked so much better than all those cotton dresses that she outgrew a year ago."

"I'm glad. I really need to go out for a visit. I have rather neglected the McKennas for the last little while. In fact, when Donald gets back, I'll ask him when I can borrow his car and we'll make a trip out. Unless you feel like coming along?"

Margaret drained her glass and then stood to go in and start on lunch. "No, you go ahead and have your visit. You have much more patience with Mr. McKenna than I do."

"He can be very dour."

"Dour? That's an understatement."

Liesbeth followed Margaret into the house. "He has a lot to deal with."

"I know, but he isn't the first." Margaret's voice softened. "I heard a rumour that he's having trouble making the mortgage payments. He may lose the place, Liesbeth."

"Oh, no. That would be so awful for all of them."

Margaret nodded. "I know. I agree. It's getting to be a common story, though. When we go up to Cape George now, you can see farms that have just been abandoned. Everything that could be sold, has been, and the family has just packed up the truck or cart and left."

"But to go where? To do what?"

"I don't know. A lot of them are going to Ontario and Alberta. I don't really think it's any better there, though. I just don't understand how the jobs just seem to be fizzling away."

Liesbeth held her glass out for a refill of tea. "Do you ever miss your job?"

Margaret topped up her own glass. "Not at all. I've been busy getting ready for the baby with sewing and knitting. And since I've joined the Women's Auxilliary, I get to keep my hand in."

"Keep up with the gossip, you mean."

"Absolutely. I have to get it from somewhere, and you're hopeless at passing along gossip."

Liesbeth was quiet as she considered Margaret's comments. "I wonder why it wasn't enough for me."

Margaret shifted in her chair to look Liesbeth fully in the face. "It's a good question, Liesbeth." She shrugged. "Perhaps I'm just a simpler person than you and more easily satisfied?"

Liesbeth leaned over to pat Margaret's hand. "You only pretend to be simple."

Margaret smiled. "Don't tell anyone."

Liesbeth leaned back again. "I think you're better at knowing what you want than I am."

Margaret frowned. "But your immigration here to Canada didn't have much to do with what you wanted, was it? I mean, you didn't want Max to mess around with another woman."

Liesbeth flushed. They had never really talked like this before. "Alida is convinced that Max didn't mess around with the woman."

Margaret's eyes widened. "But you were so sure."

"I was sure."

"Do you now doubt?"

Liesbeth sighed. "I don't know anymore. Of course it's all beside the point now."

"Is it?"

Liesbeth frowned. "Yes, of course. I've built a new life here. Without Max."

Margaret took a long sip of her drink. "It's hard on Hannah to be without her Papa."

Liesbeth nodded. "It was at first. I think she's quite used to it now."

"Perhaps." Margaret seemed to consider saying more, but at that moment Donald drove up, ending the tête-à-tête.

IX

July 1929 – Friendships Tested further

On a warm July Sunday, Liesbeth and Hannah cycled over to borrow Donald's car.

Liesbeth climbed into the driver's seat. "Are you sure you won't need the car today?"

Donald flapped his hand at her. "I'm quite sure."

Liesbeth nodded to where Margaret stood at the front door. "What if you need to take her to the hospital suddenly?"

Donald made a face. "She won't need to go, but if something did happen, Helen's husband is ready to come and take us to the hospital. Don't worry. Go and enjoy yourselves and say hello to Riley for us."

Hannah waved from the passenger seat. She grinned up at her mother. "Let's go, Mama."

"All right, let's go."

Hannah pivoted back and forth as they drove. "The front seat is way better. You can see so much. We should get a car, Mama."

Liesbeth laughed. "Wouldn't that be nice? I'm afraid it's not in the budget, sweetheart."

Hannah looked up at Liesbeth without speaking. Liesbeth glanced at her. "What is it? Is my hat twisted? I'm not used to this new cloche style."

Hannah giggled. "Your hat isn't twisted. I was just thinking that you aren't like other Mamas."

"What makes you say that?"

"They don't have jobs. And I don't think any other Mama drives a car."

"Hmm. So are these things in my favour or against?"

Hannah seemed to consider the question for longer than Liesbeth liked. "It makes you special."

Hannah turned back to look out the window and started to sing to herself.

Liesbeth smiled to herself. *Special is all right.*

Liesbeth took the drive slowly. She was enjoying herself. "Do you think that Dodie will like the blouse that Margaret sent along for her?"

Hannah nodded. "I think so. It's a pretty blue colour. She doesn't have anything like it."

They pulled into the yard and a few chickens scattered as the car came to rest. The green shutter on the left side of the front window had come loose and lay in the dirt. An untied tarp lay over some machinery and with every gust of wind expanded and deflated as though a living thing lay below, gasping its last breath.

It had been several months since Liesbeth had been here. She looked at Hannah before they climbed out. "It seems very quiet."

Hannah's hand slid into Liesbeth's as they walked to the front door. Liesbeth tapped, then stepped through the wooden screen door. "Hello? Riley?"

She saw him sitting at the kitchen table with a bottle of rum and a half-filled glass. He looked up at her with a puzzled expression on his face.

Liesbeth nudged Hannah toward the stairs. "Why don't you take the blouse up to Dodie?"

Hannah scampered up the stairs, and Liesbeth came closer to Riley. "I sent a message with Donald that we would come for a visit today. Perhaps you didn't receive it."

Riley pushed a chair away from the table with his foot and nodded that Liesbeth should sit down. "I think I remember something about it."

Liesbeth glanced around the kitchen. There were no signs of any food preparation or dishes drying from breakfast. "Is Gerard about? It seems very quiet here. Even the livestock must be napping."

Riley looked at her with bloodshot eyes. "Gerard's off somewhere. Scarpered for good, for all I know. There's nothing here for him now."

Liesbeth watched him top up his glass with rum and drink half of it down in one swallow. "What's happened, Riley?"

He gave a harsh cough of a laugh. "'What's happened?' she asks." He leaned toward her. "What do you care?"

She leaned away from his breath. "I care. Of course I do. We're friends."

She heard the girls coming down the stairs and stood up to keep them out of the kitchen.

Dodie was wearing the blouse Margaret had sent with the skirt that Liesbeth had made for her. Dodie pirouetted and grinned. "What do you think, Mrs. Bos? The blue in the blouse goes exactly with this line in the plaid, doesn't it?"

Liesbeth nodded. "It looks lovely on you, and yes, it goes together perfectly."

Liesbeth tried to shoo the girls back up the stairs when she heard the chair scrape behind her.

Riley moved to Liesbeth's side and grunted. "What are you all dolled up for?" He peered closer at Dodie. "That's not yours." He pointed at the blouse.

Dodie hung her head, too frozen to respond.

Liesbeth rested her hand on his pointing arm. "Margaret sent it along for Dodie. She doesn't wear it anymore, so it was a shame to just leave it hanging in the closet."

Riley stepped toward his daughter. "A handout? That's what we're reduced to. Handouts."

Dodie stepped back and Hannah took her hand.

Liesbeth slipped between the girls and Riley, facing him. "Now Riley, you know that Margaret loves to give little gifts. She knew the blouse would be perfect for Dodie and there's no harm in sharing something that you've enjoyed with someone else who will also get use out of it."

Instead of settling Riley down, his eyes narrowed. He gripped Liesbeth by the upper arm. "You come here pretending to want happy families, but you're a tease. You're nothing but a tease."

Liesbeth recoiled from the rotten stink of his breath and tried to pry Riley's hand off her arm. "You're hurting me, Riley. Please let go."

Instead of letting go, he leaned in close and tried to kiss her. She turned her head away and saw the two girls staring. "Dodie! Take Hannah and go to the Dekkers. Take the shortcut through the fields. Run now." She was wriggling and panting, trying to get out of his grip. Still the girls stood. "Run!"

Dodie turned, dragging Hannah, who hesitated before being pulled out the door.

Riley was slobbering against Liesbeth's neck and she tried again to push him away. "Riley McKenna! You forget yourself. Stop this instant. Let me go."

He leaned back and eyed her, then, without loosening his grip on her arm, pulled her back to the kitchen so he could take another drink.

Liesbeth saw the iron skillet on the cook stove and wondered if she should try to bang him on the head. It was far out of her reach, though, and she stood still as he swallowed the remaining drink in his glass.

She tried again, her voice soothing. "Riley, what's going on? Why are you behaving like this?"

He banged the empty glass on the table. "I seen you. You and that fella that comes to the hospital to do repairs. You two are thick as thieves now, aren't you?"

Liesbeth tried to yank her arm from his grip. "Is that what this is about? You have some notion that I'm interested in that man and you're jealous?"

"For years you've led me on, making out like you care about the kids, about me. You don't care, though. You're just a hussy. I should have known it when you arrived here with a kid and no husband. He probably doesn't even exist."

Liesbeth was hot and the pain in her arm brought tears to her eyes. "You're wrong, and if I gave you the impression that there could ever be more between us, I'm sorry. That could never happen because, despite what you may believe, I am married."

"Liar! But I was willing to take you even with a kid of your own. I would have taken you in, but you just want to play me. No one messes with me and gets away with it."

He yanked her tight against him and pushed his mouth against hers. He had dropped her arm and now had her in a bear hug.

She resorted to the one instinctive move she knew would work: she crunched her knee into his groin.

He fell away from her with a cry. "Bitch!"

He lifted his arm and slapped her with the back of his hand and she fell against the table, knocking the back of her head on its edge as she went down. She lay on the floor, stunned, tasting the copper tang of blood in her mouth. She was dizzy. She might black out in a minute. She struggled to her hands and knees when Riley's foot came up under her chin, leaving a smudge of black boot polish to be scrubbed off much later.

Liesbeth fell back again and saw him standing above her. One foot rested on either side of her. As she looked up at him, he loosened his belt, letting it hang open as he worked the buttons of his fly. Liesbeth closed her eyes, twisting her throbbing head to the side, waiting to feel the weight of him drop on top of her, helpless in her pain to fight.

She heard a loud bang and opened her eyes again. Riley was stumbling away. Yelling, thrashing shapes whirled around her, and Liesbeth slipped into blackness.

She rose to the surface when a cool cloth was being pressed to her head. Adriaan's voice: "I think she's coming to. Take the cloth away."

She opened her eyes. She was lying on the sofa. The Dekkers' oldest son, Joseph, stood holding a dripping cloth and Adriaan perched on the sofa beside her. She struggled to sit up. "Hannah?"

Adriaan pushed on her shoulders to keep her prone. "Hannah's just fine."

She turned her head, searching for Riley.

Adriaan took the cloth from Joseph, rinsing it out in a bowl of water set on the floor, and wiped her face and forehead. "Shh, now. You're safe. We have Riley locked in the barn, and by now he's probably curled up on a pile of straw to sleep it off."

Her head was splitting. The musky aroma of cows and sweat coming from Adriaan made Liesbeth's gorge rise. "Let me sit up."

Adriaan stood up to allow Liesbeth to swing her legs onto the floor. She wondered where her shoes went. Her head was swimming but she took deep, slow breaths to steady herself.

Joseph touched her shoulder. "Can I get you anything? A glass of water, maybe?"

She nodded and instantly regretted the movement. "Yes, thank you."

When Joseph stepped out of the room, Adriaan sat down beside her. "Are you all right? I think we got here in time."

Liesbeth closed her eyes. "I'll be fine. Thank you for coming. I can't imagine—"

He put an arm around her shoulders as the tears welled in her eyes. "Don't imagine anything. It's bad enough as it is."

Joseph came back in carrying the water and handed it to Liesbeth. She cried out as she lifted the glass to her lips before taking a sip. "My jaw hurts."

She handed the glass back to Joseph. He stood beside her, pale and wide-eyed.

She slid her hand across her jaw, opening and closing her mouth. "It's not broken, thank goodness."

Joseph looked at his father. "Should I go home and call the Mounties, Dad?"

Adriaan looked at Liesbeth and she shook her head. "No. No police."

Adriaan put his hand on her knee. "Are you sure, Liesbeth? He assaulted you."

"I just want to go home."

He stood up, nodding at Joseph. "Let's get her over to the house, and your Mom can make her feel better first." He looked down at Liesbeth. "We'll get a cup of tea, or maybe a brandy into you."

Joseph carried the glass and bowl into the kitchen, and Liesbeth took some deep breaths before rising.

The boy came back carrying her shoes and set them on the floor by her feet. She slipped into them, bending forward to adjust the straps, and felt dizzy again. She straightened with a small groan.

Adriaan took her under one elbow and waved at his son to take the other. "Ready now? On three we'll get you up and out of here. The car is just outside the door."

Liesbeth pointed to the kitchen table where her purse sat beside the half-bottle of rum. "My purse."

Joseph left her side and picked it up, then they continued out to the car, putting her into the passenger side.

Liesbeth felt stronger with every step, although her head and jaw throbbed.

She settled into the seat with a sigh while Adriaan climbed into the driver's seat. She heard Joseph whisper to his father. "What about Mr. McKenna? Do we just leave him?"

Adriaan's lips were pressed together in a grim line. "Damn right we do." His voice softened. "Don't worry. We'll come back later. He probably won't even move until then anyway." Adriaan waved his hand toward Donald's car. "You'll be all right driving that back to the house?"

Joseph patted his father's shoulder. "I'll be fine, Dad. Go on. I'm right behind you."

They drove down the McKennas' drive, every pothole jarring Liesbeth and making her cry out. Adriaan tried to navigate around the worst of the bumps, then they were out on route 337 and the going was better. In a minute, Adriaan turned into his own smooth driveway.

Gertrude was waiting at the front window. When she disappeared from view, Liesbeth tried to sit up straight. They rolled to a stop, and Gertrude was there at the car, pulling open the door and muttering in Dutch. "Oh girl, what's happened to you? Are you all right? You're safe now."

Adriaan jogged around the car to help his wife support Liesbeth in her walk to the door. Hannah and Dodie stood at the open door, wide-eyed. Dodie turned away and disappeared into the house, but Hannah took a tentative step toward her mother.

Liesbeth tried to smile, but the pain in her jaw was too much. She was afraid it would look more like a snarl. "It's all right, Hannah. I'm just a little bruised, but nothing is seriously wrong."

Hannah bounded toward her mother, flinging her arms around Liesbeth's waist.

There was a silence as Liesbeth rubbed the child's back. At last Hannah looked up at her mother. "Did Mr. McKenna hit you like he hits Dodie?"

Liesbeth closed her eyes. She should have listened to the child. Gertrude pulled Hannah aside. "Let's get your mama inside for now. There will be plenty of time for talking later."

Hannah whirled and led the way into the house. They settled Liesbeth in the sitting room on the chaise lounge and Gertrude went to put the kettle on. They left Liesbeth alone with Hannah for the moment. The girl knelt on the floor by her mother while Liesbeth stroked her hair. "Don't cry, Hannah. I'm fine. You can see that I'm fine."

Hannah turned her liquid blue eyes on Liesbeth. "He did, didn't he? He's mean."

Liesbeth licked her cracked lip. "He had been drinking, and that sometimes makes people do bad things. I should have taken you away the moment I saw how he was. I'm sorry, Hannah."

Adriaan and Gertrude carried in the tea things. Gertrude poured out a cup to hand to Liesbeth. "Will you be able to manage this?"

Adriaan bent down, hands on his own thighs. "Would you prefer a brandy?"

Liesbeth reached for the cup of tea. "No brandy, thank you. I'll manage this." She grimaced as the hot liquid touched her lip, but took a swallow anyway.

Liesbeth sighed, suddenly exhausted. "Adriaan, I didn't thank you. I hate to think—"

Adriaan stopped her with a wave of his hand. "Don't mention it. Thank goodness Joseph and I were on hand. When I saw Dodie and Hannah flying across the fields, I knew something was wrong." He smiled at Hannah. "You're a good runner, Hannah. You really helped your mama today by being so quick."

Liesbeth rubbed her finger against Hannah's cheek, wiping away a tear. "Why don't you go and find Dodie. She's probably worried and we should make sure she's all right."

Hannah got up off the floor and went in search of her friend.

Adriaan set his cup of tea down. "I can't excuse Riley for this, but do you know what happened to him this week?"

Liesbeth frowned. "He really wasn't talking sense when I arrived, so no."

"He lost the farm. The bank has foreclosed. He sold off most of the stock earlier in the week, and now he has to find a place to go."

Liesbeth heaved a deep sigh. "Poor man. That's why it seemed so quiet there."

Gertrude pressed her lips together. "That is no reason to forgive this."

Adriaan shook his head. "Of course not. Liesbeth, are you sure you don't want to call the police?"

"Oh, no. No authorities. Nothing's broken." She waggled her jaw again. "Just very sore. I'll have to take a couple of days off work."

Gertrude stood to take Liesbeth's empty cup away. "You two should stay here and I can look after you."

Liesbeth gave a tiny shake of her head. "No, Gertrude. Thank you, but the best place for us is at home. I have Peggy to help out, if I can just figure out how to get there. With this blinding headache, I don't think I'd be safe driving right now."

Adriaan folded his arms across his chest. "Of course not. We'll do the same as earlier. I'll drive you and Hannah, and Joseph will drive behind me with Donald's car."

"Thank you, Adriaan." Liesbeth turned to Gertrude and lowered her voice. "What will happen to Dodie? She can't go back there. Maybe Peggy wouldn't mind sharing her room."

Gertrude shook her head. "Don't think of it. She'll stay here, of course. We'll have to get a hold of that aunt in Halifax and see if she would be any help at all. The poor child. Did you see any sign of Gerard when you were at the house?"

Liesbeth repeated what Riley had said to her. "He may have left for good by the sound of it. Now I understand."

Gertrude frowned. "He's turned surly the last couple of years. I think he's got a lot of his father in him. Well then, we only have Dodie to worry about. She's welcome here until we sort something out."

Liebeth pushed a loose strand of hair behind her ear. "What if Riley insists that she go back home to look after him. Can he do that?"

Adriaan nodded. "She's his daughter. He probably could insist, but I don't think he will. It'll be easier for him to find a place and maybe some work by himself."

Liesbeth nodded. "He'll go on the road."

Adriaan shrugged. "Yes, I imagine so. There's no work around here for him. He'll have to head west."

Liesbeth touched her swelling face. "Despite all this, I feel sorry for him."

Gertrude exhaled. "He brought his troubles on himself."

Liesbeth nodded. "Some people don't know how to ask for help. When things started to go wrong, he should have said something, and I'm sure all his friends and neighbours would have rallied around."

Adriaan nodded. "I agree. He had too much pride to say anything. A couple of times when I saw something that needed to be done, I'd offer the boys or my help, but usually he just kept to himself, so we didn't realize how bad things were."

Hannah and Dodie came into the room. The older girl's eyes were red and swollen from crying. She hesitated at the doorway while Hannah came in to sit on the edge of the chaise lounge.

Liesbeth slid over, making room on the chair beside her. "Come Dodie. Give me a hug."

Dodie ran forward squeezing between Hannah and Liesbeth, and Liesbeth wrapped her arms around the thin, shaking shoulders. "Shh, you're safe now."

Dodie pulled back. "I'm sorry."

Liesbeth tilted her head. "Why are you sorry? You did exactly as I asked. You brought Hannah here where you were both safe, and told Mr. Dekker who came to help me. You did everything right."

"But my dad hurt you." Dodie's thin fingers felt like a butterfly fluttering against Liesbeth's jaw.

Liesbeth took Dodie's hand in hers. "Yes, I'm afraid your dad did hurt me. What makes me even sadder, is that I think he's probably hurt you in the past and I didn't do anything to stop it."

Dodie stared down at her hand engulfed in Liesbeth's. "What will happen now?"

Liesbeth patted Dodie's hand and released it. "Now, Mr. Dekker and Joseph are going to drive Hannah and me home, and you're going to stay here and help Mrs. Dekker. You're going to stay right here for the time being, and I think later this evening Mr. Dekker will go back to the farm and perhaps pick up some of your things so that you can stay here with them.

"But my dad will want his supper."

Gertrude almost growled. "Then he'll have to make it for himself, won't he?"

The girl's eyes were wide. "He'll be mad if I'm not there."

Liesbeth hugged Dodie again. "You don't need to be afraid, because Mr. and Mrs. Dekker are going to look after you for now. You aren't going home to your father again if any of us can help it."

Dodie looked at Gertrude, who nodded. "That's right. We'll figure out all the details, but for now you're staying with us. I'm going to teach you how to make cheese. Would you like that?"

Dodie nodded, still wide-eyed and silent.

Liesbeth pushed herself up. "Adriaan, I really would like to go home now."

Gertrude came over to support her, but Liesbeth shook her off. "I'm all right now."

Gertrude's face was wreathed in frowns. "Are you sure you won't just stay the night?"

Liesbeth straightened. "No, I'll be all right. I think my own bed is the best place for me."

Hannah took her hand. "I'll look after you, Mama."

Adriaan went to call Joseph. then they all made their way out to the cars. Liesbeth was almost surprised to see that it was still a beautiful sunny afternoon. It seemed to her that a day had passed since she'd set out this morning, but in fact it was only a few hours.

Joseph called out to Hannah before climbing into Donald's car. "Do you want to drive with me and keep me company?"

Hannah clung tight to Liesbeth's hand and shook her head.

They set off in tandem, Adriaan driving at a slow, steady pace. They didn't speak, and Liesbeth leaned back and closed her eyes. The sound of the engine and the steady motion lulled her into a light doze so she was startled when she felt the car slowing down. She blinked and saw that they were pulling up at her door.

Liesbeth sat up straighter. "I'm sorry. I dozed off there."

Adriaan glanced at her. "You needed it. You've got a bit of colour back in your face. You've lost that chalky look."

He stopped the car, and Joseph pulled in behind him. Adriaan waved to Joseph. "Just wait in the car. I'll just be a minute."

He held Liesbeth under the elbow as she walked to the house. She was glad for the support.

He helped her to the sitting room, and when she was settled on the sofa, he stood back. "Will you two be all right? Where's Peggy?"

Hannah answered quickly. "I can get her if we need her. It's her day off and she's gone to her aunt's. I can look after Mama, though."

Adriaan smiled at her. "Yes, I believe you can."

Liesbeth nodded. "Adriaan, thank you again. For everything. You go on now and don't worry about us. We're fine."

He took one more glance around to see if there was anything he could offer to do, but obviously seeing nothing, he turned to leave. "I'll stop in again in a couple of days to let you know how things are with Dodie, and to see how you're managing."

Liesbeth nodded. "Yes, please do."

After they drove away, Hannah trotted to their bedroom, coming back with Liesbeth's hairbrush and a quilt.

Liesbeth smiled as Hannah insisted on removing all the pins from her mother's disarrayed hair and began brushing it out. "You're a very good nurse, Hannah."

"You always make me feel better when I'm not well, so now it's my turn."

"Thank you. I appreciate it."

Hannah braided her mother's hair into one long braid. "Now, lay down on the sofa so I can cover you with the quilt."

"I was thinking about getting some lunch for us. With everything that's happened, we never did have lunch."

Hannah shook her head. "You lie back. I will get some bread and honey, with a glass of milk for each of us."

Liesbeth squeezed Hannah's hand. "That sounds perfect. All right, I'll just rest until you're ready, but then you call me and I'll come to the kitchen for lunch."

Liesbeth closed her eyes and listened to the sounds of her daughter in the kitchen. She thought about that other kitchen, the moment when she thought Riley would overcome her. Tears welled in her eyes. *Stop. Don't let Hannah see this.*

She kept her eyes pressed closed and swallowed several times until she felt herself under control again. She sensed Hannah more than heard her, and opened her eyes. The girl stood at her side holding a plate of sliced bread spread with honey.

Liesbeth smiled and swung herself into a sitting position. "You were supposed to call me."

Hannah shook her head. "I didn't want to wake you if you were asleep."

Liesbeth took the plate and set it on the small table in front of the sofa. "This looks perfect. Just what the doctor ordered."

Hannah retreated to the kitchen and came back carrying two glasses of milk.

"Lovely."

Liesbeth wasn't sure she'd be able to eat, but a slice of soft bread was probably a good place to start. She picked up a slice and took a small bite, then cried out, despite her best intentions.

Hannah's eyes widened. "Are you all right, Mama?"

Liesbeth nodded and managed to swallow. "My jaw is sore, so it'll take me a bit to get used to moving it, but it isn't serious."

Liesbeth managed one slice and drank her milk. "I think that's all I have an appetite for at the moment."

Hannah finished her portion, then picked up the plate. "I'll wrap yours in wax paper. You might want it later."

Liesbeth nodded. "I'm sure I will."

Hannah puttered around clearing the dishes, then returned. "Do you want to lie down here on the sofa, or go to bed?"

"Oh no, it's too early for bed. I'll just lie here for a little while, then I'll get up and we'll sort out supper."

Hannah nodded. "I'm going to get my book and I'll sit here in case you want anything."

Liesbeth smiled at her daughter who was so suddenly very grown-up. "You go out to play, sweetheart. It's such a lovely day out, it would be a shame to waste it."

Hannah shook her head. "No, Mama. I'm staying here." Her voice went back to its normal little-girl tone. "Please?"

Liesbeth felt the lump come into her throat again. "Of course you can stay here if you'd rather. I'm glad for your company, and even if I fall asleep, I'll know that you're here, watching over me."

Hannah nodded and went to the kitchen to find the book she had been reading, while Liesbeth stretched out on the sofa again.

Hannah returned and fussed with the quilt for a minute before settling herself into the chair in the corner.

X

October 1929 – New Perspectives

*D*ear Max,
I am so very sorry to hear about your mother's passing. I was quite shocked to receive the news in Alida's letter yesterday. Your mother was still quite young. I didn't realize that she was ill. I'm sure it's a terrible time for you and I'm sorry for what you are going through.

I know that Hannah will send you a letter at Christmas as she always does, but since I'm writing anyway, I'll tell you that she is turning into quite a young lady. We've had some things happen here this year that seem to have made her grow up quite quickly. She takes delight in Margaret's new baby boy and wants to spend as much time there as she can. I have to restrict her to be sure she doesn't become a nuisance. She is a little bit jealous that her good friend Dodie (who is a few years older than her) is now living with Margaret and Donald, helping out as a nanny.

She continues to do very well at school in all subjects. She has taken a keen interest in science and has borrowed a book about insects that seems to have her fascinated. You would be very proud of her and I intend to have a nice photo taken before Christmas to send to you.

In the meanwhile, I wish you strength during this difficult time.

Best regards,

Liesbeth

Liesbeth sealed the letter into an envelope. She rarely wrote to Max, only to thank him for Christmas and birthday gifts sent to Hannah. Since the episode with Riley in the summer, though, she had found herself having short conversations with him in her mind.

She had taken three days off work after the encounter. Margaret had insisted, appalled at how her face was swollen and bruised. Margaret had taken Peggy and Hannah to her house, leaving Liesbeth to sleep and apply ice to her jaw. Liesbeth had had hours to just let her mind wander, a luxury in which she rarely indulged.

Why did I insist on befriending this man? Both Margaret and Hannah knew there was something off about him. Hannah, a child for God's sake, knew, but I didn't. How come?

Max's voice in her mind had answered her question. *You're kind, and more than that, you like to be needed. He needed someone and you responded to that.*

When Liesbeth realized that it was Max's voice responding to her silent conversations, she had let herself wonder about that. *Why, after all this time, am I bringing Max into my mind?*

She couldn't quite come to a satisfactory conclusion, other than she felt comfortable thinking about him. She became accustomed to having these discussions with him. It was something new for her. She typically didn't spend much time analysing her thoughts and reasons behind her actions. *Maybe I should have.*

Now, months after the bruises had healed, she regularly had silent conversations with Max. It had truly been a shock to receive Alida's letter yesterday with the announcement of his mother's death. He was so much on her mind that it was almost as if she had known something was wrong.

That's just silly.

She did feel that the conversations were somehow helping her to a greater understanding of herself. She considered now this need she had to continue her nursing career after she was married.

Margaret had made the transition quite easily, it seemed, nurse to wife to mother with some volunteer time on the side. It seemed to be enough for her.

As if the thoughts had conjured her friend, Liesbeth heard Margaret's voice outside.

Liesbeth opened the door and welcomed Margaret and Peggy inside. Dodie and Hannah, both pushing the pram, followed a few steps behind. "My goodness, what a delegation."

Margaret held out a bag of apples. "We went apple-picking this morning and have far too many, so we brought some here. Peggy promises to make apple pies and applesauce."

Liesbeth took the bag and walked through to the kitchen to set it on the counter. "And it took all four of you—"

Margaret interrupted "All five of us."

"Of course. All five of you had to deliver the apples instead of just waiting until Peggy and Hannah came home."

Dodie and Hannah had wrestled the pram into the room and Liesbeth leaned in to look at the sleeping baby. "Donnie looks more like Donald every day, doesn't he?"

Margaret came to Liesbeth's side. "Do you think so?"

Before Liesbeth could respond, Margaret started to cough. It was a deep, chesty cough that left her gasping. Margaret moved away from the pram and dropped into a chair.

Liesbeth put a hand on Margaret's forehead. "How long have you had that cough?"

Margaret waved her hand to shoo Liesbeth away. "A couple of days. It's nothing. A fall cold."

Liesbeth frowned. "I'll get you some water."

She fetched Margaret's water, and looked at the other girls. "Why don't you three go in the kitchen and start peeling some of those apples? You have me longing for that pie now."

The three of them left, leaving Margaret and Liesbeth alone with the baby. Liesbeth watched as Margaret took a long drink of water. "Margaret, when's the last time you were at the hospital? I know you were talking about going back to the Auxilliary almost right away after Donnie was born. Have you started back already?"

Margaret sat back and studied Liesbeth. "I've been back once. With Dodie there to care for Donnie, it gives me an afternoon out."

Liesbeth shook her head. "You probably heard then that we've had two more cases of pulmonary tuberculosis. You can't be there."

Margaret frowned. "But it's all right for you to go and put yourself at risk."

"I'm taking all the precautions as a nurse. I don't think you do when you pop in and out of the rooms with magazines and fruit."

Margaret pursed her lips but didn't deny it. "Perhaps you're right. I know it's nothing, but I'll take a break for a while until Donnie is a little older."

"Tell me truthfully how you feel."

Margaret shrugged. "I'm tired, but for goodness sake, I have a newborn. Who wouldn't be tired?"

"And you're coughing."

"Yes, I'm coughing."

"I don't want to be alarmist, but why not let Dodie look after Donnie exclusively for the next couple of days and you get yourself to the doctor for a check-up?"

Margaret's eyes widened now. "You don't think I have it?"

"I'm sure you don't, but better safe than sorry."

Margaret nodded. "I'll get on home now."

Liesbeth went to get Dodie, then popped into her bedroom to fetch Margaret a large, clean linen handkerchief. Margaret took it and nodded, ready to put it before her mouth and nose if the slightest urge to cough came over her.

Hannah and Peggy came out to the living room to say goodbye. Hannah moved to give Margaret a hug but Margaret held her off. "No hugs for anyone until I've gotten rid of this cold."

Liesbeth smiled and Margaret gave a small one in return. "Let me know how you get on, Margaret."

Margaret nodded and they left, Dodie pushing the pram and Margaret walking at an arm's length to the side.

Hannah watched from the window as they walked away. "Is Tante Margaret all right, Mama?"

Liesbeth put her arm around her daughter's shoulders. "I'm sure she is, but just to be sure, she is going to see a doctor for a check-up. There is nothing for you to worry about."

Hannah turned away from the window. "But *she* seems worried. She wasn't this morning."

Liesbeth felt a pang. "I think both she and I are just being overly careful."

Hannah nodded, looking once more out the window. "Sometimes people die when you don't think they will."

Liesbeth sat down on the sofa and pulled Hannah to her in a hug. "Oh, Hannah. Are you thinking of your Oma?"

Hannah nodded. "You just think people are there somewhere and always will be, but they aren't."

Liesbeth rubbed her back. "That's true. Sometimes people do die suddenly. It's very hard to understand, but I'm sure that's not going to happen to Tante Margaret."

Hannah's face was buried in Liesbeth's neck. "Or you?"

Liesbeth leant back and looked at Hannah's tear-streaked face. "There's certainly nothing wrong with me."

Hannah looked down at the floor. "I sometimes dream that Mr. McKenna comes back. Except this time, he has a big knife."

Liesbeth pulled her close again. "Oh Hannah, Hannah, I thought you were completely over that awful day. I didn't know you were having nightmares. That man is never coming back and nothing bad is going to happen to me. You and I are safe in our snug little house, along with Peggy."

Her daughter nodded against her shoulder.

"We're all fine. Absolutely fine." Liesbeth felt an anger bubbling inside that she hadn't yet felt at Riley McKenna. *How dare he do this to my little girl?* She felt bile rising and she pushed it down as she held the small shuddering body against her.

She took a deep breath, then released Hannah. "What do you say we go in and help Peggy with the pie and the rest of supper?"

Hannah nodded and they went to the kitchen.

Liesbeth found Margaret wrapped in blankets, sitting out on her front porch. There was no sign of Dodie and the baby. Margaret had dark circles under her eyes and clutched her handkerchief in front of her mouth.

Oh God, no. Liesbeth sat down beside Margaret. "Did you get the results back?"

Margaret shook her head. "I'm still waiting. He's running some further tests. The first were inconclusive."

Liesbeth's eyes filled with tears. "It wasn't a positive, so that's good. The doctor is just being thorough."

Margaret sniffed. "Liesbeth, he took an X-ray and found a small scar on my lung."

Liesbeth bit her lip. "Margaret, you're a nurse. You know yourself that doesn't mean anything conclusive. Many of us actually get mild symptoms with associated scarring that we never even know about. We recover fully and without complications."

Margaret nodded. "I know, but I feel so exhausted, and that's a symptom as well." She stopped to cough into her handkerchief.

Liesbeth nodded at the handkerchief. "Are you seeing any blood?"

"No. Not yet."

"Don't think the worst until you know what the results are, then we'll deal with it. When will you hear?"

"Tomorrow. Liesbeth, you know how fast Pieter went. One day he was fine and then he was gone. What will happen to Donnie if that happens to me?" Margaret's hand snaked out from under the blanket to grasp Liesbeth's. "Promise me. Promise me you'll help to look after him."

Liesbeth held Margaret's hand in both of hers. "You don't need me to make a promise like that. You are going to be here to mother that child all the way through until he's your age and beyond."

"Please, Liesbeth."

Liesbeth, who had never found emotional displays easy, suddenly dropped on her knees in front of her friend. "Margaret, you can always count on me. Your son is like a child of mine already, and I promise to love him and care for him if he needs me. But I'm telling you that you need to stay strong and believe that you yourself will be here to do that job."

Margaret sighed. "Thank you. I will. I'll be positive, but thank you for your promise."

Liesbeth got to her feet. "I'm going in to rustle up a cup of tea for us. Are you all right out here in this cool morning?"

"Yes. I know that fresh air is the best possible thing."

"So is bed rest."

Margaret smiled. "All right, Nurse Bos. A cup of tea and then I'll go in and lie down."

"That's a deal."

Liesbeth was on day shift and had been assigned a new young student nurse to train. She took in the young woman's crisp uniform and stern, scraped-back hair. Liesbeth offered her hand. "I'm Sister Bos. You'll be working with me all this week, Sister Cameron."

The young woman had a firm, cold handshake. "I'm pleased to meet you. I've heard very good things of you already."

Liesbeth raised her eyebrows. "I won't ask for details."

Sister Cameron smiled.

Liesbeth led Sister Cameron through the rounds, taking pains to explain what she was doing with each patient. They wore masks when they worked with the first of the TB patients. "Miss Gillespie has had her lung collapsed through surgery and now she is resting.

Liesbeth's eyes crinkled over top of her mask and the patient smiled in return. Cameron stood by as Liesbeth reviewed the doctor's latest notes on the chart, explaining each point.

When they finished with the patient and had removed their masks, Cameron turned to Liesbeth. "I don't understand why she's here. She should have been sent to the San in Kentville."

"Ideally she would be there, and may yet be sent, but at the moment, they are full to capacity. We are working to get her stronger, then, when a bed opens up, she'll probably go."

Cameron wrinkled her forehead. "Meanwhile, she and the other TB patients here present a risk to everyone coming and going."

Liesbeth felt a ripple of anger. "That's why we have them in their own isolation rooms and we take all precautions."

Cameron sniffed. "Yes. We'll hope it's enough of a precaution."

Liesbeth gave a short nod. "Indeed we will."

Liesbeth's thoughts inevitably went to Margaret. *Please let everything be well.* If she didn't receive a message from Donald this afternoon, she and Hannah would cycle over after supper to get the news. She couldn't wait any longer to hear.

She continued showing Cameron and watching as the student performed some of the work. They took their lunch break together, and while Liesbeth would have been glad for a few moments of solitude, the younger nurse stayed by her side.

As Cameron unwrapped the waxed paper from her sandwich, she peppered Liesbeth with questions. "I understand you were in France during the war, is that right?"

Liesbeth smiled. "Yes, that's quite true."

"That must have been quite something. I'd like to get a chance like that."

Liesbeth frowned. "I hope for your sake you never get called upon to go to war."

Cameron gazed at her hands, deep in thought. "It would be an ultimate test, though. To truly use your skills. It's what I've trained for." She looked up. "Isn't that how you felt?"

Liesbeth had to be truthful. "Yes, I did feel some of that. It was quite brutal, but yes, I was glad that I could be of some comfort and help."

Cameron nodded. "That's the vocation. It's who I am." Her words were passionate, but Liesbeth was taken aback at the cool declaration. There was a certain detachment in the young woman's voice.

Liesbeth smiled. "There's more to you than nursing, I suppose."

Cameron looked at her. "You mean like you? With your daughter?"

Liesbeth tilted her head. "Well, yes. You have people in your life, I imagine, who also figure in some way."

Cameron shook her head. "No, I couldn't be like you and divide my loyalties. For me, it's all about the nursing. I think that to be the best at it, one needs to be completely focused on it. That's what I intend to do."

Liesbeth felt the rebuke. And more, the words resonated with her. It was a familiar sentiment.

Lunch over, they got back to work. By the end of the day, Liesbeth felt exhausted by the younger woman's energy and single-mindedness. *Was I like that? How insufferable. Luckily she'll only be with me for three months, then she'll be hanging on someone else's every word.*

Liesbeth hurried home after her shift. Hannah was not home from school yet, but Peggy was peeling carrots. "Is there any message from Margaret or Donald?"

Peggy shook her head. "No one's been by all afternoon."

Liesbeth sighed and slipped on an apron. "Let me help."

They worked in companionable silence, each with her own thoughts. They both leaped up at the sound of footsteps, but it was Hannah arriving home. All three chatted about Hannah's day as the child laid out her schoolbooks on the kitchen table to show the lessons she had been working on.

Liesbeth pulled a chair close to her daughter to review the pages. "You have a real talent for mathematics, Hannah. Very well done."

Peggy shook her head. "I don't know how you keep all that stuff in your head. I was hopeless at it and so glad when I could leave school."

Hannah turned the pages, looking ahead to future work. "I'm going to university someday."

Liesbeth smiled. "Are you, sweetheart? I'm very glad to hear it."

Peggy looked at Hannah, wide-eyed. "Will you go to St. Francis Xavier, then?"

Hannah shrugged. "Maybe. Or maybe I'll go to the one my Papa went to in Amsterdam."

Liesbeth sat back. "How in the world do you know that he went to the University of Amsterdam?"

Hanna blinked at Liesbeth. "You must have told me, I guess."

Liesbeth shook her head. "I can't imagine ever having told you that."

Hannah shrugged. "Maybe Tante Margaret, then." She went back to flipping through her book and asking questions about decimals.

Liesbeth and Hannah looked through the lessons while Peggy prepared supper. They were all busy, and Donald was inside the house before they heard him. Liesbeth rose and went to him, arms outstretched, steering him into the living room.

At first, his face was blank, then he put up his hands and broke out into a smile. "It's fine. It's all fine."

Liesbeth's eyes burned and she blinked. "The tests are conclusive now?"

Donald nodded. "There is some scarring on her lung, and the doctor believes she may, in fact, have contracted the TB bacteria at some previous time, but it was a mild enough infection that she fought it off. What she has now is just a bad chest cold and the scar. Nothing more."

Liesbeth held her hand to her mouth and sighed. "Thank God."

"Amen to that."

Liesbeth turned to Hannah and Peggy, who stood frozen in the kitchen. "Tante Margaret is going to be fine. There's nothing so seriously wrong that some good chicken soup won't fix."

Peggy grinned. "I'll make some tomorrow for her."

Donald nodded. "I'm sure she'll be grateful. She really is tired, and I think the worry made her even more so. Dodie's cooking is still under development, so a good chicken soup would be a welcome gift."

Liesbeth patted Donald on the arm. "Thank you for coming over to tell us the news. I'm very grateful. Go home now and look after them, your wife and son."

Donald nodded. "I will."

Hannah wriggled past her mother and threw her arms around Donald's waist. "Give her this big hug for me."

He patted her on the head. "I will, little lady. I'll do just that."

When he was gone, Peggy looked at Liesbeth. "Should I put the kettle on?"

"Why not? I should be starting on the ironing, but a cup of tea sounds lovely."

Liesbeth had Hannah read aloud to her as she relaxed with a cup of tea. Peggy set the table and the smell of fresh-baked biscuits and fish chowder filled the room with a relaxing warmth. Liesbeth felt at peace.

XI

March 1930 – Spring Fever

*D*ear Alida,
You make me very envious with your descriptions of the paper whites and crocuses. As always at this time of year, we are still under snow, although occasionally we feel a warm breeze that hints of days to come. I read in the paper last week that the Nieuw Amsterdam 1 is due into port on March 27th. Why were you asking if I ever looked at the arrivals news? Have you sent us an interesting package? You have me intrigued now. Or is someone famous arriving? I haven't heard of any Royal visits to Canada, so can't imagine what made you ask. I'll have to be patient and perhaps, in ten days, all will be revealed.

Yes, Margaret is very well again. She certainly gave us all a scare. She and Donald and little Donnie are all well and happy. I think Margaret will go to her mother's this summer and spend some months at Cape George to be close to the sea breezes of Ballentynes's Cove. We'll miss her, although Margaret is trying to convince me to let Hannah go to her on the summer vacation. We'll see. I'm not sure I can do without Hannah, although no doubt it would be lovely for her.

You sound very excited about joining the Women's Interests and Equal Citizenship group. It sounds like something you could get your teeth into. Is it one of your goals to see married women have the right to work as well? I look forward to hearing how you progress on that front. It sounds like something I would enjoy myself. In fact, I think I need something like that here. I'm feeling a little bit stale. I told you about the student nurse I had clinging to me for three months (thank goodness she's moved on to a different rotation). I have to admit that I found her intensity a little bit wearing. Don't get me wrong, nursing is still so very important to me, but I don't see it as the be-all and end-all of my life anymore. I blush a little to think that at one time I may have sounded so single-minded about it. I find myself looking through Hannah's schoolbooks and missing the challenge of studying completely new and interesting subjects. The problem is that between work and keeping this house from falling apart (I've gotten quite handy with a hammer and screwdriver), and just enjoying time with Hannah, I don't have the time or energy left for anything further.

Speaking of work, I'll need to close now and get this into the mail. I assume that Hannah continues to send her letters to you via Margaret. Perhaps this summer, she will be forced to enclose one with me again when Margaret is off on her vacation.

Love from your sister,

Liesbeth

Liesbeth sealed her letter, then looked once again at her sister's letter, received the week before. *Why in the world would she be asking me about ships coming into Halifax and if their arrival gets announced in the newspapers?* For a brief second, Liesbeth wondered if it was a subtle way of announcing that she, Alida was arriving for a visit. Liesbeth had coaxed her many times over the years, but Alida had refused. A quick look at the postmark on the letter put that thought out of her mind. The letter would have been sent just days prior to the *Niew Amsterdam 1*'s departure and Alida had mentioned a meeting she would be attending in late March. Her sister was getting a little bit eccentric. She smiled at the image of her sister taking up the cause for women's rights. She could still be a firebrand, and no one could talk people around like she could, so it might be just the fit for her.

I miss her. Liesbeth jolted at the thought. She had always been independent, her emotions buttoned away. *I'm getting soft.*

She stood up and called out for Hannah. "I'm walking down to the post office. Would you like to go with me?"

Hannah bounded out of the bedroom. "Yes, all right."

Liesbeth tickled Hannah under the chin. "What were you up to in the bedroom?"

Hannah hesitated, then confessed. "I was looking at your hats."

"My whole collection of two hats?"

"Mama, we should both get a new hat."

"I see. And why would we do that?"

"Because it's spring and we haven't had anything new for ever so long."

"You had a new dress at Christmas."

Hannah flapped her hand. "I know. I didn't mean that. But I haven't had a new hat, and that's what people see first, long before they see the dress under the coat."

Liesbeth wrinkled her brow. "What people?"

Hannah pouted. "Just people in general. You know, like when we go to church."

Liesbeth crossed her arms across her chest. "Hannah, is there a boy at church that you like? You're only nine years old. Surely you can't be thinking of boys."

Hannah made a face. "Oh Mama, I hate boys."

Liesbeth smiled. "I think you've been spending too much time around Tante Margaret with all her fine clothes."

Hannah put her coat on and pulled her woollen tam down on her head. "Can we just look in the shops at least?"

Liesbeth sighed. "We can certainly look, that doesn't cost anything, but it would have to be some real bargain for me to get you a new hat when yours is perfectly fine."

Hannah took her mother's hand. "Maybe we'll see one for you."

Liesbeth shook her head. "The one I have on my head will do for another couple of winters."

"Oh Mama, don't you want to look nice?"

Liesbeth pulled back to study her daughter. "I don't understand this sudden desire to look like a fashion model. For one thing, I have to ask you: don't I always look nice?"

Hannah scrunched up her face and Liesbeth laughed. "And secondly, why is it suddenly important to you that I look nice?"

Hannah shrugged. "I think a woman should always try to look her best."

Liesbeth shook her head. "Oh, my Lord. What magazine did you read that in?"

Hannah lifted her chin and didn't answer.

They walked to the post office in the spring sunshine. On Main Street, an auto passed by and tooted. Liesbeth waved to Mr. Arsenault. The car pulled to a stop and Mr. Arsenault got out, waiting until Liesbeth and Hannah reached him.

He doffed his cap. "Good morning, ladies."

Liesbeth stopped, despite Hannah tugging on her hand. "Good morning, Jerome. We haven't seen you for a while."

He nodded. "I did too good a job on the fall maintenance. The hospital hasn't needed my services for a while."

Hannah tugged again and Liesbeth frowned at her. "Hannah, we aren't in any sort of rush. You walk on and look in the shop windows, if you like. I'll just stop and be sociable for a moment."

Hannah gave an audible sigh, then walked on.

Liesbeth shook her head. "I'm sorry about that. I don't know what's gotten into her."

Jerome smiled. "Spring fever. Everyone's twitchy. She's like a colt who just wants to run and kick her heels a bit."

"Hmm, perhaps. It's as good an explanation as any, I suppose."

He leaned back against his car hood. "You made it through another winter, then."

She nodded. "I did."

"You're in the yellow house up on Adam, right?"

"That's the one."

"It looks like you've done a lot of work to it over the past couple of years. It looks right homey now."

"It's better than it was when we took it over, but it needs so much more work than I'll ever manage."

"It's not a long-term thing, then."

"No, it's not."

"So then, what's the plan? Are you looking to buy a home, or looking for another rental?"

Liesbeth lifted a shoulder. "Quite frankly, I'm not really sure. The budget is the concern, of course. There aren't that many options for a single mother on my income."

He nodded. "I can see that."

"And how did you fare through the winter?" Liesbeth wanted to change the subject.

He grinned. "Oh, I'm good. I have a snug place there with my brother and his family. I sometimes think I'd like to build my own place a little further out of town. Overlooking the bay somewhere would be nice. It's convenient living in town, though. I get called out on jobs at all sorts of crazy hours."

"I imagine you do." Liesbeth could see Hannah partway down the street turning back to look for her. "My daughter is keen that I join her. She would like a new hat, apparently."

Jerome's eyes twinkled. "Isn't that what ladies are always hankering for?"

Liesbeth shook her head. "Not all ladies. I'll say goodbye, then. Have a nice day."

He nodded and walked back to the driver's side of the car. "Mrs. Bos."

Liesbeth turned to look at him.

He rested his hand on the roof of his car. "Shall I keep my eyes and ears open for another place for you, if the price is right?"

Liesbeth hesitated. "Certainly, keep me in mind. The one thing that my place has going for it though, is convenience."

Jerome nodded. "I understand. I'll just keep my ear to the ground. You never know."

Liesbeth smiled and waved, then turned back to hurry over to Hannah.

The girl had a faint scowl on her face. "Why is he so friendly?"

Liesbeth raised her eyebrows. "I thought you liked him."

She shrugged. "He's nice enough, I guess."

Liesbeth put her arm around Hannah's shoulders. "Don't worry. If you think I'm going to go overboard, like I did with Mr. McKenna, you can rest easy. I've learned my lesson about being too friendly."

Hannah nodded, her face clearing. She skipped ahead to point out a hat in the dry goods store. "That would look good on you, Mama."

Liesbeth pretended to study it. "Well, perhaps one day I'll have one like that, but not today."

Hannah held still before the window. Liesbeth nudged her. "Shall we walk on?"

"Won't you try it on, Mama?"

Liesbeth felt a passing irritation. "No, Hannah. Quite honestly, there is no money in the budget for such things. It isn't long since we had Christmas and that put enough of a dent in the savings."

Hannah nodded. "All right." They walked along in silence but the joy seemed to have gone from the walk, and at the end of the block, they crossed the street to head back home.

Hannah suddenly grinned up at Liesbeth. "Maybe Tante Margaret has one she doesn't wear anymore."

Liesbeth took a breath. "Hannah, I'm not sure what has prompted your sudden obsession with hats, but neither one of us needs a new one, so don't go plaguing your Tante Margaret for one either."

Hannah's seemed to know she had pushed too far. She took her mother's hand again. "I'm sorry, Mama. I won't pester her. Don't worry."

"See that you don't. Let this be an end to the whole discussion."

Hannah nodded. "Mama, I don't mean to make you angry with me. Sometimes I get an idea in my head and it's hard to let it go."

Liesbeth's heart contracted. "I know you do, and I'm not really angry. I know you can be an independent, determined girl, and I can't be angry about that. I think perhaps I was rather like that myself sometimes when I was your age."

Hannah was thoughtful for a few moments. "So if I did things that you didn't agree with, you would forgive me, because you used to do things when you were a girl that your mama didn't agree with?"

Liesbeth pressed her lips together. "That's a very complicated question. It would depend on what the thing was, I suppose. I could be very upset with you if you went contrary to the things I hold dear."

"Like what?"

"Well, if you robbed someone, or hurt someone."

"Oh, no. I wouldn't do anything like that." Hannah sounded shocked.

"Well then, I suppose we would talk it through, and I'm sure I would always forgive you because I love you. That's unconditional."

Hannah nodded. "Yes. That's what I thought."

"Did I pass?"

Hannah looked up at her. "Pass what?"

"Whatever test this seems to be."

Hannah giggled. "It's not a test. It's just talking."

Liesbeth nodded. "All right, then."

Hannah released Liesbeth's hand and skipped ahead, her good humour restored. She stopped to pat a dog.

When they moved ahead again, Hannah spent the rest of the walk home trying to convince her mother that, despite Liesbeth deciding against a kitten, they should get a dog, and if they did get a dog, what sort it should be.

XII

April 1930 – Surprises

It was the first of April, April Fools' Day. Liesbeth wondered if it was somehow connected with this foolish day that Donald and Margaret had invited them for supper. It was a Tuesday, and they never went over for supper on a Tuesday. Margaret was very mysterious about it all, but Hannah was wild with excitement. Luckily, Liesbeth had been on day shift and would be off on Wednesday morning before the start of her afternoon rotation. As Margaret had pointed out, there was no reason not to go for supper.

Hannah came out of their room with a ribbon. "Will you tie this in my hair, please, Mama? Peggy's already gone to her aunt's place for supper."

Liesbeth took the ribbon and tied it in a bow on the back of her braid. "You're looking very fancy indeed for a supper at Tante Margaret's house."

Hannah pulled a tortoise shell comb from her pocket. "Mama, you hardly ever wear this, and it looks so nice on you. Will you wear it tonight?"

"Is this some special occasion that I've forgotten about? Someone's birthday, perhaps?"

"It's always a special occasion when we go out for supper."

"So it is. All right, give me the comb and I'll see what I can do with my hair."

Liesbeth brushed out her long hair and redid it, putting it up in a coronet pinned into place with the comb. She caught Hannah's spirit of the evening and added a scarf to trim her everyday dress. She came out to the living room where Hannah was perched on the edge of a chair, buffing her shoe with a rag. Liesbeth stopped in front of her daughter. "Ta-da. Will I do?"

Hannah smiled. "You look nice, Mama."

Liesbeth smiled. "Thank you. Now remember, despite all this celebration of a non-event, it's still a school night and we won't stay out late. So no whining when it's time to go home, right?"

Hannah nodded. "I hope we don't get all mussed when we ride our bicycles."

Liesbeth snorted. "It's not windy. I'm sure that the few minutes that we are riding our bikes won't destroy our lovely *coiffures.*"

Hannah wrinkled her forehead. "What's a *coiffure*?"

"A hairstyle. I thought you were learning French from your friends."

"That word never came up." Hannah repeated it a few times, then tried out a sentence. "Emma, I very much like your *coiffure* today."

Liesbeth smiled. "If you're finished polishing your shoes, we should go. Are you ready?"

Hannah scurried to the kitchen to put away the rag, then put on her spring coat. "Ready."

Liesbeth pinned on her Sunday hat and put on her own coat. "Let's go, then."

They rode to Donald and Margaret's house at the other end of town. It wasn't a long ride and they could have walked, but it was faster riding. Liesbeth was too Dutch not to take advantage of riding a bicycle whenever possible, and by now Hannah was as comfortable with it as well. Liesbeth knew that many people, especially women, viewed them as eccentric for riding everywhere. It wasn't quite lady-like, but it was very practical.

As they rode up to the house, Margaret was outside, holding Donnie. It was a mild spring evening and she seemed to be enjoying the last of the day. Margaret turned and said something into the house as they came up and dismounted. They pushed their bicycles up the walkway and left them just at the bottom of the steps.

Liesbeth called up to Margaret. "Are you expecting anyone else? Will our bikes be in the way here?"

Margaret shook her head. "No, they're fine there. No one else is coming."

Liesbeth walked up first while Hannah hung back. Liesbeth stopped to kiss the baby on the head. "How is Master Donnie today? Is that rash all gone?"

Margaret licked her lip. "The rash? Oh yes, that's all gone. He's right as rain again."

Liesbeth turned back to Hannah. "Go ahead, sweetheart. You know the way. You probably want to run ahead to say hello to Dodie."

Hannah stood still. "No, you go first, Mama. It's all right. I'm not in a hurry."

Liesbeth laughed. "She's been on pins and needles ever since she got home from school, and now suddenly she's not in a hurry."

Margaret smiled. "Shall we go in, then?" She led them inside and nodded toward the living room down the hall. "You go ahead. I just want to step into the kitchen to check on supper."

Liesbeth stopped. "Can I help you with anything?"

Margaret shook her head. "No, you go on. I'll be there in a moment."

Hannah pressed Liesbeth, and she obliged, heading into the living room.

In the room, Donald was speaking with a man whose back was to Liesbeth. Donald paused as Liesbeth and Hannah entered, and the man turned around.

Liesbeth felt dizzy. She opened her mouth but there were no words.

Hannah stepped around her. The child hesitated for a second, then bounded forward into the outstretched arms waiting to receive her. "Papa!"

Liesbeth continued to stand and stare. She felt Margaret come up behind her and turned to gape at her friend. "How? When?" She saw the silent pleading in Margaret's eyes. *Don't be angry with me.*

Liesbeth turned back and realized that she wasn't angry. Not at all. In fact, she felt her heart racing in a way she hadn't felt in a very long time. Max's hair was thinning; the rosy slant of late afternoon sun caused his pate to shine in a way it never had before. What hair remained was also greying at the temples, but he looked handsome nevertheless. He was slim, thinner than when she had last seen him. *Worry? Exercise?*

Finally, Max straightened up and looked at Liesbeth. He stepped over and held out his hand. "Liesbeth. How are you?"

She held out her hand and he took hers into both of his and pressed it before releasing her again. She shook her head. "Max, I'm absolutely speechless. When did you arrive?"

He pulled out his pocket watch. "Just about exactly two days ago."

Liesbeth thought for a second. "You arrived on the *Niewe Amsterdam 1*?"

He smiled. "How did you know that?"

Liesbeth nodded. "Alida mentioned that ship in her last letter, but of course didn't say why."

He nodded. "I know she wanted to tell you I was coming. She thought it would be better, but this one"—he nodded at Hannah, who stood with her arm around his waist—"wanted to keep it a surprise."

When he looked back at Liesbeth, his gaze was serious, his eyebrows drawn together. At one time, Liesbeth would have defined the look as cold or business-like, but now she could see the tremble in his tight lips. *He's nervous.*

Liesbeth looked at Hannah. "You knew about this?"

Hannah beamed and nodded.

Max continued. "Knew about it? She's the reason I'm even here."

Donald came around with a silver tray filled with glasses of wine, and apple juice in a wine glass for Hannah. "Let's sit down and have a toast."

They each lifted a glass and Donald proposed a toast "To friends, old and new."

"Cheers."

"*Prost.*" Max clinked his glass against Hannah's.

Liesbeth's heart was returning to normal. "Someone will have to explain all this. Hannah, why don't you tell me what's going on?"

Hannah set her glass on the small table beside her chair and sat up straight, taking a deep breath. Liesbeth had time to imagine an actress preparing to give a recitation. *She's practiced this moment.*

The child glanced at her father, then back at Liesbeth. "Well, a while ago, I decided to write a letter to Papa."

Liesbeth raised an eyebrow.

Hannah blinked. "I wrote him a letter folded into a letter to Tante Alida."

Liesbeth shook her head. "Why did you feel you needed to make a secret of it? I wouldn't have stopped you from writing to him."

Hannah shrugged. "I sent the first one in yours, but I asked Tante Alida to write back care of Tante Margaret."

Margaret shook her head. "I didn't know, honestly I didn't. Letters came from Alida in their own envelopes addressed to Hannah and I just thought they were playing a little game together."

Liesbeth frowned again and lifted her hands. "Were you worried I would stop you, Hannah?"

Hannah shrugged. "Not really, but I didn't want to upset you."

"Upset me?" Liesbeth was determined to explore this further when they were alone. "Go on."

Hannah smiled. "Well, then Papa and I started writing regular letters to each other." She grinned at him.

He nodded. "She's a wonderful correspondent."

Margaret nodded. "I was rather surprised at the frequency of letter-writing between Hannah and Ali, but Alida and Hannah both asked me to just let it be their secret." She looked at Liesbeth. "I'm sorry if I did wrong."

Liesbeth shook her head. "It doesn't matter. Not at all."

Hannah took another breath. "Then, after you were hurt—"

Liesbeth flushed and looked at Max, who kept his gaze averted. *He knows.*

"After you were hurt, I told Papa that we needed him."

Liesbeth bit her lip. "Hannah, that's something that you and I will have to discuss later. That was not something that your Papa needed to know, and certainly I have no idea what help he could offer."

Max interjected. "Don't be angry. She meant well. I had been in a slump for a few months anyway after my mother died, and it seemed like a perfect suggestion. A visit to Canada."

Liesbeth laughed. "You were so determined never to leave the Netherlands again."

He took another sip of wine. "Perhaps people may change their views once in a while."

She felt the sweat prickle under her arms. "Yes, of course. I didn't mean to sound churlish."

The clock on the mantelpiece chimed six o'clock and Margaret stood. "Shall we go in for supper?"

They rose and went in, Hannah staying as close to her father as possible. Now that she had overcome her initial shyness at seeing him in person, they fell into conversation easily, chatting about things over which they had corresponded.

At supper, Liesbeth asked about her sister. "So you seem to see quite a bit of Alida. How is she?"

Max nodded. "We do. She became the courier between us." Again he nodded at Hannah. He went on to talk about Alida and her work with the women's movement. "She's very energetic about it all. She organizes meetings and goes out fund raising." He waved his hand. "All that sort of thing."

Margaret shook her head. "She's so busy since she moved to Amsterdam. She sounds like she is having the time of her life."

Max nodded. "I do think she's enjoying things. This women's group is really offering her some challenges. She has become secretary there, so she spends an enormous amount of time writing letters and petitions."

Margaret laughed. "I always thought she would be the one to find romance, but then again, she was always a great talker. She could convince people of just about anything, so perhaps she's found her niche."

The evening flew past.

When it was time for Liesbeth and Hannah to go home, Max walked them to the door. "So we're agreed that I will find my way to your house by the time you get home from school, Hannah, so we can spend the evening together."

Hannah reached up to give him a hug and kiss on the cheek. "I can't wait. I'll run home so I'll be there by three-thirty, right?"

He saluted, then tilted his head at Liesbeth. "Could I interest you in going out for lunch somewhere before you go to work? Is there anywhere?"

Liesbeth laughed. "Even here there are places for lunch." She hesitated. "Yes, that would be nice. We do have a lot of years to catch up on, I suppose."

He nodded. "We do. Will you come here, then, and we'll set out from here?"

She nodded. "Yes, all right. And then you can walk back with me to ensure you make it to the house before Madam gets home."

Liesbeth and Hannah climbed aboard their bicycles and Max waved them away. Liesbeth caught sight of Margaret peeking out the living room window, and Liesbeth waved at her too. Liesbeth smiled to herself, knowing that her friend would be embarrassed at being caught spying.

XIII

April 1930 – Conversations

It was their third lunch together. The first day, they went out, the second, Margaret left lunch at the house for them while she and Donald took Donnie and Dodie out for an engagement, which Liesbeth didn't for a moment believe in. This time he was coming to the house for lunch before she went to work, then he would just stay on until Hannah got home from school. He had spent each evening with his daughter, going home after he tucked her into bed. Liesbeth felt odd, knowing that he had been in her bedroom, but tried to put the thought out of her mind.

He arrived promptly at eleven-thirty. She opened the door to his knock and he handed her a bunch of flowers.

She inhaled the fragrance. "Where in the world did you find freesias?" She wondered if he actually remembered that they were her favourite, or if he had just gotten lucky.

She knew the answer when he smiled. "I asked at the flower shop yesterday if they were ever available, and they told me that if I wanted them to, they could order them in specially. So, here they are."

Liesbeth shook her head. "They, more than anything, make me think of home."

Max laughed. "You know they are native to South Africa, not Holland, I'm sure?"

Liesbeth stuck her chin out, then took the flowers into the kitchen to put them in water. "I don't care where they come from originally. There is that wonderful flower stall in Centraal Station in Amsterdam that so often had them in abundance. The scent would lift me up the steps from the platform and carry me into the main hall."

He nodded. "I know the place you mean." He watched her snip the bottoms from the stems before putting them into the glass vase. "I'm surprised you still call Holland 'home'."

She flushed. "I didn't mean to. This is home now."

He turned back and led the way into the living room. "Hannah certainly seems all Canadian. She talks with real pride of the boys in school winning the local hockey tournament."

Liesbeth set the vase on the side table. "Thank you. They're lovely." She sat down and gestured to the sofa. "This is really the only life that Hannah remembers now. She *is* Canadian."

He bit his lip. "I think of the things in the Netherlands that I wish she could know." He nodded at the flowers. "The bulb fields in May. The food. The places where you and I grew up." He shrugged. "So many things."

Liesbeth sighed. "Perhaps one day, I'll take her back for a holiday." She smiled. "The ship goes both ways."

His lip twitched. "Yes. A holiday. It would be better than nothing."

Liesbeth's stomach clenched. He missed the child. When he was out of sight, she could put it out of mind, but here, with him sitting in front of her, it was more difficult. "Shall we eat?"

He pulled out his watch. "It's not too early for you? I know you have a long afternoon ahead."

"No, let's eat, and then perhaps we'll go for a little walk. The day is so lovely."

She served the soup that Peggy had made and laid out the fresh-baked rolls, butter, and cheese.

He sliced a small piece of cheese. "Mmm. This tastes quite like the original."

She nodded. "I wish you had time to meet Gertrude and Adriaan. I know you would like them. You only have the two weeks, though. It isn't much time."

He ate his soup, dabbing at his moustache between each bite. *I'd forgotten how tidy he is. He looks delicate against the rough-and-tumble manners of people here.*

She slid over the plate with rolls. "Have another."

He buttered a fresh roll. "I know you are working on the weekend as well, but not until three o'clock. Couldn't we go out to visit your friends on Sunday and still be back in time for you to get to work?"

She nodded. "I could borrow Donald's car, perhaps. It would be too crowded for all of us to go together, I think, but yes, if you think you'd like to go, it could probably be arranged."

He nodded. "Yes, I would like to go. I'd like to see as much as possible and meet all the people that are important to Hannah and you."

She swallowed. "All right, then. Perhaps when you go back you could ask Donald if I can use the car on Sunday. He can reach Adriaan and let them know we'll be by. He can telephone from the station."

Max raised his brows. "These people have their own telephone?"

"No, there's a party line at the wharf, but someone will pass along the message."

"Ah. A good system."

"The distances are vast here, but the community is still small. People really do help each other out more than I ever saw in the Netherlands." She was careful not to say 'home' again.

After lunch, Liesbeth washed the dishes, intending to leave them to dry in the rack. Max picked up the tea towel. "I don't know where things go, so I'll just leave them on the table."

Liesbeth tried to take the towel away. "Don't be silly. You're a guest here. Peggy will put them away later."

Max tugged back at the towel. "You're looking for a tug of war?"

Liesbeth let the towel go, surprised at his playfulness. "Good Heavens." Then she burst out laughing. After a second, he joined her.

When they both stopped laughing, Liesbeth stood looking at him. "Have we ever laughed together like that before, Max?"

He lifted a shoulder. "If we haven't, perhaps we should have."

She nodded. "I was never a laughing sort of person, but around here people laugh at everything. It's become more natural."

He dried a bowl and set it on the table. "I believe you. I hear Donald and Margaret together, and while I have no idea what they are laughing about, I feel an urge to join in."

Liesbeth nodded. "Luckily Hannah is turning out to have a wonderful sense of humour. I hear her and Peggy having the greatest fun together. I envy that freedom sometimes."

"It wasn't the way we were raised. It's very different here, I think."

She agreed. "It is. It's taken a lot for me to get used to their ways."

"But you've managed it."

"It's a work in progress." She turned to him. "You seem to have relaxed quite a bit too in the years since I've seen you."

He frowned. "I've had a lot of time to think, I suppose. I've asked myself many times what I could have done differently to change what happened between us."

"I have too."

He looked at her. "Have you come to any conclusions?"

She stalled as she took the washbasin and opened the back door to fling the water over the garden.

Instead of answering, she took the towel from him again and dried her hands before hanging it on a hook. "Let me get my hat and we'll go for a short walk. Then we'll come back and have a cup of tea before I leave for work."

He watched at the front door as she pinned her felt hat over her tightly twisted hair. "Now I understand why Hannah was so determined that I should get a new hat."

He looked at the hat. "And did you get a new one?"

She laughed. "Men. No, this one is about three years old."

He shrugged. "It looks fine to me."

She smiled in the mirror. "It looks fine to me too, but thank you for saying so. You must repeat it to Hannah."

They went out together and set off in the direction of the hospital. "I'll take you past the hospital so you can see where I work."

"I'd like that. Can you take me for a tour?"

"I'm not sure the Matron would look too kindly upon that, but we can step through the front doors to give you a sense of it."

For a moment, she thought he would offer his arm and she had a fleeting terror of not knowing how she should respond if he did, but he put his hands behind his back.

They walked in silence for a moment, then Max spoke up again. "Well? Did you reach any great conclusions?"

She took a breath. "I suppose I came to consider many things. I'm not sure how right those conclusions are, though."

"Such as?"

"Does it really matter anymore? So much time has passed."

He thought about it. "I think it does matter."

"All right, then. I think that I was lost when I came back from Paris. The war had left me unfit to take on the responsibilities of simply being a wife and a mother. The problem was that my definition of myself, if you want to call it that, was all wrapped up in being a nurse."

He glanced at her. "You were an excellent nurse. Your abilities as a nurse was one of the reasons I first noticed you."

She nodded. "Yes, I knew that. That was the problem, I suppose. Without that job, I felt I didn't have anything to offer you anymore. I lost all my confidence."

He shook his head. "But surely you understood that while I first noticed you as a nurse, I fell in love with you as a woman. It wasn't your skill at changing a dressing that made me want to marry you."

She pointed to the hospital. "There, shall we cross the road and go in?"

He shook his head. "Let's walk on for a bit and we'll stop in on the way back. Is that all right?"

She sighed. "Certainly."

She knew he was waiting for her to respond. "I'm sure I did know that it wasn't my nursing skills you wanted, but I just didn't believe that I really had any other skills that were enough to keep you interested. On top of that, I truly missed the work. I felt empty." They walked on. "Part of the problem was I didn't feel like I had anyone to talk to about it all."

He frowned. "You had me. You had your sister." He put his hand on her arm for an instant. "I'm not trying to argue with you. I'm trying to understand."

She nodded. "I know. I think in hindsight, that I just didn't know how to talk to people about my feelings. My emotions were something so buried and so, I don't know." She struggled to find the right word. "Stunted, perhaps. I didn't know how to unearth them and talk about it all."

He nodded again. "I was never terribly good at discussing feelings either."

She looked at his profile as they walked. "So what conclusions did you come to?"

He glanced at her, then looked ahead again. Now he did offer his arm to her, and she placed her hand on it without hesitation. He chewed his bottom lip. "I was perplexed for a very long time. I think that's why I contacted Alida. I needed to talk to someone and I thought perhaps she could help me muddle through it all."

Liesbeth remained silent, waiting for him to go on.

He clicked his tongue. "She didn't really help me with explanations. She seemed as bewildered as I. She did ask me finally about that Rosa woman."

Liesbeth's heart squeezed. *The woman. Will he admit now that something had gone on there?*

"She asked me outright if I had been seeing Rosa or any other woman. I told her the same as I told you at the time. Absolutely not."

They were both quiet and Liesbeth knew he was waiting for a comment from her. She sighed. "I was quite convinced that you found her attractive."

He waved his hand. "There are many women who are attractive. That doesn't mean I want a relationship with them."

She acknowledged his point. "I think my readiness to believe in your relationship with her was all mixed up with my other feelings."

He took a breath. "My conclusion was that you felt inadequate for some reason."

"Yes, I think you are probably right."

"I take just as much responsibility for that. I didn't make an effort to explain to you that it was all those things that made you a good nurse which appealed to me."

She looked at him, frowning. "What do you mean?"

"Your quiet determination. Your ability to learn and speak intelligently on all manner of subjects. Your willingness to take on new things. Yes, even your sense of adventure. I am not a particularly adventurous person, so you brought me, kicking and screaming perhaps, to new ideas."

She smiled. "Adventurous enough to immigrate to a new country."

He chuckled. "That was rather too extreme for me."

"Yes. I've sometimes thought about how you would have coped, had you come with us, and I think you're right. You wouldn't have liked it."

"You've thought about me, then?"

Liesbeth felt her face heat up. "Yes, of course. Now and then." They walked on in silence, then she took a deep breath. "Do you recall when I thought I was pregnant but hadn't been to the doctor yet?"

He nodded. "Of course."

"You said that I was usually right. You had faith in me."

Max smiled. "Yes, I remember saying that."

She stopped to face him. "Your faith was misplaced. I haven't always been right."

He touched her cheek with his finger. "Neither of us has been."

She nodded, then looked at her watch. "We'll have to turn back."

They turned, and Liesbeth slipped her hand from his arm. They picked up their pace and Liesbeth pointed out the budding hawthorn bushes and wild roses growing by the roadside, signs of the coming spring.

He stopped to look at the wild rosebush with the hips still hard and rosy from the previous autumn. "It's a much wilder sort beauty here compared to the carefully tended bulb fields and gardens at home."

"Yes, one never forgets that nature is often in charge here, not man."

"You've had some hard times here, Liesbeth."

She nodded. "Yes, it's been more difficult than I expected. The first year was hard because I just worked as a domestic. I was frustrated at not being allowed to nurse."

"But you have your wish now."

She sighed. "I'm working as a nurse, but it still seems to be a constant struggle."

"But you're managing?"

"Oh yes, we're managing. Thank goodness I have Peggy to help with Hannah. That's made all the difference."

Max smiled. "She's a lovely young lady. Hannah and Peggy clearly love each other."

"Yes. My worry is that Peggy will want to move on one of these days. I have had a hint that she's fond of a boy she's met through her aunt."

"What would you do if she wants to leave?"

Liesbeth lifted a shoulder. "I'll face that when and if it happens. Hopefully it won't be for some time yet, and by then perhaps Hannah won't need someone to look after her."

He frowned. "She couldn't stay overnight by herself, though."

"Certainly not at this age." Liesbeth dismissed the subject. "It may not be an issue for a long time to come."

They had reached the hospital again. Liesbeth gestured to the door. "Did you want to step in to see it?"

He nodded. "Yes, if it's not a problem."

They went in, and Liesbeth took him around the main reception area and pointed out the main wards and departments.

When they went back out and headed back toward the house, Max was complimentary. "It's somewhat small, but it seems very new and modern."

"Oh yes, it was just expanded in the past two years, so it has all the modern equipment. It's a good place to work. The Sisters of St. Martha's are very caring and compassionate."

"It seemed like there were quite a few young staff there."

"There's actually a nursing school associated with the hospital, so yes, we do get many new nurses to train. Then they go off to other jobs in Halifax or Ontario.

"They must be happy to have a senior nurse like you who stays."

"Possibly. At times I feel ancient, though, and I suspect the younger nurses feel that I don't practice the newest ways enough."

They made their way back to Liesbeth's house. She looked at the clock. "I have time for a quick cup of tea if you'd like."

"If you have the time."

As Liesbeth put the kettle on and set out the cups along with a pound cake, Max fiddled with a teaspoon.

When she was sitting with the teapot filled and steeping, he touched her hand. "You haven't said anything about the assault."

Liesbeth closed her eyes. She had hoped they wouldn't discuss it.

He must have seen her look. "If you don't want to tell me, you don't have to. I just know that Hannah was so very worried about you."

She poured out the tea. "No, I can tell you. I've thought so much about it naturally, wondered what I did wrong." She paused. "There had been all sorts of signs that Riley McKenna was rather a brutal man. Hannah realized it long before I did."

Max was silent.

She fiddled with a teaspoon. "I know now that I did what I often do."

"And what's that?"

"I like to be needed." She sighed. "It took me this long to realize that. I *need* to be needed. And he needed someone, so I was willing to leap into that role."

Max looked into Liesbeth's eyes. "You had a relationship?"

She shook her head. "No. I never forgot that I am a married woman, Max."

He nodded and took another sip of tea, his face colouring. "So what happened? How did that . . . friendship . . . end up in an assault?"

"While I thought I had been very clear on the boundaries of our friendship, he apparently was biding his time until it evolved into more. Even as it was, he began to feel a sense of ownership over me. I didn't understand all that until later."

"Despite you being a married woman?"

Liesbeth sighed again. "Even with that, he apparently had decided that you, my husband, were a figment of my imagination. He concluded that I was a fallen woman with a child, and he decided that he would accept me despite my dark past."

"Good Lord. But Margaret knew me. She could have told him that you really are married."

"Yes of course, but he never discussed his ideas with her. And quite honestly, I'm not sure he would have believed her." Liesbeth fell quiet.

Max sat back and folded his arms across his chest. "So he had this idea about you, and one day decided to press his position?"

Liesbeth tilted her head. "Not exactly. He had all sorts of problems that one day led him to a rage that all centered on me." Liesbeth drained her tea cup.

Max sighed and rested his hand on her arm.

She smiled and shrugged. "It could have been much worse. He bruised me somewhat, but that's all. Dodie and Hannah ran to Adriaan for help, and luckily they arrived in time, so no real damage done."

"Thank goodness for that."

"Yes. He's gone now, somewhere west. The farm is mostly abandoned. Adriaan is renting a couple of fields from the bank, but no one is buying up farms at the moment. The son has disappeared somewhere as well, and Margaret and Donald took in Dodie."

"It's all rather sad."

Liesbeth's eyes filled with tears. "Yes it is. The worst of it is what I did to Hannah with my foolishness."

Max shook his head. "I think she's fine now."

"Yes, it's long behind us now, but as her mother I'm supposed to be the wise one. Liesbeth shook her head. "My desire to be needed led me to poor choices."

"There's nothing wrong with helping people out."

"There is when you do it for the wrong reasons." Liesbeth stood and cleared off the table. "I need to go to work. You'll just stay here to wait for Hannah?"

"If you don't mind me waiting here in your house."

"Not at all. Peggy will be here any minute, anyway. You can help her peel potatoes."

He smiled. "Tomorrow is Saturday. Shall we three do something together before you go to work tomorrow afternoon?"

Liesbeth nodded. "I think Hannah has found a place that is still tapping their maple trees, even though it is rather late in the season, so we can take you there for a visit. We will see you first thing tomorrow morning."

XIV

April 1930 (continued) – Hello and Goodbye

A s Liesbeth worked her shift the following night, she caught herself smiling several times. At one point, the student nurse on duty noticed. "You seem very cheerful this evening. Did you have a nice day?"

Liesbeth smiled at her. "I did, actually. My daughter and I were showing a visitor how maple syrup is made."

The girl raised her eyebrows. "A visitor from where?"

"From the Netherlands."

"Oh, that's where you're from, isn't it?"

Liesbeth nodded.

"And what did your friend think of the whole process?"

"He was intrigued, but I think on the whole, he thought it rather a primitive way to make sugar."

The girl chuckled as she went down the hall to answer the summons of a patient's bell.

Liesbeth looked forward to tomorrow's planned visit to the Dekkers. It had been decided that they could all fit into Donald's car, with Margaret holding Donnie on her lap, of course. They would have lunch at the farm, and Margaret was preparing a basket to take along to contribute -- some cold chicken and pie.

It had been quite a while since Liesbeth had been out to see Gertrude and Adriaan. She had been self-conscious after the incident with Riley. *It'll be all right, though, because it's truly behind me now. Talking about it to Max actually helped.* Talking about things really did help. Instead of lurking somewhere, the thing just seemed to fade away. *Funny, that.*

The evening shift seemed to drag on, and she was glad when it was over.

The student nurse wished her a cheery good evening at the door. "See you tomorrow. Safe home."

Liesbeth thought about how fresh the girl looked. *Looks like she's ready to start a shift, not like she's just finished one.*

She was glad to take her shoes off at home. The clock ticked in the silence of the house. She heard Peggy's bed springs squeak as she shifted. Liesbeth warmed up some milk and sat at the kitchen table. The kitchen still smelled faintly of supper and the ever-present subtle fragrance of fresh baking. She felt the day melt away from her. She was tired. She sipped her warm milk and thought about the days ahead. In another week, Max would be going home again. He had taken a month's leave of absence, but the travel time took up a big part of that. Things would go back to normal after that. *I won't be so tired after he leaves. I'm running around burning the candle at both ends at the moment. I'll be glad when he's gone.*

But she wondered if she was being honest with herself about being glad to see him leave. She had never thought he would come to Canada, but she had occasionally pictured herself taking Hannah back to Holland for a vacation. She had imagined he'd be stiff and cold with her, although she always knew he'd be glad to see Hannah. The reality had been quite different. *I really enjoyed being with him.*

She had also imagined that he would have been settled with a new woman, and—she dared now in the quiet of her own kitchen to admit it—she believed the other woman would be Alida. They seemed to get on so well. She hadn't had the courage to ask Max about it, hoping instead that somehow what she wanted to know would be revealed without her having to ask. So far it hadn't.

He hadn't been anything like what she had imagined. Had he changed? Or had she?

She wouldn't be glad when he left. *I'll miss him.*

She washed out her cup and went to bed, sliding quietly in next to her daughter.

———

Sunday morning was bright and fresh. It had rained overnight, and now, with the warm sun, it was a perfect Canadian spring day. The blackflies hadn't arrived yet to mar the pleasure of a walk or sitting outside. Liesbeth and Hannah cycled over to Donald and Margaret's house and they all piled into the car.

Hannah sat on the edge of the seat, constantly tapping Max on the shoulder to point out scenes as they passed. "Look, Papa, you can see St. George's Bay through the trees there on the right." And then, "Look Papa, a bald eagle."

Liesbeth glanced at Margaret and reached out to touch Margaret's shoulder behind Hannah's back. "Are you all right? You seem very pale."

Margaret smiled over the top of Donnie's head. "I'm not used to sitting in the back seat."

Liesbeth frowned. "Are you sick? We must stop and you should trade places with Max."

Margaret shook her head and put a finger to her lips. "Shh. Don't make a fuss. We don't have much further to go."

When they pulled in to the Dekkers's yard, Margaret was almost green-looking. Liesbeth waited for her as Donald and Hannah led Max to the house. "You look absolutely wretched, Margaret."

Margaret swallowed and took a deep breath. "It'll pass."

"Are you sure? It's not a flare up of the TB symptoms, is it?"

As the colour returned to Margaret's face, she gave a small smile. "No, nothing like that. I get this most mornings, at the moment. In another hour I'll be right as rain again."

Liesbeth widened her eyes. "Oh!"

Margaret smiled. "Yes, I'm pregnant again, but no one knows yet. I'm just waiting another couple of weeks and then I'll start telling people."

"Donald hasn't noticed?"

"No, he's usually gone to work when I'm feeling like this." Margaret hefted her toddler on to her hip and took Liesbeth's arm with the other hand. "Come, they'll be wondering where we are."

Liesbeth leaned close to her friend. "Congratulations. You're happy, I assume?"

Margaret smiled. "Very much so. I do think it might be time to move out of town a little bit, though. I prefer to raise the children out in the fresh air and quiet somewhere."

Liesbeth nodded. "Lots for you to think about."

Margaret kissed her son's forehead. "Yes, indeed."

Gertrude came bustling out of the house. "There you two are. Come in, come in. Donald, Adriaan, and Hannah have taken Max out to meet the boys in the barn."

Liesbeth accepted Gertrude's three kisses without feeling the shame as she had on her previous visit.

Gertrude took Donnie from Margaret's arms. "I miss having a little one around. Give him here so I can give him a cuddle."

Margaret's face was still pale, but getting better by the minute. Still, to Liesbeth's eye, she looked grateful to hand over the child.

Liesbeth took Margaret's arm and linked it through hers. "Gertrude, I think Margaret would love a cup of tea after that bumpy ride, wouldn't you?"

Without waiting for an answer, Gertrude led the way in to the kitchen "The kettle's already on."

Margaret settled herself into a kitchen chair with a sigh.

Before Liesbeth sat down, she realized they had left the basket in the trunk of the car. "I'm going out to get the hamper."

Margaret nodded. "I forgot all about it."

As Liesbeth went out, she looked over at the McKenna's farm. It already had a forlorn and abandoned look, after only a few months. The hair rose on the back of her neck. *What a fool I've been.*

The sound of conversation brought her from her reverie as Hannah and the men came out of the barn and headed toward the house. Hannah was dancing backwards in front of her father, talking and gesturing. Liesbeth wanted to call out for her daughter to face forward, to be careful, but she stayed silent. Hannah wanted to keep her eyes on her father as much as possible. *She'll be so sad when he leaves.*

Max looked away from Hannah and saw Liesbeth. He waved. Hannah turned. "Come inside, Mama. We're having an early lunch." Her shrill voice scattered the chickens in the yard.

Liesbeth lifted the hamper out of the car and went back inside to join the others.

Extra chairs had been placed at the long kitchen table. There was little room for elbows, but no one seemed to mind. Liesbeth was accustomed to this chaotic sort of meal now, but she wondered what Max thought of it all. People were talking on different subjects at one time. Joseph and Donald were having a lively discussion about the Toronto Maple Leafs hockey team.

Joseph waved his knife around. "With King Clancy in the line-up, they're sure to make the playoffs next season."

Donald laughed. "Just because Smythe paid a fortune for the guy doesn't mean the team's going to do any better than they did this year."

At the other end of the table, Adriaan was explaining the benefits of his new Montgomery Ward cream separator to Max. In between, Gertrude, Margaret, and Liesbeth talked about the latest batch of cheese Gertrude was working on.

Liesbeth glanced down the table and saw a frown of concentration on Max's face. She smiled because she recognized the look. She had felt it on her own face at times as the babble seemed overwhelming. She turned back to Gertrude and listened to her frustrations with the cheese not setting the way it should.

After lunch, after the dishes were washed and put away, after one final cup of tea and an oatcake, it was time to leave.

As they all walked back out to the car, Liesbeth had a quiet word with Max. "Margaret had a bit of car sickness on the way here. I don't think that sitting in the back suits her, but I know she won't say anything to you."

Max immediately stepped up to Margaret's side. "I'm sitting in the back on the return journey. It's easier for Hannah to point out all her favourite spots to me if I'm sitting next to her."

Margaret hesitated. "Are you sure?"

Without a word, Max climbed into the rear and settled himself in the middle of the back bench, folding his arms across his chest.

Margaret laughed. "You look just like General Joffre ready to go out and inspect the battlefields."

Max waved for the others to get in the car. "You have permission to enter and be seated."

Hannah tucked in beside him behind the driver's seat. "Who is General Joffre, Papa?"

Liesbeth climbed in on the other side and listened as Max explained who some of the key men from the War had been.

As they drove off, waving to the Dekker family, Liesbeth suddenly became aware of the heat of Max's leg as it pressed against hers. There wasn't enough room to shift away without making a fuss. *Does he notice it?* Heat travelled through her body. It started as a flutter in the pit of her stomach, then a tingling in her groin and breasts. She turned to stare out the window as she realized that, for the first time since before Hannah was born, she was aroused. Sweat beaded on her brow and she didn't dare turn away from the window. As she listened to the chatter of her daughter, she calmed down and turned to look beside her.

Max sat with his arm around Hannah and peered out the window as she pointed out more interesting sights. A tree split by lightning, a pond with swans, a new foal ; Max responded with enthusiasm to them all.

Meanwhile, his leg rested against Liesbeth's.

When they arrived back in Antigonish, Max got out at Liesbeth's house.

Liesbeth gestured to the kitchen. "Why don't you two see what Peggy has planned for your supper while I get ready for work?"

When she was dressed in her uniform and ready to leave, she stepped into the kitchen. "I'm leaving now. You two have a nice evening."

Max stood up from the table. "I told Hannah I would walk with you to work."

Liesbeth tilted her head. "Are you sure?"

Max nodded. "Hannah doesn't mind. I'll be back in twenty minutes."

"All right, then. Come, Hannah, give me a kiss before I go."

Hannah gave Liesbeth a hug and a kiss. "I had a nice day so far, Mama."

"Yes, so did I. Enjoy your evening with Papa and I'll see you in the morning."

Max talked about the Dekkers as they walked toward the hospital. "I can see you've made some nice friends there. They obviously care a lot about you."

Liesbeth nodded. "Yes, I feel quite close to them. They've been a godsend. We have a common background."

"It's important to have people who understand your experience, isn't it? Perhaps that's why I always enjoy talking to your sister."

This is it. My chance to ask about Alida. "You do seem to spend quite a bit of time with her."

Max looked at her. "Now that she's moved to Amsterdam, we see each other regularly."

Liesbeth took a deep breath. "Max, are you and Alida a couple now?"

He stopped and put his hand on her arm. "Liesbeth, for goodness sake. You once before asked me something along the same line, something about preferring Alida."

Liesbeth felt her face colour.

"I told you then and I'll tell you again. No, I don't prefer Alida. She chatters like a magpie, and while I enjoy the diversion once in a while, the main reason I enjoy being with her is because she will talk to me about you."

Liesbeth bit her lip. "I'm sorry, I didn't mean to annoy you. It just seemed to me that you might be more than just friends by now."

He shook his head. "I've been spoiled." He turned to gaze at her. "I once fell in love, and so far I haven't found anyone to make my feelings change."

They arrived at the hospital doors. Liesbeth stopped and looked into Max's blue eyes. "I'm glad that we've had this time to clear the air."

Max pressed her arm and nodded. "Yes, I am too. I feel better than I've felt in a very long time."

Liesbeth smiled. "You better hurry back to Hannah. She'll be impatient for your return."

He touched the brim of his hat. "Have a good shift."

She watched for a moment as he walked back down the drive, then went in to work.

———

The day arrived. Liesbeth had taken the day off and Hannah was allowed to stay home from school as a once-only treat. They were to ride the train as far as Truro with Max.

Donald drove Max to the station with his luggage, and Liesbeth and Hannah walked over.

Hannah grasped her father's hand. "I wish you didn't have to go."

He pressed her hand between both of his and kissed her on the forehead. "I know, sweetheart, but I have to go back to work."

She pouted. "Why can't you find work here, Papa?"

He smiled and patted her hand before releasing it. "My life is back in the Netherlands. They need me there."

"Mama and I need you here."

He shook his head. "You've managed just fine for the past seven years, and I'm sure you'll manage again after I leave."

"But I want you here, Papa."

"I know you do, and I'd love to be with you, but it just isn't possible."

She heaved a great sigh and turned to Liesbeth. "Can't you convince him, Mama?"

Liesbeth smiled. "Let's make the most of these last hours that we're together instead of being sad. What was your favourite day with Papa?"

Hannah thought about it and began chattering madly.

The train pulled in with great puffs of steam and they climbed aboard. Hannah hadn't been on a train in a very long time and was diverted by the excitement of the trip.

As Hannah put her head out the window to watch the receding station, Max leaned toward Liesbeth. "I know that things aren't always easy for you financially. If you ever need help, you must let me know."

Her neck muscles tightened. "We're doing all right." She knew she sounded stiff. "Thank you, though. I do appreciate the offer."

He glanced at Hannah who was still absorbed with the rushing scenery outside. "If you ever decide you want to come home, just let me know. I'll send you the money."

Liesbeth stared at him, wide-eyed and frowning. "What do you mean?"

He lifted a shoulder. "It can mean whatever you want it to mean. I can just send you the money and you can come home and find a place of your own to live, or . . ."

"Or?"

He shrugged again. "Or perhaps we could even try again."

Liesbeth shook her head. "Max, thank you, but—"

He held up a hand. "You don't need to say anything. I'm just letting you know, so you can put it into the back of your mind, and if you ever need the information, you can pull it out again and think about it."

He turned his attention away from her and rubbed Hannah's back. The child grinned at him as the train slowed for the next station.

In Truro, they disembarked. Now it was truly time to say goodbye. Max watched to ensure his luggage was removed from the train, then after only a few moments, it was loaded on the train destined for Halifax.

Hannah was starting to sniffle already as Max held her hand. He knelt down and she threw her arms around his neck, weeping on to his shoulder. "Now, Hannah. You're a big girl and must be strong and brave. We've had such a nice time together, haven't we?"

Hannah mumbled into his neck and Max pushed her upright. She nodded. "We've had a wonderful time. I'm so glad you came, Papa."

He kissed her Dutch-style, right cheek, left, and right again. Then, for good measure, he kissed her forehead and pulled her in for another tight hug.

He straightened and, still with one hand on Hannah's shoulder, he put the other loosely around Liesbeth and kissed her, also three times.

The conductor was blowing the whistle. He let them both go and climbed into the train. Liesbeth and Hannah waited until he found a seat by the window. As the train puffed and started to move, he slid the window open and put his head out, his hat already off.

Hannah waved with both arms. "Goodbye, Papa. Goodbye."

Liesbeth called out. "Have a safe trip. Send us a letter when you are home and tell us about your trip."

He nodded. "Goodbye. I will. I'll write to each of you. One letter just for you, Hannah, and one for your mother. Goodbye." His words were almost lost in the screech of metal on metal as the train gained speed.

Hannah stood waving, even after her father had pulled his head back in and closed the window. Tears rolled down her cheeks as her arms dropped to her sides.

Liesbeth held out her hand. "Come. Let's go inside and treat ourselves to something nice in the station café while we wait for our train to go home."

Hannah continued to stand there for an instant, watching the last image of the train disappearing along the track, then took her mother's hand.

They went in, and while Liesbeth tried to make every treat sound attractive, she knew that the hot chocolate and piece of apple pie that came for Hannah probably stuck in the child's throat as much as Liesbeth's own cup of tea and piece of pie did.

XV

June 1930 – Time For A Change

The warm weather had truly arrived. Liesbeth sat out on the veranda with Margaret, drinking lemonade.

Margaret waved her hand. "Another few days of this nice weather and the blackflies will be out in force."

Liesbeth shook her head. "It's such a pity. One waits almost six months to really feel the sun again and then we get chased inside by the bugs."

Margaret laughed. "Welcome to Canada."

"I should be used to it by now."

"Indeed. Are you used to it, though?"

Liesbeth looked at Margaret. "What do you mean?"

Margaret tilted her head. "I sometimes feel that you have never really truly settled here. You haven't developed a large circle of friends or interests."

Liesbeth pursed her lips. "Look what happened when I tried to develop a friendship."

Margaret shook her head. "You certainly can't judge everyone by Riley McKenna."

Liesbeth sighed. "I know. Of course not. I enjoy the people I work with. I've met a couple of the mothers of Hanna's friends."

Margaret raised an eyebrow. "I'm not sure that counts."

Liesbeth bit her lip. "I don't feel the need for a large circle of friends. I never have. Never mind me. Tell me how you're feeling. Of course, Donald was delighted when you told him?"

Margaret smiled and rubbed the small swell of her growing baby. "Yes, he's over the moon. Thank goodness I seem to be over the morning sickness, and now I feel great. I have all sorts of energy, in fact."

"That's great. Are you planning to do some rearranging? I thought I saw some boxes in the corner of your dining room."

Margaret's face coloured. "Well, here's the thing, I'm starting to pack."

"Pack?"

Margaret placed a hand on Liesbeth's arm. "Yes. It's all finalized now so I can talk about it. While it was still just a vague plan, we didn't want to say anything to anyone."

"Tell me, then."

"Well, we are moving out to Cribbon's Point. We've gotten a very good deal on a house there. So much so that, by selling this house, we'll have enough money left over to buy a fishing boat."

Liesbeth's voice went up a notch. "A fishing boat?"

"Well, Donald always wanted to go back to fishing. You know his father was a fisherman, as were his mother's people, who are Boyds and live all around Cribbon's Point. So Donald and his brother are buying a boat together and are going to make a go of it."

Liesbeth hardly knew what to say. "My goodness. That's a whole lifestyle change for you all."

Margaret's eyes shone. "It's so wonderful. You know, it's so much closer to my mother, so I can help her out more, and in fact she can come and help me when the baby comes. The property is lovely. It needs fixing up, but Donald can do that. It sits on five acres, so I can have some chickens, perhaps a goat or two, and of course, a nice big vegetable garden."

Liesbeth smiled. "You're a country girl at heart, aren't you?"

Margaret nodded. "I am. And Donald can't wait to give up his job at the station to get back to the sea. It's hard work, he's going to have to toughen up some, but I know he can do it."

"So when does all this happen?"

Margaret bit her lip. "That's a good question. The house is already empty, so we're trying to negotiate that Donald actually go in and start working on the most immediate things before we take possession. I think the bank will let us do it. We might have to rent it on paper for a month or two, but they seem keen to try to make something work because, of course, the bank doesn't like it to stand empty if they can help it."

Liesbeth swept her hand across the veranda. "What about this place? When will it go up for sale?"

Margaret shook her head. "It's already sold. Donald knew a fellow who always said he loves the place, so when we were starting to think about this, he went and talked to him, and yes, the man wants it. It's a private sale, so he's pretty open to setting the closing date to suit us."

"You have it all worked out."

"Yes, it really has all come together. We want to be in the new house before the baby comes, so I would say we're looking at moving in late June if possible."

"My goodness, so soon." Liesbeth had a thought. "What about Dodie?"

"Oh, Dodie will come with us. I talked to her and she would love to move out of town again." Margaret pulled a wry face. "Her cooking skills leave something to be desired, but she's so good with Donnie. I'll be so very glad for her help when the new baby comes. I know I said my mother would come, but truly, I think Mother will just sit with the baby in her arms and look out at sea the whole day."

"You will have a sea view?"

"Yes, it's up on a hill so you can't get down to the water, but it's a lovely view."

Liesbeth squeezed Margaret's hand. "It sounds absolutely perfect. I know you'll be very happy there."

Margaret put her other hand on top of Liesbeth's. "Yes, I know we will. The one thing that worries me is you."

"Why do I worry you?"

Margaret clicked her tongue. "When we move out, you'll be rather lonely, I think."

Liesbeth lifted a shoulder. "Perhaps it will force me to make new friends. That's what you want, isn't it?"

Margaret took Liesbeth's hand in hers. "Liesbeth, what really happened all those years ago with Max? I had imagined you'd parted under terrible circumstances, yet when I saw you together, you seemed like the best of friends. I had been so afraid that first evening when you saw him standing in our living room. I didn't know if you would just turn and walk out again. Instead, you both seemed glad to see each other. I haven't wanted to pry, but well, now I am."

Liesbeth gazed out at the large maple tree in the front yard. "I think we were both different people then. I know I am. You ask what happened, and I hardly know what to tell you. I felt lost. I felt that unless I was using my skills as a nurse, helping people, I just wasn't myself. I wasn't Liesbeth. And if I wasn't Liesbeth, then who was I? I didn't know, and I suppose I imagined that Max couldn't possibly want this less-than-Liesbeth person."

Margaret squeezed and released Liesbeth's hand. "How very sad for you."

Liesbeth glanced at her and gave her a thin smile before looking away again. "I can say it now. I probably—yes, I believe I did—*imagine* that Max was interested in that Rosa woman."

"But he wasn't?"

"No, I don't think he was."

"So all of this was for nothing?"

Liesbeth frowned and shook her head. "No, I can't say that. I needed to see all that for myself. No one could have convinced me."

Margaret smiled. "You can be somewhat stubborn."

Liesbeth nodded her head. "Yes. I can be."

"So you've come all this way. And now what?"

Liesbeth looked at her friend. "And now what? Well, now I know myself better, and indeed, I have come a very long way. I have made a new life for myself and for Hannah. Canada is our home now and"—she slapped a blackfly—"despite its aggravations, it's a beautiful place full of good opportunities."

Margaret stood up. "Well, let's go in and you can help me pack up some of that good china I won't be using again until we are in the new house."

———

It was the third week of June. The final move would take place the following week, and much had already been moved into the house. Liesbeth and Hannah were at the new house to help.

Margaret set Donnie down between Hannah and Dodie. "Why don't you two take Donnie outside for a walk?"

Hannah and Dodie wandered around outside, holding Donnie's hands as he toddled between them on chubby legs. Liesbeth watched Hannah through the window. "Poor mite will miss you all when you move out of town."

Margaret had followed her gaze. "Hannah seems very quiet these days. Is she doing all right in school?"

"Oh yes. She's a good student and, of course, all that letter-writing between her and her father and her aunt are honing her penmanship and reading skills."

"You'll have to let her come here for her summer vacation."

Liesbeth smiled. "She'll love spending some time here, but I can't manage without her for weeks at a time. Now, let's tackle this unpacking."

———

Days later Liesbeth was still thinking about Margaret's move as she cycled to town. Hannah really would be lost without Dodie and the rest of the family. Of course, Peggy would ensure that Hannah was well looked after, and they would have plenty of activities to enjoy together, but still. Liesbeth was trying to think of something special that could be planned yet not cost a lot. Something to which Hannah could look forward.

She was startled out of her deep thoughts by a car honking behind her. She wobbled the bicycle and steered into the ditch, falling into the grass.

The car pulled over and the driver jumped out. "Good Lord, Mrs. Bos. Are you hurt? I didn't mean to startle you like that."

Liesbeth stood and brushed herself off. She smiled ruefully at Jerome Arsenault. "It's my fault entirely. I wasn't paying attention."

He picked up her bicycle and rolled it forward. "It doesn't seem to be damaged. I'm so sorry. I only meant to say hello. I thought you heard the car coming behind you."

She took the bicycle from him. "Please don't be sorry. I should have heard. I was lost in thought, but there's no harm done. I'm fine and my trusty vehicle is fine, so all is well."

She prepared to climb back on the bicycle, but he continued to stand there, so she hesitated.

He stuffed his hands in his pockets. "Mrs. Bos."

Liesbeth shook her head. "I've told you before, please call me Liesbeth."

He nodded. "Liesbeth, then. Would you go out for a coffee or a meal with me sometime?"

Liesbeth felt her heart thump. *Oh dear.* "Jerome, I'm very tied up between work and my daughter. I really don't think I can take time away from her."

He looked at her with a slight frown. "You can't just work and look after your daughter. That's not much of a life for you. What about taking some time to do something that makes you happy?"

She smiled. "Being with my daughter does make me happy."

He shrugged. "Yes, of course, but that isn't all there is to life."

She tilted her head. "You may be right, Jerome, but at the moment it will have to do."

He scuffed the dirt and then nodded. "Sure. I understand. No problem."

She felt that she had hurt him. "Thank you, though, for the invitation. It's very kind and I'm sure I'd very much enjoy it, but at the moment it just isn't possible."

He seemed to brighten a little. "Maybe another time then?"

"Perhaps. Let's see how it goes after the summer."

He nodded. "All right. Well then. I better get going."

She nodded. "Yes, me too."

After he had driven off and Liesbeth continued her own journey, she considered Jerome Arsenault's words. Margaret had hinted at much the same thing. Going to work and being at home with Hannah wasn't a full life. *Are they right? Jerome's a nice man. Not at all like Riley. But not Max either.*

Liesbeth's head ached by the time Hannah got home from school. What constituted a full life? How did she truly feel about the life she was leading?

School was out, and the next day, Hannah was going to spend three days at Cribbon's Point. She was excited. Donald had promised he would take her for a ride on their new fishing boat.

Liesbeth sat at the kitchen table with her daughter and listened as she talked about the upcoming visit. *Hannah misses Margaret as much as I already do. This must be how it felt for Alida when I left her behind.* It was a shock to realize that. "You'll have a lovely time with them."

Hannah nodded. "I can't wait."

Liesbeth waited until Hannah finished the last of her supper, then sighed, hesitating to pull the letter from her pocket. "Hannah, you're getting to be such a big girl now. You're at an age where I think you deserve to have an opinion on our life together."

Hannah pushed her plate away and folded her arms in front of her. "What do you want my opinion about?"

Liesbeth read the wariness on the child's face. "I have a letter from your father here."

Immediately a smile came to her daughter's face, then a shadow chased it away. "Is Papa all right? He's not sick, is he?"

Liesbeth shook her head and touched her daughter's cheek with her finger. "No, no. He's fine. Absolutely fine."

Hannah frowned. "What is it? What's the matter?"

Liesbeth licked her lips and then began. "Hannah, this is the only life you really know. This is your home and I know that you have friends here, and you have Tante Margaret and Uncle Donald. They're our family now, aren't they?"

"Yes."

"What if I asked you to leave them all? What if I asked you to move back to Holland?"

Hannah's mouth fell open. "Leave Antigonish forever?"

Liesbeth shrugged. "Forever is a long time, but certainly for the foreseeable future."

"I don't speak Dutch anymore."

"I think there's a lot of it still hiding inside you. I think you would learn it pretty quickly again."

Hannah's eyes widened. "Would we live with Papa?"

Liesbeth took a deep breath. "Yes, I think we would try that. We've been apart for a very long time, so it may not work out, but even if we decided not to live with Papa, we would live very close by so that you could spend as much time with him as with me."

Hannah nodded. "And does Tante Alida live close by also?"

"Quite close by. Only a tram ride or a bicycle ride away."

"So I would be writing letters to Tante Margaret instead."

Liesbeth smiled. "Yes, I'm sure she would love that. She's a very good letter-writer herself."

Liesbeth leaned over and took Hannah's two hands in her own. "So tell me what you think? Do you need time to consider it? Perhaps think about it while you are visiting with Tante Margaret?"

Liesbeth felt a lump in her throat as she saw a grin dawning on Hannah's face.

Hannah pulled her mother's hands up to her lips and kissed the work-hardened fingers. "When can we leave?"

Acknowledgments

As with any work of historical fiction, the years of research included more books, articles, and war diaries than I can list here. Some of my key resources included:

A.E. Snell's *The C.A.M.C. With the Canadian Corps During The Last Hundred Days of the Great War*, Ian Beckett's *The Great War, Diary of a Nursing Sister on the Western Front, From a Surgeon's Journal* by Harvey Cushing, and Tom Scotland's *War Surgery, 1914-1918, A Bittersweet Land, The Dutch Experience in Canada, 1890-1980* by Herman Ganzevoort.

Special thanks to Le Pré Catelan in the Bois de Boulogne for allowing me to tour and poke around this spectacular building. I'd also like to acknowledge the curators of the Musée de l'Armée in Paris who do such a wonderful job of bringing history to life.

Closer to home, thanks to Prof. James Wood of Trent University who helped steer me through the course on WW1. As always, thanks to my family both in Ontario and the Netherlands for their contributions of encouragement and ideas. Also thanks to my family in Antigonish Nova Scotia who, over the years, showed me what an ideal setting the location is for story-telling.

Thanks to my writerly friends at 'the Guild' for your passion and encouragement, especially Vera Constantineau, Matthew Del Papa and Liisa Kovala – all very fine writers themselves. Thank you again to my editorial team of Tiffany Maxwell-Graovac and Sharron Elkouby. Last but not least, thanks to Jimmy Carton for your early reading and feedback on the manuscript.

Last Words

I am indebted to my grandmother Mary Thomson-Meijer from whom I inherited a photo album containing a record of her time as a Dutch nurse working with the Netherlands Ambulance in Paris during WW1. Although this is a work of fiction, I was inspired by that album to write this story.

Anyone interested in viewing some of those photos can check out my website: http://rennydegroot.com.

AMBULANCE NÉERLANDAISE EN FRANCE — Hôpital du Pré-Catelan (Neuilly-sur-Seine)